William Wordsworth
Concerning the Convention of Cintra

William Wordsworth
Concerning the Convention of Cintra
A Critical Edition

edited by Richard Gravil
and W. J. B. Owen

with a Critical Symposium by
Simon Bainbridge, David Bromwich
Timothy Michael and Patrick Vincent

𝓗𝓕𝓡 ✧ Humanities-Ebooks, Tirril , 2009

Text derived from *The Prose Works of William Wordsworth*, first published in 1974 by the Clarendon Press, Oxford and digitized by Humanities-Ebooks in 2008

This edition published electronically in 2009 by *Humanities-Ebooks.co.uk*
Tirril Hall, Tirril, Penrith CA10 2JE

ISBN 978-1-84760-063-9 Ebook
ISBN 978-1-84760-074-5 Paperback

Contents

Preface

The reason for this critical edition of *Concerning the Convention of Cintra*, Words-worth's most ambitious prose work, is not far to seek: 2008 saw the bicentennial of the Convention itself, and 2009 sees the bicentennial of Wordsworth's belated tract upon that event—a tract which expresses with extraordinary passion the anger of many at such an egregious instance of a victorious army of liberation treating its defeated and imperial opponent to the spoils of victory, and, more generally, the fury of a generation at the imperial use made by Napoleon of France's erstwhile patriotic armies.

The text for this edition is extracted from Volume 1 of the electronic version (2008) of *The Prose Works of William Wordsworth* (1974), as edited by W. J. B. Owen and Jane Worthington Smyser. Professor Owen's general and textual introductions, tex-tual notes, appendices, and his commentary, still invaluable at this date, are retained in full (Professors Owen and Smyser divided the prose works between them, and the Cintra editing was solely his). This paperback inevitably lacks the advantages of the electronic edition of which it is a print-on-demand version. The ebook is, of course, searchable, and the table of contents is itself hyperlinked, and is duplicated in the form of hyperlinked bookmarks at the left of the screen, enabling instant navigation between the general introduction, the textual introduction, Wordsworth's text and appendices (themselves hyperlinked to and from the appropriate page of text), the editorial appendices, and the commentary. Two advantages of the ebook are retained in the paperback: the presence of editorial commentary is indicated by the symbol ¶ in the margin, or by the line number being in in a lighter shade, and the separate line-ation of columnized textual notes is designed to make these features of the editorial apparatus clearer and easier to construe than in the Clarendon edition.

It is hoped that this digital and paperback edition will enable scholars, critics and students to access the work in affordable form, so as to reach an informed judge-ment—whatever that judgment may be—on the curious critical controversies that recur from time to time as to the nature of its politics. And to stimulate the search for such judgement, the volume includes a critical symposium made up of a Foreword by the present editor, two short contributions, by Simon Bainbridge and David Bromwich to a debate at the 2008 Wordsworth Summer Conference on the place of the *Cintra* in Wordsworth's life and work, and two longer papers, by Timothy Michael and Patrick Vincent presented at the same conference.

In the Critical Symposium, references to the the text are cited by line number (that is, the line numbers in this electronic text) and by page references to the Clarendon edition of the *Prose Works* [Clarendon].

I am grateful, for varieties of help with the production of this text, to John Beer, Jeff Cowton, Michael John Kooy, Sam Ward, and Averill Buchanan, and of course to Betty and Lynette Owen, representing the estate of W. J. B. Owen, for their agreement to its production.

Richard Gravil, Tirril, 2009

Extract from the Preface to the Clarendon edition of Wordsworth's Prose Works

The texts of our edition, whether of works published by Wordsworth or of works left unpublished in manuscript, are, with one exception, the last to have been corrected by him. [The exception is the Preface to *Lyrical Ballads*] Throughout the whole of our edition, variants, both from manuscripts and earlier editions, are preserved in textual notes and occasionally in longer appendices. The last versions to be corrected by Wordsworth have been adopted as the main texts not only because of the great importance which he attached 'to following strictly the last Copy of the text of an Author' (L.T., p. 473), but also because of the kinds of revisions that are peculiar to his prose. In the case of unpublished manuscripts, the last corrected version provides almost invariably the only coherent and clearly intelligible text, for earlier versions are little more than fragmentary rough drafts, with numerous deletions and rewritings. In the case of published works, with the exception just mentioned, Wordsworth did not alter the main arguments of his prose or contradict the original spirit and intent. He merely corrected misprints and factual errors, made stylistic improvements, clarified ambiguous statements, and expanded earlier texts or added new sections. (On the rare occasions when an error was introduced into the final text, we relegate it to the textual apparatus and print instead the most recent correct version.)

In separate introductions we describe in detail not only the various manuscripts but also any departures from our standard procedure in editing them. Here it is only necessary to set forth briefly a few of the principles governing our editorial practice: we preserve the manuscript spellings and abbreviations, with all their inconsistencies; where the manuscript lacks pointing, we silently insert it for the sake of intelligibility, but wherever we alter a mark of punctuation, we record that alteration in a textual note; although we have endeavoured to preserve all deletions, we have not recorded the striking out and the immediate rewriting of identical words and phrases; we have also not recorded transpositions within a sentence of identical words, phrases, and clauses, and only rarely have we recorded the fact that some of the text was inserted, usually by means of a caret, at the very moment of composition. A table of sigla used in the textual notes will be found on p. [11].

Our general introductions are concerned primarily with defining the date, occasion, and background of the particular work, and we have usually refrained from comment on its literary qualities. In our commentaries where we quote or cite the poetry of any major English poet without referring to a specific edition, we are using the edition of his work in the series known as the Oxford Standard Authors. Otherwise, works frequently cited are identified in the list of abbreviations.

For permission to publish manuscripts of Wordsworth's prose and other related manuscripts, we are indebted to the Wordsworth Library in Grasmere, the British Museum, the Victoria and Albert Museum, the Pierpont Morgan Library, the Cornell University Library, Harvard University Library, Northwestern University Library, and Yale University Library. The specific manuscripts of these libraries are all identified and described in subsequent introductions appropriate to them. But it should be added here that the numbering of the manuscripts in the Wordsworth Library at Grasmere, both those which we edit and those to which we briefly refer, is what will some day, no doubt, be called 'Old Style'. New numbers were assigned to all the manuscripts after this edition had gone into page proof, but scholars seeking to examine the manuscripts at Grasmere will find there a table of correspondences for the old and new numbering.

Professor Owen's research has been generously supported by the Humanities Research Council of Canada, the Canada Council, and McMaster University, and Professor Smyser's by a grant from the American Council of Learned Societies and frequent research grants from Connecticut College.

We are also grateful to many scholars and friends who have assisted us in numerous ways and it is pleasant here to express our gratitude to them. Helen Darbishire comes first to mind for she welcomed us to Grasmere and aided us at the very beginning of this undertaking; her wisdom and generosity are unforgettable. The loyal support of Professor Basil Willey, as chairman of the Dove Cottage Trustees, has, over a long period of time, been invaluable; indeed, he and his fellow Trustees have made this edition possible. At Grasmere too we have found in the librarians allies par excellence: first, Miss Phoebe Johnson and later and for a longer time, Miss Nesta Clutterbuck. To them especially, but also to Dr. Stephen Gill, whose librarianship more briefly overlapped our days of research, we are deeply grateful. By their admirable publications Professor Zera S. Fink, the late Professor George H. Healey, Mr. Alan G. Hill, Mrs. Mary Moorman, Professor Mark L. Reed, and Professor Chester L. Shaver have advanced the work of all Wordsworth scholars; in addition they have personally assisted us in prompt and generous ways, which are greatly appreciated. At the Cornell University Library Professor Donald D. Eddy continues the cordial traditions of George Healey and we acknowledge with thanks his many kindnesses. For generous aid of various kinds we are also indebted to Miss Helen K. Aitner, Connecticut College Library; the Revd. T. E. H. Baily, Shap; Dr. Paul F. Betz, Georgetown University; Dr. F. W. Bradbrook, University College of North Wales; Dr. Elizabeth M. Brennan, Westfield College, University of London; Professor A. D. Fitton Brown, University of Leicester; Professor M. L. Clarke, University College of North Wales; Miss Martha A. Connor, Swarthmore College Library; the late Professor John F. Danby, University College of North Wales; Miss Vera Farnell, Grasmere; Mrs. Sylvia Harris, Ambleside; the late Mrs. Beatrix Hogan; Mr. Wilmarth Lewis, Farmington, Connecticut; Mr. J. R. T. Pollard, University College of North Wales; Professor Frederick A. Pottle, Yale University; Professor T. M. Raysor, University of Nebraska; Mr. Kenneth Smith, Tullie House Library; Mr. J. H. Watkins, University College of North Wales; Dr. George J. Willauer, Jr., Connecticut College; Miss Marjorie G. Wynne, Yale University Library.

Finally, to Betty Owen and Hamilton Smyser, our shadow collaborators in countless ways, we give our heartfelt thanks. One particularly generous contribution of Betty Owen's must, however, be permitted to emerge into full light: she compiled for us a file of all proper names and all place-names that are now entered in our Index. If there are errors there, they are, like errors elsewhere in this work, ours.

W. J. B. OWEN, McMaster University
JANE WORTHINGTON SMYSER, Connecticut College

Table of Sigla and Abbreviations

MS.	the first version in the manuscript
MS.^{2}	the second version or first correction
MS.^{3}	the third version or first correction
A^2	he second version or first correction of MS. A.
[ ]	a blank space in the manuscript
[?]	an illegible letter or letters, or an illegible word or words
[? there]	the word may be *there*
[?there *or* their]	the word is either *there* or *their*
[there]	an editorial interpolation
273/4	occurring between lines 273 and 274
corr.	corrected
del.	deleted
ins.	inserted
om.	omitted
subs.	substituted

A sample note:

there 1822: their MS.: here MS.^{2}, 1810–20.

The first occurrence of *there* is in the edition of 1822; the first version of the manuscript reads *their* (we avoid the use of sic); the second version of the manuscript and the editions of 1810 to 1820 read *here*

Abbreviations

Ad. Cintra	Advertisement to *Concerning ... the Convention of Cintra*
Address	[Address on the Convention of Cintra]
Ap. Cintra	Appendix to *Concerning ... the Convention of Cintra*
Bord.	*The Borderers*
Burns	*Letter to a Friend of Robert Burns*
Cintra	*Concerning ... The Convention of Cintra*
Clarendon	*The Prose Works of William Wordsworth*, ed. W. J. B. Owen and Jane Worthington Smyser (Oxford, 1974).
C.L.	*Collected Letters of Samuel Taylor Coleridge*, ed. Earl Leslie Griggs (Oxford, 1956-71)
C.N.B.	*The Notebooks of Samuel Taylor Coleridge*, ed. Kathleen Coburn (New York, 1957–)
C.R.	*The Correspondence of Henry Crabb Robinson with the Wordsworth Circle*, ed. Edith J. Morley (Oxford, 1927)
D.N.B	*Dictionary of National Biography*
E.E.	Essays upon Epitaphs
E.S.	Essay, Supplementary to the Preface
Exc.	*The Excursion*, in *P.W.* v.
E.Y.	*The Letters of William and Dorothy Wordsworth: The Early Years, 1787–1806*, ed. Ernest de Selincourt; second edition, revised by Chester L. Shaver (Oxford, 1967)
Freeholders	*Two Addresses to the Freeholders of Westmorland*
H.C.R.	*Henry Crabb Robinson on Books and their Writers*, ed. Edith J. Morley (London, 1938)
Healey	George Harris Healey, *The Cornell Wordsworth Collection* (Ithaca, N.Y., 1957)
Jordan	John E. Jordan, *De Quincey to Wordsworth* (Berkeley and Los Angeles, CA., 1962)
Knight, *Prose Works*	*The Prose Works of William Wordsworth*, ed. William Knight (London, 1896)

Llandaff	A Letter to the Bishop of Llandaff …
L.Y.	*The Letters of William and Dorothy Wordsworth: The Later Years,* ed. Ernest de Selincourt (Oxford, 1939)
Mathetes	Letter of 'Mathetes' (John Wilson) to *The Friend*
Moorman, i.	Mary Moorman, *William Wordsworth, a Biography: The Early Years, 1770–1803* (Oxford, 1957)
Moorman, ii.	Mary Moorman, *William Wordsworth, a Biography: The Later Years, 1803–1850* (Oxford, 1965)
M.Y.	*Letters of William and Dorothy Wordsworth: The Middle Years,* ed. Ernest de Selincourt; second edition, revised by Mary Moorman and Alan G. Hill (Oxford, 1969–70)
Nat. Ind. and Lib.	*Poems Dedicated to National Independence and Liberty* in *P.W.* iii
O.E.D.	*Oxford English Dictionary*
Oman	Charles Oman, *History of the Peninsular War* (Oxford, 1902, etc.)
P. 1815	Preface to the Edition of 1815
P. Bord.	Preface to *The Borderers*
P. Exc.	Preface to *The Excursion*
P.L.B.	Preface to *Lyrical Ballads*
Prel.	*The Prelude,* ed. Ernest de Selincourt; second edition, revised by Helen Darbishire (Oxford, 1959). The text of 1805 is cited unless otherwise stated.
Priestley, *Oratory*	Joseph Priestley, *A Course of Lectures on Oratory and Criticism* (London, 1775)
P.W.	*Poetical Works of William Wordsworth,* ed. Ernest de Selincourt and Helen Darbishire (Oxford, 1940–9, and revised issues, 1952–9)
R.E.S.	*Review of English Studies*
R.M.	[Reply to 'Mathetes']
Rydal Mount Catalogue	*Catalogue of the Varied and Valuable Historical, Poetical, Theological, and Miscellaneous Library of the late venerated Poet-laureate, William Wordsworth* … (Preston, 1859); reprinted in *Transactions of the Wordsworth Society,* No. VI, pp. [195]–257 (Edinburgh, n.d.)
S.H., Letters	*The Letters of Sara Hutchinson,* ed. Kathleen Coburn (London, 1954)

[Southey,] *Life and Correspondence*	C. C. Southey, *Life and Correspondence of Robert Southey* (London, 1849, etc.)
[Southey,] *Selections*	J. W. Warter, *Selections from the Letters of Robert Southey* (London, 1856)
Subl. and Beaut.	The Sublime and the Beautiful
Wells	John Edwin Wells, 'The Story of Wordsworth's *Cintra*', *Studies in Philology*, xviii (1921), 15–77
Wordsworth as Critic	W. J. B. Owen, *Wordsworth as Critic* (Toronto and London, 1969)

A Critical Symposium
introduced and edited by Richard Gravil

A NOTE ON REFERENCES

In the essays that follow, the line numbers are those of this electronic edition, and page references are to the Clarendon edition cited as [Clarendon].

Foreword: Richard Gravil

Wordsworth as Partisan

Of Wordsworth's many ways of characterising Napoleon, the aptest is perhaps 'the intoxicated setter-up of Kings': by 1808, Michael Glover points out in *Britannia Sickens*, the Corsican was Emperor of France, King of Italy, Mediator of the Swiss Republic, and 'Protector' of the Rhine; one of his brothers was King of Holland, another of Naples, a third of Westphalia; Spain, Dalmatia and the Hanseatic states were his clients; and after defeating Austria, Prussia and Russia he had concluded a treaty with the Tsar, dividing Europe between them.[1] The major obstacle to perfection of the 'continental system', whereby France attempted to end British trade with Europe and control internal trade to the benefit of Paris as the hub of Empire, was the efficacy of Britain's naval blockade of such external trade as remained. A minor flaw was the refusal of Portugal to join the system. To punish Portugal, Napoleon therefore decided to dismember it into three principalities—one for the General entrusted with invading this small and relatively enlightened state; one to be kept under permanent military occupation; and one to reward the Spanish Prime Minister, Manuel Godoy, for his compliance. A further inducement to this policy was the possibility that annexing Portugal's naval fleet would help Napoleon achieve his goal of maritime supremacy.

While sensible enough, by mercenary standards, the invasion was only half-hearted in execution. Inadvertently, Napoleon started a train of events that led (though not quite inexorably) to Waterloo. Britain had, hitherto, found no viable employment on the continent for its small army of 60,000 regular troops. Now it was impelled to act, by the imminent threat to its naval security, and gifted with a winnable land campaign. Napoleon, Michael Glover says, 'solved the British problem for them'.[2] He not only entrusted the annexation of Portugal to a small, probably beatable force of about

---

1 *Britannia Sickens: Sir Arthur Wellesley and the Convention of Cintra* (London, Leo Cooper, 1970) 16–18.
2 *The Peninsular War, 1807–1814* (Newton Abbot: David & Charles, 1974), 26

30,000 troops, but his treachery to Spain—sending 75,000 troops to occupy all of the fortresses on the Spanish side of the Pyrenees, including Barcelona, on the pretext of reinforcing and supplying his Portuguese forces—turned Spain from ally into a ferocious enemy. By March 1808 the Imperial army had occupied Madrid, and the effect upon Spain can be seen from Wordsworth's copious quotations from the proclamations of various provincial Juntas that sprang into existence to avenge such treachery. For the next six years, Napoleon's overwhelming numerical superiority in the Peninsula was nullified by the need to police Spain's regular and guerrilla forces. These, however inept (and for the most part they were tragically inept) proved inexhaustible.

By a series of accidents, some of which are made clear in Wordsworth's tract and some in W. J. B. Owen's general introduction, the first major engagement of British troops in the Peninsular War was led not by the general nominally in charge, Sir Hew Dalrymple, but by a younger lieutenant-general, Sir Arthur Wellesley, who had gained something of a reputation in India for decisiveness and despatch. On 21 August 1808, at Vimiero, Wellesley's trade-mark exploitation of imaginatively chosen defensive positions and superior use of infantry fire-power inflicted a major defeat on General Junot. Junot's modest army was saved from immediate pursuit and probable destruction only by the timidity of Wellesley's immediate superior, Sir Harry Burrard. The French commander then converted deliverance to diplomatic triumph by negotiating a favourable armistice and convention with Sir Hew. As Byron put it in *Childe Harold*: 'Here folly dashed to earth the victor's plume / And policy regain'd what arms had lost'.

Junot's army was repatriated at his Britannic Majesty's expense, landed just over the border at Bayonne, with all its equipment, horses and considerable plunder (plundered from museums and churches as well as the people) without even the customary undertaking not to return to the same theatre. Some of these same forces harried General Moore's evacuation from Corunna in January 1809—a Dunkirk moment—and half of them confronted Wellington again at Torres Vedras in 1810, in the second invasion of Portugal under Marshals Soult and Massena. The convention is criticised by Wordsworth on both military and diplomatic grounds. Articles 4 and 6 insulted the Portuguese by making undertakings on behalf of the Portuguese civil government, without consulting them—including an undertaking that there would be no reprisals of any sort against Portuguese collaborators. These articles offended not only Wordsworth's sense of the respect due to allies, but the King's also. Article 7 annoyed the British Navy, by laying down how it should deal with a Russian fleet then blockaded in the Port of Lisbon. Article 3 left the French in possession of the most defensible territory, should hostilities be resumed. Article 8—despite the fact that a shortage of cavalry was Burrard's most convincing excuse for not allowing Wellesley to pursue Junot's retreat in the first place—undertook that the Royal Navy would transport 800 horses, three times as many as were available to the British, to France. Article 9 required 48 hours notice of any resumption of hostilities if a Convention could not be concluded. In Michael Glover's apt summary, 'Never has a victorious army with every advantage in its hand signed an agreement which gave so much to its defeated enemies with so little to itself' (*Britannia Sickens*, 139).

It took until 1814 for Viscount Wellington of Talavera, Marquess of Torres Vedras, Count of Vimeiro, Marshal General of Portugal and Captain-General of Spain (to give Sir Arthur some of his later titles) to secure Portugal, achieve his first victories in Spain, become (sometimes more in name than in practice) commander-in-chief of the allies in the peninsula and drive Napoleon's armies back to Bayonne, Bordeaux and Toulouse, after successive victories over Marshals Soult, Victor, Massena, Marmont and Clausel. Wordsworth's account is, of course, unaware of this later progress, and he pins as much blame as possible on the future Duke. Junot, like many of Napoleon's commanders had aggravated his catalogue of offences in Portugal by assuming a local aristocratic title, in his case 'Duc d'Abrantes'. Wellesley's unthinking use of that title in his report on the engagement—perhaps vain of having defeated 'the duc d'Abrantes *in person*' (line 930)—is enough for Wordsworth to pick on Wellesley in his remorseless indictment of the military mind: 'It was plain', W writes, 'that here was a man, who, having not any fellow-feeling with the people whom he had been commissioned to aid, could not know where their strength lay, and therefore could not turn it to account, … but that, if his future conduct should be in the same spirit, he must be a blighting wind wherever his influence was carried' (1030 ff): this diagnosis is repeated in Miltonic parlance at the close of the pamphlet, when Wordsworth cites Milton's *History of Britain* (1670) to indict those who are 'Valiant indeed, and prosperous to win a field; but to know the end and reason of winning, injudicious, and unwise' (4370). Wordsworth—wishing Britain could find another Marlborough—was not to know that he was slighting Napoleon's eventual Nemesis. And to do him credit, the principled basis of his criticism remains unaffected by Wellington's military success. In 1815, Wellington's victory at Waterloo and his magnanimous conduct at the surrender of Paris earned him an unqualified eulogy from Helen Maria Williams. A year later, Wordsworth still insisted that 'the constitution of [Wellington's] mind is not generous, nor will he pass with posterity for a hero' (*MY*, 2: 280).

The armistice was, in Wellesley's words, a 'very remarkable document'; and though he signed it at the request of his commanding officer, he let it be known through his Military Secretary, Colonel Torrens (according to the latter's evidence), that he 'totally disapproved of many points in it and of the tone of the language in which it was drawn up'.[1] 'Many' is more damning than it sounds. As the document (given by Wordsworth as an Appendix entitled 'Suspension of Arms') contains only seven substantive points, other than the agreement that there should be a convention, and how it should be arranged, total disapproval of 'many' of its points, along with the tone of the whole, sounds fairly comprehensive. The only aspects of the convention that we know he did agree with were that the French should be permitted to depart with their property, provided that this meant only 'military baggage and equipment',[2] and that Burrard's decision not to pursue the defeated French army until it was 'broken' created circumstances in which evacuation was warranted. As Wellesley pointedly remarked to the Inquiry on 14 November 1808:

> I am decidedly of opinion that the most decisive consequences would have resulted from the march as proposed, and the pursuit of the enemy on the 21st August after the battle, yet it does not follow that the measure of allowing the French to evacuate Portugal was not right on the evening of the 22nd. On the 21st August the enemy were defeated and in confusion; and I have explained the grounds which I have for thinking that the most advantageous consequences would have resulted from a pursuit. On the 22nd, in the evening, when the question of the evacuation was considered and decided, the enemy was no longer in confusion.

Why does Wordsworth ignore such evidence as was available to him in the reports of the Inquiry (and, by the time he composed his appendices, its published report) that Wellesley was an unwilling, indeed outraged, partner?

It is partly, perhaps, that his temper cannot have been improved by knowing that his attempt to orchestrate constitutional protest in Cumbria has been frustrated by what W. J. B. Owen calls Lord Lowther's 'covert threats [of] organized rowdyism'. He seems, quite simply, and despite his posture of almost Olympian retirement, to have been blinded by partisan prejudice against one who was both a soldier and a Tory minister. Like Hunt's *Examiner*, which made similar points on 25 September 1808, Wordsworth depicts Wellesley's return to the Peninsula as commander-in-chief, as a

---

1 *Proceedings upon the Inquiry relative to the Armistice and Convention & made and concluded in Portugal in 1808* (London, 1809) 104, 116.
2 As developed in the Convention, by the astute Junot and Kellerman, the protection afforded to French 'property', however acquired, extended even to real estate ('property ... immoveable': see Article XVI of the Convention itself).

reward for influence rather than a welcome sign of recognition for superior abilities. He even argues (in a strangely tangential paragraph) that Castlereagh should be 'impeached' for advising Dalrymple to heed Wellesley's advice. In short, he joins in the general hue and cry and decides to hunt with the pack.

Wordsworth's intervention, though instigated by the events of 9–30 August 1808, was not published in full until May 1809. By then, Sir John Moore had died during his defence of Corunna, and Palafox, Augustina and the people of Saragossa had entered legend for their heroic resistance to siege.[1] But Wellington's remarkable campaign had hardly begun. Wordsworth wrote, of course, without benefit of hindsight, and his work is as coloured as any journalistic effusion about fresh starts in human affairs— such as 1789 or the 'Prague Spring' of 1968—must be by half-knowledge, partisanship (the word is doubly apt) and unrealistic expectations. It was a remarkably heady moment. The Spanish rising, combined with the overt demonstration of Napoleon's increasingly megalomaniacal and imperial tendencies, united Whig opinion for the first time in many years, and the Convention put the Whigs in the novel position of being able to criticise Tory ministers for lack of vigour in prosecuting a war they had hitherto been at best lukewarm in supporting.

Optimism was in the air. The expulsion of Napoleon from Spain seemed imminent; the indiscriminate banditry of Spain's guerrilla forces had not yet become as notorious as the systematic terror practised by Imperial France; and Spain's ineptly led 'regular' armies had barely begun the long catalogue of ignominious and bloody defeats that followed their surprise victory at Baylen in July 1808 (see 1402, 2708). A country that had long seemed incapable of constitutional renovation, and whose civil and religious institutions symbolized all that was vile in feudalism, now struck many as engaged in a popular awakening such as France herself had achieved in 1789. The revival in Wordsworth of the feelings of that revolutionary moment is patent.

It is clear from the note of ecstasy that sounds again and again in this text, that Wordsworth exulted to find himself at one with liberal sentiment—one might say, with the movement of history—for the first time in many years. His sense of belonging to an outraged and united opposition is not greatly exaggerated, as is easily shown by citing one not known for making common cause with William Wordsworth, namely Francis Jeffrey. Jeffrey wrote in the *Edinburgh Review*:[2]

---

1 Sir David Wilkie's 'Augustina, Maid of Saragossa' (1828; see cover) is still a popular subject for reproductions and copies in oil.
2 The article may have been co-authored, Deirdre Coleman has suggested, by Henry Brougham. See 'Re-Living Jacobinism: Wordsworth and the Convention of Cintra', in J. R. Watson, ed., *The French Revolution in English Literature and Art*, *The Yearbook of English Studies*, vol 19, 1989, 144–61, 144–5.

The people, then, and, of the people, the middle, and, above all, the lower orders, have alone the merit of raising this glorious opposition to the common enemy of national independence. Those who had so little of what is commonly termed interest in the country,—those who had no stake in the community…– the persons of no consideration in the state—they who could not pledge their fortunes, having only lives and liberty to lose,—the bulk,—the mass of the people—alone, uncalled, unaided by the higher classes … raised up the standard of insurrection … a cheering example to every people. (*Edinburgh Review* 13, Oct 1808)

The term 'the people' is a notoriously slippery one, but there is no more doubt what Jeffrey mean by it in this passage, than there is about what Wordsworth means by it. Both Wordsworth and the *Edinburgh* celebrate what they see as a genuine people's uprising in the Peninsula. Spain's patriots, born again in the revolutionary hour of uprising, are busily generating a new and vital state in place of the feudal one with which they had been encumbered. Unfortunately, however, they were let down by Britain's effete military class, with their 'rotten customs and precedents':

Then it was—when the people of Spain were thus rouzed; after this manner released from the natal burthen of that government which had bowed them to the ground; in the free use of their understandings, and in the play and 'noble rage' of their passions; *while yet the new authorities, which they had generated, were truly living members of their body, and (as I have said) organs of their life*; when that numerous people were in a stage of their journey which could not be accomplished without the spirit which was then prevalent in them, and which (as might be feared) would too soon abate of itself;—then it was that we—not we, but the heads of the British army and nation—when, if they could not breathe a favouring breath, they ought at least to have stood at an awful distance—stepped in with their forms, their impediments, their rotten customs and precedents, their narrow desires, their busy and purblind fears; and called out to these aspiring travellers to halt— [2816 ff, my italics]

What caused Britain's leaders to betray the mission with which they had been entrusted? It is, the pamphlet explicitly argues, the pernicious effect of class and the disabling effects of an education designed to separate rulers from the ruled; to inculcate pride and a feeling of superiority, and a disabling cynicism about human nature, which cynicism is 'mistaken for a knowledge of human kind' (3018).

It might have been a narrow step from sympathizing with such a movement abroad, to envisaging similar renewal at home. Both Wordsworth and Jeffrey, the latter in a eulogistic review of a posthumous work by Charles James Fox, feel at liberty to invoke, once more, the heroes of the Commonwealth and Republican tradition.[1] Neither, however, travels far under that momentary re-identification.

As a guide to what happened after Vimeiro, or who was responsible for the Convention; or why Sir John Moore retreated to Corunna, and what condition his Spanish allies were then in; and the variant ideologies and motivations of competing factions in Spain, Wordsworth's *Convention* is only partly reliable. It is, in fact, for all its ponderous rhetoric, a remarkably Romantic—even romantic—text, to be valued primarily as a surprising expression of Wordsworth's capacity for idealization. He was still seeing the shield of human nature 'from the golden side' as he had put it in *The Prelude* three years earlier. The text expresses an ardent self-vindication as a consistent man of the people—the Spanish people as much as the English people. It expresses a quite unwarranted faith in the ability of Spain's leaders to learn from their mistakes. Wordsworth's pamphlet is still cited for its exposition of the virtues of guerrilla warfare—he was aware of the analogies to be made between the Peninsula War and the American 'Revolution'—and the not inconsiderable strategic sense of the pamphlet is worth some attention: what Wordsworth thinks should happen in 1808–09 is, by and large, what did happen—militarily and politically—between 1809 and 1814.[2] It is equally remarkable, however, for looking forward to such events as the Italian *Risorgimento*. Wordsworth identifies (as Byron and Shelley and Keats will do) with one of the great engines of nineteenth-century liberation—the nationalism that, after the luminous example of the United States, inspired Poland, Greece, and eventually Italy, to assert their identity against the hegemonic powers of continental Europe.

At the same time, however, the text's rhetorical qualities lead many to follow James K. Chandler in finding the text thoroughly 'Burkean', a matter that is addressed from several perspectives in the essays that follow in the present volume. Certainly, Wordsworth, like Whitman, does indeed agree with Burke and with the Apostles creed that in common human experience 'the living and the dead' ('les vivants et les morts', both 'vivos et mortuos') compose one community. But a test case of whether the Cintra exhibits *substantively* Burkean politics might be found in the following passage. Its immediate topic is the failure of Spain's own rulers to trust 'the People' when establishing a Supreme Junta in place of a constitutional assembly,

---

1   See Francis Jeffrey, *Contributions to the Edinburgh Review*(2 vols, London 1844), vol 2, 16): In the 1790s 'it was thought as well to say nothing in favour of Hamden, or Russell, or Sidney, for fear it might give spirits to Robespierre, Danton, or Marat.' In the 1802 sonnet Wordsworth invoked 'Sidney, Harrington, young Vane', and in the *Cintra*, England's 'Alfred, her Sidneys, and her Milton'.
2   See lines 3370–81 ('let there be floating armies'); and 4032–44 envisaging the necessary conjunction of Spanish 'patriots', Britain's disciplined troops, and (regrettably) Austria.

a move referred to a 'second delegation' of power:

> Much therefore was wanting to direct the general judgement in the choice of persons, when the second delegation took place; which was a removal (the first, we have seen, had not been so) of the power from the People. But, when a common centre became absolutely necessary, the power ought to have passed from the provincial Assemblies into the hands of the Cortes; and into none else. A pernicious Oligarchy crept into the place of this comprehensive—this constitutional—this saving and majestic Assembly. Far be it from me to speak of the Supreme Junta with ill-advised condemnation: every man must feel for the distressful trials to which that Body has been exposed. But eighty men or a hundred, with a king at their head veiled under a cloud of fiction (we might say, with reference to the difficulties of this moment, begotten upon a cloud of fiction), could not be an image of a Nation like that of Spain, or an adequate instrument of their power for their ends. The Assembly, from the smallness of its numbers, must have wanted breadth of wing to extend itself and brood over Spain with a quickening touch of warmth every where. If also, as hath been mentioned, there was a want of experience to determine the judgment in choice of persons; this same smallness of numbers must have unnecessarily increased the evil—by excluding many men of worth and talents which were so far known and allowed as that they would surely have been deputed to an Assembly upon a larger scale. Gratitude, habit, and numerous other causes must have given an undue preponderance to birth, station, rank, and fortune; and have fixed the election, more than was reasonable, upon those who were most conspicuous for these distinctions;—men whose very virtue would incline them superstitiously to respect established things, and to mistrust the People.

Only a representative assembly, truly from the People, can give rise to new institutions that are 'living members of their body, and (as I have said) organs of their life'. What Spain still needs, Wordsworth comes very close indeed to saying, is the kind of popular constitution that France achieved in 1794—but without the subsequent perversion of that constitution to despotic purposes.[1]

---

1   See lines 67–11, 292 ff, 2780ff, with their positive reflections on the early stages of the French Revolution, and even the interesting parenthesis in this sentence (3268ff):—'The feebleness of despotic power we have had before our eyes in the late condition of Spain and Prussia; and in that of France before the Revolution; and in the present condition of Austria and Russia. But, in a new-born arbitrary and military Government (especially if, like that of France, it have been immediately preceded by a popular Constitution), not only this weakness is not found; but it possesses, for the purposes of external annoyance, a preternatural vigour'. Note also the endorsement of 'careers open to all talents' (a principle established in the *Droits de L'Homme et du Citoyen*) in the subsequent sentence. 'Many causes contribute to this: we need only mention that, fitness—real or supposed—being necessarily the

In 1810, as if in answer to Wordsworth's advice concerning breadth of representation, a reformed Cortes duly assembled in Cadiz and began work on the liberal Spanish Constitution promulgated in March 1812.[1] As it happens, Wordsworth disowned the result, and by 1816 he has to deal with the growing suspicion that he had become carried away in 1809. Writing to John Scott, he confesses that in the *Cintra* he had indeed 'boldly' called for a reformed Cortes and a popular constitution—i.e. that that is indeed what he is arguing in the passage just cited—but he now derides the result as the product of men 'liable to French delusions' (*MY*, 2: 283).[2]

So one cannot conclude from this eloquent passage that Wordsworth thoroughly understood the fissures in Spain—between (a) autocrats, (b) 'afrancesados' who looked to Napoleonic intervention to sweep away Spain's feudal institutions, and (c) those liberals who combined similarly reformist objectives with a passion for independence—or that he identified primarily with the third faction, even though (as his 1816 letter recognized) *the logic of the passage points indubitably in that direction*. Nor, however, can one yet enlist him under Burke's counter-revolutionary banner. It is true that such phrases as 'Gratitude, habit and numerous other causes' and 'this saving and majestic Assembly' may appear to invoke Burkean values as well as Burkean periods. And many phrases throughout the *Cintra* suggest an affection for Burkean metaphors for the organic growth of institutions, such as 'young scions of polity must be grafted onto the time-worn trunk, a new fortress ... reared upon the ancient and living rock of justice' (4342). But, surely, Wordsworth's emphatic derision for 'eighty men ... with a king at their head', and for those who give 'undue preponderance to birth, station, rank and fortune' does not consort with what people imagine they mean when they use the short-hand epithet 'Burkean'.

The immediate reference of the long passage just quoted is to the power struggle between the Supreme Junta and the Cortes, but its theme—it arises so often in the

---

chief (and almost sole) recommendation to offices of trust, it is clear that such offices will in general be ably filled; and their duties, comparatively, well executed: ...'. French tyranny, that is, is based on the perversion of revolutionary renewal.

1   For a succinct appraisal see http://en.wikipedia.org/wiki/Spanish_Constitution_of_1812. Though annulled by the absolutist Ferdinand VII after the restoration, this document inspired political reform in Portugal, Mexico and Italy in the years of the Carbonari.

2   c.f. 281: 'They [the Cortes] thirsted after the independence of their country, and many of them nobly laboured to effect it; but, as to civil liberty and religious institutions, their notions were as wild as the most headstrong Jacobins of France, Their plan was to erect an Iberian Republic—and they were pushing matters desperately to that extremity. Think of a Republic in Spain—what horror to go through before such a thing could be brought about; and what worse than horrors would have attended its rapid destruction' (*MY*, 2: 281; c.f. 283.). In 1822, however, Wordsworth deplored the Bourbon intervention of in favour of the absolutist Ferdinand who had abolished that Constitution (*MY* 3: 179–80).

Cintra as to be its *leitmotiv*—is the unfitness of rulers to rule. What went wrong with Britain's first venture into the Peninsula, the argument is repeatedy insisted upon, is that it was entrusted to people whose background, education and above all, class, unfitted them for the task of liberation. Because Sir Harry Burrard, Sir Hew Dalrymple and Sir Arthur Wellesley were pre-destined from childhood for political power in a stratified society, they had been subjected to an education which, because it separated them from 'the People', made them unfit for purpose.

Similarly radical motifs include the pamphlet's internationalism, expressed most forcibly in its outrage at the convention's disregard of Portuguese interests; its crisply expressed agenda for Spain ('the first end to be secured by Spain is riddance of the enemy: the second, permanent independence: and the third, a free constitution of government; which will give their main [though far from sole] value to the other two; and without which little more than a formal independence, and perhaps scarcely that, can be secured'); its denunciation of Spain's lethargic government ('imbecile even to dotage, whose very selfishness was destitute of vigour .... whose sole aim it had been to prop up the last remains of its own decrepitude'); and a passionate belief in 'the People', redolent of *The Prelude*'s declaration 'I became a patriot':

> the cause of the People, in dangers and difficulties issuing from this quarter of oppression, is safe while it remains not only in the bosom but in the hands of the People; or (what amounts to the same thing) in those of a government which, being truly *from* the People, is faithfully *for* them.'

Much critical legerdemain would be required to reconcile this passage with Burke's famous equation of 'the People' with four hundred thousand people with a stake in the country, minus of course some 80,000 'pure Jacobins'.[1]

Yet the man who in 1808/09 criticises Spain's leaders for their failure to trust the people will, ten years later, be supporting the Lowther interest and 'old corruption' in

---

1 'I have often endeavoured to compute and to class those who, in any political view, are to be called the people. Without doing something of this sort we must proceed absurdly. We should not be much wiser, if we pretended to very great accuracy in our estimate. But I think, in the calculation I have made, the error cannot be very material. In England and Scotland, I compute that those of adult age, not declining in life, of tolerable leisure for such discussions, and of some means of information, more or less, and who are above menial dependence, (or what virtually is such) may amount to about four hundred thousand. ... This is the British publick; and it is a publick very numerous. The rest, when feeble, are the objects of protection; when strong, the means of force. ... Of these four hundred thousand political citizens, I look upon one fifth, or about eighty thousand, to be pure Jacobins; utterly incapable of amendment; objects of eternal vigilance; and when they break out, of legal constraint.' *Two Letters Addressed to A Member of the Present Parliament, on the Proposals for Peace with the Regicide Directory of France*, [Second Edition. Rivingtons, 1796.] 105–6.

his *Two Addresses to the Freeholders of Westmorland*:

> The basis of the elective Franchise being property, the legal condition of eligibil-
> ity to a seat in Parliament is the same. Our ancestors were not blind to the *moral*
> considerations which, if they did not suggest these ordinances, established a con-
> fidence in their expediency. Knowing that there could be no *absolute* guarantee
> for integrity, and that there was no *certain* test of discretion and knowledge, for
> bodies of men, the prudence of former times turned to the best substitute human
> nature would admit of, and civil society furnished. This was property; which
> shewed that a man had something that might be impaired or lost by mismanage-
> ment; something which tended to place him above dependence from need; and
> promised, though it did not insure, some degree of education to produce requisite
> intelligence. To be a Voter required a fixed Property, or a defined privilege; to
> be voted for, required more; and the scale of demand rose with the responsibil-
> ity incurred. A Knight of the Shire must have double the Estate required from a
> Representative of a Borough. This is the old Law; and the course of things, since,
> has caused, as was observed above, that high office to devolve almost exclusively
> on Persons of large Estate, or their near connections. And why is it desirable, that
> we should not deviate from this track?

This argument involves an utter recantation of the position maintained in the *Cintra*, just five years before, yet what makes the *Cintra* fascinating, is an undertow in
its rhetoric hinting at the *volte face* that is to come. In 1808, Wordsworth deplores
the Spaniards giving 'an undue preponderance to birth, station, rank, and fortune'
and electing men 'whose very virtue would incline them superstitiously to respect
established things, and to mistrust the People'. In 1818, in a polar reversal, the *Two
Addresses* advocate *precisely* such deference at home. The *Cintra* is a critique of the
British ruling class by one who, having got that off his chest, will soon decide (with
Sir George Beaumont and the Earl of Lonsdale demonstrating their taste and civility
on a regular basis), to throw in his lot with that same class. The author of the *Cintra*,
one might say, resembles an avalanche waiting to happen.

As is shown by the contentious critical history of the text, in which Stephen Gill,
Gordon Thomas, James K. Chandler and Deirdre Coleman have taken very different
views of its political stance, the text is by no means easy to read.[1] Deirdre Coleman's
1989 essay, already cited, sets out the text's ambivalences in exemplary fashion:

---

1   See Stephen Gill, *William Wordsworth: A Life* (Oxford and new York: Oxford University Press, 1989),
Gordon Kent Thomas, *Wordsworth's Dirge and Promise: Napoleon, Wellington, and the Convention of
Cintra* (Lincoln: University of Nebraska Press, 1971), James Chandler, *Wordsworth's Second Nature:
A Study of the Poetry and Politics* (Chicago: University of Chicago Press, 1984).

she adduces some persuasive indications that in 1806 to 1809 Wordsworth is indeed surprisingly wedded to confidence in the (British) people, and even parliamentary reform,[1] and, reading more closely than Chandler, she offers a deft analysis of Wordsworth's counter-Burkean application of Burke's metaphors (154–5). Tom Duggett, too, has recently offered a richly informed argument which situates the text in terms of what he (a shade problematically) calls 'a progressive 'Gothic' politics'.[2] The *Cintra*'s difficulty as text proceeds in part from the unaccustomed attempt of a reclusive and philosophic poet to engage successfully in contemporary political debate, and in part, no doubt, from the editorial collaboration of Coleridge and De Quincey. As prose the *Cintra* sometimes combines the worst features of all three authors, and its occasional impenetrability—arising partly from its preference for Miltonic over Paineite style—is perhaps responsible for the numerous misconstructions now extant, particularly on the internet, but even in scholarly journals, including naive readings founded in an anachronistic sense of what is implied by 'nationalism', and more serious distortions of its politics.

Much of Wordsworth's tract is perhaps best read less as journalism than as a prose poem in celebration of human nature and human possibility.[3] See, for instance the astonishing periodic sentence (truncated here, at some cost to its magnificent rhythms) which makes up most of lines 4119–4231 on the passions of human life:

> The history of all ages; tumults after tumults; ... wars—why and wherefore? yet with courage, with perseverance, with self-sacrifice, with enthusiasm...; the senseless weaving and interweaving of factions—vanishing and reviving and piercing each other like the Northern Lights; public commotions, and those in the bosom of the individual; the long calenture of fancy to which the Lover is subject; ... the slowly quickening but ever quickening descent of appetite down which the Miser is propelled; the agony and cleaving oppression of grief; the ghost-like hauntings

---

1 Coleman 'Reliving Jacobinism', 146; *MY*, 1: 11, 296; Coleman 154–5..
2 Tom Duggett, 'Wordsworth's Gothic Politics and The Convention of Cintra', *Review of English Studies*, n.s. 58:234 (2007), 186–211. Duggett uses the terms 'Gothic' and 'Saxon' as virtually interchangeable, as some Whig writers (including Locke's disciple Montesquieu) did. Certainly the myth of Saxon liberty is sometimes associated with 'Gothic' challenges to Rome. Confusion arises, however, because among more radical reformists and Commonwealthmen, such as John Thelwall and Obadiah Hulme, the terms Gothic and Saxon are used in binary opposition, and the father of Commonwealth theory, James Harrington, was at pains to desynonymise what he called a 'Gothic or feudal' constitution from that of a Commonwealth.
3 It is not merely, Coleridge irritably complained, 'a self-robbery from some great philosophical poem'—i.e. yet another distraction from *The Recluse*—but one without 'Shade and Background', 'all foreground, all in hot tints', the 'depth of Feeling .... so incorporated with depth of Thought, that the Attention is kept throughout at its utmost Strain and Stretch' (*C.L.* 3:214).

of shame; the incubus of revenge; the life-distemper of ambition;—these inward existences, and the visible and familiar occurrences of daily life in every town and village; the patient curiosity and contagious acclamations of the multitude in the streets of the city and within the walls of the theatre; a procession, or a rural dance; a hunting, or a horse-race; a flood, or a fire; rejoicing and ringing of bells for an unexpected gift of good fortune, or the coming of a foolish heir to his estate;—*these demonstrate incontestibly that the passions of men ... do immeasurably transcend their objects.*

'The true sorrow of humanity', Wordsworth concludes,

> consists in this;—not that the mind of man fails; but that the course and demands of action and of life so rarely correspond with the dignity and intensity of human desires: and hence that, which is slow to languish, is too easily turned aside and abused.

The passage is at once an almost Elian celebration of the variety of human existence, and a plea for human possibility—an exemplary formulation of that fundamental Romantic and *progressive* persuasion that man's state is inadequate to his conceptions. It introduces, in the next paragraph, Wordsworth's famous announcement that 'there is a spiritual community binding together the living and the dead; the good, the brave, and the wise, of all ages'. What unites this community, it is implied, is an inherited aspiration to a state of affairs more fitted to human possibility, and as his exemplar of that 'community' Wordsworth invokes Sir Philip Sidney as one who who saw himself engaged in '"the great work indeed in hand against the abusers of the world"'. The phrase reminds one of Wordsworth's imprecation against 'the unthinking Masters of the earth' in *The Pedlar*, retained in *The Excursion*. See also, in this context of resistance to oppressions, the strangely Shelleyan invocations of those Promethean virtues, hope and endurance, at Cintra 399–405 and elsewhere.

In the short essays that follow immediately upon this Foreword, Simon Bainbridge, David Bromwich, Timothy Michael and Patrick Vincent tease out some of the text's richness of implication. Each of these contributions notes its fascinating ambivalence and offers a different standpoint from which to assess that ambivalence. Simon Bainbridge, appraising 'Wordsworth's peninsular campaign [as] essentially literary, even poetic, and fought in the minds of men', argues that the tract's imaginative and poetic qualities are self-defeating. He points to how the 'oracular [and Miltonic] tone' raises Napoleon to the status of the great Satan, contributing to the myth he wishs to deflate, and how, despite the considerable pains taken by Wordsworth to root the argument in ascertainable fact, his decision to pitch its rhetoric somewhere between Milton and

Burke caused readers to focus upon its problematic style and disables it as polemic.

David Bromwich ponders the curious blend of exhortations—'at once republican, nationalist, and cosmopolitan'—in this work of 'moral suasion', an argument arriving at 'an ideology of republican nationalism' through 'vicarious association with another people's act of resistance'. Such vicarious resistance, it is argued, may be sufficient to reanimate an allied people's spirit of liberty. Obeying a familiar pattern in Wordsworth's compositional habits, as Wordsworth reconnects himself with the arguments of 1791–2 his essay of 1808–9 ends by challenging 'the habits and customs that seal the legitimacy of an aristocratic society'.

Timothy Michael's paper, which sees Wordsworth as closer to Milton than to Burke, meditates the Kantian question of what precisely is that 'knowledge of human nature' that Wordsworth accuses Sir Hew, Sir Harry and Sir Arthur of not possessing; what does it consist in and how do we come by it? 'Knowledge', as a word-search of its 43 uses will soon persuade the reader, is a key term in the *Cintra*, and the essay sees Wordsworth as engaged in an immanent (that is, non-Coleridgean and counter Humean) critique of Enlightenment thinking, seeking to rehabilitate Bacon's 'identification of knowledge with power' but in the context of the realization of human freedom.

Pointing out that liberal disenchantment with the Peninsular War arose from a suspicion that, unlike Wordsworth, the government's war aims included national independence but not 'a free constitution', Patrick Vincent points to Wordsworth's tactical difficulty and the eakness of his solution. Wishing Spain to achieve civil liberty, but determined that it must achieve national independence, Wordsworth persuades himself that 'liberty must ensue' from independence, a belief closely related to his tenacious upholding of 'the myth of Swiss liberty'. While overtly critical of government policy, and explicitly committed to classical republican values, Wordsworth thus allies himself implicitly (and, in the light of his later decisions, prophetically) with those for whom 'non-domination', without 'civil liberty', is a sufficient goal.

Simon Bainbridge

A Self-Defeating Campaign

WORDSWORTH'S imaginative campaign against Napoleon in the *Convention of* Cintra was, I shall argue, self-defeating. I begin by quoting what for me is one of the crucial passages in the *Convention of Cintra*, one which exemplifies Wordsworth's key rhetorical strategy in the tract. Writing of Wellington's initial victories over the French armies at Rolica and Vimiero, he comments:

> It was not for the soil, or for the cities and forts, that Portugal was valued, but for the human feeling which was there; for the rights of human nature which might be there conspicuously asserted; for a triumph over injustice and oppression there to be atchieved, which could neither be concealed nor disguised, and which should penetrate the darkest corner of the dark Continent of Europe by its splendour. We combated for victory in the empire of reason, for strong-holds in the imagination. Lisbon and Portugal, as city and soil, were chiefly prized by us as a *language*; but our generals mistook the counters of the game for the stake played for. (1401–9 [Clarendon 261–2])

There's much of interest in Wordsworth's key statement: his juxtaposition of the material with the emotional, the real with the symbolic; his construction of the war as a set of binary oppositions; his surprising adoption of a discourse of darkness more frequently applied to Africa than Europe; and his appropriation of elements of political discourse from both ends of the spectrum of the revolution debate of the previous decade. But what I particularly want to highlight here is Wordsworth's construction of the peninsular war as pre-eminently imaginative and discursive. As Wordsworth comments elsewhere in the Tract, Napoleon's 'power is strongest, in the imaginations of men, which are sure to fall under the bondage of long-continued success' (945–7 [249]), and it is this essentially imaginative nature of the war that the British generals who ratified the convention have failed to grasp – 'our Generals mistook the counters of the game for the stake played for.'

In the *Convention of Cintra*, then, Wordsworth tackles head on what we might see as the fundamental question addressed by critics of Romanticism over the last three decades, the relationship between politics or history and the imagination. And in a work in which he took enormous trouble to check and ascertain historical and military facts and details, Wordsworth gives a forceful answer: it is in the imaginations of men rather than on the battlefield that the decisive campaigns of world history are fought. Events themselves count for nothing if they are not seen or understood in the right way. In his pamphlet, Wordsworth sets out to fight this imaginative war against Napoleon, and he does so by producing a work that is highly literary in its style, its quotations and its allusions. Wordsworth deploys passages from Virgil, Dante, Sidney, Petrach and Plutarch, as well as from the Biblical books of Paul, Acts, Matthew and Daniel to create a work that is both 'dirge' and 'prophecy', to draw on two of the words he himself used in his sonnet on the composition of the tract beginning 'I dropped my pen;—and listened the wind'.[1] A key model for Wordsworth in his creation of this elevated work was John Milton, not only as a political prose writer, but also as the author of *Paradise Lost*, the inspirational epic for all the Romantic poets. The events of the Peninsular War offered Wordsworth a modern equivalent to the 'old / Romantic tale by Milton left unsung' which the poet had considered as a fit subject for his own epic ambition in the opening book of *The Prelude* (I, 179–80).[2] Indeed, as Coleridge indicates, the *Convention* can be seen as a displaced version of *The Recluse*, commenting that 'a considerable part [of the pamphlet] is almost a self-robbery from some great philosophical poem, of which it would form an appropriate part, & be fitlier attuned to the high dogmatic Eloquence, the oracular [tone] of inspired Blank Verse'.[3]

Wordsworth draws specifically on the language of Milton's blank verse epic as part of his attempt to drive Napoleon from the imagination; the French emperor haunts the text as the 'Fallen Spirit' possessed of 'satanic pride', and as the 'adversary of all good' who performs 'the worst deeds of darkness' (2866 [301]). More generally, Napoleon is described as 'the evil-doer' (877 [247]), who pursues 'nefarious purposes' and threatens the destruction of 'every thing which gives life its value–of virtue, of reason, of repose in God, or in truth' (641–2 [241]) Wordsworth frequently alludes

---

1 William Wordsworth, *Shorter Poems, 1807–1820*, edited by Carl H. Ketcham (Ithaca and London: Cornell University Press, 1989), p. 53.
2 References to *The Prelude* are by book and line number and are to the 1805 version in William Wordsworth, *the Prelude: 1799, 1805, 1850*, ed. Jonathan Wordsworth, M. H. Abrams, and Stephen Gill (New York and London; W. W. Norton and Co., 1979).
3 Quoted in Stephen Gill, *William Wordsworth: A Life* (Oxford and new York: Oxford University Press, 1989), p. 100.

to Milton's Satan in his descriptions of Napoleon and this provides him with both a way of explaining Bonaparte's power and a plot for his downfall. According to Wordsworth, Napoleon's power is 'not laid in any superiority of talents in him, but in his utter rejection of the restraints of morality – in wickedness which acknowledges no limit but the extent of its own power' (3285f [312]). Such a conception of power is Satanic, as Coleridge would clarify in his 'Letters on the Spaniards' when he repeated Wordsworth's argument, adding the phrase 'Evil be thou my good' from book 4 of *Paradise Lost*.[1] Through a series of allusions to Satan, Wordsworth also uses the parallel to present the inevitability of Napoleon's fall, reinforcing the literary prophecy with a series of more pragmatic arguments. There is an irony here, of course, in that in seeking to drive Napoleon from the imagination Wordsworth could be seen to make him all the more powerful; an irony enjoyed and exploited by the radical pro-Bonaparte essayist, who revelled in the fact that Napoleon had 'realised a conception of himself in the minds of his enemies on a par with the most stupendous creations of the imagination'.[2]

I've been arguing that Wordsworth's peninsular campaign is essentially literary, even poetic, and fought in the minds of men. To conclude, I want to draw attention to what I see as two aspects of this imaginative campaign, points that I hope will introduce issues we might debate later. The first of these issues is that I think in striving to enact the imaginative defeat of Napoleon, Wordsworth produces not only a version of *The Recluse*, as Coleridge suggested, but also a version of *The Prelude*, in the sense that he gives us another epic in which he himself is the hero. What the *Convention of Cintra* celebrates is a way of seeing, a way of responding to world affairs, which is essentially poetic and which is embodied by the narrator who addresses us. Indeed, Wordsworth turns to Coleridge's line 'I see, not feel, how beautiful they are' from 'Dejection: an Ode' when discussing 'the majority of men, who are usually found in high stations under old governments' as 'spectators who neither see nor feel'. Ultimately, it is the poet, the 'dauntless Bard' to quote a sonnet of 1806, who will raise and dignify our mortal state during a time of national and international crisis.

The second element I wish to highlight is something of the flip side of this claim for the poet's supreme role in international affairs. Despite Wordsworth's attempt to address his Countrymen, there is a striking tension between what is said in the

---

1 Samuel Taylor Coleridge, *Essays On His Times – in The Morning Post and the* Courier, 3. Vols, ed. David V. Erdman, Bollingen Series (London: Routledge and Princeton University Press, 1978), II, 63.
2 William Hazlitt, *The Complete Works*, 21 vols., ed. P. P. Howe (London: J. M. Dent, 1930–4), XVII, 22.

Convention of Cintra and how it is said, between the idea of the people Wordsworth describes and the status of the people it addresses. While writing the tract, Wordsworth feared that its publication might 'call forth the old yell of Jacobinism',[1] and in many ways, the *Convention* does seems to me to offer a continuation of Wordsworth's politics of the 1790s, in its celebration of the idea of the people as constituting the nation, in its positive recollection of the spirit of the French revolution, in its denunciation of allied aggression towards the revolution in the early 1790s, in its rejection of social hierarchy, in its emphasis on the corrupting effects of power, and in its critique of conventional forms of military and political leadership. But while these may seem like republican or reformist sentiments that we might trace back to Milton—and Southey did identify Wordsworth's admiration for Milton's prose as one of the reasons for its lack of perspicuity—contemporary readers much more often turned to another political writer for comparison, Edmund Burke, whether seeking to praise or criticize the tract. While Anthony Robinson commented that 'In true poetical inspiration & the bursting language of passion, he is infinitely above Burke', Thomas Quayle remarked that 'His Style resembles the worst of Burke's'; both were agreed, however that what were frequently identified as the Burkean elements of the tract–its prolixity, its long and complex sentences, its repetitions—would prevent it from having any widespread impact; Robinson argued that only one man in ten thousand will relish the work, though to him 'it will be the Bible of his Life', while Quayle concluded that 'I do not expect that he himself will be a Model to any body else'. [2] One of the most surprisingly astute comments on the Tract came from Lord Lonsdale, who commented that it was 'written in a very bad taste, not with plainness & simplicity such [as]is proper to a political subject, but in a style inflated & ill suited to it'.[3] While perhaps hostile to the politics of the tract, Lonsdale does seem to recognise that Wordsworth might have been better served by an adoption of the rhetorical qualities we might associate with the radical Thomas Paine, rather than those characteristic of his conservative antagonist, Burke.

1   Quoted Gill, *William Wordsworth*, p.275.
2   Quoted in Gordon Kent Thomas, *Wordsworth's Dirge and Promise: Napoleon, Wellington, and the Convention of Cintra* (Lincoln: University of Nebraska Press, 1971), pp. 137–8.
3   Quoted Gill, *William Wordsworth*, p, 276.

David Bromwich

Vicarious Feeling:
Spanish Independence, English Liberty

THE *Convention of Cintra* seems to me one of the great political essays of the Romantic era, but to call it a political essay is only a convenience. It begins as analysis and ends as a work of moral suasion, an eloquent statement of enthusiasm that means to convert its readers to a larger cause than the author can specify. Wordsworth wrote it with an urgency as driving as one feels in his major poems; yet its argument, plainly advancing a local cause under pressure of circumstance, remains difficult to reduce to practical wisdom. Its exhortations are at once republican, nationalist, and cosmopolitan: a curious blend. If, finally, Wordsworth professes an ideology of republican nationalism, the reader is made to arrive at national self-feeling by vicarious association with another people's act of resistance; it is resistance itself that comes to be identified with the spirit of revolution. So complete is this equation that Wordsworth can say that the spirit of the French Revolution is most alive in the work of destroying 'the child of the revolution,' Napoleon.

He wrote it not long after he had finished writing his Intimations Ode. He was even more concerned at this than at other periods with demonstrating the coherence of his life and feelings; and it is fair to say *The Convention of Cintra* means to prove his days 'Bound each to each by natural piety' in the realm of politics, just as the ode meant to prove them so in the realm of imagination and personal identity.

Politics, for Wordsworth, no less than poetry is subject to a test of sincerity, which means a test of sensation. Recall his words in the Preface to *Lyrical Ballads* about the natural interest taken by the poet in 'the goings-on of the Universe' (Clarendon, 1: 138); the same interest is shown by the citizen, in *The Convention of Cintra*, who pursues 'the appearances and intercourse of daily life' (2956 [Clarendon, 404]). The first of these concerns is abstract, the second particular and gregarious, but both are outward-looking and tend toward civic-mindedness. In *The Convention of Cintra*, too, Wordsworth cares for 'that knowledge which is founded not upon things but upon sensations;—sensations which are general, and under general influences (and this it is which makes them what they are, and gives them their importance);—not upon things which may be brought; but upon sensations which may be met' (2992–96 [304–05]). *To repel an invader* may afford the purest of all the sensations that war brings into being; it has that effect from the depth of the natural feelings connected with the idea of home. Such feelings, says Wordsworth, are neither gross nor uncontrolled; he speaks of 'the delicacy of moral honour which pervades the minds of a people, when despair has been suddenly thrown off and expectations are lofty' (3021 [305]).

If there is a particle of skepticism or self-distrust in the *Convention*, it relates to the wildness of the passions that war feeds. In the Preface to *The Borderers*, he had adverted to 'a kind of superstition which makes us shudder when we find moral sentiments to which we attach a sacred importance applied to vicious purposes'—as for example when a bad man convinces a good to commit murder out of loyalty. 'In real life,' Wordsworth adds, 'this is done every day' (Clarendon, 79); we do not see the commonness of the shift, because the 'superstition' makes us avert our eyes. At the time of the wars against Napoleon, it cannot have escaped his notice that such sacred sentiments were applied to vicious purposes most of all by the powerful, who lead nations into wars; the sacred attachment to home only adds to the power of such men, and in their own minds serves to acquit them of responsibility for acts not purely wicked, or for which high-sounding pretexts can be found. To Napoleon, in particular, a related perception of the Preface to *The Borderers* clearly pertains: 'a bad man may be furnished with sophisms in support of his crimes which it would be difficult to answer' (80) By contrast with the glamour of arbitrary power, true virtue may be known by a simplicity and a gravity that approach the condition of speechlessness; as Wordsworth remarks in his *Essay on Morals*, 'we do not *argue* in defence of our good actions' (304).

Clearly the Spanish resistance to Napoleon presents an example of such virtue; but how does Wordsworth know it? What is the immediate unarguable sensation of the Spanish people against the imposition of French power? The desire to throw off oppression might seem enough in itself; but it does not satisfy Wordsworth:

> Riddance, mere riddance—safety, mere safety—are objects far too defined, too inert and passive in their own nature, to have ability either to rouze or to sustain. They win not the mind by any attraction of grandeur or sublime delight, either in effort or in endurance: for the mind gains consciousness of its strength to undergo only by exercise among materials which admit the impression of its power,— which grow under it, which bend under it,—which resist,—which change under its influence,—which alter either through its might or in its presence, by it or be-

fore it. These, during times of tranquility, are the objects with which, in the studious walks of sequestered life, Genius most loves to hold intercourse; by which it is reared and supported;—these are the qualities in action and in object, in image, in thought, and in feeling, from communion with which proceeds originally all that is creative in art or science, and all that is magnanimous in virtue.—Despair thinks of *safety*, and hath no purpose; fear thinks of safety; despondency looks the same way:—but these passions are far too selfish, and therefore too blind, to reach the thing at which they aim; even when there is in them sufficient dignity to have an aim.—All courage is a projection from ourselves; however short-lived, it is a motion of hope. But these thoughts bind too closely to something inward,—to the present and to the past,—that is, to the self which is or has been. Whereas the vigour of the human soul is from without and from futurity,—in breaking down limit, and losing and forgetting herself in the sensation and image of Country and of the human race; and, when she returns and is most restricted and confined, her dignity consists in the contemplation of a better and more exalted being, which, though proceeding from herself, she loves and is devoted to as to another (2510–34 [291–92]).

In this tremendous passage, we can feel him pressing beyond political expectation to a more-than-political hope. The spirit of self-surpassing, here, also suggests a moral problem about the limits of politics. What if the *justice* of the cause extends only to mere 'riddance'? What, then, becomes of the vast radiations of a feeling that cannot contain itself, or rest content with so merely negative a triumph?

By hope, Wordsworth means solidarity of feeling that extends from people to people; the British sympathy for Spanish resistance is evoked to illustrate the broader phenomenon of such enthusiasm:

This just and necessary war, as we have been accustomed to hear it styled from the beginning of the contest in the year 1793, had, some time before the Treaty of Amiens, viz. after the subjugation of Switzerland, and not till then, begun to be regarded by the body of the people, as indeed both just and necessary; and this justice and necessity were by none more clearly perceived, or more feelingly bewailed, than by those who had most eagerly opposed the war in its commencement, and who continued most bitterly to regret that this nation had ever borne a part in it. Their conduct was herein consistent: they proved that they kept their eyes steadily fixed upon principles; for, though there was a shifting or transfer of hostility in their minds as far as regarded persons, they only combated the same enemy opposed to them under a different shape; and that enemy was the spirit of selfish tyranny and lawless ambition (67–79 [226]).

What is surprising is Wordsworth's eagerness to connect his sense of the purity of heart of the English people with a vindication of his own consistency. Thus, he suggests that the argument for regicide, which fifteen years earlier he had applied to Louis XVI, may be transferred to the war against Napoleon. And he goes still further in identifying his sentiments with those of his countrymen: the English people, he surmises in a parenthesis, actually favored in secret the French revolution in all its early stages. He refers first more narrowly to the 'class of persons' who shared the spirit he himself espoused, but adds: '(and I would now be understood, as associating them with an immense majority of the people of Great Britain, whose affections, notwithstanding all the delusions which had been practiced upon them, were, in the former part of the contest, for a long time on the side of their nominal enemies)' (80–84 [226]). Elsewhere in the *Convention*, he will go out of his way to connect the wisdom of the people of France with their support for the French Assembly, and to instruct the Spanish people to look back on the first years of the revolution as no unhappy example: 'Much, in the outward manner, might there be found worthy of qualified imitation. … Spain has nothing to dread from Jacobinism' (3973 [332]).

Articulate opponents (like himself) of the first stage of the war with France underwent a change of heart when the enemy became Napoleon, but they only did so initially 'in order to be preserved from spirit-breaking submissions' (92 [226]). So the motive was no more than resistance to self-subjection; riddance, one might say, practiced from a secure distance:

> But from the moment of the rising of the people of the Pyrenean peninsula, there was a mighty change; we were instantaneously animated; and, from that moment, the contest assumed the dignity, which it is not in the power of any thing to bestow: and, if I may dare to transfer language, prompted by a revelation of a state of being that admits not of decay or change, to the concerns and interests of our transitory planet, from that moment 'this corruptible put on incorruption, and this mortal put on immortality' (127–33 [Clarendon 227–28]).

The difference between the political aim of the war and its moral object opens here as wide the difference between an ordinary motive and a sublime reason:

> We were intellectualized also in proportion; we looked backward upon the records of the human race with pride, and, instead of being afraid, we delighted to look forward into futurity (140 [Clarendon, 228]).

In that sentence, effort and expectation and desire form a complex of feeling against tyranny; it is the same emotion, more abstractly directed and considered, that Wordsworth comes to know in *The Prelude* after crossing the Alps.

By comparison, the patriotic motive of the *Convention* seems almost commonplace. Yet, even here, Wordsworth holds himself answerable to a faith in human dignity that has deep roots in sensation: 'labouring under these violations done to their moral nature,' he observes, the Spanish people 'describe themselves, in the anguish of their souls, treated as a people at once dastardly and *insensible*' (708 [243]). It is that elemental, sensible denial of human status, that prompts Wordsworth at last to describe Napoleon as satanic. He is said to exemplify 'that blind energy and those habits of daring which are often found in men who, checked by no restraint of morality, suffer their evil passions to give extraordinary strength in extraordinary circumstances' (2884–6). And yet, his wish for his own countrymen is that they should 'so far imitate our enemies as, like them, to shake off these bonds; but not, like them, from the worse—but from the worthiest impulse' (2891 [302]). Self-knowledge will thereby enforce a lesson of humility in judging the French; the character of their leader is that of 'the Fallen Spirit, triumphant in misdeeds, which was formerly a blessed Angel' (2908 [302]). This amounts to a metaphysical statement on the nature of the French empire as evil incarnate—though in a key more charitable than that of Burke, who never speaks of the innocence of Lucifer before his rebellion. Such is the strange versatility of Wordsworth's choice of tactics that he elects to describe the 'Enemy of mankind,' at the same time, in altogether historical language, as a backward character. 'In vindication of the dignity of human nature,' he remarks that Napoleon does not altogether deserve either credit or blame for his dominion: 'it has risen from circumstances over which he had no influence; circumstances which, with the power they conferred, have stimulated passions whose natural food hath been and is ignorance; from the barbarian impotence and insolence of a mind—originally of ordinary constitution—lagging, in moral sentiment and knowledge, three hundred years behind the age in which it acts' (3301–2 [313]). Paradoxically, the proof of the existence of a more-than-historical agency, which renders Napoleon a vehicle for moral progress, is precisely the fact that his character and formation were primitive and regressive.

We come now to the most perplexing feature of Wordsworth's argument; for the essence of his doctrine of hope is not personal faith but vicarious feeling. Yet a feeling with broad consequences: the revolutionary defense of Spanish independence is made to issue in a prophecy of a revival of English liberty. We infer that sympathy with the Spanish cause cannot but lead the people of England to re-examine their own social arrangements and conspire to make a revolution at home. Some such appeal from participation abroad to the inevitability of domestic reform is familiar from other instances. (George Orwell in *The Lion and the Unicorn* made a similar argument, during the Second World War. The unity of the common people in the struggle against fascism would produce a social revolution and indeed would assure the acceptance of socialism in England.) Hence, for Wordsworth, the logical progression in such a passage as the following, from local sympathy to general commitment; the English people know, he says, that the privilege of complaint and petition, 'a privilege, the exercise of which implies condemnation of something complained of, followed by a prayer for its removal or correction—not only is established by the most grave and authentic charters of Englishmen, who have been taught by their wisest statesmen and legislators to be jealous over its preservation' but is also 'an indispensable condition of all civil liberty' (2273–4 [285]). The enjoyment of English liberty implicates the liberty of mankind; and on this occasion the English have responded accordingly, to Spain, as if its call emanated from all men and women: 'The object was at a distance; and it rebounded upon us, as with force collected from a mighty distance; we were calm till the very moment of transition; and all the people were moved—and felt as with one heart, and spake as with one voice' (2438–41 [289]). Such unity among an entire people, when directed upon an unselfish object, Wordsworth takes to signify a directive of human nature itself.

But what English popular feeling had realized early and by intuition, English force had nearly suppressed in the government policy toward Spain. The cry of sympathy was 'the power of popular resistance rising out of universal reason, and from the heart of human nature' (1074–5 [253]): it is the nature of such stirrings that they add fresh power to the body they affect. The fear that the Spanish resistance would be colored by Spanish prejudice was thus misguided:

> Short-sighted despondency! Whatever mixture of superstition there might be in the religious faith or devotional practices of the Spaniards; this must have necessarily been transmuted by that triumphant power, wherever that power was felt, which grows out of intense moral suffering—from the moment in which it coalesces with fervent hope. The chains of bigotry, which enthralled the mind, must have turned into armour to defend and weapons to annoy. Wherever the heaving and effort of freedom was spread, purification must have followed it (2571–78 [Clarendon 293]).

The act of revolt improves the revolutionist—it is a claim one might expect to hear from the Wordsworth of 1793. This happens, he thinks, because the person who chooses to act at all and is ready to suffer, has moved himself toward exposure to sensation, and hence toward radical sympathy and imagination. He is more alive than other men in spirit because he is more active in mind. Voluntary activity itself, indeed, Wordsworth would have us associate with moral purification.

In the continuation of the passage above, he speaks of the credulous faith in 'miraculous interposition' as a form of mental dependency that in times of crisis may be spurred to effects beyond itself. Religious faith becomes 'a power added to a power; a breeze which springs up unthought-of to assist the strenuous oarsman' until at last 'it passes into a habit of obscure and infinite confidence of the mind in its own energies' (2611–16 [294]). In the naturalized psychology of religion that Wordsworth here suggests, faith gives support to human confidence that is beyond the reach of other explanations. And, just as faith is a breeze that assists the 'strenuous oarsman' of physical resistance, so emancipation may serve to enlighten the practice of faith. Once the Spanish people had thrown off oppression, it was it was noticeable to Wordsworth how far 'the perceptions—the impulses—and the actions also' far outstripped what might have been expected from the history of the Spanish character. So, in all cases, 'how much farther ... the principles and practice of a people, with great objects before them to concentrate their love and their hatred, transcend the principles and practice of governments' (2811–14 [300]). The laws grow barbarous when a people forget their liberty, but, with the recovery of liberty, when their spirits are united for the common good, people may give an intimation of laws more perfect than any they have known. The only reason that governments can be good is that people transcend their governments.

What finally is the practical meaning of Wordsworth's vicarious love of Spanish independence? We must work with hints, for he writes ostensibly of Spain alone. But near the end of the *Convention*, he offers a radical challenge, not to the system of property, title, and rank as such—as he had done in *A Letter to the Bishop of Llandaff*—but rather to the habits and customs that seal the legitimacy of an aristocratic society. Chief among those habits in Spain is gratitude—a conventional virtue that Wordsworth (like Godwin and Shelley) treats as a vice:

> Gratitude, habit, and numerous other causes must have given an undue preponderance to birth, station, rank, and fortune; and have fixed the election, more than was reasonable, upon those who were most conspicuous for these distinctions;—men whose very virtue would incline them superstitiously to respect established things, and to mistrust the People—towards whom not only a frank confidence but a forward generosity was the first of duties (3528–33 [319]).

The value placed in such habits of deference served to retard the cause of Spanish liberty; we are left to draw the appropriate conclusion regarding the people and the aristocracy of England.

The largest enemy of a free life of the spirit, as Wordsworth translates his politics into moral prophecy, would seem to be mere labor, or toil:

> The great end and difficulty of life for men of all classes, and especially difficult for those who live by manual labour, is a union of peace with innocent and laudable animation. Not by bread alone is the life of Man sustained; not by raiment alone is he warmed;—but by the genial and vernal inmate of the breast, which at once pushes forth and cherishes; by self-support and self-sufficing endeavours; by anticipations, apprehensions, and active remembrances; by elasticity under insult, and firm resistance to injury; by joy, and by love; by pride which his imagination gathers in from afar; by patience, because life wants not promises; by gratitude which—debasing him not when his fellow-being is his object—habitually expands itself, for his elevation, in complacency towards his Creator (3753–63 [Clarendon 326]).

The intransitive use of *cherishes* is notable here for its resemblance to a similar inventive usage in the Intimations Ode. Spontaneous feeling presses outward from the heart as a plant from its soil—-upholds us, cherishes, and testifies to the energetic continuity of mere being. The 'gratitude' in question here is to be distinguished from the vice of gratitude observed under an aristocracy. It comes now from an experience of equality, and expresses a feeling one has toward a 'fellow being.' As for the things by which man does live, for Wordsworth they appear to be friendship, leisure, and self-exertion, the last always heightened by the possibility of contest. Strife, or war, he regards as an extreme, obtrusively material, and perhaps dispensable form of contest.

War inspires acts of self-sacrifice that human nature would be better for owning without the impetus of war. Yet here once more we confront the puzzle of a sublime motive called into being by an exertion in itself destructive and undesirable—the exalted sentiment that comes to be applied to a vicious purpose. It seems a tragedy of our nature that 'disaster opens the eyes of conscience' (4071 [335]). We could be seated more happily (but also more sedately?) in our lives if conscience did not require to be thus shaken. Better, however, Wordsworth implies, to know unsettling sensations than not to feel at all: the condition, he suspects, of most of the men in high stations in the old regime of Europe. 'These spectators neither see nor feel' (3049 [306]). The danger is lest in reaction against the 'insensibility of these, and the train whom they draw along,' men of energy like Wordsworth—in this resembling Napoleon after all—should grow too attached to exultations and agonies. 'Magnificent desires,' he warns, 'when least under the bias of personal feeling, dispose the mind—more than itself is conscious of—to regard commotion with complacency, and to watch the aggravations of distress with welcoming; from an immoderate confidence that, when the appointed day shall come, it will be in the power of intellect to relieve' (3074–78 [307]). One is compelled to read the admonition as a conclusive praise of the spirit of resistance, an acknowledgment of its kinship with the spirit of conquest, but also as a self-correction by Wordsworth: not to confuse the enchantment of vicarious patriotism with the purer and less betrayable hopes of intellect and imagination. Yet such hopes have politics always in view among the fields of action in which they become vivid to themselves. In this sense, the spirit of national liberty that Wordsworth discovers in 1807–08 is a direct descendant of his experience and thinking in 1791–92. As the foregoing quotations show, the displacement of the scene to the Spanish peninsula created, for his moral energy and political passion, a surer focus than he had found at any time in the preceding decade.

Timothy Michael

The State of Knowledge
in *The Convention of Cintra*

FOURTEEN years before composing *The Convention of Cintra* (1809), Wordsworth wrote to his Cambridge friend, William Matthews, who had recently visited the Iberian Peninsula. Wordsworth asks: 'What rema[rks] do you make on the Portuguese? in what state is knowledge with them? and have the principles of free government any advocate there? or is Liberty a sound, of which they have never heard? Are they so debased by superstition as we are told, or are they improving in anything?' (Letter to William Matthews, 17 February, 1794).[1] Wordsworth would assume a more forgiving tone regarding Portuguese superstition in *Cintra*, but his interest in the 'state of knowledge' with them, and with British statesmen, would remain undiminished. The state and status of knowledge are, I argue, at the center of Wordsworth's political pamphlet ('state,' with its senses of both 'condition' and 'body politic,' and 'status' share, of course, an etymological root [L, *status*, 'condition'], which would also give rise to 'estate'). The immediacy with which Wordsworth inquires into the Portuguese state of knowledge, and the question's contiguity with a question about the 'principles of free government,' is telling. The argument of *The Convention of Cintra* is premised on an intimate connection between knowledge and liberty ('Wherever the heaving and effort of freedom was spread, [mental] purification must have followed it' [2577-78]).[2] The pamphlet defines knowledge in such a way as to justify a militaristic defense of freedom.

The argument of *Cintra* is straightforward: in allowing the defeated French army to leave the Iberian Peninsula on the most favourable terms, the British generals who

---

1   *The Early Letters of William and Dorothy Wordsworth (1785–1805)*, ed. Ernest de Selincourt (London: Oxford University Press, 1935), p.110
2   William Wordsworth, *The Convention of Cintra* in *The Prose Works of William Wordsworth*, Vol. I, ed. W. J. B Owen and Jane Worthington Smyser (Oxford: Clarendon Press, 1974), p.293 [all subsequent references to *Cintra* given with line numbers only]

negotiated the treaty disgraced Great Britain and offended, in the parlance of the time, something called 'the spirit of liberty.' It is an extraordinary document, exhibiting a keen and undervalued political intellect, a prescient understanding of power relations in global politics, and remarkable rhetorical efficacy. The influence of Burke on Wordsworth's rhetoric in *Cintra* has been pursued by Alfred Cobban and, later, by James Chandler in *Wordsworth's Second Nature* (1984). Stephen Gill adds that 'If Wordsworth has a model it is Milton rather than Burke, but again and again in images and manner of address the *Reflections* are evoked and *Cintra* is not damaged by the comparison.'[1]

The relative indebtedness of *Cintra* to Burke and Milton, discussed by Chandler and Gill primarily in stylistic terms, raises the crucial question of what kind of pamphlet this is, politically and ideologically. Gordon Kent Thomas, in the most extensive treatment of the tract, *Wordsworth's Dirge and Promise* (1971), correctly situates the tract in the tradition of English liberalism.[2] Thomas dismisses poorly founded charges that Wordsworth's doctrine of 'National Happiness' in *Cintra* is an early manifestation of more pernicious twentieth-century forms of nationalism and that Wordsworth, in the words of one critic, 'enunciated an anti-democratic doctrine of leadership which foreshadows the 'hero-worship' of Carlyle.'[3] Wordsworth's doctrine of National Happiness, Thomas observes, should be understood in the context of his definition in *Cintra* of a nation as 'nothing but aggregates of individuals;' the charge of hero-worship disappears after even the most cursory reading of the pamphlet, which argues for the necessity of challenging the authority of those who claim to speak on behalf of the people and which belittles the souls and minds of men like Napoleon ('... a Tyrant's domain of knowledge is narrow ...' [2764]). The tract is a powerful statement of democratic principles—its repeated emphasis is on the value of 'a government which, being truly *from* the People, is faithfully *for* them' (3491–92). In terms of doctrine, Wordsworth is considerably closer to Milton than he is to Burke. He commends the Spanish for respecting 'established laws, forms, and practices,' but, he argues, 'when old and familiar means are not equal to the exigency, new ones

---

1   Cf. James Chandler, *Wordsworth's Second Nature: A Study of the Poetry and Politics* (Chicago: University of Chicago Press, 1984), pp.42–44; Alfred Cobban, *Edmund Burke and the Revolt Against the Eighteenth-Century* (New York: Barnes and Noble, 1929), pp. 140–52; Stephen Gill, *Wordsworth: A Life* (Oxford: Clarendon Press, 1989), pp.274–277
2   Gordon Kent Thomas, *Wordsworth's Dirge and Promise* (Lincoln: University of Nebraska Press, 1971)
3   Albert C. Baugh, ed., *A Literary History of England*, vol. 4, Samuel C. Chew, *The Nineteenth Century and After* (New York: Appleton-Century-Crofts, 1948), p.1145

must, without timidity, be resorted to' (314–15). Wordsworth praises the Spanish people, 'whose failing of excess, if such there exist, is assuredly on the side of loyalty to their Sovereign, and predilection for all established institutions' (371–73). *Cintra* ends, significantly, with a passage from Milton's *History of Great Britain*, criticizing 'our ancestors' who were 'valiant, indeed, and prosperous to win a field; but, to know the end and reason of winning, injudicious and unwise' (4370).

The knowledge of means and ends, one of the crucial forms of political knowledge for Wordsworth, is a dominant motif in *Cintra*.[1] In addition to the instances just mentioned, Wordsworth uses the means/end distinction to frame the broader significance of the conflict. Moving from the 'contemplation of their errors in the estimate and application of means to the contemplation of their heavier errors and worse blindness in regard to ends,' Wordsworth laments that 'the British Generals acted as if they had no purpose but that the enemy should be removed from the country in which they were, upon *any* terms' (1394–96). The stakes of the conflict, for Wordsworth, are much higher than 'mere riddance' of the French. 'We combated for victory in the empire of reason, for strong-holds in the imagination. Lisbon and Portugal, as city and soil, were chiefly prized by us as a *language*; but our Generals mistook the counters of the game for the stake played for' (1406–09). Winning the battle of 'mere riddance' means little in the context of a broader spiritual and imaginative war, in which the conquest of cities signifies greater victories in an inexorable 'march of Liberty' (3949).

Wordsworth quite obviously saw the treaty as part of a broader drama between liberty and injustice. This drama, I am suggesting, revolves around the definition of knowledge: knowledge may be defined in the service of conflicting interests, and it is crucial for the interests of liberty that it be defined in sufficiently liberal terms. Knowledge is a keyword in the essay, appearing with remarkable frequency. The communication of knowledge provides the justification of the essay: 'For all knowledge of human nature leads ultimately to repose; and I shall write to little purpose if I do not assist some portion of my readers to form an estimate of the grounds of hope and fear in the present effort of liberty against oppression' (482–485). Wordsworth writes that this '[most sacred cause] calls aloud for the aid of the intellect, knowledge, and love' (884–85). He goes on: 'It is not from any thought that I am communicating

---

1   Cf. 4472–78 [Clarendon p.331] for Wordsworth's explicit invocation of the liberal Kantian distinction between means and ends. There is, it should be noted, a tension in Wordsworth's recognition of the Spanish and Portuguese people as rational creatures, worthy to be treated as ends themselves, and his view of the conflict as a mere signifier of a broader historical drama.

new information, that I have dwelt thus long upon this subject, but to recall to the reader his own knowledge, and to re-infuse into that knowledge a breath and life of appropriate feeling' (889–92). Wordsworth implies the existence of knowledge of which one is unaware, of a kind of unconscious knowledge, and intends to 're-infuse' into that knowledge the 'breath' and 'life' of feeling. Knowledge, then, is not dead matter—independent facts about the mechanical operation of the physical world, for example—but something capable of being resuscitated. The inspiring function of the inspired poet is here transferred to the political essayist, as Wordsworth hopes to breathe new life into a kind of unrealized knowledge. The conjunction of knowledge with the 'breath and life of appropriate feeling' suggests an associated sensibility that, Wordsworth contends, is the precondition of any solution to the political crisis (what constitutes 'appropriate' feeling is something we may wish to consider). The conjunction of knowledge and tranquility, or repose, is repeated in a rejection of the claim that submission to Napoleon's authority would result in peace and happiness: '[P]eace and happiness can exist only by knowledge and virtue; slavery has no enduring connection with tranquillity or security' (1283–85). Wordsworth implies that knowledge, along with virtue, is the condition of both political security and individual tranquility, a variation of the claim made in the 1802 Preface that pleasure is the condition of knowledge.

Knowledge is again at the centre of Wordsworth's political argument, as he contends that a lack of knowledge was the cause of this national disgrace and that its only solution consists in the establishment of a particular kind of knowledge, what Coleridge, Shelley and others would call 'political knowledge.' Inquiring into the 'original sources of our miscarriages,' Wordsworth declares 'First; a want, in the minds of the members of government and public functionaries, of knowledge indispensable for this service; and, secondly, a want of power, in the same persons acting in their corporate capacities, to give effect to the knowledge which individually they possess' (2914–18). Wordsworth stops short of identifying knowledge with power, as he does in the eventually deleted passage on Bacon, but he does assert an intimate connection: power 'gives effect' to knowledge. Godwinian optimism in inevitable progress based on human reason is discarded, as Wordsworth argues for the necessity of applying knowledge through political and social institutions, i.e. recognized individuals acting in their 'corporate capacities.' This, then—'the want of appropriate and indispensable knowledge' and the power to apply that knowledge—is the cause of the problem. The solution follows from this. 'How far,' Wordsworth asks, 'is it in our power to make amends for the harm done?,' acknowledging that Britain has a responsibility to make reparations to a country it has treated unjustly. 'We may confidently affirm that nothing, but a knowledge of human nature directing the operations of our government, can give it a right to an intimate association with a cause which is that of human nature. I say, an intimate association founded on the right of thorough knowledge' (2970–74). A science of human nature (and indeed a poetry of human nature) thus has considerable political value.

The British government, according to Wordsworth, has a right to interfere in the Portuguese cause only if it proceeds from a thorough knowledge of human nature. What this knowledge of human nature looks like, or what it consists of, is not entirely clear, although Wordsworth attempts to define it in opposition to other foundations of right. He proposes first 'to contradistinguish this best mode of exertion from another which might find *its* right upon a vast and commanding military power put forth with manifestation of sincere intentions to benefit our allies' (2974–78). British interference is justified insofar as it proceeds from a knowledge of human nature, but not if it is justified on the basis of military might and noble intentions. He also distinguishes 'this best mode of exertion' from a 'conviction merely of policy that their liberty, independence, and honour, are our genuine gain' (2977–78). British association with the Portuguese cause cannot be self-serving, motivated by the assumption that a free and stable Iberian Peninsula is essential to the security and prosperity of Great Britain.

These distinctions do not, however, specify what is meant by 'knowledge of human nature.' What, then, does the phrase signify? Wordsworth enumerates many of its possible forms: knowledge of 'the instincts of natural and social man,' 'the deeper emotions,' 'the simpler feelings,' 'the spacious range of the disinterested imagination,' 'the pride in country for country's sake, when to serve has not been a formal profession,' 'the instantaneous accomplishment in which they start up who, upon a searching call, stir for the land which they love,' 'the delicacy of moral honour,' 'the apprehensiveness to a touch unkindly or irreverent,' and 'the power of injustice and inordinate calamity' to bring out the best in men (3011–32). There does not appear to be any necessary connection between these various forms of knowledge—that is, it is not immediately obvious how knowledge of the 'spacious range of the disinterested imagination' is the same in kind as knowledge of 'the power of injustice'—but Wordsworth's catalogue suggests some form of entailment. Knowledge of human nature, an apparently descriptive science, somehow entails knowledge of just political arrangements, or alleged 'knowledge' of normative propositions.

These are, for Wordsworth, the 'indispensable' forms of political knowledge, conspicuously absent in the British generals, Wellesley and Dalyrymple, who negotiated the treaty. 'It is plain *a priori*,' Wordsworth writes, 'that the minds of Statesmen and Courtiers are unfavorable to the growth of this knowledge'[1] (that this is plain *a priori* is a strange claim). This is so because they 'are in a situation exclusive and artificial,' cut off from the real world in an environment designed to increase their pride, and because this knowledge is 'founded not upon things but upon sensations;—sensations which are general and under general influences (and this it is which makes them what they are, and gives them their importance);—not upon things which may be *brought*; but upon sensations which must be *met*' (2985–96). This knowledge comes only from an active, empirical engagement with, in the words of the Preface, the world of 'real men,' 'real life,' and 'real events,' and is denied to those whose intellects have been weakened by inherited wealth and privilege. 'Hence, where higher knowledge is a prime requisite, [practical statesmen] not only are unfurnished; but, being unconscious that they are so, they look down contemptuously upon those who endeavor to supply (in some degree) their want' (3008–11). Wordsworth is, of course, speaking of himself here, but he is also speaking of the poet more generally. As he says in the Preface, the poet has a 'greater knowledge of human nature, and a more comprehensive soul.'[2] This 'greater knowledge of human nature' is precisely the kind of political knowledge Wordsworth addresses in *The Convention of Cintra*: knowledge of the passions of real men. Lest one think that Wordsworth's aim is to 'disparage the characters of men high in authority,' he assures the reader that his purpose is to guard against unreasonable expectations: 'That specific knowledge,—the paramount importance of which, in the present condition of Europe, I am insisting upon,—they, who usually fill places of high trust in old governments, neither do—nor, for the most part, can—possess: nor is it necessary, for the administration of affairs in ordinary circumstances, that they should' (3058–62). These, though, are extraordinary circumstances, demanding 'that specific knowledge' unfortunately denied to those accustomed to power. 'The fact is certain—that there is an unconquerable tendency in all power, save that of knowledge acting by and through knowledge, to injure the mind of him who exercises that power' (3111–13). Power corrupts, but power, however absolute, does not necessarily corrupt absolutely. Power that begins in knowledge and that is exercised through knowledge need not be injurious to the powerful.

    So much for the powerful, but what of the powerless—the conquered people of

---

1   2985 (Clarendon, p. 304)

2   William Wordsworth, Preface to the *Lyrical Ballads*, in *The Prose Works of William Wordsworth*, Vol. I, ed. W. J. B. Owen and Jane Worthington Smyser (Oxford: Clarendon Press, 1974), p.138

Spain and Portugal? Of all possible responses to French aggression, Spanish and Portuguese submission is, for Wordsworth, the least desirable. Justification for submission based on the idea that they would somehow benefit materially from French domination is particularly worrisome. Allowing, Wordsworth says, 'that the mass of the Population would be placed in a condition outwardly more thriving—would be *better off* (as the phrase in conversation is); it is still true that—in the act and consciousness of submission to an imposed lord and master, to a will not growing out of themselves....there would be the loss of a sensation within for which nothing external ...can make amends' (3699–709). Economic security is meager recompense for spiritual submission. Wordsworth's discomfort in even entertaining the idea—an idea so foreign to him that he is forced to borrow the common '*better off*' to express it (presumably one of the 'real defects' of the language that would be purified in his poetry)—is not merely indicative of Romantic bourgeois ideology or the struggle for cultural capital in which Wordsworth and Coleridge were engaged. The discomfort reflects fundamental principles of Wordsworth's immanent critique of the pre-Kantian Enlightenment. Just as the minds of men have been atrophied to state of almost 'savage torpor' by inferior cultural products, so have the minds of men, specifically their imaginations, been atrophied by the narrow pursuits of the experimental philosophy.

> [I]n many parts of Europe (and especially in our own country), men have been pressing forward, for some time, in a path which has betrayed by its fruitfulness; furnishing them constant employment for picking up things about their feet, when thoughts were perishing in their minds. While Mechanic Arts, Manufactures, Agriculture, Commerce, and all those products of knowledge which are confined to gross—definite—and tangible objects, have, with the aid of the Experimental Philosophy, been every day putting on more brilliant colours; the splendour of the Imagination has been fading: Sensibility, which was formerly a generous nursling of rude Nature, has been chased from its ancient range in the wide dominion of patriotism and religion with the weapons of derision by a shadow calling itself Good Sense: calculations of presumptuous Expediency—groping its way among the partial and temporary consequences—have been substituted for the dictates of paramount and infallible Conscience, the supreme embracer of consequences: lifeless and circumspect Decencies have banished the graceful negligence and unsuspicious dignity of Virtue. (3723–38)

Material progress has outpaced spiritual progress, with disastrous moral, political, and religious consequences. To suggest that the benefits of entering the Continental System compensate for the absence of self-determination is to lose sight of the positive freedom that is only afforded by the unrestrained use of the creative imagination. The 'calculations of presumptuous Expediency' can only yield 'partial and temporary consequences' (the frequent reference to 'expediency' and 'fixed 'principles' in *Cintra* reflects perhaps the influence of Coleridge, who in the same year was writing on theories of expediency and the principles of political knowledge in *The Friend*). Recall Wordsworth's professed aim in writing *The Convention of Cintra*, quoted above: 'to re-infuse' into the reader's 'knowledge a breath and life of appropriate feeling' (891–2). Here, again, Wordsworth values animated thought: real thoughts are unfortunately 'perishing' while gross, definite, and tangible forms of knowledge are lifeless 'things' to be picked up from the ground. There are at least two kinds of knowledge, then, both with political relevance: indefinite, animated knowledge infused with feeling and definite, inanimate knowledge that is somehow less real, or less important. The failure to distinguish between the two has led to a misunderstanding of liberty, knowledge of which can only be gained in conjunction with the sensibility and the imagination and not through the 'calculations of presumptuous expediency.' Wordsworth departs from Coleridge here, exhibiting some reservations regarding the political theory of expediency promoted in *The Friend*.

The distinction between material and spiritual progress is pursued in a lengthy passage eventually deleted from the pamphlet. In it, Wordsworth goes to an origin of the English Enlightenment as part of a larger critique its eighteenth-century manifestations:

> Lord Bacon two hundred years ago announced that knowledge was power and strenuously recommended the process of experiment and induction for the attainment of knowledge. But the mind of this philosopher was comprehensive and sublime and must have had intimate communion of the truth of which experimentalists who deem themselves his disciples are for the most part ignorant viz. that knowledge of facts conferring power over the combinations of things in the material world has no determinate connection with power over the faculties of the mind. Nay so far is such encrease from being a necessary result that it is scarcely possible to [? strengthen] and unite the two species of power in such a manner that the more noble shall not lag behind in proportion to the rapid and eager advancement of the less noble. (3727 n.)

Wordsworth suggests that the project of spiritual, or non-material, enlightenment (what he would broadly define as poetry) cannot employ the same method as the 'mechanical arts.' Bacon's dictum that knowledge is power is true enough so long as it remains confined to the material world. One cannot assume that knowledge of mental events confers power over the mind in the same way that knowledge of physical events confers power over matter. Wordsworth's appropriation of Bacon's formulation is part of an immanent critique of the pre-Kantian Enlightenment ('immanent' as opposed to, for example, Coleridge's transcendent and transcendental critiques of empiricism and materialism). Adorno and Horkheimer would perform a similar manoeuvre at the beginning of their *Dialectic of Enlightenment*, where the identification of knowledge and power is preserved but knowledge is understood primarily as power over the material world and other people. Technology, for Adorno and Horkheimer, is the essence of this knowledge. It refers not to concepts, but to method: the exploitation of others' work and capital. Wordsworth cannot be said to anticipate precisely this kind of critique of the Enlightenment, but he shares its method: a critique of the Enlightenment undertaken from within its ideological center and that proceeds dialectically outward (progress in technology, or the 'mechanical arts,' defined in opposition to non-domination, or the positive freedom of the imaginative life).

Bacon's identification, though, is predicated on a particular notion of causality: 'Human knowledge and power come to the same thing, for ignorance of the cause puts the effect beyond reach. For nature is not conquered save by obeying it' (*Novum Organum*, 65).[1] Knowledge of causal relationships, a form of knowledge denied in Hume's scepticism, is thus the ground of action in the material world. Hume's claim that we cannot know with certainty the necessary connection between two events introduces certain ethical problems, at least when treated in isolation. This was immediately obvious to common-sense philosophers such as Beattie, who argued that the result of Hume's scepticism is 'to disqualify man for action, and to render him useless and wretched.'[2] It was also obvious to poets such as Wordsworth, for whom certainty, if one allows the term, was the product of moral and aesthetic intuition and not of consecutive reasoning, either inductive or deductive. The identification of this knowledge with power is accepted not so that one may dominate nature, as Bacon suggests ('For nature is not conquered save by obeying it'), but so that the individual consciousness may realize itself to be the free and unrestricted child of nature. This self-realization of consciousness involves the acquisition of, in the terms of *Cintra*, a 'higher knowledge' that subsumes the knowledge provided by inductive reasoning. *The Convention of Cintra* presents an aggressively liberal understanding

---

1   Francis Bacon, *The Instauratio Magna, Part II: Novum Organon and Associated Texts*, ed. Graham Rees with Maria Wakely (Oxford: Clarendon Press, 2004).
2   James Beattie, *An Essay on the Nature and Immutability of Truth, in Opposition to Sophistry and Scepticism*, 1770. Reprint, intro. Roger J. Robinson (Bristol: Thoemmes Press, 1999), p. 4

of knowledge, grounded in the power to inflict material and symbolic punishment in the defence of individual liberty against imperial ambition.

Patrick Vincent

Sleep or Death?
Republicanism in *The Convention of Cintra*

In his account of a meeting with the Lake Poets at Grasmere in October 1810, the Franco-American travel writer Louis Simond wryly notes that after having planned to emigrate to America,

> At present, these gentlemen seem to think that there is no need of going so far for liberty, and that there is a reasonable allowance of it at home. Their democracy is come down to Whiggism, and may not even stop there.[1]

Simond, in the words of Thomas De Quincey, 'was a thorough knowing man of the world, keen, sharp as a razor, and valuing nothing but the tangible and the ponderable'. Married to the niece of John Wilkes and related to Swiss historian Jean-Charles Simonde de Sismondi, Simond was a committed liberal, with little patience for poetry or for political romanticism, as may be gathered from his brief conversation with Wordsworth during a walk to Easedale Tarn: 'They met, they saw, they interdespised.'[2] Commenting on the Lake Poets' views on the Peninsular War, Simond is particularly taken aback by what he sees as a case study in political accommodation:

> But it is remarkable, that this strange Spanish cause is one of the watch–words of party, to which I have alluded to before. By a strange perversion of the human mind, those liberal and independent opinions in matter of government, which one of the parties professes, are generally found associated with a certain toleration of usurpation and tyranny in certain situations; which is, on the contrary, held in utter abhorrence by the other party, although accused of being, otherwise, less nice on those points than its adversary. This might well raise uncharitable suspicions

---

1   Louis Simond, *Journal of a Tour and Residence in Great Britain in the years 1810 and 1811*, London: Longman, 1815, volume 1, p. 350.
2   Thomas De Quincey, 'Lake Reminiscences from 1807 to 1830', *The Works of Thomas De Quincey*, Gen. Ed. Grevel Lindop, London: Pickering and Chatto, 2003, vol. 11, pp. 187–189.

of the candour and sincerity of both [...] These two parties, having, however, many points of contact and natural sympathies, individuals slide easily and un-consciously from one to the other; and when the metamorphosis takes place, it happens frequently that the new insect, fresh out of his old skin, drags still some fragments of it after him,—just enough to indicate what he was before.[1]

For Simond, the Whigs' pacifist policy after 1809, as opposed to the Tories' dogged support for their Spanish and Portuguese allies, not only suggests insincerity on both sides, but also indicates the ideological permeability of Britain's two-party system. This was particularly striking in regard to figures such as Lord Grenville, whose almost schizophrenic stance toward the war must have been especially incompre-hensible to foreign observers. According to historian Godfrey Davies, the Whigs' enthusiasm for the Spanish cause waned rapidly when they realized that 'they were fighting solely to expel the French and not for constitutional liberty'.[2] The Tories, on the other hand, believed that the restoration of independent states and of the rule of law in Europe superseded any demand for individual rights. In other words, the Peninsular War, and Napoleon's annexations more generally, brought to the fore a split between two kinds of liberty, civil freedom and national independence, that had largely been indistinguishable in the Whiggish rhetoric of patriotism deployed by both parties right up to the French Revolution.

Simond's difficulty in perceiving any real difference between Whig and Tory reminds us of the problems critics have also faced in precisely identifying William Wordsworth's political position, especially around the time of Simond's meeting with the poet in 1810. In *The Convention of Cintra*, a vital document to map out the poli-tics of his middle years, the poet distances himself from both parties, self-consciously casting himself as 'a man of disciplined spirit, who withdrew from the too busy world' in order to gain a 'wider compass of eye-sight, that he might comprehend and see in just proportions and relations'.[3] His stance of virtue and of philosophical retreat at Grasmere not only imitates heavyweight precursors such as Petrarch and Milton, but also the eighteenth-century patrician ideal of the patriot hero, whose material independence and disinterestedness make him the best defender of Britain's political liberties. As in progress poems such as Thompson's *Liberty* (1734), Collins's 'Ode to Liberty' (1746) and Goldsmith's *The Traveller* (1764) written in the same tradition,

---

1   Simond, vol. 1, pp. 350–352.
2   Godfrey Davies, 'The Whigs and the Peninsular War', *Transactions of the Royal Historical Society*, Fourth Series, vol. 2 (1919), 130.
3   *Cintra*, 4352-4355 in this text [Clarendon, p. 342].

Cintra vacillates between Whig panegyric of British liberty and jeremiad-like attacks on Britain's moral decline. It also gives a distinctly cosmopolitan flavor to patriotism, imagining the progress of liberty as European, if not global, so that one state's freedom is dependent on the freedom of all others. Unlike these progress poems, however, it introduces modern political concepts such as the nation and the people that had emerged out of Rousseau and the French Revolution. To complicate matters, it adds a layer of Burkean rhetoric, criticizing abstract principles, privileging organic metaphors of rootedness and emphasizing the links between the living and the dead. Finally, it relies heavily on terms such as duty and spirit normally associated with German idealism. The ambiguity surrounding the ideas and diction in *Cintra* is such that critics such as Michael Friedman and James Chandler have been able to claim Wordsworth's pamphlet as a central statement proving the poet's so-called apostasy, while others, including Deirdre Coleman and Gregory Dart, have used it to argue just as convincingly that the poet was still faithful to his early, radical beliefs.[1]

In this essay, I wish to ask whether Benjamin Constant's chronologically minded distinction between the liberty of the Ancients and the Moderns, rather than the more common opposition between Painite Radicalism and Burkean conservatism, may not be a more helpful way to try to view what Coleman has called *Cintra*'s 'kaleidoscope of political perspectives'.[2] The pamphlet's apparent lack of coherence stems less from its ideological inconsistencies than from what liberals such as Constant and Simond would have considered as its anachronistic, or perhaps simply romantic, understanding of liberty, suggested in Simond's statement that 'their democracy is come down to Whiggism, and may not even stop there'.[3] The liberty of the An-

---

1   Michael Friedman, *The Making of a Tory Humanist: William Wordsworth and the Idea of Community*, New York: Columbia University Press, 1979; James Chandler, *Wordsworth's Second Nature : A Study of the Poetry and the Politics*, Chicago : University of Chicago Press, 1984; Deirdre Coleman, 'Re-Living Jacobinism: Wordsworth and the Convention of Cintra', *The Yearbook of English Studies*, 19 (1989): 144–161; Gregory Dart, *Rousseau, Robespierre and English Romanticism*, Cambridge: Cambridge University Press, 1999.
2   Coleman, p. 146.
3   In his essay on *Cintra*, Tom Duggett also focuses on the text's anachronisms, arguing for the 'oxymoron' of a progressive gothic politics adumbrating between past radical and future loyalist sympathies. Yet the English Commonwealth tradition that revived this Gothicism owes as much to its Classical, southern influences, including the Greek and Roman tradition and Machiavelli, writers who also directly informed Wordsworth's politics. See Tom Duggett, 'Wordsworth's Gothic Politics and the Convention of Cintra', *The Review of English Studies*. 58 (2007): 186–211. For more on Wordsworth and various strands of the republican tradition, see Jane Worthington, *Wordsworth's Reading of Roman Prose*, New Haven: Yale University Press, 1946; Zera Fink, 'Wordsworth and the English Republican Tradition', *JPEG*, 47 (1948): 107–126; and Alan Hill, 'Wordsworth and the Two Faces of Machiavelli', *Review of English Studies*, 31: 123 (Aug. 1980): pp. 285–304.

cients and the Moderns, theorized by the Coppet circle and first put down on paper in 1806, refers to an opposition between a republican and a liberal tradition of political thought as the principle source of ideological division in early nineteenth-century political culture. Republicanism is the shared political culture of the Ancients. Keeping in mind historians' caveats concerning the a-historicity or conceptual vagueness of the term, particularly in its relation to liberalism,[1] I will define it as a tradition that places a supreme value on independence from arbitrary power as a means to safeguard the citizen's liberty to actively participate in the *res publica*. Liberalism, on the other hand, seeks to safeguard individual civil liberties by limiting government intervention in the private sphere. Republican theorists such John Pococke, Quentin Skinner and Mauricio Viroli have identified a form of positive liberty, non-domination, closely tied with the *ex post facto* concept of civic humanism, the idea that the republic depends on widespread civic virtue, and with what Viroli has labeled republican patriotism, which he defines as the love of common liberty in opposition to nationalism's emphasis on shared cultural, linguistic and ethnic features. Not only did Whigs and Tories often tout these republican ideals, hence Simond's difficulty in distinguishing the two parties. Republican principles also place Rousseau and Burke together as unlikely bedfellows and feed French Revolutionary ideology, explaining the difficulty we have in deciding whether Wordsworth is in fact politically progressive or conservative, and reminding us how far we have drifted from the communitarian ideals of all these eighteenth-century writers.

During the 1980s, so-called communitarian moral philosophers such as Alisdair McIntyre and Charles Taylor, drawing in part on the classical republican tradition, argued for a renewed sense of civic humanism as a progressive, leftist alternative to what they perceived as liberalism's over-emphasis on the self.[2] In a similar vein, *Cintra* is an anti-establishment essay that attempts to salvage the language and principles of patriotism derived from Classical republicanism out of the wreck of the French Revolution, this as a radical response to what its author also perceives as the selfishness of his own age. Nancy Rosenblum, writing in defense of the liberal tradition in *Another Liberalism*, quite rightly identifies Wordsworth's pamphlet as stemming from his insatisfaction with liberal politics and with modern life more generally. But she argues that his response, which she labels 'Romantic militarism,' finds its source

---

1   See, for example, Daniel Rodgers, 'Republicanism: The Career of a Concept', *The Journal of American History*, vol. 79, n. 1 (June 1992): pp. 11–38.
2   For a useful review of this debate, see Stephen Mulhall and Adam Swift, *Liberals and Communitarians*, Oxford: Blackwell, 1992.

within liberalism itself, namely in individual self-expression and intensity of desire, rather than in civic virtue: 'One possible reading [...] is as a classical republican warning: if a people has nothing to fear from without, it risks enervation within [...] It would be a mistake to think that Wordsworth intended to draw the moral lessons of republicanism'. [1] While individual passages of the pamphlet may justify Rosenblum's claim, the overall text privileges virtue over self-expression and the will of the community over that of the individual. Wordsworth makes this explicit when, referring as examples to Abdiel and Satan, and to Leonidas and Napoleon, he writes that 'the splendid qualities of courage and enthusiasm' are 'the frequent companions [...] and the necessary agents of virtue', but should not be confused with virtue itself. [2]

The pamphlet's frequent references to civic virtue are only one of many indications that Wordsworth did in fact intend us to 'draw the moral lessons of republicanism'. Another obvious and self-conscious way in which the text inscribes itself in the republican tradition is by comparing the cause of the Spaniards to that of the Greeks against Persia[3] and recollecting England's 'long train of deliverers and defenders, her Alfreds, her Sidneys, her Miltons'. [4] Its sublime *energia*, like the enthusiasm it is meant to generate, is a standard feature of republican rhetoric, inspired by a Machiavellian sense of *occasione*, or crisis moment of disorder that gives the possibility of a new beginning. The real crisis here is not the Peninsular War so much as the 'calculation', 'good sense' and 'expediency' back home, in other words the sort of cynical *Realpolitik* that drove the Government to ratify the Convention. [5] Wordsworth, like Machiavelli but also Rousseau, calls for the recovery of an original essence, what he calls an 'authentic voice', [6] to shore up this crisis, so that not only Great Britain, but the whole of Europe can be regenerated in the wake of Napoleon. [7] Key principles that the pamphlet shares with the Classical republican tradition include the idea of

1   Nancy L. Rosenblum, *Another Liberalism: Romanticism and the Reconstruction of Liberal Thought*, Cambridge, Mass.: Harvard University Press, 1987, p. 12.
2   Wordsworth, *Cintra*, ll. 428ff [Clarendon, pp. 235-236]. One may further argue that Wordsworthian imagination, ascribed in the text to the Spanish, cannot be distinguished from republican feeling, as Gregory Dart and others have shown.
3   *Cintra*, ll. 207-208 [Clarendon, p. 229].
4   *Cintra*, 2405ff [p. 286].
5   *Cintra*, 3734 [p. 325].
6   *Cintra*, 105 [p. 327].
7   For more on what J. G. A. Pocock has called 'The Machiavellian Moment', see part I of J.G.A. Pocock, *The Machiavellian Moment: Florentine Political Thought and the Atlantic Republican Tradition*, Princeton: Princeton University Press, 1975; see also Maurizio Viroli, *Jean-Jacques Rousseau and the Well-Ordered Society*, Cambridge: Cambridge University Press, 2003, p. 6.

power as corrupting, the importance of a citizen soldier army, the notion that love of common liberty of one's people can easily extend beyond national boundaries and the analogy between the freedom of the citizen and the independence of the republic. Republican terms that appear most frequently are of course, 'liberty' and 'virtue,' followed by 'independence' and 'tyranny.' Tyranny is synonymous with lack of independence, the 'spirit-breaking submission' that Wordsworth like all republicans virulently attacks for violating human dignity. 'Spirit,' which is as prominent a term as 'liberty,' is mainly used in the same sense as in Machiavelli's *Discorsi* (e.g. Book III, chapter 31) to refer to the combined civic and military virtue of a people in a republic, although it also sometimes refers to a sense of traditional political community, as in the often quoted lines 'there is a spiritual community of the living and the dead'.[1] As David Cameron has shown, however, such a non-intellectual attachment to one's country and its institutions was as much a Rousseauvian as a Burkean ideal.[2]

Rousseau's modern republicanism, blending the stoic ideals of the Ancients with Social Contract Theory, is far more present in Wordsworth's pamphlet than critics have asserted, but 'in a suitably subdued and repatriated form' as Gregory Dart aptly puts it.[3] This may explain Wordsworth's defensive mention in the text of 'the paradoxical reveries of Rousseau', one of the first times he cites the Genevan philosopher since the mid-1790s.[4] Yet *Cintra*'s positive and frequent references to the 'People' both of Spain and of Britain are completely foreign to the author of the *Reflections*, and take us back instead to Book II, chapters 8–10 of the *Social Contract* entitled 'The People'. Here, Rousseau introduces two ideas particularly relevant to the situation of Bonaparte in Spain, the argument that freedom can only be acquired once, either through a slow process of growth or, more rarely, through a revolution that is a form of rebirth, and the prophetic distinction between lawgiver and tyrant. For Wordsworth, the 'voice of the people' arising in Spain and Portugal, harmoniously blended with that of their forefathers, is a 'pure' and 'mighty' revolutionary 'stream'[5] on par with the *journées révolutionnaires* of 1789.[6] This revolutionary voice, perhaps best summarized in the passage beginning with the 'instincts of natural and social

---

1   *Cintra*, 4235–4236 [Clarendon, p. 339].
2   David Cameron, *Rousseau and Burke: A Comparative Study*, London: Weidenfeld and Nicolson, 1973, pp. 127–128.
3   Dart, p. 182.
4   *Cintra*, 3985 [Clarendon, p. 332].
5   *Cintra*, 864, 886–7 [Clarendon, pp. 247–248].
6   *Cintra*, 886–887, 3968ff [Clarendon, pp. 226, 302].

man',[1] is not the shared national language and culture advocated by Herder but rather the values advanced by Rousseau of a people fit to receive laws, including the sense of independence and of social equality, as well as the necessary combination between 'the stability of an ancient people with the malleability of a new one'.[2] Wordsworth furthermore goes to great lengths to show how Napoleon is not the lawgiver meant to help the Spanish achieve their self-determination. Using the metaphor of the 'underground part of the tree of liberty', he argues that whatever superficial civil liberties the French 'Usurper' may have given to the Spanish are irrelevant to what he calls 'true Liberty' which relies on the slow development of a society 'growing out' of itself.[3] Again, although this passage sounds unmistakably Burkean, Rousseau does often rely, like Herder, on organic metaphors to fuse nature and culture, as we see for instance in the opening pages of *Considerations on the Government of Poland* (1772), and he shares with Burke the basic view of individual rights as grounded as much in history as in nature.[4] As evidence, Cameron cites the dedication to Geneva in the Second Discourse: 'I would therefore have chosen as my country a happy and peaceful republic whose origins were lost in the midst of the past [...] ; a republic [...] in which the citizens, long accustomed to wise independence, were not only free, but worthy of freedom.'[5]

Rousseau's idealized description of Geneva as a republican seat of virtue is closer to the primitive democracies of Central Switzerland than to Geneva's commercial oligarchy. Cited six times in *Cintra*, I would argue that Switzerland is as present in Wordsworth's mind as Rousseau, helping to inscribe the pamphlet in the republican tradition but also to restore the republican energies of the poet's youth. Switzerland is made into a touchstone vouchsafing for the validity of Wordsworth's republican theory. He thus mentions the Swiss alongside the Greek republics in discussing the right to petition as indispensable to liberty, points out that some French officers were grieved by the injustice of the invasion of Switzerland, and likewise, that many Swiss enlisted in the Napoleonic army in Spain deserted to British side, and finally gives Britain and Switzerland as counter-examples of the notion that a peasant with no

---

1   *Cintra*, 3011ff [Clarendon, pp. 305–306].
2   Jean-Jacques Rousseau, 'The Social Contract', *The Essential Rousseau*, trans. Lowell Blair, New York: Signet Classics, 1974, p. 44.
3   *Cintra*, 3656ff [Clarendon, pp. 322–324].
4   Cameron, pp. 56–57, 136; see also F.M. Barnard, 'National Culture and Political Legitimacy: Herder and Rousseau', *Journal of the History of Ideas*, 44, 2 (April–June 1983): 233.
5   Jean-Jacques Rousseau, 'Discourse on Inequality among Men', *The Essential Rousseau*, trans. Lowell Blair, New York: Signet Classics, 1974, p. 129.

liberties can be patriotic.[1] Switzerland was of course a staple of eighteenth-century progress poems, in which it served as a convenient pit-stop for liberty on its way to Britain, but also, under the influence of Rousseau, as an alternative, oppositional form of democratic liberty. Many liberals in Britain claimed that after the 1798 subjugation by the French, Switzerland could never again be the same paragon of republican liberty and virtue—they were briefly filled with hope, but then also sorely disappointed by the failure of two successive popular uprisings in 1798 and 1802, which dispelled the republican myth that a free people could not be invaded. As an editorial in *The Morning Chronicle* bluntly states it, 'The day that saw a French army in their country extinguished their liberties for ever. The charm which has so long defended them amidst the rage of surrounding wars, and the mad ambition of surrounding Potentates, was dissolved'.[2] In *Cintra*, Wordsworth himself identifies the subjugation of Switzerland as the turning point in the British people's and in his own opposition to Revolutionary France.[3] Unlike the Whig journalist, however, he does not abandon hope that Switzerland's mythic liberty can be restored. 'There is sleep, but not death, among the mountains of Switzerland', he declares toward the end of the pamphlet, casting the patriot hero's 'wide-compass of eyesight' to the long-term situation in Europe.[4]

Wordsworth needs to keep the myth of Swiss liberty alive because his ideal of an agrarian civic virtue,[5] linked to his reinhabitation project in the Lake District, is imaginatively dependent on the cultural authority of Switzerland as a primitive mountain republic. This becomes particularly important after the Jacobins, indistinguishable in the poet's mind from Bonaparte, usurped the notions of popular liberty, civic virtue and patriotism that were dear to the young Wordsworth and that he sought to discover on his 1790 walking tour. The irony, obviously, is that the mountain shepherd with book in one hand and sword in the other celebrated in 1793 in the *Descriptive Sketches* and the *Letter to Bishop Llandaff* feels his rights yet is unprepared to guard his blessings when the French invade, whereas the Spanish who are not free, heroically fight off the French in the first full blown partisan war in modern history. Bonaparte's occupation of Switzerland presented the additional paradox

---

1   *Cintra*, 2276, 3318, 3793, 4054 [Clarendon, pp. 80, 302, 313, 334].
2   'From the Paris Papers', *The Morning Chronicle*, 10, 405 (September 24, 1802)
3   *Cintra*, 70 [p. 226].
4   4301-4302 [p. 341].
5   This is David Simpson's term. See chapter one of *Wordsworth's Historical Imagination: The Poetry of Displacement,* London: Methuen, 1987.

of freedom without independence. Writing about Switzerland, Louis Simond argues that its Revolution was justified and that 'the Swiss had enjoyed for ten years a tolerable share of independence under the constitution called 'The Act of Mediation''.[1] This is a point-of-view shared by modern historians who argue that Switzerland was treated better than any other of France's satellites and that the Act imposed by the First Consul in 1803 and still invoked with respect after 1815, was in many ways the founding document of Switzerland as a modern, liberal state. As Hans Kohn writes, Bonaparte 'found in Switzerland a similar spirit of traditionalism and of liberty as in his native island'.[2]

That Napoleon may have admired the Swiss for the very same reasons as Wordsworth points to the imaginative hold of the republican myth of Switzerland, but also to its increasingly conservative cultural signification in the early nineteenth century. To keep the myth alive and untainted by the French Revolution, Wordsworth had to ignore the increased civil freedom and national unity that Napoleon introduced in Switzerland under the Helvetic Republic, instead blindly privileging national independence and the spirit of republican freedom over concrete change. As another journalist in the *Morning Chronicle* of 1 January 1803 puts it: 'It is of little consequence what constitution is given to the people of Helvetia. The essential aim of it must be, to repress every thing like a national spirit.'[3] The Peninsular War provided Wordsworth with the ideal opportunity to do so, serving as a proxy battle ground to defend the republican virtues traditionally emblematized by the Swiss. Analogies between Switzerland and Spain were in fact fairly common during and after the Peninsular War, as suggested by James Sheridan Knowles's 1825 production of *William Tell* at Drury Lane, dedicated to Spanish general Francisco Espoz y Mina.[4] Like the Spanish, but on a smaller scale, the Swiss had had their own violently repressed popular uprisings in the primitive Catholic cantons that had briefly inflamed the British imagination. At the same time, as we see in his 1807 sonnet 'Thought of a Briton on the Subjugation of Switzerland', analogies between Britain and Switzerland were also common. As such, Wordsworth's call for Britain to participate in the Peninsular war is also an indirect way to reawaken Switzerland's voice of the mountains.

1 Louis Simond, *Switzerland; or, a Journal of a Tour and Residents in that Country in the Years 1817, 1818, and 1819*, two volumes, Boston: Wells and Lilly, 1822, II, p. 372.
2 Hans Kohn, *Nationalism and Liberty: The Swiss Example*, London: G. Allen and Unwin, 1956, pp. 25, 49.
3 Editorial, *The Morning Chronicle*, 10, 480 (January 1, 1803)
4 James Sheridan Knowles, *William Tell, a Play in Five Acts*, first performed at the Theatre Royal Drury Lane, May 11, 1825, London: Thomas Dolby, 1825.

For all the above reasons, *The Convention of Cintra* may be viewed as one of the nineteenth century's boldest and most ambitious pieces of republican writing. But what Wordsworth did not understand, or did not want to understand, was that the republican voice of the mountains was already dead. Switzerland's mythic communal liberty, associated with the harshness of pastoral life, was inextricably tied to Old Order Europe, and for better or worse Bonaparte had opened the way to the individual freedom of modern liberalism.[1] At the same time, the absence of liberal institutions in Spain forced the poet to give more weight to the independence of the republic than to individual liberty. Claiming at several points that 'liberty must ensue' from independence, he also argues that a society can possess 'the feeling of being self-governed' without civil liberty, but never without national independence.[2] Here, I believe, lies the crux of Wordsworth's thesis in *Cintra*, but also its most vulnerable point. By insisting on a positive, republican idea of freedom as non-domination, while at the same time downplaying the importance of negative or civil liberty, Wordsworth goes against the liberal spirit of the age invoked by Constant: 'To claim today that one can console men for the loss of their civil liberty by giving them political liberty, is to go against the tide of the present spirit of the human race.'[3] Wordsworth's pamphlet blurs the line between radical and conservative republicanism, a strategy which Simond, as a liberal, criticizes as hypocritical, and which anticipates the political right's monopoly on the language of patriotism and virtue throughout much of nineteenth- and twentieth-century British history.[4] Thinking about *Cintra* in terms of republican theory and of Switzerland therefore can help us see how Wordsworth, as Alan Hill writes, 'remained a true son of the republican tradition to the end of his days', but also how this tradition remained anachronistically tied to the positive liberty of the Ancients.[5]

---

1   Benjamin Barber, *The Death of Communal Liberty: A History of Freedom in a Swiss Mountain Canton*, Princeton: Princeton University Press, 1974, pp. 97-98.
2   Wordsworth,*Cintra*, 2129, 3772 [pp. 374, 327].
3   Benjamin Constant, *Principes de Politique*, ed. Etienne Hoffmann, Paris: Hachette, 1997, p. 373 (my translation).
4   Viroli writes about 'the process of absorption of patriotism into Liberal and later Conservative patriotism' under Palmerston, Gladstone and especially Disraeli who 'explicitly proclaimed the Tory party as the national and patriotic party of England'. Maurizio Viroli, *For Love of Country: An Essay on Patriotism and Nationalism*, Oxford: Oxford University Press, 1995, p. 156.
5   Alan Hill, 'The Two Faces of Machiavelli': p. 304.

The Convention of Cintra
edited by W. J. B. Owen

INTRODUCTION: GENERAL

IN August 1807 Napoleon attempted to bring Portugal within the Continental System by demanding that by 1 September the Prince-Regent should declare war on Great Britain and seize British subjects and property in Portugal. After some temporizing by the Prince-Regent, unsatisfactory to France, the French and Spanish ambassadors left Lisbon on 30 September; and in October a French army under Junot entered Spain on its way to Portugal. It reached Salamanca on 12 November; thereafter it hastened its march by way of Alcantara, the Tagus valley, and Abrantes; and, with considerable difficulty and loss of men and armament, though without significant Portuguese opposition, began to arrive in Lisbon on 30 November. The day before, the Prince-Regent, who had meanwhile complied with most of Napoleon's demands without being able thereby to conciliate him, had set sail with his court for Rio de Janeiro. Junot settled down in Lisbon to rule and tyrannize over the Portuguese; there was no organized opposition for some months.

Meanwhile disturbances in the Spanish Court, arising from the incompetence of King Charles IV and the hostility of his son Ferdinand, Prince of the Asturias, towards the Court favourite Manuel Godoy, provided a favourable opportunity for French interference. On 27 October 1807 Ferdinand was arrested on a charge of treason; on the day of his arrest there was signed by France and Spain the secret Treaty of Fontainebleau, which proposed a division of Portuguese territory between France and Spain, and which permitted the entry of French troops into Spain to ensure this division.[1] By 22 November a force of 25,000 under Dupont had crossed the Spanish border from Bayonne, and on 8 January 1808 another force of 30,000 under Moncey entered Spain. These forces occupied strong positions in northern Spain without attempting to enter Portugal, where, indeed, they were not required. Between mid-February and mid-March 1808 French forces, casting aside the pretence that they were in passage for Portugal, seized four Spanish border fortresses (Pampeluna, Barcelona, San Sebastian, and Figueras), and advanced towards Madrid; their command was taken over by Murat. The Spanish Court, already removed to Aranjuez, prepared to move to Seville. Riots aimed at Godoy at Aranjuez on 17 March prevented this; they

---

1   The text was printed in *Courier*, 10 Oct. 1808.

were quietened when Ferdinand was produced and Godoy's dismissal promised, and on 19 March Charles abdicated in favour of Ferdinand.

Instead of opposing the French, Ferdinand entered Madrid on 24 March, one day after Murat's arrival, and proposed co-operation and marital alliance with Napoleon. Murat ignored him, and entered into communication with Charles and the Queen; and Charles prepared a protest against his abdication, claiming that it had been forced upon him. Early in April, Ferdinand was lured north to meet a proposed visit by Napoleon; he arrived at Bayonne on 20 April, ostensibly to confirm his throne in the eyes of Napoleon, but actually to receive the news that a French king would assume the rule of Spain. After ten days of argument and protest, Napoleon confronted Ferdinand with Charles and the renunciation of his abdication. Further debates ensued between Ferdinand and his parents as to who should rule; but by 6 May news arrived of the riots of 2 May in Madrid against Murat; whereupon Napoleon's tone became threatening, and Ferdinand resigned his throne in favour of his father. Charles had already signed a treaty resigning his throne to Napoleon; and Ferdinand being compelled to sign away his expectations on 10 May, the way was clear for the appointment of Joseph Bonaparte as King of Spain.

By the end of April the early events of this series were known to the people of Madrid; on 1 May Murat proposed to send relatives of Ferdinand after him to Bayonne; and on 2 May riots broke out in protest against their removal. These were savagely put down by Murat's troops. A deputation of Spaniards nominated by Napoleon went to Bayonne in late May to beg from him that Joseph Bonaparte might be appointed to rule Spain.[1]

News of the Madrid riots and of their suppression called forth a general revolt in Spain, beginning in Asturias on 24 May, then in Galicia (where there was appreciable Spanish military strength) on 30 May. Asturian envoys to Britain secured promises of British aid in early June.

The French authorities, in the early stages of the struggle, appear to have underestimated the size of the Spanish revolt, and proposed to deal with it by means of comparatively small and isolated forces. Bessières was to watch the northern lines of communication, detaching a force against Saragossa. Dupont moved south from Madrid on Cordova and Seville, and Moncey south-east to Valencia. Dupont took and sacked Cordova on 7 June, but shortly found his communications to Madrid cut by revolt in his rear, and a Spanish army under Castanos advancing on his front. He withdrew on 16 June to Andujar, where he remained for a month.

---

1 Cf. *Cintra*, 642 ff.

Meanwhile Moncey pressed on towards Valencia, avoiding Spanish forces which might have ambushed his small army at suitable points; and on 26 June he began a siege. He was repulsed with considerable losses in two assaults, and, like Dupont, had had his communications cut. He withdrew without meeting further opposition, and reached Madrid on 15 July.

The French had greater success in the north-west, where detachments of Bessières's force under Lasalle and Merle defeated Cuesta on 12 June at Cabezon; a month later, on 13–14 July, Bessières won a crushing victory over Cuesta and Blake at Medina de Rio Seco. This success cleared the French lines from Bayonne to Madrid, and Joseph Bonaparte entered the capital on 20 July. In the north-east, however, Saragossa under Joseph Palafox withstood its first siege by Lefebvre-Desnouettes, and subsequently by Verdier, in June, July, and August.

Joseph Bonaparte had hardly entered Madrid when he moved out again (1 August); for news shortly arrived of the defeat and surrender of Dupont's army at Baylen (13–19 July). The resulting convention between Dupont and Castanos removed some 17,000 French troops from the war.

The Spanish revolt cut the communications of Junot's force in Portugal, and encouraged Portuguese resistance. In early June a Spanish division under Belesta, which had been garrisoning northern Portugal on behalf of Junot, moved into Spain, taking with it General Quesnel, the French governor of Oporto, and other prisoners. Junot prevented a similar defection of the Spanish troops at Lisbon under Caraffa, by disarming them (9 June) and imprisoning them in hulks covered by the Lisbon artillery. Oporto rose in revolt on 18 June, and there were minor risings in the south. Junot concentrated his troops in and near Lisbon by early July, and during that month sent out small forces on local expeditions. But on 1 August the British expeditionary force under Wellesley was landing on the Portuguese coast at Mondego Bay.

Wellesley began to advance on Lisbon on 9 August; he was hampered by lack of horses and vehicles, and by the unco-operative attitude of the Portuguese forces under General Freire. He was opposed on 17 August at Roliça by a small French force underDelaborde, who retreated skilfully before superior strength. Wellesley took up positions at Vimiero, covering the landing of two reinforcing brigades at Maceira. Here, on 21 August, he was attacked by Junot, who suffered a severe defeat. Pursuit was prevented by the arrival of Wellesley's successor, Sir Harry Burrard, on 22 August. Sir Hew Dalrymple, who almost immediately superseded Burrard, landed and confirmed the policy of caution, at any rate until the support of Sir John Moore's division should have been obtained. But on the same day Kellermann, who had commanded Junot's reserve in the battle, appeared in the British camp to appeal for a convention, which was negotiated between 23 and 30 August. The text of this document, which was to occupy Wordsworth's attention for some time to come, is given in his Appendix.

II

News of the Convention of Cintra was published in British newspapers on 16 September 1808. By 27 September 1808 Wordsworth was complaining to Richard Sharp: 'We are all here cut to the heart by the conduct of Sir Hew and his Brother Knight in Portugal' (*M.Y.* i. 267, cf. i. 269). A Board of Inquiry began to sit on the subject of the Armistice and Convention on 14 November 1808. During October and November Wordsworth and others made efforts to follow, and to better, the example of the City of London by holding a public meeting which might approve an address to the King on the subject of the Convention. The following documents[1] indicate the course of these efforts, and their eventual failure, which led to Wordsworth's voicing of his discontent in *Cintra:*

(l) Southey to Humphrey Senhouse, 19 October 1808 *(Life and Correspondence,* iii. 175–7; our text mainly from Raymond D. Havens, 'A Project of Wordsworth's', *R.E.S.* v (1929), 320–2):

> I have had a visit this morning from Wordsworth & Spedding upon the subject of this accursed convention in Portugal. They & some of their friends are very desirous of bringing before the country in some regular form the main iniquity of the business ... these sentiments [on Dalrymple's conduct] would appear with most effect if they were embodied in a County Address, of which the ostensible purport might be to thank his Majesty for having instituted an Enquiry, and to request that he would be pleased to appoint a day of national humiliation for this grievous national disgrace. This would not be liable to the reproof with which he thought proper to receive the city address, because it prejudges nothing.... Spedding & Calvert know many persons who will come forward at such a meeting.

---

1   The following authorities, as well as others in more general use, are referred to in the ensuing discussion and in our Commentary: C. C. Southey, *Life and Correspondence of Robert Southey* (London, 1849, etc.; cited as *'Life and Correspondence')* ; J. W. Warter, *Selections from the Letters of Robert Southey* (London, 1856; cited as *'Selections');* John E. Jordan, *De Quincey to Wordsworth* (Berkeley, Calif., 1962; cited as 'Jordan'); J. E. Wells, 'The Story of Wordsworth's *Cintra', S.P.* xviii (1921), 15–77 (cited as 'Wells'). Where we have been able to discover them, we have used the manuscripts of Southey's letters rather than the printed texts cited above; and as our transcripts of De Quincey's correspondence were made before the appearance of Professor Jordan's book, we have used these rather than his.

Coleridge or Wordsworth will be ready to speak, & will draw up resolutions to be previously approved, & brought forward by some proper person. We will prepare the way by writing in the county papers.

(2) Southey to Tom Southey, 30 October 1808 (B.M. Add. MS. 30927, fol. 143; cf. *Selections,* ii. 116–17):

There is a talk [sic] of an address from this county,—but Lord Lonsdale will do all he can to prevent a meeting, or oppose any thing that may be done at once. ... If anything is done in Cumberland here it will originate with Wordsworth, he & I & Coleridge will set the business in its true light in the county newspapers,— & frame the resolutions, to be brought forward by some weighty persons,—& Wordsworth will speak at the meeting, he being a freeholder. We are all to meet Curwen ... at Calverts on Friday next:—& then I suppose the plan of operations will be settled. It was wished not to make this a party matter, & therefore Lord Lonsdale was applied to thro H. Senhouse,—but it seems he 'views the Convention in a very different light!' God help poor England!

(3) Southey to Walter Scott, 6 November 1808 *(Life and Correspondence,* iii. 180):

Wordsworth ... left me to-day ... he is about to write a pamphlet upon this precious convention, which he will place in a more philosophical point of view than any body has yet done.

(4) Southey to Tom Southey, 22 November 1808 (B.M. Add. MS. 30927, fol. 146):

Our projected county meeting came to nothing. Lord Lonsdale set his face against it, & upon consultation with Curwen, we were convinced that it was hopeless to muster force against his merry men, who would have bellowed as loudly against us at the meeting, as they would have done against the cursed Convention before they were under orders of mum. So Wordsworth went home to ease his heart by writing a pamphlett, which you may be sure will be a right good one, & contain more true philosophy & true patriotism than has for many a long year appeared in such a form. How he gets on with it I have not heard.

(5) Southey to W. S. Landor, 26 November 1808 (MS. F.48.D.32, Forster Collection, Victoria and Albert Museum, fol. 6; cf. *Life and Correspondence,* iii. 197):

We used our endeavours here to obtain a County Meeting & send in a petition which should have taken up the damned Convention upon its true grounds of honour & moral feeling, keeping all pettier considerations out of sight. But Lord Lonsdale had received Mum as the word of command from those who move his strings, & he moves the puppets of two Counties! Wordsworth who left me when we found the business hopeless, went home to ease his heart in a pamphlett, which I daily expect to hear he has completed.

In brief, Wordsworth and his friends made efforts to arrange a public meeting, for which Wordsworth appears to have drafted the speech mentioned by Southey in documents (1) and (2) above (see our Appendix I); but these efforts were frustrated by what seem to have been covert threats by Lord Lonsdale to break up the meeting with organized rowdyism. In consequence, Wordsworth, as he says in the Advertisement to *Cintra,* began to write the pamphlet in November 1808, probably in the first half of the month.

III

Southey's expectation that Wordsworth's pamphlet would be completed by late November 1808 was excessively optimistic, and the lengthy and complex progress of the work towards publication falls into three more or less distinct phases during the next six months: (A) publication by instalments in Daniel Stuart's daily newspaper *The Courier;* (B) publication in book form under the supervision of Stuart; and (C) publication in book form under the supervision of De Quincey.

Phase A.

The following documents trace the early stages of the book's development:

(6) Wordsworth to Wrangham, 3 December 1808 *(M.Y.* i. 278): Wordsworth is
> very deep in this subject [Spain], and about to publish upon it; first, I believe in a newspaper for the sake of immediate and wide circulation; and next, the same matter in a separate pamphlet.

(7) Dorothy Wordsworth to Jane Marshall, 4 December 1808 *(M.Y.* i. 280):
> my brother is deeply engaged in writing a pamphlet upon the Convention of Cintra ...

(8) Coleridge to Poole, 4 December 1808 *(C.L.* iii. 131):
> ... the Cintra Convention—on which Wordsworth has nearly finished a most eloquent & well-reasoned Pamphlet.

(9) (*a*) Coleridge to Daniel Stuart, *c.* 6 December 1808 (*C.L.* iii. 134):
> Wordsworth has nearly finished a series of most masterly Essays on the affairs of Portugal & Spain—and by my advice he will first send them to you, that if they suit the Courier, they may be inserted;

(and so (*b*) Coleridge to Humphry Davy, 7 December 1808 (*C.L.* iii. 136)).

(10) Coleridge to T. G. Street, 7 December 1808 *(C.L.* iii. 137):

> Wordsworth has nearly finished a series of most masterly Essays on [the Convention]—and I shall send the two first to Mr Stuart by the next post—and the others, as soon as ever I hear from him or you.

(11) Dorothy Wordsworth to Catherine Clarkson, 8 December 1808 (*M. Y.* i. 282–3):

> William and Mary ... in William's study, where she is writing for him (he dictating). He is engaged in ... a pamphlet of considerable length. ... I believe it will first appear in the *Courier* in different sections.

(12) Coleridge to Stuart, *c.* 14 December 1808 (*C.L.* iii. 142):

> Wordsworth's first Essay, I hope, the two first, will be sent to you by this or the following Post.

(13) Stuart to Coleridge, 16 December 1808 (ms. in Wordsworth Library, Grasmere):

> The Essays on Spain & Portugal from Mr Wordsworth have not arrived; but we shall be very glad indeed to receive them, & to pay for them too, if you think that will be agreeable. But at any rate let us have them.

(14) Stuart to Coleridge, P.S. of 24 December to letter of 17 December 1808 (manuscript in Wordsworth Library, Grasmere):

> I have just received Mr Wordsworth's Packet & shall take it to Brompton to read.

(15) *The Courier,* 27 December 1808, prints *Cintra,* 1–187; see *Ad. Cintra,* 6–7, and n.

(16) Coleridge to Stuart, 28 December 1808 (*C.L.* iii. 151):

> I am afraid that Wordsworth's fifth cannot go off, as was intended, in this Frank—it is finished all but the corrections—but [Wordsworth has been ill]. Consequently, such are our Posts, it cannot go off from Kendal till Saturday Morning [31 December 1808].

(17) Coleridge to Stuart, 3 January 1809 (*C.L.* iii. 160):

> William received your Letter this Morning at 11 o/clock—we have been hard at work ever since ... the Essay has probably benefited by the accident—at all events, it has been increased in size—We are very sorry, you should have had so much ... anxiety about the loss of the papers.

(18) Coleridge to Basil Montagu, 7 January 1809 (*C.L.* iii. 161):

In the Courier one Essay of [Wordsworth's] has appeared, signed G.—the second was lost in London, and so was re-written & sent again.

(19) Coleridge to Stuart, 9 January 1809 (*C.L.* iii. 164):

You will long ere this (on Friday Morning [6 January], I calculate) have received Wordsworth's second Essay re-written by me, and in some parts re-composed.

(20) *The Courier,* 13 January 1809, prints *Cintra,* 188–503; see *Ad. Cintra,* 6–7, and n.

From documents (12)–(20) it appears that the first instalment of *Cintra* was sent to Stuart in the third week of December 1808 for publication in *The Courier;* whether this copy coincided with the instalment actually printed in *The Courier* of 27 December, or exceeded it, cannot be determined. Further copy must have been sent before 28 December, when Coleridge promises that the 'fifth' part will leave Kendal by 31 December. Of this further copy, all or some was lost in the post (cf. *Ad. Cintra,* 11–13), and, in response to a letter from Stuart received 2 or 3 January 1809, Wordsworth and Coleridge rewrote what was necessary.[1] This material was published, or forms part of what was published, in *The Courier,* 13 January 1809.

Phase B.

There were no further instalments in *The Courier.* The reason is given by Wordsworth: 'the pressure of public business rendering it then [mid-January 1809] improbable that room could be found, in the columns of the paper, regularly to insert matter extending to such a length—this plan of publication was given up' *(Ad. Cintra,* 13–15; see n. ad loc.). This decision was perhaps taken by about 20 January, in view of (21) Coleridge to Stuart, 23 January 1809 (*C.L.* iii. 169): 'In answer to that part of your Letter (which I have just now received) respecting Wordsworth's Copy . . .'; almost certainly by 26 January, when Stuart writes to Coleridge (22), giving specimen printing charges, in connection with *The Friend,* and states that 'For such as Wordsworths Pamphlet [I was asked] 2 G^s [a sheet] for 500 [copies]' (manuscript in Wordsworth Library, Grasmere); and certainly by 3 February, in view of (23) Coleridge to Poole, 3 February 1809 (*C.L.* iii. 174):

An accident in London delayed the publication ten days—the whole therefore is

---

1   See Coleridge, *EOT,* 3, 98.n. for Coleridge's claim to have in some sense 're-composed' or at least amplified several hundred lines from draft. The passage in question is lines 375–536. I am indebted to Michael John Kooy for drawing this to my attention and to Jeff Cowton for providing a scan of EOT 3: 98–103 containing Coleridge's supposed 'recomposition' [RG].

now publishing as a Pamphlet, & I believe, with a more comprehensive Title.

This procedure had, of course, been envisaged from the first conception of the work (documents (3)–(8) above), and early in January, or even late in December, Stuart had been negotiating, or offering to negotiate, for a publisher on Wordsworth's behalf (*C.L.* iii. 160; 3 January 1809). He was shortly engaged in supervising the printing; this is probably indicated by document (21) above, and is clear from (24) Coleridge to Stuart, 4 June 1809 (*C.L.* iii. 210):

> I was forced to be so troublesome just at the very time when your Kindness had prompted you to take upon yourself the equal or greater Task of superintending the interests of W. Wordsworth's Pamphlet;

and from (25) *M.Y.* i. 288 (postmarked 9 February 1809, written 'Sunday', i.e. 5 February), which indicates that Wordsworth was sending copy to Stuart.

In spite of Stuart's supervision, Wordsworth continued to read proofs of the book at this time; for (26) De Quincey on 25 March 1809 (Jordan, p. 119) mentions '[sheet] M, which was the last proof that Mr. Wordsworth saw'. Moreover, it is obvious that the main reason for De Quincey's taking over the supervision was so that proofs could be read in London rather than in Grasmere; so Wordsworth told Stuart (27) on 25 May (*M.Y.* i. 344):

> My inducement for placing it in Mr De Quincey's hands was to save time and expense (our situation being so inconvenient for the post) and also to save you trouble;

and so (28) *M.Y.* i. 351 (? 28 May 1809).

Phase C.

When the decision to entrust the supervision to De Quincey was taken is not clear. It is perhaps indicated by Coleridge to Stuart, 8 February 1809 (*C.L.* iii. 177), where Coleridge gives Stuart a description of De Quincey, as if Stuart was expecting to meet De Quincey shortly. Stuart replies (to Coleridge, 14 February 1809; manuscript in Wordsworth Library, Grasmere): 'I recollect M^r De Quincey perfectly & envy him the pleasure he will feel in pursuing his proposed Plan.' At any rate, De Quincey left Grasmere about 20 February 1809 and arrived in London on 25 February (Jordan, pp. 91–5). The progress of *Cintra* under his supervision can be traced in some detail, though not with absolute completeness, from his correspondence with the Wordsworths; the Wordsworthian half of this correspondence is by no means complete.

At the time of De Quincey's arrival in London Wordsworth himself had seen proof of the book up to and including sheet M (document (26) above). Again, De Quincey writes on 28 March 1809 that 'up to page 96 [the last page of sheet M] inclusively, none of the errors are imputable to me' (Jordan, p. 124). Thus De Quincey's handling of the printing begins, generally speaking, with sheet N of the text of 1809 (in our text, 'people knew', 2162). However, the printer had manuscript material later than sheet M which passed through De Quincey's hands only in proof; for on 1 April he writes that the phrase 'at least from the animating efforts of the Peninsula' (*Cintra*, 2425–6; in 1809, p. 108, sheet O) occurs 'in a part of the M.S. sent up to London before I arrived' (Jordan, p. 136). Moreover, on 14 March he reports that he has emended 'refined' to 'defined' (*Cintra*, 2511; cf. *M.Y.* i. 298) in proof (Jordan, p. 110); and, as his habit was, obviously, to check Wordsworth's copy before handing it to the printer, this passage also must belong to copy sent before his arrival.

On 5 March he acknowledges receipt, on 4 March, of '2 packets (containing 4 M.S. sheets)' (Jordan, p. 97), and, according to the same letter, these four sheets contained *Cintra*, 2925–30: 'The former source ... stock of knowledge', and 3083–4: 'for reasons ... given'. Thus when De Quincey reached London, the printer had already received copy, either directly from Wordsworth or through Stuart, which extends at least up to *Cintra*, 2511, and at most up to *Cintra*, 2925.

On 11 March De Quincey reports the receipt, on 7 March, of '1 single letter', which may have contained text, or at least emendations. On 9 March he received '2 [single letters] containing the winding-up of the pamphlet'; and on 10 March he received *M.Y.*, Letters 140 and 141; Letter 141 must be dated 6 March (Jordan, pp. 104–5).[1] On 11 March he received 'the supplementary intercalation, beginn^g—'*In Madrid, in Ferrol, in Corunna*' ' (*Cintra*, 3539; Jordan, pp. 106–7). This last is evidently the additional matter promised on 7 March *(M.Y.* i. 294), which was to extend to 'about a Folio sheet', and which was to be inserted after 'career in the fulness of [her joy]' (*Cintra*, 4313). But it was later moved to an earlier position; for on 25 March De Quincey writes: 'I *believe* that I have made out, in Mr Wordsworth's note (contained in your last letter) where the addition—'In Madrid—Ferrol' &c. is to come in' (Jordan, p. 120). At this date, 'your last letter' (unpreserved) means a letter of 'Friday afternoon', 17 March, received by De Quincey on 21 March (Jordan, p.

---

1   Mrs. Moorman follows de Selincourt's dating of Letter 141 (26 Mar.), on the grounds that 'D. W.'s postscript makes it clear that she wrote on Monday, 27 Mar.' *(M.Y.* i. 294). Dorothy's postscript appears to us to prove nothing except that it was written on a Monday. De Quincey's letter of 11 March, however, acknowledges receipt of a letter 'dated Monday morn^g before your walk to Rydale'; Dorothy's postscript is dated 'Monday Morning', and says that 'Wm and I proceed to the post at Rydale where we hope to find a letter from you.'

114, cf. p. 119). On 28 March (Jordan, p. 125), De Quincey says that he has inserted 'In Madrid', etc., 'Directly after *'and hope has inwardly accompanied me to the end'* ' (*Cintra,* 3537), 'all along to the *end* of the addition. Then, in a new parag. I resume *'Whilst I was writing the earlier part of this tract'* up to *'feed and uphold'* the bright *consum. flower* [*Cintra,* 4289] —where the press will stop.' The final text of *Cintra* contains no such 'new parag.', but the significance of the passage concerned will appear shortly.

In the letter just quoted (Jordan, p. 124), De Quincey tells Dorothy Wordsworth that he has not *'yet* (viz. Tuesday, after the delivery of the letters) received anything from you since this day last week [21 March], when I had your letter.—However, I dare say, something will come tomorrow or Thursday; and (if there does) not the least delay will have been occasioned at the press by this long pause on your part', because the printers have, for various reasons, been fully occupied. Again, on 29 March, he writes that Stuart thinks that 'the remainder of the copy should be sent up' (Jordan, p. 131). These passages, and the promise of 28 March to stop the press, indicate that in late March De Quincey and Stuart were expecting further copy from Wordsworth; and on 30 March De Quincey received four letters sent off from Grasmere on 26 March (Jordan, p. 132).

Of these four letters, one was *M.Y.* Letter 143, to be dated about 26 March. Some or all of the remaining three were copy, or copy was sent off at approximately the same time *(M.Y.* i. 295: 'the last sheets of the Pamphlet'). This copy was matter to be *inserted,* since De Quincey had received 'the winding-up' on 9 March; it concerns 'the hopes of the Spaniards and principles of the contest' *(M.Y.* i. 296), and 'the great body' of it begins at *Cintra,* 3539, or, more precisely, at 3537: 'But I began' (*M.Y.* i. 299). The limits of these additions we shall now attempt to define.

In a series of letters, beginning 26 March, Wordsworth makes various corrections to, or comments on, the text of *Cintra,* in such a way as to suggest that he is correcting, or commenting on, matter recently written. We shall therefore assume that all or most of these corrections refer to copy sent to De Quincey on 26 March. Except for corrections concerned with (*a*) *Cintra,* 3537 ff., (*b*) passages which Wordsworth suspected to be libellous, and (*c*) a passage in the Advertisement, the passages concerned are as follows, in the order in which Wordsworth corrects them: *Cintra,* 3905–08 and Appendix E, 4019–21 and Appendix F (*M.Y.* i. 299–300); 2998-9, 3718, 3796 (*M.Y.,* i. 300–1); 3770–76, 4061–2, 4080, 4085 (*M.Y.* i. 304).

Again, on 1 April, when he acknowledges receipt of the four letters sent on 26 March, De Quincey comments on two passages in the manuscript which is 'sent to the printer' (Jordan, p. 134). These passages were presumably part of the copy which he has just received; they are *Cintra,* 4077–8 and 3805–7.

It will be seen that, with one exception (*Cintra,* 2998–9), all these passages fall within a well-consolidated continuum of writing extending from *Cintra,* 3718 to 4085, or, from beginning to end of paragraphs, from *Cintra,* 3700 to 4087.

The limits just arrived at, however, are minimal, in that the addition of 26 March may begin earlier than *Cintra,* 3700, and may end later than 4087. That it does begin earlier is indicated by *M.Y.* i. 299, which says that 'The great body of additions sent, since the conclusion was sent [i.e. after the matter received by De Quincey on 9 March], will begin' at *Cintra,* 3537. The passage beginning here, or rather at 3539, is, as we have seen, the 'supplementary intercalation' received by De Quincey on 11 March and promised by Wordsworth on 7 March (*M.Y.* i. 294); it was to be 'about a Folio sheet', it was originally to be inserted after 'fulness of her joy' (*Cintra,* 4313), but, as we have also seen, it was moved to its present position in accordance with instructions issued by Wordsworth about 17 March).

A folio sheet, regularly written, corresponds to about 150 lines of our text, so that the matter concerned extends from *Cintra,* 3539 to about 3632, or, to end of paragraph, 3666; and the addition of 26 March begins at *Cintra,* 3667.

This point, thus hypothetically arrived at, in fact corresponds with the beginning of the text in a sheet of manuscript preserved in the Wordsworth Library, Grasmere, and more fully described elsewhere in this Introduction. We suggest that this manuscript is the first sheet of the copy (or, rather, a draft of it) sent from Grasmere on 26 March, received by De Quincey on 30 March, and acknowledged by him on 1 April (Jordan, p. 132). Since it is cued to follow 3666, and since 3666 at this date occupied approximately its present position (Jordan, p. 125; Wordsworth's instructions of ?17 March), the general disposition of the added matter must have been clear in Wordsworth's mind at this date. This is indeed indicated by *M.Y.* i. 299, 305, where Wordsworth repeats instructions requiring a general removal of inserted material from somewhere 'near the conclusion' to an earlier position; but we make the point, since it is to be suspected that in mid-March Wordsworth proposed to make a major insertion after 4289 'where the press will stop' (Jordan, p. 125, referring to Wordsworth's instructions of ?17 March). Such a proposal would account, generally, for De Quincey's and Stuart's expectation of the copy of 26 March before it arrived (Jordan, p. 131), and also for Wordsworth's dismissal, in late March, of a large insertion 'near the conclusion' of the work *(M.Y.* i. 299). In fact, there is now no evidence of an insertion or a stopping of the press at 4289; for the paragraph which now follows after this point belongs, in some form or other, to the early 'winding-up' of the work, since its last phrase is mentioned on 7 March *(M.Y. i.* 294). In sum: we suggest that on 21 March De Quincey received, with Dorothy's letter of 17 March, 'Mr Wordsworth's note' which gave new directions for inserting 'In Madrid, in Ferrol,' etc., in its present position, 3539, rather than after 4313 as is suggested by *M.Y.* i. 294; that the note forecast a bulky insertion to be placed after 4289 (Jordan, p. 125); but that when the insertion actually arrived on 30 March it was cued to follow 3666.

Where the addition of 26 March ends is more difficult to determine. On 6 March, immediately after sending the 'winding-up' of the work, Wordsworth sent to De Quincey corrections of *Cintra,* 4200–06 and 4274–5 *(M.Y. i.* 294–5, to be dated 5 or 6 March). Therefore the original text of *Cintra* contained 4205 ff., and the additions of 26 March must precede, or be interpolated into, 4205–4376. The bulk of the matter which precedes 4205 extends, as we saw above, probably to 4087 at least; so that between 44088 and 4205 we must seek a point of junction between the original matter and that of 26 March.

The paragraphs 4088–126 appear to belong to the addition, since they mention the second siege of Saragossa as completed. The fall of Saragossa, which occurred on 20 February 1809, was first heard of by De Quincey on 10 March (Jordan, p. 112). These passages, therefore, must have been written, or substantially revised, by Wordsworth after 10 March (probably after 13 or 14 March).

The paragraph 4125–73, concerned mainly with quotations from Sir Philip Warwick and Charles Vaughan, does not seem to offer any evidence, unless a date can be established for Wordsworth's reading of the second edition of Vaughan's pamphlet (see Commentary, n. on 4161).

The paragraph beginning at 4174 seems to show signs of patching in its early sentences. The phrase 'in the earlier part of this tract' (4175) appears to be a remnant of a 'new parag. ... 'Whilst I was writing the earlier part of this tract' ' at which the text was, in De Quincey's understanding on 28 March, to 'resume' after 'the *end* of the addition' (Jordan, p. 125). The present paragraph refers to 'details given, in the earlier part of this tract, concerning the course which ... might with advantage be pursued in Spain', i.e. to the argument either for a very large military effort, or for helping Spain 'rather in *Things* than in Men' (3214–381), a passage which closely precedes the point (3405) at which Wordsworth, obviously writing in late February or early March, describes himself as 'drawing towards a conclusion' (see Commentary, nn. on 3214 ff., 3405–08). Further, these early sentences of the paragraph beginning at 4174 echo phrases in the same earlier region of the work, shortly preceding the point

(3537) at which we know that 'the great body of additions' begins (*M.Y.* i. 299): note 3502: 'the same disinterested generous passions', and 4180: 'the grand and disinterested passions'; 3501: 'a blessing', and 4195: 'this of blessedness'. These references and echoes suggest that in the early sentences of 4174 ff. Wordsworth is endeavouring to knit together two portions of his original argument (one ending at 3536/9, the other beginning at some point closely preceding 4205) which have become separated by the insertion of 'the great body of additions' made after 5 March. The precise point at which this patching ends and Wordsworth's original text recommences is impossible to define without manuscript evidence. But we may guess that it lies between about 4187 or 4189 (where the last of the summarizing, retrospective perfect tenses occurs) and 4200, where the sentence emended by Wordsworth on 6 March begins. Thus, if for 'the action of these powers' (4190) we were to write 'hope', then the sentence beginning 'If, however, there should be men' (4188), or that beginning 'Oppression, its own blind' (4194) would follow satisfactorily after '. . . justified my hope' (3539). We suggest tentatively that the major interpolation in *Cintra*, comprising both the 'intercalation' of early March and the additions of late March, begins at 3536/9 and ends at about 4188 or 4194.

At least one other paragraph, lying outside these limits, must be an interpolation or revision, since it too refers to the fall of Saragossa. This is 4314–36, which follows the phrase 'fulness of her joy', in a position which was once to be occupied by the 'intercalation' of early March, beginning 'In Madrid, in Ferrol'. We suggest that the present paragraph 4314–36 is part of the addition of 26 March; cf. *M.Y.* i. 298, on 'what is now sent' concerning Saragossa. This suggestion is consistent with Jordan, pp. 155–6 (10 May 1809), which reports that

> the final part beginning at—'feed and uphold the bright consummate flower' [*Cintra*, 4289]—having been sent on a sheet containing a letter to me—and having besides a Latin quotation [? *Cintra*, 4358–67] in it which was not written quite distinctly enough to prevent the printer fm making blunders—and being, in a manner, matted into the preface (which, from the alterations and insertions since sent, it was necessary should be written out fair)—for all these reasons I thought it better to write all this over again . . .

De Quincey's transcript of the passage concerned, beginning at 'feed and uphold' (*Cintra*, 4289) and proceeding to 'fulness of her joy' (4313), is preserved in the Cornell MS. of his Postscript, pp. 56–7. After 'joy.' this transcript proceeds: 'But we may turn &c. [from these thoughts; for the present juncture is most auspicious. &c. *del.*] see page marked III.' We may infer from De Quincey's breaking off at this point that the paragraph beginning 'But we may turn' (4314–36) was on a sheet ('marked III') other than that which De Quincey thought it necessary to transcribe, and that the sheet 'marked III' was, unlike De Quincey's exemplar both before and after this paragraph, legible enough for the printer. It is therefore likely to have been an insertion. It is unlikely that the insertion extended beyond 4336, since the following paragraph, 4337–77, is probably that referred to by Wordsworth, in terms suggesting that it was part of the original version, as 'the Paragraph before' the concluding quotation, containing a 'simile not … sufficiently upon a level with ordinary imaginations' to stand at the end of the book (*M.Y.* i. 299).[1]

The original text of *Cintra*, therefore, the latter parts of which were received by De Quincey in six or seven sheets of manuscript by 9 March 1809, seems to have been approximately 1–3536, 4188–313, and 4337–77. The extent of these six or seven sheets cannot be defined with precision, since we are not in fact certain whether they numbered six or seven, nor of the exact extent of a single sheet of manuscript. We know of them that they included (*a*) *Cintra*, 2975–80 and 3083–4 (Jordan, p. 97; 5 March 1809; included in the four sheets received on that date); (*b*) a passage about 'the incompetence of ordinary Statesmen to deal with indefinite things', probably *Cintra*, 2985 ff. (Jordan, p. 107; 11 March 1809); (*c*) a quotation at the end of the work, either 4358–67, or 4370–7, or both (ibid.); (*d*) *Cintra*, 3230, 3473, 3176, 3393–5, passages commented on by De Quincey on 14 March 1809 (Jordan, pp. 110–11).

---

1   On 11 March 1809 De Quincey had regretted 'that the work ends with a *quotation*' (Jordan, p. 107); Wordsworth here replies to this comment. There are various passages in this and another letter which, as Wells (p. 36) pointed out, indicate Wordsworth's confusion as to the paragraphing of the final pages of *Cintra*. He proceeds immediately: 'Does what you will now find added require an alteration in the first words of the last Paragraph?' Later in the same letter (*M.Y.* i. 302), he writes: 'N.B.—If Austria should not appear to join in the war, the two last paragraphs will require a slight alteration, an *'if'* or something that you can easily give.' And on 29 March he writes (*M.Y.* i. 309): 'The concluding paragraph need not be altered on account of Palafox's reported Death.' In the first of these passages Wordsworth must refer, if our assumptions are correct, to the first words of the paragraph 4337–49, which is the third from the end of *Cintra*. In the second passage, he appears to refer to the paragraph 4314–36, which mentions Austria twice, as 'the two last paragraphs'; or, if we take the reference to Hungary (4307) as relevant, he refers to the two paragraphs 4292–336 as 'the two last paragraphs'. In the third passage he again refers to the paragraph 4314–36 as 'The concluding paragraph'. If all this is not mere confusion, we may attempt to clarify Wordsworth's remarks thus: in the first passage cited (*M.Y.* i. 299), 'the last Paragraph' should be interpreted as 'the last [mentioned] Paragraph', that containing the 'simile': Wordsworth is asking whether the insertion of 4314–36 requires alteration of the words immediately following (for instance, the word 'surviving', 4337, might have been inserted by De Quincey to take account of Palafox's reported Death'). In the second and third passages (*M.Y.* i. 302, 309) Wordsworth is thinking of the paragraph 4314–36 as the last of the matter sent on 26 March.

The six or seven sheets therefore begin at earliest at 2511, at latest at 2925. Their maximum extent is thus 2511–3536, 4188–313, and 4337–77, a total of about 1191 lines; and their minimum extent is 2925–3536, 4188–313, and 4337–77, about 691+143+46 = 776 lines of our text. The maximum extent postulates manuscript at the rate of 198 (six sheets) or 170 (seven sheets) lines of our text per sheet; the minimum postulates manuscript at 129 or 110 lines per sheet.

Any of these rates is theoretically possible. The manuscript of *Cintra* seems to have been written in the first instance by Mary Wordsworth from Wordsworth's dictation (*M.Y.* i. 283); whether this arrangement persisted throughout the composition is uncertain. The printer's copy, however, was not, or not usually, the work of the original amanuensis, since various passages indicate that Wordsworth retained the original manuscript, and that a fair copy was sent to De Quincey (*M.Y.* i. 299: 'I cannot find the passage in my MS. ... I cannot find the MS.'; i. 315: 'We have hunted out the MS. from which your copy was taken and it is exactly as you say'). The scribes of the printer's copy were in fact mainly Sara Hutchinson and Dorothy Wordsworth (Jordan, p. 196). A 'single sheet' in the terminology used for describing letters at this date is what we should call a double foolscap sheet, i.e. four pages approximately 13 in. x 8 in. The manuscript of *Cintra*, 3667–785, preserved at Grasmere, is such a sheet; it is written (probably) in the hand of Sara Hutchinson, and shows that a regularly written page in a largish, fairly formal hand corresponds to about 37 lines of our text (about 148 lines of our text to a four–page sheet).[1] A sheet containing an address panel (about four inches deep) might be 11 or 12 lines shorter (136 or 137 lines of our text). A cramped page may contain noticeably more: the last page of the sheet at Grasmere, even though it contains an address panel, contains the equivalent of about 46 lines of our text, and, if the address panel had been used for text, might have contained 56 or 58 lines of our text; so that a 'single sheet' so written might contain as much as 232 lines of our text. (That the Grasmere sheet effectively contains only 134 lines of our text is explained by the large deletions eventually made in it.) The first sheet of the Yale manuscript of *P.L.B.*, wholly in the hand of Dorothy Wordsworth and containing an address panel, contains about 255 lines of our text. The manuscript of *R.M.*, in the hand of Mary Wordsworth, contains 48–50 lines of our text per page, i.e. 192–200 lines per four-page sheet. Thus the printer's copy for *Cintra* might contain as much as about 250 lines of our text per sheet or as little as about 150, or less in

---

1   I have not attempted to recalculate the figures in this paragraph, that is, relating to the number of lines in our [Clarendon] text accounted for by a page of manuscript. References to line numbers in the Cintra text have, however, all been changed to the line numbers in the e-text. [RG]

a sheet which was not full or which was much emended or cancelled. Six (or seven) sheets at 250 lines per sheet will more than fill the gap postulated above (1371 lines at most); we therefore give two specimen calculations, assuming manuscript at the rate of 200 and 150 lines of our [Clarendon] text per sheet:

(*a*) 200 [Clarendon] lines per sheet. The two sheets of the 'winding-up' are the last 400 lines of the original text as defined above, i.e. 3348–3536 (188 lines), 4188–313 (125 lines), and 4337–77 (41 lines). The other sheets (800 or 1000 lines) are 2633–3347 or 2486–3347; the latter figure comes within thirty lines of the postulated earliest possible point at which the passage can begin (2511).

(*b*) 150 [Clarendon] lines per sheet. The two sheets of the 'winding-up' are the last 300 lines of the original text, i.e. 3438–3536 (98 lines), 4188–313 (125 lines), and 4337–77 (41 lines). The remaining four or five sheets (600 or 750 lines) are 2907–3437 or 2795–3437.

It is clear from these calculations that the extent of a 'single sheet' of manuscript cannot be defined with sufficient precision to give a clear indication of the point at which the six or seven sheets concerned begin; moreover, all calculations are based on the assumptions that the scribe or scribes maintained a constant rate per sheet, and that all sheets were filled with the text of *Cintra.* Neither of these assumptions is true: the first because of the variation in rate revealed by the Grasmere manuscript, the second because we know that the sheet containing 4289 ff. contained also a letter to De Quincey, and all or some of *Ad. Cintra* (Jordan, p. 155). However, the calculations will serve to show that six (and, *a fortiori,* seven) sheets of manuscript, written at credible rates, will amply fill the gap which has to be accounted for. They are, moreover, consistent with the following points which have not so far appeared in our arguments:

(1) On 25 March (Jordan, p. 119) De Quincey states that the printer is ready to print off 'at least' sheets N, O, P, Q. These correspond to *Cintra,* 2162 ('people knew')—2895 ('Power of'). Copy for this, according to our calculations, was in the printer's hands well before 25 March.

(2) On 1 April (Jordan, p. 133) De Quincey says that sheet P has been printed by that date (it was later cancelled because Wordsworth rejected De Quincey's note on Saragossa), and that Q, R, S, T, U have been composed. Sheets Q–U now correspond to *Cintra,* 2895–3649, i.e. to matter received by De Quincey by 11 March. This matter, moreover, was at the time swollen by De Quincey's note on Saragossa, so that sheet U must, on 1 April, have ended rather earlier than 3649 of the present text.

(3) The reference to Lord Henry Petty's motion in the Commons of 22 February

(*Cintra*, 3402 ff.) as a recent event is placed either in the 'winding-up' itself (calculation *a* above), or very near the end of the sheets received by De Quincey by 4 or 7 March, within sight of the 'winding-up' (calculation *b* above). In either case, it belongs to writing of late February or early March, when Wordsworth was, as he says, 'drawing towards a conclusion' (3405).

(4) Wordsworth's second reference to Lord Peterborough (*Cintra*, 4034–8) draws on a book which he mentions on 26 March as having been procured, presumably recently; this reference, therefore, belongs to the additions of 26 March, where our calculations place it.

The difficulties and delays in publication did not by any means end with De Quincey's receipt and correction of Wordsworth's manuscript. His letters are full of complaints about the inefficiency of Baldwin's compositors. As early as 7 March he mentions that the compositor 'was [on 6 March] (according to established practice) celebrating the orgies of St Monday' (Jordan, p. 101). On 11 March he records that composing is going on 'rather slowly;—chiefly on account of Mrs. Clarke; whose Memoirs &c. are now pleaded at every press in London as an apology for neglecting all other business' (Jordan, p. 107).[1] On 21 March he records remodelling Appendix A 'since the appearance of an official Report of the Board of Inquiry's proceedings' (Jordan, p. 116) . On 25 March he writes that, because of 'proneness to modify any word, though misspelt, into the word which one is anticipating—added to the daily instances of extreme carelessness of the compositor', he is now insisting on seeing three proofs (Jordan, p. 119). In punctuation, 'the stupid compositor [has] attended to my alterations, or not, *ad libitum*' (Jordan, p. 123; 28 March 1809). Moreover,

> (partly in consequence of neither Mr Stewart's nor the pressmen's having discovered a line of the *interlineary corrections* until I came to Town) there was a good deal of time spent in getting the press to rights—which, added to the different Monthly publications ... and to Mrs Clarke's memoirs, so delayed the printing for the 1st fortnight—that I shall not receive a 1st proof of the *last part of the M.S. which can be printed before the whole arrives* until to-morrow morning [29 March] [Jordan, p. 124].

On 30 March, as we have seen, De Quincey received additional copy to be inserted into the text, and instructions which involved cancelling sheet P. Nevertheless, he writes on 1 April that he has 'explained to the printer that no further delay will arise on the part of the author; ... the utmost expedition shall be used to get the work out

---

1   Sara Hutchinson to Mary Monkhouse, 19 Apr. 1809, in *S. H., Letters*, pp. 20–1, is based on this information.

(if possible) by Monday after Easter:[1] I will take care that they shall not wait for me' (Jordan, p. 136). On 5 April he reports receipt on 3 April of '*both* the letters relating to the note on Sir J. Moore [*M.Y.* Letter 145 and another]; which shall be done as well as I can do it' (Jordan, pp. 137–8); the Cornell manuscript of De Quincey's Postscript shows the extent of his labour, some passages existing in as many as six versions. He complains in the same letter that, because of Easter holidays, 'the pamphlet has languished since Saturday [1 April]: however to-day, if the men can be made to attend, the overseer promises that it shall begin to advance again by forced marches ... if I give [the printers] half an hour's respite, they are ready to make that an excuse for going off to some other work ... the pamphlet [may be] out (as I am promised) by Monday next [10 April]' (Jordan, p. 139). On 15 April, however,

> The pamphlet ... is not yet finished: what is the cause of the delay, I cannot learn ... there remains at least a whole sheet of which I have not yet seen a proof; and the whole of the Appendix (about 3 half-sheets).[2] ... I fear therefore that it is in vain to hope that the pamphlet can be ready for publication before Wednesday night next [19 April] ... Mʳ Baldwin ... assured me that his 'best endeavours' &c. should be used to get it done as soon as possible: but this it is impossible to believe from the pace at which they have advanced since.—Easter Week, however, accounts for some part of the delay; as most of the workmen made a jubilee week of it—seldom staying but a few hours of the day—and many of them none at all [Jordan, pp. 143–4].

> [On 25 April,] it is not yet finished ... last week, out of the six days, the man attended *two;* and must then undoubtedly have been drunk from the absurd blunders and omissions which he made;—and they will not (they say, *cannot*) put any other compositor to the work ... [Stuart] has either guessed—or been told at the press—that it is the multitude of my corrections which causes [the delay; but the real point is that] if I have troubled them with numerous corrections—it is because they have troubled me with numerous blunders [Jordan, pp. 144–6].[3]

---

1   Probably Monday, 10 April, rather than the day commonly called Easter Monday, 3 April.
2   Sheets Bb, Cc, Dd.
3   On 26 April Stuart writes to Coleridge: 'I ... was much vexed to hear Mʳ Baldwins account of [*Cintra*]. He says that in the whole course of his Business, he never knew so much chopping & changing, so much cancelling & correction, that he supposes he has got the whole but in forming that supposition he has several times already been deceived, & that he cannot say when it will be done, till it is done. He plainly told me that the multitude of alterations, corrections & cancels would greatly [? inflame] the expence of printing. ... I of myself changed the long notes into an appendix as I know notes inflame the expence, & I ordered only 500 to be printed distinctly stating to Wordsworth that there would soon be an opportunity to making a second Edition in which he might set all to rights. ... About 3 or 4 weeks

On 29 April, 'though the pamphlet is not finished, it will go on without stopping; as they promised on Thursday [27 April] to put a new workman to it ... on Wednesday [3 May], I should hope, it will be published' (Jordan, pp. 147–8). On 9 May De Quincey records receipt of '3 letters from Grasmere' (*M.Y.* Letters 154, 156, 158), the second of which initiates further disorder arising from Wordsworth's fears that he has written libel, especially at *Cintra,* 2170 ff.; De Quincey, Stuart, and Baldwin have attended to the cancellation of leaf N1 (Jordan, pp. 151–3). De Quincey has in proof 'only the 1st half sheet of the Appendix'; but two compositors are now working, and he has 'hopes that the last proof (i.e. the Title-page and Advertisement) should be in my hands on Wednesday [10 May] and that the pamphlet should be in Longman's hands for publication on Thursday [11 May]' (Jordan, p. 152). His letter of 10 May gives a long report of delays concerned with the last pages of 'the *body* of the pamphlet' and the Appendix: he has been accused, evidently by the printers through Stuart,[1] of holding back copy; but in fact the only copy he has held back is matter for which the compositors were not ready (Jordan, pp. 155–8). On 12 May he reports that the pamphlet is almost finished (Jordan, p. 161); on 13 May he receives 'Mr Wordsworth's letter of Wednesday night' *(M.Y.* Letter 159), which delays progress further with more Wordsworthian fears about libel. He extracts possible libels for Stuart's opinion; Stuart inspects them on Monday, 15 May, and thinks 'not one of these libellous;—but ... thought one which I had not suspected ... a libel' (*Cintra,* 3384). He disagrees with Stuart and is confirmed in his opinion by Baldwin, thereby arousing Wordsworth's displeasure (Jordan, pp. 162–6; *M.Y.* i. 342, 344). On 16 May 'there remains now only the last half-sheet and the advertisement—to be *corrected'* (Jordan, p. 166) by the compositor. On Wednesday (17 May) he makes his final proof-corrections; dates the Advertisement 20 May, alters the date in his Postscript on Moore 'from April 20th to May 18th that I might lie with consistency'; and only the printing of corrected sheets remains (Jordan, pp. 167–8). He sends off four advance copies to Wordsworth on 17 May (Jordan, p. 168; cf. *M.Y.* i. 341); the printing is finished on 18 May, in spite of instructions from Stuart not to print till he gives permission (cf. *M.Y.* i. 349–50);

---

ago I informed Mr De Quincey to the same effect & even remonstrated against notes & many great alterations; urging the necessity of publishing immediately after the Easter Holidays & making him promise to write to Wordsworth. Now the whole of my prudence is upset. The Expence of printing will be great, the Edition small, the Season nearly expired. ... I wish Mr Wordsworth had trusted to himself to send the Pamphlet to Press. We got on much faster when it was in his own hands. I am quite satisfied of Mr de Quinceys amiable character & kind intentions;—but these are nothing on such an occasion' [Grasmere manuscript].

1   See the letter cited in the last note. Stuart was asked by Wordsworth on 26 April *(M.Y.* i. 321) to 'procure the immediate finishing of the work'.

but the sheets will take till Monday (22 May) to dry. However, Orme of Longman's 'promised me that, if 50 for immediate distribution could be sent up, they should be stitched and circulated in 2 hours: accordingly by 6 that evening (Thursday last [18 May]), 50 were sent up to [*tear*] by the fire' (Jordan, p. 171). Yet on 24 May, to De Quincey's mystification, the book remains unpublished (Jordan, p. 173). On 27 May he reports that he 'was at Longman's last night; and I had at length the pleasure of finding that the pamphlet was in a course of delivery; Mr Orme has promised to send up the remaining 10 copies for you this morning'[1] (Jordan, p. 181). The book was advertised in *The Courier* of 27 May; the advertisement, appropriately, as it were, to the general progress of the book, misprints 'CENTRA' and 'WONDSWORTH'.

Here the record of *Cintra* from De Quincey's side ends, except for a discussion about misprints on 31 May 1809 (Jordan, pp. 192–6), and a report to Dorothy Wordsworth, 7 July 1809, that by 30 June 170 copies of the book had been sold (Jordan, p. 238). As to Wordsworth, he found the delays in publication tiresome. He learned 'from Coleridge, that the Printers accuse Mr. de Quincey and myself of being the cause of the delay of the publication, by the chopping and changing that has taken place. As for myself, the charge gives me no concern; whatever harm has been occasioned by the delay cannot now be remedied' (*M.Y.* i. 328; 3 May 1809). He returns to this charge in another letter to Stuart of 25 May: 'I have no doubt that Mr De Quincey was the *occasion,* though I am at the same time assured that he neither was, nor could be, the necessary *cause* of the delay. The MSS was transmitted to him, now nearly two months ago, nor has a single syllable of the *body of the work* been altered, either by him or me, since that time—it is now printed exactly as I sent it at that time' (*M.Y.* i. 344). This statement is not, of course, true, for many alterations of word and phrase were made by De Quincey and Wordsworth, as their correspondence makes clear; but it is also clear that De Quincey made nearly all of them in copy, before it reached the printer, and the only major alterations affecting the printing were the removal of De Quincey's note on Saragossa and the cancellation of leaf N1 because of Wordsworth's fear of libel. It is obvious that 'Mr De Quincey must have insisted upon his punctuation being attended to', but Wordsworth's inference that 'the Printer must have been put out of humour by this and therefore refused to go on with the work' (*M.Y.* i. 344, cf. i. 351) does not necessarily follow. De Quincey was over-meticulous in his anxiety to serve Wordsworth, as Coleridge saw (*C.L.* iii. 205–6), and as a glance at De Quincey's prolix explanations in his letters will show; but, except for his insist-

---

1   Wordsworth had asked for fourteen copies for himself on 6 March *(M.Y.* i. 295); he had already had four, sent on 17 May.

ence on three proofs in the latter stages of the printing, most of his fussiness seems to have been exercised before the manuscript reached the printer. And there seem to have been gaps in the compositor's work which are hardly explicable except on the grounds that he or his employer preferred to spend his time on other work, such as Mrs. Clarke's memoirs or 'Monthly publications (of which this printer prints a great many)' or '*bills* &c.' (Jordan, pp. 124, 143). And whatever the printer or Coleridge (*C.L.* iii. 213) thought of De Quincey's system of punctuation, Wordsworth thought it 'admirable' (*M.Y.* i. 348). De Quincey, again, could hardly be blamed for the errors of collation of which Wordsworth complained on 4 June (*M.Y.* i. 353–4).

At some time, perhaps up to the point when he sent the 'winding-up' to De Quincey on 5 March, Wordsworth must have been at least considering a sequel to *Cintra.* On 11 March De Quincey speaks of the work 'as being only a *first* part' (Jordan, p. 107). Some trace of this intention seems to remain in the present text at 4263 ff., and as late as 5 April De Quincey questioned whether this passage ought to stand. He evidently received no instructions to cancel it; but on 26 March Wordsworth had already stated that 'The Title-Page need not state 'first part'. I do not wish to engage myself so far, having now said so much' (*M.Y.* i. 302). This passage suggests that the ground of the proposed sequel, or comparable ground, was covered by the additions of 26 March; other suggestions are made in our note on *Cintra,* 4263. In a letter to Stuart of 2 May, Coleridge, regretting De Quincey's 'unwise anxiety to let nothing escape', commented that had Wordsworth 'brought it out, such as it was, he might now have been adding all, he wished, to a second Edition' (*C.L.* iii. 206). Wordsworth himself had hopes of a second edition (*M.Y.* i. 354, 358), which he did not propose to revise except by correcting errors. A few weeks later Dorothy Wordsworth sadly records that 'nobody buys' *Cintra* (*M.Y.* i. 370); and the dry records of Longman's accounts show that, two years after publication, the 178 copies of the book which remained were sold as waste paper.[1]

Certain bibliographical peculiarities in the book emerged from the long and complicated printing. In some copies leaf N1 remained un-cancelled, as Wordsworth complained to Stuart on 4 June; he was the more mystified because the uncorrected copies he saw 'contain ... the errata which were printed on another part of the same half sheet' (*M.Y.* i. 354; cf. Jordan, p. 152).[2]

---

1 See W. J. B. Owen, 'Costs, Sales, and Profits of Longman's Editions of Wordsworth', *The Library,* 5th Ser. xii (1967), 93–107.

2 'The cancel [N1] has luckily been so contrived by a fortunate spare leaf which they calculate on having at the end ... that only one leaf of that half-sheet will be lost.' This seems to be the basis of Wordsworth's statement. T. J. Wise *(Bibliography,* p. 79) claimed that the paper of the errata leaf is

A variant title-page was reported by T. J. Wise in his *Bibliography* ... of *William Wordsworth* (London, 1916), pp. 74–6: it reads, in Wise's copy of *Cintra* (B.M. Ashley 4628): 'CONCERNING/ THE / CONVENTION OF CINTRA, / *IN RELATION TO* / THE PRINCIPLES BY WHICH THE INDEPENDENCE OF / NATIONS MUST BE PRESERVED OR RECOVERED. / [rule] / LONDON: / PRINTED FOR LONGMAN, HURST, REES, AND ORME, / PATERNOSTER ROW. / [rule] / 1809.' Two other copies of the book are known to preserve this version; in each case the usual title-page is present also (Healey, item 22). The usual arrangement of the book is described by Healey as follows: 'The old title-page was A1 of a quarto gathering. It was replaced not by a single leaf but by a two-leaf fold; the second leaf carried a new addition to the book, the 'Advertisement'. Furthermore, an errata leaf was printed and inserted in the middle of this new fold. Cancellandum A1 was replaced, therefore, by three leaves.' The reason for the existence of two title-pages is not fully explicable. Two preliminary versions, nearly identical, are given in *M.Y.* i. 278, 283 (early December 1808), and two further versions appear at the head of the two instalments in *The Courier* (see Commentary, n. on *Ad. Cintra*, 6–8). These versions and the earlier title-page all give prominence to the matter beginning at *'those Principles'* in the later and commoner title-page; so that Wordsworth's revision is concerned with widening the scope of the title to include 'the relation of Great Britain, Spain, and Portugal, to each other, and to the common enemy'. This version is first announced in a letter to Stuart of 26 March (*M.Y.* i. 295–6, cf. *M.Y.* i. 310, 312);[1] and Wells (p. 42) may have been correct in inferring that Wordsworth made the change in order to take account of the additions made to *Cintra* in late March. Yet as early as 3 February Coleridge had mentioned 'a more comprehensive Title' than that used in *The Courier* (*C.L.* iii. 174); and it would seem that the change must have been made before the copy for the additions of late March was received by De Quincey, for on 29 March, in urging early completion of the book, De Quincey says that 'The change in the title would indeed alone have secured it a better chance for immediate circulation' (Jordan, pp. 131–2). The last letter he had had from the Wordsworths at this date seems to have been from Dorothy, 17 March, receipt of which he acknowledges on 21 March. This letter of Dorothy's is not preserved, but may have contained the revised title designed to cover the additions which Wordsworth was in

---

'slightly thinner than that employed for the body of the work, and for the two cancel-leaves', but Wells (p. 74) doubted this.

1   This letter to Wrangham, dated April 1809 by de Selincourt, must belong to the last week of March, where Mrs. Moorman places it: note 'I sent off the last sheets only a day or two since', and cf. *M.Y.* i. 295.

mid-March in process of writing.[1] The early title-page seems to exist because it was set at the beginning of the printing of the book. For originally it occupied A1^r; the text of *Cintra* begins on A2^r, not, as might have been expected, on A1^r, with title-page and preliminaries on unsigned sheets.

On 5 April De Quincey is inquiring whether to add after the author's name on the title-page 'Author of 'the Lyrical Ballads' and of other 'Poems' ' (Jordan, p. 139); on 9 April he is told that this 'must by no means be done' (*M.Y.* i. 320), perhaps, as we have suggested elsewhere, because Wordsworth was still smarting at the reception of the *Poems* of 1807, and thought that such a reminder to the public would be injudicious. On 9 May 'the Title-page and Advertisement' is 'the last proof to be corrected; on 13 May 'printing the New title-page and the advertisement' remains to be done, and so again on 17 May, though De Quincey has on this day 'gone—for the last time—over last half-sheet—title-page—advertisement—table of Errata'.

The dubious readings of all copies of 1809 that we have seen at *Cintra,* 131, are mentioned in Commentary, n. ad loc. Another curious typographical feature of the book is the presence in the edition of 1809 of abnormally long dashes at certain points in the latter half [not replicated in the Clarendon edition or here]: It is possible that the dashes at 2674 after Madrid; and 2685 after slavery were used to fill space which fell vacant with the removal of De Quincey's note on Saragossa, which must once have stood on sheet P in their neighbourhood; no such explanation presents itself for the other instances.

We have preserved in our text the variant spellings 'Portugueze/ Portuguese' from 1809. The first of these is confined to parts of the book proof-read by Wordsworth, the second to parts proof-read by De Quincey; and we assume that the difference arises from the difference in proof-readers.

Our Commentary on this, Wordsworth's largest work in prose, is necessarily less close than elsewhere. We have, however, tried to identify Wordsworth's literary sources, to clarify his references to current affairs, and to give the sources of his information on current affairs where we have been able to discover them. It is clear

---

1   It may have been sent even earlier, if not as early as Coleridge's reference of 3 February. Some, perhaps the major part, of *Ad. Cintra* was sent with the last parts of the manuscript which De Quincey received by 9 March. De Quincey had to transcribe these parts for the sake of legibility (see above). Since the printing of the Advertisement was involved with the printing of the new title-page, the final version of the title-page may have been sent at the same time, i.e. by 9 March. If this is so, the revision of the title does not depend on the additions sent on 26 March. Sheet A, containing the original title-page, must have been read by Wordsworth well before this date, since he had read as far as sheet M when De Quincey reached London.

that Wordsworth relied almost entirely on daily newspapers for his information about the Peninsula, and wherever possible we have looked for his sources in *The Courier,* which he obviously read regularly: see the references in *M.Y.,* Index, i. 532–3; and De Quincey, *Reminiscences of the English Lake Poets,* ed. Jordan (Everyman's Library, London, 1961), p. 122, fn. Where *The Courier* lacks information, or where its files in the British Museum and the Library of Guildhall are deficient, we have used *The Times.* From these journals we have given, as well as references for Wordsworth's citing of documents, a certain amount of editorial comment on current affairs which parallels Wordsworth's. In citing such comment we have not meant to suggest so much that Wordsworth necessarily borrowed it (though he may have done so), as that many of his feelings on Peninsular affairs were shared by contemporary Opposition journalists.

For general historical information on the war in our Introduction and Commentary we have relied primarily on Charles Oman, *History of the Peninsular War* (Oxford, 1902, etc.), and occasionally on W. F. P. Napier, *History of the War in the Peninsula* (London, 1828, etc.).

A Bibliographical Note:

Other relevant works, mostly published since the preparation of W. J. B. Owen's Introductions include: Gabriel H. Lovett, *Napoleon and the Birth of Modern Spain,* 2 vols. (New York, 1965), Michael Glover, *Britannia Sickens: Sir Arthur Welles-ley and the Convention of Cintra* (London, 1970), Gordon K.Thomas, *Wordsworth's Dirge and Promise: Napoleon, Wellington, and the Convention of Cintra* (Lincoln: U of Nebraska P, 1971), Michael Glover, *The Peninsula War, 1807–1814* (Haden CT, 1974), David Gates, *The Spanish Ulcer: A History of the Peninsular War* (New York, 1986), Charles Esdaile, *The Peninsula War* (London, 2002).

[R.G.]

INTRODUCTION: TEXTUAL

Our text of *Cintra* is derived primarily from the printed text of 1809, the genesis of which has been described above; see also Healey, item 22. Corrections to the text of 1809 are provided by its own list of *Errata* (so referred to in our apparatus), and by a list of errata appended to Wordsworth's letter to De Quincey, 24 May 1809, printed in *M.Y.* i. 342–3. A similar list of errata is appended to Wordsworth to Daniel Stuart, p.m. 31 May 1809 (*M.Y.* i. 350–1); this list omits the corrections given in *M.Y.* i. 342–3, for *Cintra,* 3359, 3477, and 3854, confuses the correction given there for 2780 by requiring 'to' (the reading of 1809) to be read for 'of' (which does not occur in 1809 at all), and, in giving the correction for 4103, reads 'honour' instead of 'triumph'.

Variants from the text of *Cintra,* 1–503, as printed in *The Courier,* 27 December 1808 and 13 January 1809 (see *Ad. Cintra,* 6–8, and n.), are referred to in our apparatus as *Courier.*

Our apparatus records also the significant variants from 1809 of two fragmentary manuscript drafts of *Cintra.* The first of these, in Wordsworth's hand, appears deleted at the head of Wordsworth to Daniel Stuart, p.m. 9 February 1809, dated 'Sunday Evening', presumably 5 February 1809 (*M.Y.* i. 288; B.M. Add. MS. 34046, fol. 207). This draft, cited as BM in our apparatus, corresponds to *Cintra,* 2239–65; the reason for its revision in early February 1809 is suggested in our note ad loc.

The second manuscript draft is a single sheet, i.e. four foolscap pages, 12.9 in. x 7.8 in., preserved in the Wordsworth Library, Grasmere. It has been folded as a letter and is addressed to De Quincey at Great Titchfield Street, London. It has been sealed and opened, but not, apparently, postmarked. The first page opens with the following, in Wordsworth's hand:

> My dear Friend I am very sorry that I must [?draw] upon your patience for two days more—I [was *del.*] had a miserable head-ache yesterday and was occupied with visitors a great part of the day before
> I don't remember the last words but they were about avoided

In the left-hand margin, also in Wordsworth's hand:

> you filled up the [lacu *del.*] gap with the proper word

The last sentence of the note places the text of the manuscript where it now stands, after *Cintra,* 3666: 'much to be avoided', etc.; the marginal remark replies to De Quincey's request for something to fill 'a *lacuna,* as the critics say' (Jordan, p. 97; 5 March 1809). The text, written in the hand of Sara Hutchinson (probably) or Mary Wordsworth, begins at 'There is yet' and ends at 'position' (*Cintra,* 3667–3785). This manuscript is cited as G in our apparatus.

Jordan (p. 66) thinks that this sheet was sent early in the period of De Quincey's supervision of the printing; but he gives no evidence for this view, and there are reasons against it, and, indeed, reasons for thinking that the sheet now preserved at Grasmere was never sent to De Quincey. We think it probable that the matter on the sheet is part of Wordsworth's addition to *Cintra* finally sent to De Quincey on 26 March and received by him on 30 March, but that, though the sheet preserved at Grasmere was prepared for posting to the extent of being sealed, it was subsequently opened by the Wordsworths and copied, with revisions, in more legible form. Indeed, if this is not so, it is hard to account for the preservation of one particular sheet out of the many which made up the copy for 1809.

As to the date: the marginal note quoted above, by its use of the word 'lacu[na]', evidently refers to De Quincey's letter of 5–7 March (Jordan, p. 97), which could not have been received by the Wordsworths before 10 or 11 March; by which date Wordsworth had sent, and De Quincey had received, not only the original 'winding-up' of *Cintra* but also 'the supplementary intercalation', *Cintra,* 3539 ff. (Jordan, pp. 104–7). As there is no evidence that De Quincey received further copy until 30 March (Jordan, p. 132), it seems clear that the Grasmere manuscript must be later than 10–11 March, and therefore part of, or a draft of part of, the copy sent on 26 March.

As to the nature of the manuscript: the absence of postmark is consistent with our views, but can also be accounted for by supposing that the sheet was enclosed in a packet (cf. Jordan, p. 97: '2 packets'); and that this sheet was one of several written about the same date is clear from the fact that it breaks off in the middle of a sentence, and also from a direction to 'see the end of last sheet' (3727, textual n., ad fin.) which is repeated in Sara Hutchinson's hand on the address panel: 'You will find the interlined passage, which may be difficult to read plainly written at the end of the *last* Sheet. God bless you!' There are other characteristics of the sheet, however, which suggest that it did not reach De Quincey. It shows no signs of having been handled by a printer; its punctuation is inadequate (as may be seen from 3727, textual n.), whereas De Quincey's letters of 5 March and 25 April (Jordan, pp. 97, 145–6) indicate that he punctuated the copy before passing it to the printer; and certain variants from the text of 1809 suggest the revision of the author at first-hand rather than by letter. Thus, whereas the comparatively lengthy passage 3769–76 is inserted by Wordsworth in a letter sent immediately after the additions of 26 March (*M.Y.* i. 304), the substitution of a single word for another (see, e.g., textual notes to 3684, 3691, 3726, 3743, 3757) does not seem a revision of a kind commonly made by Wordsworth in his letters; at least two examples (3726 and 3757) are so insignificant that it is hard to imagine Wordsworth taking the trouble to write about them, though they are revisions (if indeed they are not slips) such as could easily emerge in the recopying of a manuscript. Further, at 3758 the word 'anticipations' is clearly deleted from the manuscript; its appearance in the printed text suggests restoration by the author reconsidering his manuscript rather than in a written instruction. The absence from Wordsworth's letters of all revisions to the text contained in the manuscript, except the addition 3769–76, is consistent with these views, though not evidence for them, since letters may have been lost; at least one, of possibly relevant date, has been (Jordan, p. 137). Again, the manuscript is legible in parts only with difficulty, and would have been recopied with advantage; and Wordsworth's own scribbled efforts to write the sentence 3753–5 on the address panel have made the address itself almost illegible. Lastly, since the passage recorded in 3727, textual n., is in fact eventually deleted entirely, we should expect that, if the manuscript had been sent to De Quincey, Sara Hutchinson's note concerning this passage would have been deleted accordingly from the address panel.

CONCERNING

THE RELATIONS

OF

GREAT BRITAIN,
SPAIN, AND PORTUGAL,

TO EACH OTHER, AND TO THE COMMON ENEMY,

AT THIS CRISIS;

AND SPECIFICALLY AS AFFECTED BY

THE

CONVENTION OF CINTRA:

*The whole brought to the test of those Principles, by which
alone the Independence and Freedom of Nations
can be Preserved or Recovered.*

———

Qui didicit patriae quid debeat;——
Quod sit conscripti, quod judicis officium; quae
Partes in bellum missi ducis.

———

BY WILLIAM WORDSWORTH.

———

London:

PRINTED FOR LONGMAN, HURST, REES, AND ORME,
PATERNOSTER-ROW.

———

1809.

[MOTTO]   ▶

BITTER and earnest writing must not hastily be condemned; for men cannot contend coldly, and without affection, about things which they hold
dear and precious. A politic man may write from his brain, without touch
and sense of his heart; as in a speculation that appertaineth not unto
him;—but a feeling Christian will express, in his words, a character of
hate or love,

Lord Bacon.

ADVERTISEMENT

The following pages originated in the opposition which was made by his Majes-
ty's ministers to the expression, in public meetings and otherwise, of the opinions
and feelings of the people concerning the Convention of Cintra. For the sake of
immediate and general circulation, I determined (when I had made a consider-
able progress in the manuscript) to print it in different portions in one of the 5
daily newspapers. Accordingly two portions of it (extending to page [111]) *were*
printed, in the months of December and January, in the Courier,—as being one
of the most impartial and extensively circulated journals of the time. The reader
is requested to bear in mind this previous publication: otherwise he will be at a
loss to account for the arrangement of the matter in one instance in the earlier 10
part of the work. An accidental loss of several sheets of the manuscript delayed
the continuance of the publication in that manner, till the close of the Christmas
holidays; and—the pressure of public business rendering it then improbable that
room could be found, in the columns of the paper, regularly to insert matter ex- ▶
tending to such a length—this plan of publication was given up. 15

MOTTO:
hate *M.Y.* i. 342: zeal 1809.

It may be proper to state that, in the extracts which have been made from the ▶
Spanish Proclamations, I have been obliged to content myself with the transla-
tions which appeared in the public journals; having only in one instance had
access to the original. This is, in some cases, to be regretted—where the lan-
guage falls below the dignity of the matter: but in general it is not so; and the **20**
feeling has suggested correspondent expressions to the translators; hastily as,
no doubt, they must have performed their work.

   I must entreat the reader to bear in mind that I began to write upon this sub-
ject in November last; and have continued without bringing my work earlier to
a conclusion, partly from accident, and partly from a wish to possess additional **25**
documents and facts. Passing occurrences have made changes in the situation
of certain objects spoken of; but I have not thought it necessary to accommodate
what I had previously written to these changes: the whole stands without altera-
tion; except where additions have been made, or errors corrected.

   As I have spoken without reserve of things (and of persons as far as it was **30**
necessary to illustrate things, but no further); and as this has been uniformly
done according to the light of my conscience; I have deemed it right to prefix
my name to these pages, in order that this last testimony of a sincere mind
might not be wanting.

May 20th, 1809.   **35**

CONCERNING THE
CONVENTION OF CINTRA

THE CONVENTION, recently concluded by the Generals at the head of the British
army in Portugal, is one of the most important events of our time. It would be
deemed so in France, if the Ruler of that country could dare to make it public
with those merely of its known bearings and dependences with which the English people are acquainted; it has been deemed so in Spain and Portugal as far 5
as the people of those countries have been permitted to gain, or have gained, a
knowledge of it; and what this nation has felt and still feels upon the subject is
sufficiently manifest. Wherever the tidings were communicated, they carried
agitation along with them—a conflict of sensations in which, though sorrow
was predominant, yet, through force of scorn, impatience, hope, and indigna- 10
tion, and through the universal participation in passions so complex, and the
sense of power which this necessarily included—the whole partook of the energy and activity of congratulation and joy. Not a street, not a public room, not
a fire-side in the island which was not disturbed as by a local or private trouble;
men of all estates, conditions, and tempers were affected apparently in equal 15
degrees. Yet was the event by none received as an open and measurable affliction: it had indeed features bold and intelligible to every one; but there was an
under-expression which was strange, dark, and mysterious—and, accordingly
as different notions prevailed, or the object was looked at in different points of
view, we were astonished like men who are overwhelmed without forewarn- 20
ing—fearful like men who feel themselves to be helpless, and indignant and
angry like men who are betrayed. In a word, it would not be too much to say
that the tidings of this event did not spread with the commotion of a storm
which sweeps visibly over our heads, but like an earthquake which rocks the
ground under our feet.   25

---

4 dependences ... acquainted 1809:
  dependences which the English people are
  acquainted with *Courier*.

11 and through the ... included 1809: and the
  universal participation in passion ... which it
  necessarily included *Courier*.

20 astonished 1809: astounded *Courier*.

How was it possible that it could be otherwise? For that army had been sent upon a service which appealed so strongly to all that was human in the heart of this nation—that there was scarcely a gallant father of a family who had not his moments of regret that he was not a soldier by profession, which might have made it his duty to accompany it; every high-minded youth grieved that his first impulses, which would have sent him upon the same errand, were not to be yielded to, and that after-thought did not sanction and confirm the instantaneous dictates or the reiterated persuasions of an heroic spirit. The army took its departure with prayers and blessings which were as widely spread as they were fervent and intense. For it was not doubted that, on this occasion, every person of which it was composed, from the General to the private soldier, would carry both into his conflicts with the enemy in the field, and into his relations of peaceful intercourse with the inhabitants, not only the virtues which might be expected from him as a soldier, but the antipathies and sympathies, the loves and hatreds of a citizen—of a human being—acting, in a manner hitherto unprecedented under the obligation of his human and social nature. If the conduct of the rapacious and merciless adversary rendered it neither easy nor wise—made it, I might say, impossible to give way to that unqualified admiration of courage and skill, made it impossible in relation to him to be exalted by those triumphs of the courteous affections, and to be purified by those refinements of civility which do, more than any thing, reconcile a man of thoughtful mind and humane dispositions to the horrors of ordinary war; it was felt that for such loss the benign and accomplished soldier would upon this mission be abundantly recompensed by the enthusiasm of fraternal love with which his Ally, the oppressed people whom he was going to aid in rescuing themselves, would receive him; and that this, and the virtues which he would witness in them, would furnish his heart with never-failing and far nobler objects of complacency and admiration. The discipline of the army was well known; and as a machine, or a vital organized body, the Nation was assured that it could not but be formidable; but thus to the standing excellence of 55

33 or 1809: of *Courier*.
36 private 1809: meanest *Courier*.
38 virtues *Errata*: virtue *Courier*, 1809.
43–5 to give way ... exalted 1809: to give way in connection with him to that unqualified admiration of courage and skill, to be exalted *Courier*.

45–6 to be purified 1809: purified *Courier*.
46 do, ... reconcile 1809: do more than anything to reconcile *Courier*.
47 humane 1809: benign *Courier*.
48–9 for such ... mission 1809: upon this mission the soldier would *Courier*.
49 fraternal 1809. paternal *Courier*.

mechanic or organic power seemed to be superadded, at this time, and for this ▶
service, the force of *inspiration:* could any thing therefore be looked for, but
a glorious result? The army proved its prowess in the field; and what has been
the result is attested, and long will be attested, by the downcast looks—the
silence—the passionate exclamations—the sighs and shame of every man who 60
is worthy to breathe the air or to look upon the green-fields of Liberty in this
blessed and highly-favoured Island which we inhabit.

If I were speaking of things however weighty, that were long past and
dwindled in the memory, I should scarcely venture to use this language; but
the feelings are of yesterday—they are of to-day; the flower, a melancholy 65
flower it is! is still in blow, nor will, I trust, its leaves be shed through months
that are to come: for I repeat that the heart of the nation is in this struggle. This ◀
just and necessary war, as we have been accustomed to hear it styled from the
beginning of the contest in the year 1793, had, some time before the Treaty ◀
of Amiens, viz. after the subjugation of Switzerland, and not till then, begun 70
to be regarded by the body of the people, as indeed both just and necessary;
and this justice and necessity were by none more clearly perceived, or more ◀
feelingly bewailed, than by those who had most eagerly opposed the war in
its commencement, and who continued most bitterly to regret that this nation
had ever borne a part in it. Their conduct was herein consistent: they proved 75
that they kept their eyes steadily fixed upon principles; for, though there was
a shifting or transfer of hostility in their minds as far as regarded persons,
they only combated the same enemy opposed to them under a different shape;
and that enemy was the spirit of selfish tyranny and lawless ambition. This
spirit, the class of persons of whom I have been speaking, (and I would now 80
be understood, as associating them with an immense majority of the people of
Great Britain, whose affections, notwithstanding all the delusions which had
been practised upon them, were, in the former part of the contest, for a long
time on the side of their nominal enemies,) this spirit, when it became undeni-
ably embodied in the French government, they wished, in spite of all dangers, 85
should be opposed by war; because peace was not to be procured without submission, which could not but be followed by a communion, of which the word
of greeting would be, on the one part, insult,—and, on the other, degradation.
The people now wished for war, as their rulers had done before, because open

60 exclamations 1809: exclamation *Courier.*   81 associating them with 1809: including with
                                                     them *Courier.*

war between nations is a defined and effectual partition, and the sword, in the **90**
hands of the good and the virtuous, is the most intelligible symbol of abhorrence. It was in order to be preserved from spirit-breaking submissions—from
the guilt of seeming to approve that which they had not the power to prevent,
and out of a consciousness of the danger that such guilt would otherwise actually steal upon them, and that thus, by evil communications and participations, 95▶
would be weakened and finally destroyed, those moral sensibilities and energies, by virtue of which alone, their liberties, and even their lives, could be
preserved,—that the people of Great Britain determined to encounter all perils
which could follow in the train of open resistance.—There were some, and
those deservedly of high character in the country, who exerted their utmost **100**
influence to counteract this resolution; nor did they give to it so gentle a name
as want of prudence, but they boldly termed it blindness and obstinacy. Let
them be judged with charity! But there are promptings of wisdom from the
penetralia of human nature, which a people can hear, though the wisest of their
practical Statesmen be deaf towards them. This authentic voice, the people of **105**
England had heard and obeyed: and, in opposition to French tyranny growing
daily more insatiate and implacable, they ranged themselves zealously under
their Government; though they neither forgot nor forgave its transgressions,
in having first involved them in a war with a people then struggling for its
own liberties under a twofold affliction—confounded by inbred faction, and **110**
beleaguered by a cruel and imperious external foe. But these remembrances
did not vent themselves in reproaches, nor hinder us from being reconciled to
our Rulers, when a change or rather a revolution in circumstances had imposed
new duties: and, in defiance of local and personal clamour, it may be safely
said, that the nation united heart and hand with the Government in its resolve **115**
to meet the worst, rather than stoop its head to receive that which, it was felt,
would not be the garland but the yoke of peace. Yet it was an afflicting alternative; and it is not to be denied, that the effort, if it had the determination,
wanted the cheerfulness of duty. Our condition savoured too much of a grind-
ing constraint—too much of the vassalage of necessity;—it had too much of **120**
fear, and therefore of selfishness, not to be contemplated in the main with rue-
ful emotion. We desponded though we did not despair. In fact a deliberate and
preparatory fortitude—a sedate and stern melancholy, which had no sunshine

94–5 actually *Errata*: aetually 1809.   111 beleaguered *Fdd · beleagured Courier*, 1809.
97 their lives 1809: lives *Courier*.   111 external 1809: eternal *Courier*.

and was exhilarated only by the lightnings of indignation—this was the highest and best state of moral feeling to which the most noble-minded among us 125
could attain.

▶

But, from the moment of the rising of the people of the Pyrenean peninsula, ¶
there was a mighty change; we were instantaneously animated; and, from that
moment, the contest assumed the dignity, which it is not in the power of any
thing but hope to bestow, and, if I may dare to transfer language, prompted by 130
a revelation of a state of being that admits not of decay or change, to the con- ¶
cerns and interests of our transitory planet, from that moment 'this corruptible ¶
put on incorruption, and this mortal put on immortality.' This sudden elevation
was on no account more welcome—was by nothing more endeared, than by
the returning sense which accompanied it of inward liberty and choice, which 135
gratified our moral yearnings, inasmuch as it would give henceforward to our
actions as a people, an origination and direction unquestionably moral—as it
was free—as it was manifestly in sympathy with the species—as it admitted
therefore of fluctuations of generous feeling—of approbation and of complacency. We were intellectualized also in proportion; we looked backward upon 140
the records of the human race with pride, and, instead of being afraid, we de-
lighted to look forward into futurity. It was imagined that this new-born spirit
of resistance, rising from the most sacred feelings of the human heart, would
diffuse itself through many countries; and not merely for the distant future, but
for the present, hopes were entertained as bold as they were disinterested and 145
generous.

Never, indeed, was the fellowship of our sentient nature more intimately ¶
felt—never was the irresistible power of justice more gloriously displayed
than when the British and Spanish Nations, with an impulse like that of two
ancient heroes throwing down their weapons and reconciled in the field, cast 150
off at once their aversions and enmities, and mutually embraced each other—
to solemnize this conversion of love, not by the festivities of peace, but by
combating side by side through danger and under affliction in the devotedness
of perfect brotherhood. This was a conjunction which excited hope as fervent
as it was rational. On the one side was a nation which brought with it sanction 155
and authority, inasmuch as it had tried and approved the blessings for which
the other had risen to contend: the one was a people which, by the help of the

127 *Errata indicates a new paragraph at this point;*   131 of a state *Courier recte:* ofa state *or* oft state
    Courier and 1809 *run on from* 141.   1809. *See note.*

surrounding ocean and its own virtues, had preserved to itself through ages ▶
its liberty, pure and inviolated by a foreign invader; the other a high-minded ⸙
nation, which a tyrant, presuming on its decrepitude, had, through the real 160
decrepitude of its Government, perfidiously enslaved. What could be more
delightful than to think of an intercourse beginning in this manner? On the part
of the Spaniards their love towards us was enthusiasm and adoration; the faults
of our national character were hidden from them by a veil of splendour; they
saw nothing around us but glory and light; and, on our side, we estimated *their* 165
character with partial and indulgent fondness;—thinking on their past greatness, not as the undermined foundation of a magnificent building, but as the
root of a majestic tree recovered from a long disease, and beginning again to
flourish with promise of wider branches and a deeper shade than it had boasted
in the fulness of its strength. If in the sensations with which the Spaniards 170
prostrated themselves before the religion of their country we did not keep pace
with them—if even their loyalty was such as, from our mixed constitution
of government and from other causes, we could not thoroughly sympathize ▶
with,—and if, lastly, their devotion to the person of their Sovereign appeared ⸙
to us to have too much of the alloy of delusion,—in all these things we judged 175
them gently: and, taught by the reverses of the French revolution, we looked
upon these dispositions as more human—more social—and therefore as wiser,
and of better omen, than if they had stood forth the zealots of abstract principles, drawn out of the laboratory of unfeeling philosophists. Finally, in this
reverence for the past and present, we found an earnest that they were prepared 180
to contend to the death for as much liberty as their habits and their knowledge
enabled them to receive. To assist them and their neighbours the Portuguese in
the attainment of this end, we sent to them in love and in friendship a powerful army to aid—to invigorate—and to chastise:—they landed; and the first
proof they afforded of their being worthy to be sent on such a service—the first 185
pledge of amity given by them was the victory of Vimiera; the second pledge ⸙
(and this was from the hand of their Generals,) was the Convention of Cintra.

    The reader will by this time have perceived, what thoughts were uppermost
in my mind, when I began with asserting, that this Convention is among the
most important events of our times:—an assertion, which was made deliber- 190
ately, and after due allowance for that infirmity which inclines us to magnify
things present and passing, at the expence of those which are past. It is my aim

185 on 1809: upon *Courier.*   189 among 1809: aiming *Courier.*

to prove, wherein the real importance of this event lies: and, as a necessary preparative for forming a right judgment upon it, I have already given a representation of the sentiments, with which the people of Great Britain and those 195 of Spain looked upon each other. I have indeed spoken rather of the Spaniards than of the Portuguese; but what has been said, will be understood as applying in the main to the whole Peninsula. The wrongs of the two nations have been equal, and their cause is the same: they must stand or fall together. What their wrongs have been, in what degree they considered themselves united, and 200 what their hopes and resolutions were, we have learned from public Papers issued by themselves and by their enemies. These were read by the people of this Country, at the time when they were severally published, with due impression.—Pity, that those impressions could not have been as faithfully retained as they were at first received deeply! Doubtless, there is not a man in these Is- 205 lands, who is not convinced that the cause of Spain is the most righteous cause in which, since the opposition of the Greek Republics to the Persian Invader ◀▶ at Thermopylae and Marathon, sword ever was drawn! But this is not enough. We are actors in the struggle; and, in order that we may have steady PRINCIPLES to controul and direct us, (without which we may do much harm, and can do 210 no good,) we ought to make it a duty to revive in the memory those words and facts, which first carried the conviction to our hearts: that, as far as it is possible, we may see as we then saw, and feel as we then felt. Let me therefore entreat the Reader seriously to peruse once more such parts of those Declarations as I shall extract from them. I feel indeed with sorrow, that events are 215 hurrying us forward, as down the Rapid of an American river, and that there is too much danger *before,* to permit the mind easily to turn back upon the course which is past. It is indeed difficult.—But I need not say, that to yield to the difficulty, would be degrading to rational beings. Besides, if from the retrospect, we can either gain strength by which we can overcome, or learn prudence by 220 which we may avoid, such submission is not only degrading, but pernicious. I address these words to those who have feeling, but whose judgment is overpowered by their feelings:—such as have not, and who are mere slaves of curiosity, calling perpetually for something new, and being able to create nothing new for themselves out of old materials, may be left to wander about under 225

200 have 1809: had *Courier.*
207 Republics 1809: Republic *Courier.*
218 not say *Errata, Courier:* not to say 1809.

221 avoid, such submission is 1809: avoid such submission, is *Courier.*
225 out of 1809: from *Courier.*

the yoke of their own unprofitable appetite.—Yet not so! Even these I would include in my request: and conjure them, as they are men, not to be impatient, while I place before their eyes, a composition made out of fragments of those Declarations from various parts of the Peninsula, which, disposed as it were in a tesselated pavement, shall set forth a story which may be easily understood; 230 which will move and teach, and be consolatory to him who looks upon it. I say, consolatory: and let not the Reader shrink from the word. I am well aware of the burthen which is to be supported, of the discountenance from recent calamity under which every thing, which speaks of hope for the Spanish people, and through *them* for mankind, will be received. But this, far from deterring, 235 ought to be an encouragement; it makes the duty more imperious. Nevertheless, whatever confidence any individual of meditative mind may have in these representations of the principles and feelings of the people of Spain, both as to their sanctity and truth, and as to their competence in ordinary circumstances to make these acknowledged, it would be unjust to recall them to the public 240 mind, stricken as it is by present disaster, without attempting to mitigate the ◀▶ bewildering terror which accompanies these events, and which is caused as much by their nearness to the eye, as by any thing in their own nature. I shall, however, at present confine myself to suggest a few considerations, some of which will be developed hereafter, when I resume the subject.   245

It appears then, that the Spanish armies have sustained great defeats, and have been compelled to abandon their positions, and that these reverses have been effected by an army greatly superior to the Spanish forces in number, and far excelling them in the art and practice of war. This is the sum of those tidings, which it was natural we should receive with sorrow, but which too 250 many have received with dismay and despair, though surely no events could be more in the course of rational expectation. And what is the amount of the evil?—It is manifest that, though a great army may easily defeat or disperse another *army*, less or greater, yet it is not in a like degree formidable to a determined *people*, nor efficient in a like degree to subdue them, or to keep them 255 in subjugation—much less if this people, like those of Spain in the present instance, be numerous, and, like them, inhabit a territory extensive and strong by nature. For a great army, and even several great armies, cannot accomplish this by marching about the country, unbroken, but each must split itself into

238–9 both ... truth, 1809: *om. Courier.*   253 It 1809: Now, it *Courier.*
244 suggest 1809: point out *Courier.*   284 success 1809: final success *Courier.*

many portions, and the several detachments become weak accordingly, not **260**
merely as they are small in size, but because the soldiery, acting thus, necessarily relinquish much of that part of their superiority, which lies in what may
be called the enginery of war; and far more, because they lose, in proportion as
they are broken, the power of profiting by the military skill of the Commanders, or by their own military habits. The experienced soldier is thus brought **265**
down nearer to the plain ground of the inexperienced, man to the level of
man: and it is then, that the truly brave man rises, the man of good hopes and
purposes; and superiority in moral brings with it superiority in physical power.
Hence, if the Spanish armies have been defeated, or even dispersed, it not
only argues a want of magnanimity, but of sense, to conclude that the cause **270**
therefore is lost. Supposing that the spirit of the people is not crushed, the war
is now brought back to that plan of conducting it, which was recommended
by the Junta of Seville in that inestimable paper entitled "PRECAUTIONS," which ◀▶
plan ought never to have been departed from, except by compulsion, or with a
moral certainty of success; and which the Spaniards will now be constrained **275**
to re-adopt, with the advantage, that the lesson, which has been received, will
preclude the possibility of their ever committing the same error. In this paper
it is said, "let the first object be to avoid all general actions, and to convince
ourselves of the very great hazards without any advantage or the hope of it, to
which they would expose us." The paper then gives directions, how the war **280**
ought to be conducted as a war of partizans, and shews the peculiar fitness
of the country for it. Yet, though relying solely on this unambitious mode of
warfare, the framers of the paper, which is in every part of it distinguished by
wisdom, speak with confident thoughts of success. To this mode of warfare,
then, after experience of calamity from not having trusted in it; to this, and to **285**
the people in whom the contest originated, and who are its proper depository,
that contest is now referred.

Secondly, if the spirits of the Spaniards be not broken by defeat, which is
impossible, if the sentiments that have been publicly expressed be fairly characteristic of the nation, and do not belong only to particular spots or to a few **290**
individuals of superior mind,—a doubt, which the internal evidence of these
publications, sanctioned by the resistance already made, and corroborated by
the universal consent with which certain qualities have been attributed to the
Spaniards in all ages, encourages us to repel;—then are there mighty resources

292 sanctioned by 1809: in addition to *Courier.*   295 not yet 1809: not *Courier.*

in the country which have not yet been called forth. For all has hitherto been **295**
done by the spontaneous efforts of the people, acting under little or no compulsion of the Government, but with its advice and exhortation. It is an error to suppose, that, in proportion as a people are strong, and act largely for
themselves, the Government must therefore be weak. This is not a necessary
consequence even in the heat of Revolution, but only when the people are **300**
lawless from want of a steady and noble object among themselves for their
love, or in the presence of a foreign enemy for their hatred. In the early part of
the French Revolution, indeed as long as it was evident that the end was the
common safety, the National Assembly had the power to turn the people into
any course, to constrain them to any task, while their voluntary efforts, as far **305**
as these could be exercised, were not abated in consequence. That which the
National Assembly did for France, the Spanish Sovereign's authority acting
through those whom the people themselves have deputed to represent him,
would, in their present enthusiasm of loyalty, and condition of their general
feelings, render practicable and easy for Spain. The Spaniards, it is true, with **310**
a thoughtfulness most hopeful for the cause which they have undertaken, have
been loth to depart from established laws, forms, and practices. This dignified
feeling of self-restraint they would do well to cherish so far as never to depart
from it without some reluctance;—but, when old and familiar means are not
equal to the exigency, new ones must, without timidity, be resorted to, though **315**
by many they may be found harsh and ungracious. Nothing but good would result from such conduct. The well-disposed would rely more confidently upon a
Government which thus proved that it had confidence in itself. Men, less zealous, and of less comprehensive minds, would soon be reconciled to measures
from which at first they had revolted; the remiss and selfish might be made **320**
servants of their country, through the influence of the same passions which had
prepared them to become slaves of the Invader; or, should this not be possible,
they would appear in their true character, and the main danger to be feared
from them would be prevented. The course which ought to be pursued is plain.
Either the cause has lost the people's love, or it has not. If it has, let the strug- **325**
gle be abandoned. If it has not, let the Government, in whatever shape it may
exist, and however great may be the calamities under which it may labour, act

297 with 1809: from *Courier.*   309 condition 1809: the condition *Courier.*
298 a people 1809: the people *Courier.*   315 ones 1809: one *Courier.*
299 themselves, the 1809: themselves, that the 316 harsh 1809: hard *Courier.*
     Courier.

up to the full stretch of its rights, nor doubt that the people will support it to the full extent of their power. If, therefore, the Chiefs of the Spanish Nation be men of wise and strong minds, they will bring both the forces, those of the 330 Government and of the people, into their utmost action; tempering them in such a manner that neither shall impair or obstruct the other, but rather that they shall strengthen and direct each other for all salutary purposes.

Thirdly, it was never dreamt by any thinking man, that the Spaniards were to succeed by their army; if by their *army* be meant any thing but the people. 335 The whole people is their army, and their true army is the people, and nothing else. Five hundred men, who in the early part of the struggle had been taken ▶ prisoners,—I think it was at the battle of Rio Seco—were returned by the French General under the title of Galician Peasants, a title, which the Spanish General, Blake, rejected and maintained in his answer that they were genuine 340 soldiers, meaning regular troops. The conduct of the Frenchman was politic, ▶ and that of the Spaniard would have been more in the spirit of his cause and of his own noble character, if, waiving on this occasion the plea of any subordinate and formal commission which these men might have, he had rested their claim to the title of Soldiers on its true ground, and affirmed that this was no 345 other than the rights of the cause which they maintained, by which rights every Spaniard was a soldier who could appear in arms, and was authorized to take that place, in which it was probable, to those under whom he acted, and on many occasions to himself, that he could most annoy the enemy. But these patriots of Galicia were not clothed alike, nor perhaps armed alike, nor had the 350 outward appearance of those bodies, which are called regular troops; and the Frenchman availed himself of this pretext, to apply to them that insolent language, which might, I think, have been more nobly repelled on a more comprehensive principle. For thus are men of the gravest minds imposed upon by the presumptuous; and through these influences it comes, that the strength of a 355 tyrant is in opinion—not merely in the opinion of those who support him, but alas! even of those who willingly resist, and who would resist effectually, if it were not that their own understandings betray them, being already half enslaved by shews and forms. The whole Spanish nation ought to be encouraged to deem themselves an army, embodied under the authority of their country 360 and of human nature. A military spirit should be there, and a military action,

334 or 356 to 478 See Commentary: Coleridge claims to have composed or 'recomposed' this long paragraph (or possibly from the dash in line 356) from WW's draft.

not confined like an ordinary river in one channel, but spreading like the Nile
over the whole face of the land. Is this possible? I believe it is: if there be
minds among them worthy to lead, and if those leading minds cherish a *civic*
spirit by all warrantable aids and appliances, and, above all other means, by 365
combining a reverential memory of their elder ancestors with distinct hopes of
solid advantage, from the privileges of freedom, for themselves and their posterity—to which the history and the past state of Spain furnish such enviable
facilities; and if they provide for the sustenance of this spirit, by organizing it
in its primary sources, not timidly jealous of a people, whose toils and sacri- 370
fices have approved them worthy of all love and confidence, and whose failing
of excess, if such there exist, is assuredly on the side of loyalty to their Sovereign, and predilection for all established institutions. We affirm, then, that a
universal military spirit may be produced; and not only this, but that a much
more rare and more admirable phenomenon may be realized—the civic and 375
military spirit united in one people, and in enduring harmony with each other.
The people of Spain, with arms in their hands, are already in an elevated mood,
to which they have been raised by the indignant passions, and the keen sense
of insupportable wrong and insult from the enemy, and its infamous instruments. But they must be taught, not to trust too exclusively to the violent pas- 380
sions, which have already done much of their peculiar task and service. They
must seek additional aid from affections, which less imperiously exclude all
individual interests, while at the same time they consecrate them to the public
good.—But the enemy is in the heart of their land! We have not forgotten this.
We would encourage their military zeal, and all qualities especially military, 385
by all rewards of honourable ambition, and by rank and dignity conferred on
the truly worthy, whatever may be their birth or condition, the elevating influence of which would extend from the individual possessor to the class from
which he may have sprung. For the necessity of thus raising and upholding the
military spirit, we plead: but yet the *professional* excellencies of the soldier 390
must be contemplated according to their due place and relation. Nothing is
done, or worse than nothing, unless something higher be taught, *as* higher,
something more fundamental, *as* more fundamental. In the moral virtues and
qualities of passion which belong to a people, must the ultimate salvation of a
people be sought for. Moral qualities of a high order, and vehement passions, 395

365 by all warrantable aids and appliances   power *Courier.* warrantable, by all aids and
    Errata: by all aids and appliances in their   appliances 1809.

and virtuous as vehement, the Spaniards have already displayed; nor is it to be anticipated, that the conduct of their enemies will suffer the heat and glow to remit and languish. These may be trusted to themselves, and to the provocations of the merciless Invader. They must now be taught, that their strength *chiefly* lies in moral qualities, more silent in their operation, more permanent 400 in their nature; in the virtues of perseverance, constancy, fortitude, and watchfulness, in a long memory and a quick feeling, to rise upon a favourable summons, a texture of life which, though cut through (as hath been feigned of the bodies of the Angels) unites again—these are the virtues and qualities on which the Spanish People must be taught *mainly* to depend. These it is not in the 405 power of their Chiefs to create; but they may preserve and procure to them opportunities of unfolding themselves, by guarding the Nation against an intemperate reliance on other qualities and other modes of exertion, to which it could never have resorted in the degree in which it appears to have resorted to them without having been in contradiction to itself, paying at the same time an 410 indirect homage to its enemy. Yet, in hazarding this conditional censure, we are still inclined to believe, that, in spite of our deductions on the score of exaggeration, we have still given too easy credit to the accounts furnished by the enemy, of the rashness with which the Spaniards engaged in pitched battles, and of their dismay after defeat. For the Spaniards have repeatedly proclaimed, 415 and they have inwardly felt, that their strength was from their cause—of course, that it was moral. Why then should they abandon this, and endeavour to prevail by means in which their opponents are confessedly so much superior? Moral strength is their's; but physical power for the purposes of immediate or rapid destruction is on the side of their enemies. This is to them no disgrace, 420 but, as soon as they understand themselves, they will see that they are disgraced by mistrusting their appropriate stay, and throwing themselves upon a power which for them must be weak. Nor will it then appear to them a sufficient excuse, that they were seduced into this by the splendid qualities of courage and enthusiasm, which, being the frequent companions, and, in given cir- 425 cumstances, the necessary agents of virtue, are too often themselves hailed as virtues by their own title. But courage and enthusiasm have equally characterised the best and the worst beings, a Satan, equally with an ABDIEL—a BONA- PARTE equally with a LEONIDAS. They are indeed indispensible to the Spanish soldiery, in order that, man to man, they may not be inferior to their enemies 430

419 power 1809: powers *Courier.*

in the field of battle. But inferior they are and long must be in warlike skill and coolness; inferior in assembled numbers, and in blind mobility to the preconceived purposes of their leader. If therefore the Spaniards are not superior in some superior quality, their fall may be predicted with the certainty of a mathematical calculation. Nay, it is right to acknowledge, however depressing to 435 false hope the thought may be, that from a people prone and disposed to war, as the French are, through the very absence of those excellencies which give a contra-distinguishing dignity to the Spanish character; that, from an army of men presumptuous by nature, to whose presumption the experience of constant success has given the confidence and stubborn strength of reason, and who 440 balance against the devotion of patriotism the superstition so naturally attached by the sensual and disordinate to the strange fortunes and continual felicity of their Emperor; that, from the armies of such a people a more manageable enthusiasm, a courage less under the influence of accidents, may be expected in the confusion of immediate conflict, than from forces like the Spaniards, unit- 445 ed indeed by devotion to a common cause, but not equally united by an equal confidence in each other, resulting from long fellowship and brotherhood in all conceivable incidents of war and battle. Therefore, I do not hesitate to affirm, that even the occasional flight of the Spanish levies, from sudden panic under untried circumstances, would not be so injurious to the Spanish cause; no, nor 450 so dishonourable to the Spanish character, nor so ominous of ultimate failure, as a paramount reliance on superior valour, instead of a principled reposal on superior constancy and immutable resolve. Rather let them have fled once and again, than direct their prime admiration to the blaze and explosion of animal courage, in slight of the vital and sustaining warmth of fortitude; in slight of 455 that moral contempt of death and privation, which does not need the stir and shout of battle to call it forth or support it, which can smile in patience over the stiff and cold wound, as well as rush forward regardless, because half senseless of the fresh and bleeding one. Why did we give our hearts to the present cause of Spain with a fervour and elevation unknown to us in the commence- 460 ment of the late Austrian or Prussian resistance to France? Because we attrib- ◀ ▶ uted to the former an heroic temperament which would render their transfer to such domination an evil to human nature itself, and an affrightening perplexity in the dispensations of Providence. But if in oblivion of the prophetic wisdom

447–8 brotherhood ... | 1809. brotherhood.—In   therefore | *Courier.*
    all conceivable incidents of war and battle

of their own first leaders in the cause, they are surprised beyond the power of 465
rallying, utterly cast down and manacled by fearful thoughts from the first
thunder-storm of defeat in the field, wherein do they differ from the Prussians
and Austrians? Wherein are they a People, and not a mere army or set of armies? If this be indeed so, what have we to mourn over but our own honourable
impetuosity, in hoping where no just ground of hope existed? A nation, with- 470
out the virtues necessary for the attainment of independence, have failed to
attain it. This is all. For little has that man understood the majesty of true national freedom, who believes that a population, like that of Spain, in a country
like that of Spain, may want the qualities needful to fight out their independence, and yet possess the excellencies which render men susceptible of true 475
liberty. The Dutch, the Americans, did possess the former; but it is, I fear, more
than doubtful whether the one ever did, or the other ever will, evince the nobler morality indispensible to the latter.

   It was not my intention that the subject should at present have been pursued
so far. But I have been carried forward by a strong wish to be of use in raising 480
and steadying the minds of my countrymen, an end to which every thing that
I shall say hereafter (provided it be true) will contribute. For all knowledge of ◄ ►
human nature leads ultimately to repose; and I shall write to little purpose if I
do not assist some portion of my readers to form an estimate of the grounds of
hope and fear in the present effort of liberty against oppression, in the present 485
or any future struggle which justice will have to maintain against might. In
fact, this is my main object, "the sea-mark of my utmost sail:" in order that,
understanding the sources of strength and seats of weakness, both in the tyrant
and in those who would save or rescue themselves from his grasp, we may act
as becomes men who would guard their own liberties, and would draw a good 490
use from the desire which they feel, and the efforts which they are making, to
benefit the less favoured part of the family of mankind. With these as my ultimate objects, I have undertaken to examine the Convention of Cintra; and, as
an indispensible preparative for forming a right judgment of this event, I have
already faithfully exhibited the feelings of the people of Great Britain and of 495
Spain towards each other, and have shewn by what sacred bonds they were
united. With the same view, I shall next proceed to shew by what barrier of
aversion, scarcely less sacred, the people of the *Peninsula* were divided from

468 Austrians 1809: Austrian *Courier.*   475 which 1809: that *Courier.*
468 set 1809: sets *Courier.*   481 that 1809: which *Courier.*

their enemies,—their feelings towards them, and their hopes for themselves; trusting, that I have already mitigated the deadening influences of recent ca- **500** lamity, and that the representation I shall frame, in the manner which has been promised, will speak in its true colours and life to the eye and heart of the spectator.

The government of Asturias, which was the first to rise against their op- pressors, thus expresses itself in the opening of its Address to the People of **505** that Province. "Loyal Asturians! beloved Countrymen! your wishes are al- ready fulfilled. The Principality, discharging those duties which are most sa- cred to men, has already declared war against France. You may perhaps dread this vigorous resolution. But what other measure could or ought we to adopt? Shall there be found one single man among us, who prefers the vile and igno- **510** minious death of slaves, to the glory of dying on the field of honour, with arms in his hand, defending our unfortunate monarch, our homes, our children, and our wives? If, in the very moment when those bands of banditti were receiving the kindest offices and favours from the inhabitants of our Capital, they mur- dered in cold blood upwards of two thousand people, for no other reason than **515** their having defended their insulted brethren, what could we expect from them, had we submitted to their dominion? Their perfidious conduct towards our king and his whole family, whom they deceived and decoyed into France un- der the promise of an eternal armistice, in order to chain them all, has no prec- edent in history. Their conduct towards the whole nation is more iniquitous, **520** than we had the right to expect from a horde of Hottentots. They have profaned our temples; they have insulted our religion; they have assailed our wives; in fine, they have broken all their promises, and there exists no right which they have not violated. To arms, Asturians! to arms!" The Supreme Junta of Gov- ernment, sitting at Seville, introduces its declaration of war in words to the **525** same effect. "France, under the government of the emperor Napoleon the First, has violated towards Spain the most sacred compacts—has arrested her mon- archs—obliged them to a forced and manifestly void abdication and renuncia- tion; has behaved with the same violence towards the Spanish Nobles whom he keeps in his power—has declared that he will elect a king of Spain, the most **530** horrible attempt that is recorded in history—has sent his troops into Spain, seized her fortresses and her Capital, and scattered his troops throughout the country—has committed against Spain all sorts of assassinations, robberies, and unheard-of cruelties; and this he has done with the most enormous in-

gratitude to the services which the Spanish nation has rendered France, to the **535**
friendship it has shewn her, thus treating it with the most dreadful perfidy,
fraud, and treachery, such as was never committed against any nation or monarch by the most barbarous or ambitious king or people. He has in fine declared, that he will trample down our monarchy, our fundamental laws, and
bring about the ruin of our holy catholic religion.—The only remedy therefore **540**
to such grievous ills, which are so manifest to all Europe, is in war, which we
declare against him." The injuries, done to the Portuguese Nation and Government, previous to its declaration of war against the Emperor of the French, are
stated at length in the manifesto of the Court of Portugal, dated Rio Janeiro, ◀▶
May 1st, 1808; and to that the reader may be referred: but upon this subject I **545**
will beg leave to lay before him, the following extract from the Address of the ◀▶
Supreme Junta of Seville to the Portuguese nation, dated May 30th, 1808.
"PORTUGUESE,—Your lot is, perhaps, the hardest ever endured by any people on
the earth. Your princes were compelled to fly from you, and the events in Spain
have furnished an irrefragable proof of the absolute necessity of that meas- **550**
ure.—You were ordered not to defend yourselves, and you did not defend
yourselves. Junot offered to make you happy, and your happiness has consisted
in being treated with greater cruelty than the most ferocious conquerors inflict
on the people whom they have subdued by force of arms and after the most
obstinate resistance. You have been despoiled of your princes, your laws, your **555**
usages, your customs, your property, your liberty, even your lives, and your
holy religion, which your enemies never have respected, however they may,
according to their custom, have promised to protect it, and however they may
affect and pretend to have any sense of it themselves. Your nobility has been
annihilated,—its property confiscated in punishment of its fidelity and loyalty. **560**
You have been basely dragged to foreign countries, and compelled to prostrate
yourselves at the feet of the man who is the author of all your calamities, and
who, by the most horrible perfidy, has usurped your government, and rules you
with a sceptre of iron. Even now your troops have left your borders, and are
travelling in chains to die in the defence of him who has oppressed you; by **565**
which means his deep malignity may accomplish his purpose,—by destroying
those who should constitute your strength, and by rendering their lives subservient to his triumphs, and to the savage glory to which he aspires.—Spain beheld your slavery, and the horrible evils which followed it, with mingled sensations of grief and despair. You are her brother, and she panted to fly to your **570**

assistance. But certain Chiefs, and a Government either weak or corrupt, kept ▶
her in chains, and were preparing the means by which the ruin of our king, our
laws, our independence, our liberty, our lives, and even the holy religion in
which we are united, might accompany your's,—by which a barbarous people
might consummate their own triumph, and accomplish the slavery of every 575
nation in Europe:—our loyalty, our honour, our justice, could not submit to
such flagrant atrocity! We have broken our chains,—let us then to action." But
the story of Portuguese sufferings shall be told by Junot himself; who, in his
proclamation to the people of Portugal (dated Palace of Lisbon, June 26,) thus
speaks to them: "You have earnestly entreated of him a king, who, aided by the 580
omnipotence of that great monarch, might raise up again your unfortunate
Country, and replace her in the rank which belongs to her. Doubtless at this
moment your new monarch is on the point of visiting you.—He expects to find
faithful Subjects—shall he find only rebels? I expected to have delivered over
to him a peaceable kingdom and flourishing cities—shall I be obliged to shew 585
him only ruins and heaps of ashes and dead bodies?—Merit pardon by prompt
submission, and a prompt obedience to my orders; if not, think of the punishment which awaits you.—Every city, town, or village, which shall take up
arms against my forces, and whose inhabitants shall rise upon the French
troops, shall be delivered up to pillage and totally destroyed, and the inhabit- 590
ants shall be put to the sword—every individual taken in arms shall be instantly shot." That these were not empty threats, we learn from the bulletins
published by authority of the same Junot, which at once shew his cruelty, and
that of the persons whom he employed, and the noble resistance of the Portuguese. "We entered Beia," says one of those dismal chronicles, "in the midst 595
of great carnage. The rebels left dead on the field of battle; all those taken with
arms in their hands were put to the sword, and all the houses from which we
had been fired upon were burned." Again in another, "The spirit of insanity,
which had led astray the inhabitants of Beia and rendered necessary the terrible chastisement which they have received, has likewise been exercised in the 600
north of Portugal." Describing another engagement, it is said, "the lines endeavoured to make a stand, but they were forced; the massacre was terrible—
more than a thousand dead bodies remained on the field of battle, and General
Loison, pursuing the remainder of these wretches, entered Guerda with fixed
bayonets." On approaching Alpedrinha, they found the *rebels* posted in a kind 605
of redoubt— "it was forced, the town of Alpedrinha taken, and delivered to the

flames:" the whole of this tragedy is thus summed up— "In the engagements ▶
fought in these different marches, we lost twenty men killed, and 30 or 40
wounded. The insurgents have left at least 13000 dead in the field, the melan- ¶
choly consequence of a frenzy which nothing can justify, which forces us to 610
multiply victims, whom we lament and regret, but whom a terrible necessity
obliges us to sacrifice." "It is thus," continues the writer, "that deluded men,
ungrateful children as well as culpable citizens, exchange all their claims to
the benevolence and protection of Government for misfortune and wretched-
ness; ruin their families; carry into their habitations desolation, conflagrations, 615
and death; change flourishing cities into heaps of ashes—into vast tombs; and
bring on their whole country calamities which they deserve, and from which
(feeble victims!) they cannot escape. In fine, it is thus that, covering themselves with opprobrium and ridicule at the same time that they complete their
destruction, they have no other resource but the pity of those they have wished 620
to assassinate—a pity which they never have implored in vain, when acknowledging their crime, they have solicited pardon from Frenchmen, who, incapable of departing from their noble character, are ever as generous as they are
brave.—By order of Monseigneur le duc d'Abrantes, Commander in chief."—
Compare this with the Address of Massaredo to the Biscayans, in which there 625
is the like avowal that the Spaniards are to be treated as Rebels. He tells them,
that he is commanded by his master, Joseph Bonaparte, to assure them—"that,
in case they disapprove of the insurrection in the City of Bilboa, his majesty
will consign to oblivion the mistake and error of the Insurgents, and that he
will punish only the heads and beginners of the insurrection, with regard to 630
whom *the law must take its course."*

To be the victim of such bloody-mindedness is a doleful lot for a Nation;
and the anguish must have been rendered still more poignant by the scoffs and
insults, and by that heinous contempt of the most awful truths, with which
the Perpetrator of those cruelties has proclaimed them.—Merciless ferocity 635
is an evil familiar to our thoughts; but these combinations of malevolence
historians have not yet been called upon to record; and writers of fiction, if
they have ever ventured to create passions resembling them, have confined,
out of reverence for the acknowledged constitution of human nature, those
passions to reprobate Spirits. Such tyranny is, in the strictest sense, intoler- 640
able; not because it aims at the extinction of life, but of every thing which

624 brave.—*Edd.:* brave."—1809

gives life its value—of virtue, of reason, of repose in God, or in truth. With
what heart may we suppose that a genuine Spaniard would read the following impious address from the Deputation, as they were falsely called, of his ▶
apostate countrymen at Bayonne, seduced or compelled to assemble under 645
the eye of the Tyrant, and speaking as he dictated? "Dear Spaniards, Beloved
Countrymen!—Your habitations, your cities, your power, and your property,
are as dear to us as ourselves; and we wish to keep all of you in our eye, that
we may be able to establish your security.—We, as well as yourselves, are
bound in allegiance to the old dynasty—to her, to whom an end has been put 650
by that God-like Providence which rules all thrones and sceptres. We have
seen the greatest states fall under the guidance of this rule, and our land alone
has hitherto escaped the same fate. An unavoidable destiny has now overtaken
our country, and brought us under the protection of the invincible Emperor of
France.—We know that you will regard our present situation with the utmost 655
consideration; and we have accordingly, in this conviction, been uniformly
conciliating the friendship to which we are tied by so many obligations. With
what admiration must we see the benevolence and humanity of his imperial
and royal Majesty outstep our wishes—qualities which are even more to be
admired than his great power! He has desired nothing else, than that we should 660
be indebted to him for our welfare. Whenever he gives us a sovereign to reign
over us in the person of his magnanimous brother Joseph, he will consummate
our prosperity.—As he has been pleased to change our old system of laws, it
becomes us to obey, and to live in tranquillity: as he has also promised to re-
organize our financial system, we may hope that then our naval and military 665
power will become terrible to our enemies, &c."—That the Castilians were
horror-stricken by the above blasphemies, which are the habitual language of
the French Senate and Ministers to their Emperor, is apparent from an address ▶
dated Valladolid,—"He (Bonaparte) carries his audacity the length of holding
out to us offers of happiness and peace, while he is laying waste our country, 670
pulling down our churches, and slaughtering our brethren. His pride, cherished
by a band of villains who are constantly anxious to offer incense on his shrine,
and tolerated by numberless victims who pine in his chains, has caused him
to conceive the fantastical idea of proclaiming himself Lord and Ruler of the
whole world. There is no atrocity which he does not commit to attain that end 675
* * * * * *. Shall these outrages, these iniquities, remain unpunished while
Spaniards—and Castilian Spaniards—yet exist?"

Many passages might be adduced to prove that the carnage and devastation spread over their land have not afflicted this noble people so deeply as this more searching warfare against the conscience and the reason. They groan 680 less over the blood which has been shed, than over the arrogant assumptions of beneficence made by him from whose order that blood has flowed. Still to be talking of bestowing and conferring, and to be happy in the sight of nothing but what he thinks he has bestowed or conferred, this, in a man to whom the weakness of his fellows has given great power, is a madness of 685 pride more hideous than cruelty itself. We have heard of Attila and Tamer-lane who called themselves the scourges of God, and rejoiced in personat-ing the terrors of Providence; but such monsters do less outrage to the rea-son than he who arrogates to himself the gentle and gracious attributes of the Deity: for the one acts professedly from the temperance of reason, the other 690 avowedly in the gusts of passion. Through the terrors of the Supreme Ruler of things, as set forth by works of destruction and ruin, we see but darkly; we may reverence the chastisement, may fear it with awe, but it is not natural to incline towards it in love: moreover, devastation passes away—a perishing power among things that perish: whereas to found, and to build, to create and 695 to institute, to bless through blessing, this has to do with objects where we trust we can see clearly,—it reminds us of what we love,—it aims at perma-nence,—and the sorrow is, (as in the present instance the people of Spain feel) that it may last; that, if the giddy and intoxicated Being who proclaims that he does these things with the eye and through the might of Providence be not 700 overthrown, it will last; that it needs must last:—and therefore would they hate and abhor him and his pride, even if he were not cruel; if he were merely an image of mortal presumption thrust in between them and the piety which is natural to the heart of man; between them and that religious worship which, as authoritatively as his reason forbids idolatry, that same reason commands. 705 Accordingly, labouring under these violations done to their moral nature, they describe themselves, in the anguish of their souls, treated as a people at once dastardly and *insensible.* In the same spirit they make it even matter of com-plaint, as comparatively a far greater evil, that they have not fallen by the brute violence of open war, but by deceit and perfidy, by a subtle undermining, or 710 contemptuous overthrow of those principles of good faith, through prevalence of which, in some degree, or under some modification or other, families, com-munities, a people, or any frame of human society, even destroying armies themselves can exist.   ▶

But enough of their wrongs; let us now see what were their consolations, 715
their resolves, and their hopes. First, they neither murmur nor repine; but with
genuine religion and philosophy they recognize in these dreadful visitations
the ways of a benign Providence, and find in them cause for thankfulness. The
Council of Castile exhort the people of Madrid "to cast off their lethargy, and
purify their manners, and to acknowledge the calamities which the kingdom 720
and that great capital had endured as a punishment necessary to their correction." General Morla in his address to the citizens of Cadiz thus speaks to
them:— "The commotion, more or less violent, which has taken place in the
whole peninsula of Spain, has been of eminent service to rouse us from the state
of lethargy in which we indulged, and to make us acquainted with our rights, 725
our glory, and the inviolable duty which we owe to our holy religion and our
monarch. We wanted some electric stroke to rouse us from our paralytic state
of inactivity; we stood in need of a hurricane to clear the atmosphere of the
insalubrious vapours with which it was loaded."—The unanimity with which
the whole people were affected they rightly deem an indication of wisdom, an 730
authority, and a sanction,—and they refer it to its highest source. "The defence
of our country and our king," (says a manifesto of the Junta of Seville) "that of
our laws, our religion, and of all the rights of man, trodden down and violated
in a manner which is without example, by the Emperor of the French, Napoleon I. and by his troops in Spain, compelled the whole nation to take up arms, 735
and choose itself a form of government; and, in the difficulties and dangers
into which the French had plunged it, all, or nearly all the provinces, as it were
by the inspiration of heaven, and in a manner little short of miraculous, created
Supreme Juntas, delivered themselves up to their guidance, and placed in their
hands the rights and the ultimate fate of Spain. The effects have hitherto most 740
happily corresponded with the designs of those who formed them."

With this general confidence, that the highest good may be brought out of
the worst calamities, they have combined a solace, which is vouchsafed only
to such nations as can recal to memory the illustrious deeds of their ancestors.
The names of Pelayo and The Cid are the watch-words of the address to the 745
people of Leon; and they are told that to these two deliverers of their country,
and to the sentiments of enthusiasm which they excited in every breast, Spain
owes the glory and happiness which she has *so long* enjoyed. The Biscayans
are called to cast their eyes upon the ages which are past, and they will see

their ancestors at one time repulsing the Carthaginians, at another destroying 750
the hordes of Rome; at one period was granted to them the distinction of serving in the van of the army; at another the privilege of citizens. "Imitate," says
the address, "the glorious example of your worthy progenitors." The Asturians,
the Gallicians, and the city of Cordova, are exhorted in the same manner. And
surely to a people thus united in their minds with the heroism of years which 755
have been long departed, and living under such obligation of gratitude to their
ancestors, it is not difficult, nay it is natural, to take upon themselves the highest obligations of duty to their posterity; to enjoy in the holiness of imagination
the happiness of unborn ages to which they shall have eminently contributed;
and that each man, fortified by these thoughts, should welcome despair for 760
himself, because it is the assured mother of hope for his country.— "Life or
Death," says a proclamation affixed in the most public places of Seville, "is in ▶
this crisis indifferent;—ye who shall return shall receive the reward of gratitude in the embraces of your country, which shall proclaim you her deliverers;—ye whom heaven destines to seal with your blood the independence of 765
your nation, the honour of your women, and the purity of the religion which
ye profess, do not dread the anguish of the last moments; remember in these
moments that there are in our hearts inexhaustible tears of tenderness to shed
over your graves, and fervent prayers, to which the Almighty Father of mercies
will lend an ear, to grant you a glory superior to that which they who survive 770
you shall enjoy." And in fact it ought never to be forgotten, that the Spaniards
have not wilfully blinded themselves, but have steadily fixed their eyes not
only upon danger and upon death, but upon a deplorable issue of the contest.
They have contemplated their subjugation as a thing possible. The next extract, from the paper entitled Precautions, (and the same language is holden by 775
many others) will show in what manner alone they reconcile themselves to it.
"Therefore, it is necessary to sacrifice our lives and property in defence of the
king, and of the country; and, though our lot (which we hope will never come
to pass) should destine us to become slaves, let us become so fighting and dying like gallant men, not giving ourselves up basely to the yoke like sheep, as 780
the late infamous government would have done, and fixing upon Spain and her
slavery eternal ignominy and disgrace."

But let us now hear them, as becomes men with such feelings, express
more cheering and bolder hopes rising from a confidence in the supremacy
of justice,—hopes which, however the Tyrant from the iron fortresses of his 785

policy may scoff at them and at those who entertained them, will render their
memory dear to all good men, when his name will be pronounced with universal abhorrence. ▶

"All Europe," says the Junta of Seville, "will applaud our efforts and hasten
to our assistance: Italy, Germany, and the whole North, which suffer under the 790
despotism of the French nation, will eagerly avail themselves of the favourable opportunity, held out to them by Spain, to shake off the yoke and recover
their liberty, their laws, their monarchs, and all they have been robbed of by
that nation. France herself will hasten to erase the stain of infamy, which must
cover the tools and instruments of deeds so treacherous and heinous. She will 795
not shed her blood in so vile a cause. She has already suffered too much under
the idle pretext of peace and happiness, which never came, and can never be
attained, but under the empire of reason, peace, religion, and laws, and in a
state where the rights of other nations are respected and preserved." To this
may be added a hope, the fulfilment of which belongs more to themselves, 800
and lies more within their own power, namely, a hope that they shall be able
in their progress towards liberty, to inflict condign punishment on their cruel
and perfidious enemies. The Junta of Seville, in an Address to the People of
Madrid, express themselves thus: "People of Madrid! Seville has learned, with
consternation and surprize, your dreadful catastrophe of the second of May; the 805
weakness of a government which did nothing in our favour,—which ordered
arms to be directed against you; and your heroic sacrifices. Blessed be ye, and
your memory shall shine immortal in the annals of our nation!—She has seen
with horror that the author of all your misfortunes and of our's has published
a proclamation, in which he distorted every fact, and pretended that you gave 810
the first provocation, while it was he who provoked you. The government was
weak enough to sanction and order that proclamation to be circulated; and saw,
with perfect composure, numbers of you put to death for a pretended violation
of laws which did not exist. The French were told in that proclamation, that
French blood profusely shed was crying out for vengeance! And the Span- 815
ish blood, does not *it* cry out for vengeance? That Spanish blood, shed by an
army which hesitated not to attack a disarmed and defenceless people, living
under their laws and their king, and against whom cruelties were committed,
which shake the human frame with horror. We, all Spain, exclaim—the Spanish blood shed in Madrid cries aloud for revenge! Comfort yourselves, we are 820
your brethren: we will fight like you, until we perish in defending our king and

country. Assist us with your good wishes, and your continual prayers offered
up to the Most High, whom we adore, and who cannot forsake us, because he ▶
never forsakes a just cause." Again, in the conclusion of their address to the ¶
People of Portugal, quoted before, "The universal cry of Spain is, we will die 825
in defence of our country, but we will take care that those infamous enemies
shall die with us. Come then, ye generous Portugueze, and unite with us. You
have among yourselves the objects of your vengeance—obey not the authors
of your misfortunes—attack them—they are but a handful of miserable panic-
struck men, humiliated and conquered already by the perfidy and cruelties 830
which they have committed, and which have covered them with disgrace in
the eyes of Europe and the world! Rise then in a body, but avoid staining your
honourable hands with crimes, for your design is to resist them and to destroy
them—our united efforts will do for this perfidious nation; and Portugal, Spain,
nay, all Europe, shall breathe or die free like men."—Such are their hopes; and 835
again see, upon this subject, the paper entitled "*Precautions*;" a contrast this ¶
to the impious mockery of Providence, exhibited by the Tyrant in some passages heretofore quoted! "Care shall be taken to explain to the nation, and to
convince them that, when free, as we trust to be, from this civil war, to which
the French have forced us, and when placed in a state of tranquillity, our Lord 840
and King, Ferdinand VII, being restored to the throne of Spain, under him and
by him, *the Cortes will be assembled, abuses reformed,* and such laws shall
be enacted, as the circumstances of the time and experience may dictate for
the public good and happiness. Things which we Spaniards know how to do,
which we have done as well as other nations, without any necessity that the 845
vile French should come to instruct us, and, according to their custom, under
the mask of friendship, should deprive us of our liberty, our laws, &c. &c."

One extract more and I shall conclude. It is from a proclamation dated Oviedo, ¶
July 17th. "Yes—Spain with the energies of Liberty has to contend with France
debilitated by slavery. If she remain firm and constant, Spain will triumph. A 850
whole people is more powerful than disciplined armies. Those, who unite to
maintain the independence of their country, must triumph over tyranny. Spain
will inevitably conquer, in a cause the most just that has ever raised the deadly
weapon of war; for she fights, not for the concerns of a day, but for the security
and happiness of ages; not for an insulated privilege, but for the rights of human 855
nature; not for temporal blessings, but for eternal happiness; not for the benefit
of one nation, but for all mankind, and even for France herself."

I will now beg of my reader to pause a moment, and to review in his own mind the whole of what has been laid before him. He has seen of what kind, and how great have been the injuries endured by these two nations; what they have suffered, and what they have to fear; he has seen that they have felt with that unanimity which nothing but the light of truth spread over the inmost concerns of human nature can create; with that simultaneousness which has ▶ led Philosophers upon like occasions to assert, that the voice of the people is the voice of God. He has seen that they have submitted as far as human nature could bear; and that at last these millions of suffering people have risen almost like one man, with one hope; for whether they look to triumph or defeat, to victory or death, they are full of hope—despair comes not near them—they will die, they say—each individual knows the danger, and, strong in the magnitude of it, grasps eagerly at the thought that he himself is to perish; and more eagerly, and with higher confidence, does he lay to his heart the faith that the nation will survive and be victorious;—or, at the worst, let the contest terminate how it may as to superiority of outward strength, that the fortitude and the martyrdom, the justice and the blessing, are their's and cannot be relinquished. And not only are they moved by these exalted sentiments of universal morality, and of direct and universal concern to mankind, which have impelled them to resist evil and to endeavour to punish the evil-doer, but also they descend (for even this, great as in itself it is, may be here considered as a descent) to express a rational hope of reforming domestic abuses, and of re-constructing, out of the materials of their ancient institutions, customs, and laws, a better frame of civil government, the same in the great outlines of its architecture, but exhibiting the knowledge, and genius, and the needs of the present race, harmoniously blended with those of their forefathers. Woe, then, to the unworthy who intrude with their help to maintain this most sacred cause! It calls aloud for the aid of intellect, knowledge, and love, and rejects every other. It is in vain to send forth armies if these do not inspire and direct them. The stream is as pure as it is mighty, fed by ten thousand springs in the bounty of untainted nature; any ▶ augmentation from the kennels and sewers of guilt and baseness may clog, but cannot strengthen it.—It is not from any thought that I am communicating new information, that I have dwelt thus long upon this subject, but to recall to the reader his own knowledge, and to re-infuse into that knowledge a breath and life of appropriate feeling; because the bare sense of wisdom is nothing without its powers, and it is only in these feelings that the powers of wisdom exist.

If then we do not forget that the Spanish and Portugueze Nations stand upon
the loftiest ground of principle and passion, and do not suffer on our part those   895
sympathies to languish which a few months since were so strong, and do not ▶
negligently or timidly descend from those heights of magnanimity to which ¶
as a nation we were raised, when they first represented to us their wrongs and
entreated our assistance, and we devoted ourselves sincerely and earnestly
to their service, making with them a common cause under a common hope;   900
if we are true in all this to them and to ourselves, we shall not be at a loss to
conceive what actions are entitled to our commendation as being in the spirit
of a friendship so nobly begun, and tending assuredly to promote the common
welfare; and what are abject, treacherous, and pernicious, and therefore to be
condemned and abhorred. Is then, I may now ask, the Convention of Cintra an   905
act of this latter kind? Have the Generals, who signed and ratified that agreement, thereby proved themselves unworthy associates in such a cause? And
has the Ministry, by whose appointment these men were enabled to act in this
manner, and which sanctioned the Convention by permitting them to carry it
into execution, thereby taken to itself a weight of guilt, in which the Nation   910
must feel that it participates, until the transaction shall be solemnly reprobated
by the Government, and the remote and immediate authors of it brought to
merited punishment? An answer to each of these questions will be implied in
the proof which will be given that the condemnation, which the People did
with one voice pronounce upon this Convention when it first became known,   915
was just; that the nature of the offence of those who signed it was such, and established by evidence of such a kind, making so imperious an exception to the
ordinary course of action, that there was no need to wait here for the decision
of a Court of Judicature, but that the People were compelled by a necessity involved in the very constitution of man as a moral Being to pass sentence upon   920
them. And this I shall prove by trying this act of their's by principles of justice
which are of universal obligation, and by a reference to those moral sentiments
which rise out of that retrospect of things which has been given.

I shall now proceed to facts. The dispatches of Sir Arthur Wellesley, con- ¶
taining an account of his having defeated the enemy in two several engage-   925
ments, spread joy through the nation. The latter action appeared to have been
decisive, and the result may be thus briefly reported, in a never to be forgotten
sentence of Sir Arthur's second letter. "In this action," says he, "in which the
whole of the French force in Portugal was employed, under the command of

the Duc d'Abrantes in person, in which the enemy was certainly superior in 930
cavalry and artillery, and in which not more than half of the British army was
actually engaged, he sustained a signal defeat, and has lost thirteen pieces of
cannon, &c. &c." In the official communication, made to the public of these
dispatches, it was added, that "a General officer had arrived at the British
head-quarters to treat for terms." This was joyful intelligence! First, an imme- 935
diate, effectual, and honourable deliverance of Portugal was confidently expected: secondly, the humiliation and captivity of a large French army, and just
punishment, from the hands of the Portugueze government, of the most atrocious offenders in that army and among those who, having held civil offices
under it, (especially if Portugueze) had, in contempt of all law, civil and mili- 940
tary, notoriously abused the power which they had treasonably accepted: thirdly, in this presumed surrender of the army, a diminution of the enemy's military ▶
force was looked to, which, after the losses he had already sustained in Spain,
would most sensibly weaken it: and lastly, and far above this, there was an
anticipation of a shock to his power, where that power is strongest, in the im- 945
aginations of men, which are sure to fall under the bondage of long-continued
success. The judicious part of the nation fixed their attention chiefly on these
results, and they had good cause to rejoice. They also received with pleasure
this additional proof (which indeed with the unthinking many, as after the victory of Maida, weighed too much,) of the superiority in courage and discipline 950
of the British soldiery over the French, and of the certainty of success whenever our army was led on by men of even respectable military talents against
any equal or not too greatly disproportionate number of the enemy. But the
pleasure was damped in the minds of reflecting persons by several causes. It
occasioned regret and perplexity, that they had not heard more of the Portugu- 955
eze. They knew what that People had suffered, and how they had risen;—remembered the language of the proclamation addressed to them, dated August
the 4th, and signed Charles Cotton and Arthur Wellesley, in which they
(the Portugueze) were told, that "The British Army had been sent in consequence of ardent supplications from all parts of Portugal; that the glorious 960
struggle, in which they are engaged, is for all that is dear to man; that the noble
struggle against the tyranny and usurpation of France will be *jointly* maintained by Portugal, Spain, and England." Why then, it was asked, do we not
hear more of those who are at least coequals with us, if not principals, in this
contest? They appeared to have had little share in either engagement; (*See* 965

Appendix A.) and, while the French were abundantly praised, no word of commendation was found for *them*. Had they deserved to be thus neglected? The body of the People by a general rising had proved their zeal and courage, their animosity towards their enemies, their hatred of them. It was therefore apprehended, from this silence respecting the Portugueze, that their Chiefs might 970 either be distracted by factions, or blinded by selfish interests, or that they mistrusted their Allies. Situated as Portugal then was, it would argue gross ignorance of human nature to have expected that unanimity should prevail among all the several authorities or leading persons, as to the *means* to be employed: it was enough, that they looked with one feeling to the *end,* namely, an 975 honourable deliverance of their country and security for its Independence in conjunction with the liberation and independence of Spain. It was therefore absolutely necessary to make allowance for some division in conduct from difference of opinion. Instead of acquiescing in the first feelings of disappointment, our Commanders ought to have used the best means to win the confi- 980 dence of the Portugueze Chiefs, and to induce them to regard the British as dispassionate arbiters; they ought to have endeavoured to excite a genuine patriotic spirit where it appeared wanting, and to assist in creating for it an organ by which it might act. Were these things done? or, if such evils existed among the Portugueze, was *any* remedy or alleviation attempted? Sir Arthur 985 Wellesley has told us, before the Board of Inquiry, that he made applications ▶ to the Portugueze General, FRERE, for assistance, which were acceded to by General FRERE upon such conditions only as made Sir Arthur deem it more advisable to refuse than accept his co-operation: and it is alleged that, in his general expectations of assistance, he was greatly disappointed. We are not 990 disposed to deny, that such cause for complaint *might* exist; but that it *did,* and upon no provocation on our part, requires confirmation by other testimony. And surely, the Portugueze have a right to be heard in answer to this accusation, before they are condemned. For they have supplied no fact from their own hands, which tends to prove that they were languid in the cause, or that 995 they had unreasonable jealousies of the British Army or Nation, or dispositions towards them which were other than friendly. Now there is a fact, furnished by Sir Arthur Wellesley himself, which may seem to render it in the ▶ highest degree probable that, previously to any recorded or palpable act of disregard or disrespect to the situation and feelings of the Portugueze, the gen- 1000 eral tenour of his bearing towards them might have been such that they could not look favourably upon him; that he was not a man framed to conciliate them, to compose their differences, or to awaken or strengthen their zeal. I allude to the passage in his letter above quoted, where, having occasion to speak of the French General, he has found no name by which to designate him but 1005 that of Duc d'Abrantes—words necessarily implying, that Bonaparte, who had taken upon himself to confer upon General Junot this Portugueze title with Portugueze domains to support it, was lawful Sovereign of that Country, and that consequently the Portugueze Nation were rebels, and the British Army, and he himself at the head of it, aiders and abettors of that rebellion. It would 1010 be absurd to suppose, that Sir Arthur Wellesley, at the time when he used these words, was aware of the meaning really involved in them: let them be deemed an oversight. But the capability of such an oversight affords too strong suspicion of a deadness to the moral interests of the cause in which he was engaged, and of such a want of sympathy with the just feelings of his injured Ally as 1015 could exist only in a mind narrowed by exclusive and overweening attention to the *military* character, led astray by vanity, or hardened by general habits of contemptuousness. These words, "Duke of Abrantes *in person,*" were indeed words of bad omen: and thinking men trembled for the consequences. They saw plainly, that, in the opinion of the exalted Spaniards—of those assuredly 1020 who framed, and of all who had felt, that affecting Proclamation addressed by the Junta of Seville to the Portugueze people, he must appear utterly unworthy of the station in which he had been placed. He had been sent as a deliverer—as an assertor and avenger of the rights of human nature. But these words would carry with them every where the conviction, that Portugal and Spain, yea, all 1025 which was good in England, or iniquitous in France or in Frenchmen, was forgotten, and his head full only of himself, miserably conceiting that he swelled the importance of his conquered antagonist by sounding titles and phrases, come from what quarter they might; and that, in proportion as this was done, he magnified himself and his atchievements. It was plain, then, that 1030 here was a man, who, having not any fellow-feeling with the people whom he had been commissioned to aid, could not know where their strength lay, and therefore could not turn it to account, nor by his example call it forth or cherish it; but that, if his future conduct should be in the same spirit, he must be a blighting wind wherever his influence was carried: for he had neither felt the 1035 wrongs of his allies nor been induced by common worldly prudence to affect to feel them, or at least to disguise his insensibility; and therefore what could follow, but, in despite of victory and outward demonstrations of joy, inward disgust and depression? These reflections interrupted the satisfaction of many; but more from fear of future consequences than for the immediate enterprize, **1040** for here success seemed inevitable; and a happy and glorious termination was confidently expected, yet not without that intermixture of apprehension, which was at once an acknowledgment of the general condition of humanity, and a proof of the deep interest attached to the impending event.

Sir Arthur Wellesley's dispatches had appeared in the Gazette on the 2d of **1045** September, and on the 16th of the same month suspence was put an end to by the publication of Sir Hew Dalrymple's letter, accompanied with the Armistice and Convention. The night before, by order of ministers, an attempt had been made at rejoicing, and the Park and Tower guns had been fired in sign of good news.—Heaven grant that the ears of that great city may be preserved from **1050** such another outrage! As soon as the truth was known, never was there such a burst of rage and indignation—such an overwhelming of stupefaction and sorrow. But I will not, I cannot dwell upon it—it is enough to say, that Sir Hew Dalrymple and Sir Arthur Wellesley must be bold men if they can think of what must have been reported to them without awe and trembling; the heart of **1055** their country was turned against them, and they were execrated in bitterness.

For they had changed all things into their contraries, hope into despair; triumph into defeat; confidence into treachery, which left no place to stand upon; justice into the keenest injury.—Whom had they delivered but the Tyrant in captivity? Whose hands had they bound but those of their Allies, who were able **1060** of themselves to have executed their own purposes? Whom had they punished but the innocent sufferer? Whom rewarded but the guiltiest of Oppressors? They had reversed every thing:—favour and honour for their enemies—insult for their friends—and robbery (they had both protected the person of the robber and secured to him his booty) and opprobrium for themselves;—to those **1065** over whom they had been masters, who had crouched to them by an open act of submission, they had made themselves servants, turning the British Lion into a beast of burthen, to carry a vanquished enemy, with his load of iniquities, when and whither it had pleased him.

Such issue would have been a heavy calamity at any time; but now, when **1070** we ought to have risen above ourselves, and if possible to have been foremost in the strife of honour and magnanimity; now, when a new-born power had been arrayed against the Tyrant, the only one which ever offered a glimpse of hope to a sane mind, the power of popular resistance rising out of universal reason, and from the heart of human nature,—and by a peculiar provi- 1075 dence disembarrassed from the imbecility, the cowardice, and the intrigues of a worn-out government—that at this time we, the most favoured nation upon earth, should have acted as if it had been our aim to level to the ground by one blow this long-wished-for spirit, whose birth we had so joyfully hailed, and by which even our own glory, our safety, our existence, were to be maintained; 1080 this was verily a surpassing affliction to every man who had a feeling of life beyond his meanest concerns!

As soon as men had recovered from the shock, and could bear to look somewhat steadily at these documents, it was found that the gross body of the ▶ transaction, considered as a military transaction, was this; that the Russian 1085 fleet, of nine sail of the line, which had been so long watched, and could not have escaped, was to be delivered up to us; the ships to be detained till six months after the end of the war, and the sailors sent home by us, and to be by us protected in their voyage through the Swedish fleet, and to be at liberty to fight immediately against our ally, the king of Sweden. Secondly, that a French 1090 army of more than twenty thousand men, already beaten, and no longer able to appear in the field, cut off from all possibility of receiving reinforcements or supplies, and in the midst of a hostile country loathing and abhorring it, was to be transported with its arms, ammunition, and plunder, at the expence of Great Britain, in British vessels, and landed within a few days march of the Spanish 1095 frontier,—there to be at liberty to commence hostilities immediately!

Omitting every characteristic which distinguishes the present contest from others, and looking at this issue merely as an affair between two armies, what stupidity of mind to provoke the accusation of not merely shrinking from future toils and dangers, but of basely shifting the burthen to the shoulders of an 1100 ally, already overpressed!—What infatuation, to convey the imprisoned foe to the very spot, whither, if he had had wings, he would have flown! This last was an absurdity as glaring as if, the French having landed on our own island, we had taken them from Yorkshire to be set on shore in Sussex; but ten thousand times worse! from a place where without our interference they had been 1105 virtually blockaded, where they were cut off, hopeless, useless, and disgraced, to become an efficient part of a mighty host, carrying the strength of their numbers, and alas! the strength of their glory, (not to mention the sight of their plunder) to animate that host; while the British army, more numerous in the

proportion of three to two, with all the population and resources of the penin- 1110
sula to aid it, within ten days sail of it's own country, and the sea covered with
friendly shipping at it's back, was to make a long march to encounter this same
enemy, (the British forfeiting instead of gaining by the treaty as to superiority
of numbers, for that this would be the case was clearly foreseen) to encounter,
in a new condition of strength and pride, those whom, by its deliberate act, it 1115
had exalted,—having taken from itself, meanwhile, all which it had conferred,
and bearing into the presence of its noble ally an infection of despondency and
disgrace. The motive assigned for all this, was the great importance of gaining
time; fear of an open beach and of equinoctial gales for the shipping; fear that
reinforcements could not be landed; fear of famine;—fear of every thing but 1120
dishonour! (*See Appendix, B.*)

The nation had expected that the French would surrender immediately at
discretion; and, supposing that Sir Arthur Wellesley had told them the whole
truth, they had a right to form this expectation. It has since appeared, from the
evidence given before the Board of Inquiry, that Sir Arthur Wellesley earnestly 1125
exhorted his successor in command (Sir Harry Burrard) to pursue the defeated
enemy at the battle of Vimiera; and that, if this had been done, the affair, in Sir
Arthur Wellesley's opinion, would have had a much more satisfactory termination. But, waiving any considerations of this advice, or of the fault which
might be committed in not following it; and taking up the matter from the 1130
time when Sir Hew Dalrymple entered upon the command, and when the two
adverse armies were in that condition, relatively to each other, that none of the
Generals has pleaded any difference of opinion as to their ability to advance
against the enemy, I will ask what confirmation has appeared before the Board
of Inquiry, of the reasonableness of the causes, assigned by Sir Hew Dalrym- 1135
ple in his letter, for deeming a Convention adviseable. A want of cavalry, (for
which they who occasioned it are heavily censurable,) has indeed been proved;
and certain failures of duty in the Commissariat department with respect to
horses, &c; but these deficiencies, though furnishing reasons against advancing upon the enemy in the open field, had ceased to be of moment, when the 1140
business was to expel him from the forts to which he might have the power of
retreating. It is proved, that, though there are difficulties in landing upon that
coast, (and what military or marine operation can be carried on without difficulty?) there was not the slightest reason to apprehend that the army, which
was then abundantly supplied, would suffer hereafter from want of provisions; 1145

proved also that heavy ordnance, for the purpose of attacking the forts, was
ready on ship-board, to be landed when and where it might be needed. There- ▶
fore, so far from being exculpated by the facts which have been laid before the
Board of Inquiry, Sir Hew Dalrymple and the other Generals, who deemed *any*
Convention necessary or expedient upon the grounds stated in his letter, are 1150
more deeply criminated. But grant, (for the sake of looking at a different part
of the subject,) grant a case infinitely stronger than Sir Hew Dalrymple has
even hinted at;—why was not the taste of some of those evils, in apprehension
so terrible, actually tried? It would not have been the first time that Britons had
faced hunger and tempests, had endured the worst of such enmity, and upon 1155
a call, under an obligation, how faint and feeble, compared with that which
the brave men of that army must have felt upon the present occasion! In the
proclamation quoted before, addressed to the Portugueze, and signed Charles
Cotton and Arthur Wellesley, they were told, that the objects, for which they
contended, "could only be attained by distinguished examples of fortitude and 1160
constancy." Where were the fortitude and constancy of the teachers? When
Sir Hew Dalrymple had been so busy in taking the measure of his own weakness, and feeding his own fears, how came it to escape him, that General Junot
must also have had *his* weaknesses and *his* fears? Was it nothing to have been
defeated in the open field, where he himself had been the assailant? Was it 1165
nothing that so proud a man, the servant of so proud a man, had stooped to
send a General Officer to treat concerning the evacuation of the country? Was
the hatred and abhorrence of the Portugueze and Spanish Nations nothing? the
people of a large metropolis under his eye—detesting him, and stung almost to
madness, nothing? The composition of his own army made up of men of dif- 1170
ferent nations and languages, and forced into the service,—was there no cause
of mistrust in this? And, finally, among the many unsound places which, had
his mind been as active in this sort of inquiry as Sir Hew Dalrymple's was, he
must have found in his constitution, could a bad cause have been missed—a
worse cause than ever confounded the mind of a soldier when boldly pressed 1175
upon, or gave courage and animation to a righteous assailant? But alas! in Sir
Hew Dalrymple and his brethren, we had Generals who had a power of sight
only for the strength of their enemies and their own weakness.

Let me not be misunderstood. While I am thus forced to repeat things, which
were uttered or thought of these men in reference to their military conduct, as 1180
heads of that army, it is needless to add, that their personal courage is in no

wise implicated in the charge brought against them. But, in the name of my countrymen, I do repeat these accusations, and tax them with an utter want of *intellectual* courage—of that higher quality, which is never found without one or other of the three accompaniments, talents, genius, or principle;—talents 1185 matured by experience, without which it cannot exist at all; or the rapid insight ▶ of peculiar genius, by which the fitness of an act may be instantly determined, and which will supply higher motives than mere talents can furnish for encountering difficulty and danger, and will suggest better resources for diminishing or overcoming them. Thus, through the power of genius, this quality of intel- 1190 lectual courage may exist in an eminent degree, though the moral character be greatly perverted; as in those personages, who are so conspicuous in history, conquerors and usurpers, the Alexanders, the Caesars, and Cromwells; and in that other class still more perverted, remorseless and energetic minds, the Catilines and Borgias, whom poets have denominated "bold, bad men." But, 1195 though a course of depravity will neither preclude nor destroy this quality, nay, in certain circumstances will give it a peculiar promptness and hardihood of decision, it is not on this account the less true, that, to *consummate* this species of courage, and to render it equal to all occasions, (especially when a man is not acting for himself, but has an additional claim on his resolution from the 1200 circumstance of responsibility to a superior) *Principle* is indispensibly requisite. I mean that fixed and habitual principle, which implies the absence of all selfish anticipations, whether of hope or fear, and the inward disavowal of any tribunal higher and more dreaded than the mind's own judgment upon its own act. The existence of such principle cannot but elevate the most commanding 1205 genius, add rapidity to the quickest glance, a wider range to the most ample comprehension; but, without this principle, the man of ordinary powers must, in the trying hour, be found utterly wanting. Neither, without it, can the man of excelling powers be trustworthy, or have at all times a calm and confident repose in himself. But he, in whom talents, genius, and principle are united, will have 1210 a firm mind, in whatever embarrassment he may be placed; will look steadily at the most undefined shapes of difficulty and danger, of possible mistake or mischance; nor will they appear to him more formidable than they really are. For his attention is not distracted—he has but one business, and that is with the object before him. Neither in general conduct nor in particular emergencies, 1215 are his plans subservient to considerations of rewards, estate, or title: these are

1188 than *Edd.*: that 1809.

not to have precedence in his thoughts, to govern his actions, but to follow in ▶
the train of his duty. Such men, in ancient times, were Phocion, Epaminondas,
and Philopoemen; and such a man was Sir Philip Sidney, of whom it has been
said, that he first taught this country *the majesty of honest dealing.* With these 1220
may be named, the honour of our own age, Washington, the deliverer of the
American Continent; with these, though in many things unlike, Lord Nelson,
whom we have lately lost. Lord Peterborough, who fought in Spain a hundred
years ago, had the same excellence; with a sense of exalted honour, and a tinge
of romantic enthusiasm, well suited to the country which was the scene of his 1225
exploits. Would that we had a man, like Peterborough or Nelson, at the head
of our army in Spain at this moment! I utter this wish with more earnestness,
because it is rumoured, that some of those, who have already called forth such
severe reprehension from their countrymen, are to resume a command, which
must entrust to them a portion of those sacred hopes in which, not only we, 1230
and the people of Spain and Portugal, but the whole human race are so deeply
interested. (*See Appendix C.*)

I maintain then that, merely from want of this intellectual courage, of courage as generals or chiefs, (for I will not speak at present of the want of other
qualities equally needful upon this service,) grievous errors were committed 1235
by Sir Hew Dalrymple and his colleagues in estimating the relative state of
the two armies. A precious moment, it is most probable, had been lost after
the battle of Vimiera; yet still the inferiority of the enemy had been proved;
they themselves had admitted it—not merely by withdrawing from the field,
but by proposing terms:—monstrous terms! and how ought they to have been 1240
received? Repelled undoubtedly with scorn, as an insult. If our Generals had
been men capable of taking the measure of their real strength, either as existing
in their own army, or in those principles of liberty and justice which they were
commissioned to defend, they must of necessity have acted in this manner;—if
they had been men of common sagacity for business, they must have acted in 1245
this manner;—nay, if they had been upon a level with an ordinary bargain-
maker in a fair or a market, they could not have acted otherwise.—Strange
that they should so far forget the nature of their calling! They were soldiers,
and their business was to fight. Sir Arthur Wellesley had fought, and gallantly;
it was not becoming his high situation, or that of his successors, to treat, that 1250
is, to beat down, to chaffer, or on their part to propose: it does not become any

general at the head of a victorious army so to do.* They were to *accept,*—and, if the terms offered were flagrantly presumptuous, our commanders ought to have rejected them with dignified scorn, and to have referred the proposer to the sword for a lesson of decorum and humility. This is the general rule of all 1255 high-minded men upon such occasions; and meaner minds copy them, doing in prudence what they do from principle. But it has been urged, before the Board of Inquiry, that the conduct of the French armies upon like occasions, and their known character, rendered it probable that a determined resistance would in the present instance be maintained. We need not fear to say that this 1260 conclusion, from reasons which have been adverted to, was erroneous. But, in the mind of him who had admitted it upon whatever ground, whether false or true, surely the first thought which followed, ought to have been, not that we should bend to the enemy, but that, if they were resolute in defence, we should learn from that example to be courageous in attack. The tender feelings, 1265 however, are pleaded against this determination; and it is said, that one of the motives for the cessation of hostilities was to prevent the further effusion of human blood.—When, or how? The enemy was delivered over to us; it was not to be hoped that, cut off from all assistance as they were, these, or an equal number of men, could ever be reduced to such straits as would ensure their 1270 destruction as an enemy, with so small a sacrifice of life on their part, or on ours. What then was to be gained by this tenderness? The shedding of a few drops of blood is not to be risked in Portugal to-day, and streams of blood must shortly flow from the same veins in the fields of Spain! And, even if this had not been the assured consequence, let not the consideration, though it be one 1275 which no humane man can ever lose sight of, have more than its due weight. For national independence and liberty, and *that* honour by which these and other blessings are to be preserved, honour—which is no other than the most elevated and pure conception of justice which can be formed, these are more precious than life: else why have we already lost so many brave men in this 1280 struggle?—Why not submit at once, and let the Tyrant mount upon his throne of universal dominion, while the world lies prostrate at his feet in indifference and apathy, which he will proclaim to it is peace and happiness? But peace and happiness can exist only by knowledge and virtue; slavery has no enduring

* Those rare cases are of course excepted, in which the superiority on the one side is not only fairly to be presumed but positive—and so prominently obtrusive, that to *propose* terms is to *inflict* terms.

connection with tranquillity or security—she cannot frame a league with any 1285
thing which is desirable—she has no charter even for her own ignoble ease and ▶
darling sloth. Yet to this abject condition, mankind, betrayed by an ill-judging
tenderness, would surely be led; and in the face of an inevitable contradiction!
For neither in this state of things would the shedding of blood be prevented,
nor would warfare cease. The only difference would be, that, instead of wars 1290
like those which prevail at this moment, presenting a spectacle of such character that, upon one side at least, a superior Being might look down with favour
and blessing, there would follow endless commotions and quarrels without the
presence of justice any where,—in which the alternations of success would not
excite a wish or regret; in which a prayer could not be uttered for a decision 1295
either this way or that;—wars from no impulse in either of the combatants, but
rival instigations of demoniacal passion. If, therefore, by the faculty of reason
we can prophecy concerning the shapes which the future may put on,—if we
are under any bond of duty to succeeding generations, there is high cause to
guard against a specious sensibility, which may encourage the hoarding up 1300
of life for its own sake, seducing us from those considerations by which we
might learn when it ought to be resigned. Moreover, disregarding future ages,
and confining ourselves to the present state of mankind, it may be safely affirmed that he, who is the most watchful of the honour of his country, most
determined to preserve her fair name at all hazards, will be found, in any view 1305
of things which looks beyond the passing hour, the best steward of the *lives* of
his countrymen. For, by proving that she is of a firm temper, that she will only
submit or yield to a point of her own fixing, and that all beyond is immutable
resolution, he will save her from being wantonly attacked; and, if attacked,
will awe the aggressor into a speedier abandonment of an unjust and hopeless 1310
attempt. Thus will he preserve not only that which gives life its value, but life
itself; and not for his own country merely, but for that of his enemies, to whom
he will have offered an example of magnanimity, which will ensure to them
like benefits; an example, the re-action of which will be felt by his own countrymen, and will prevent them from becoming assailants unjustly or rashly. 1315
Nations will thus be taught to respect each other, and mutually to abstain from
injuries. And hence, by a benign ordinance of our nature, genuine honour is
the hand-maid of humanity; the attendant and sustainer—both of the sterner
qualities which constitute the appropriate excellence of the male character,
and of the gentle and tender virtues which belong more especially to motherli 1320

ness and womanhood. These general laws, by which mankind is purified and
exalted, and by which Nations are preserved, suggest likewise the best rules ▶
for the preservation of individual armies, and for the accomplishment of all
equitable service upon which they can be sent.

Not therefore rashly and unfeelingly, but from the dictates of thoughtful 1325
humanity, did I say that it was the business of our Generals to fight, and to
persevere in fighting; and that they did not bear this duty sufficiently in mind;
this, almost the sole duty which professional soldiers, till our time, (happily for
mankind) used to think of. But the victories of the French have been attended
every where by the subversion of Governments; and their generals have ac- 1330
cordingly united *political* with military functions; and with what success this
has been done by them, the present state of Europe affords melancholy proof.
But have they, on this account, ever neglected to calculate upon the advantages which might fairly be anticipated from future warfare? Or, in a treaty
of to-day, have they ever forgotten a victory of yesterday? Eager to grasp at 1335
the double honour of captain and negociator, have they ever sacrificed the one
to the other; or, in the blind effort, lost both? Above all, in their readiness to
flourish with the pen, have they ever overlooked the sword, the symbol of their
power, and the appropriate instrument of their success and glory? I notice this
assumption of a double character on the part of the French, not to lament over 1340
it and its consequences, but to render somewhat more intelligible the conduct
of our own Generals; and to explain how far men, whom we have no reason
to believe other than brave, have, through the influence of such example, lost
sight of their primary duties, apeing instead of imitating, and following only to
be misled.   1345

It is indeed deplorable, that our Generals, from this infirmity, or from any
other cause, did not assume that lofty deportment which the character and relative strength of the two armies authorized them, and the nature of the service
upon which they were sent, enjoined them to assume;—that they were in such
haste to treat—that, with such an enemy (let me say at once,) and in such cir- 1350
cumstances, they should have treated at all. Is it possible that they could ever
have asked themselves who that enemy was, how he came into that country,
and what he had done there? From the manifesto of the Portugueze government, issued at Rio Janeiro, and from other official papers, they might have
learned, what was notorious to all Europe, that this body of men commissioned 1355
by Bonaparte, in the time of profound peace, without a declaration of war, had

invaded Portugal under the command of Junot, who had perfidiously entered
the country, as the General of a friendly and allied Power, assuring the people,
as he advanced, that he came to protect their Sovereign against an invasion of
the English; and that, when in this manner he had entered a peaceable king- 1360
dom, which offered no resistance, and had expelled its lawful Sovereign, he
wrung from it unheard-of contributions, ravaged it, cursed it with domestic
pillage and open sacrilege; and that, when this unoffending people, unable to
endure any longer, rose up against the tyrant, he had given their towns and
villages to the flames, and put the whole country, thus resisting, under mili- 1365
tary execution.—Setting aside all natural sympathy with the Portugueze and
Spanish nations, and all prudential considerations of regard or respect for *their
feelings* towards these men, and for *their expectations* concerning the manner
in which they ought to be dealt with, it is plain that the French had forfeited
by their crimes all right to those privileges, or to those modes of intercourse, 1370
which one army may demand from another according to the laws of war. They
were not soldiers in any thing but the power of soldiers, and the outward frame
of an army. During their occupation of Portugal, the laws and customs of war
had never been referred to by them, but as a plea for some enormity, to the
aggravated oppression of that unhappy country! Pillage, sacrilege, and mur- 1375
der—sweeping murder and individual assassination, had been proved against
them by voices from every quarter. They had outlawed themselves by their
offences from membership in the community of war, and from every species
of community acknowledged by reason. But even, should any one be so insensible as to question this, he will not at all events deny, that the French ought 1380
to have been dealt with as having put on a double character. For surely they
never considered themselves merely as an army. They had dissolved the established authorities of Portugal, and had usurped the civil power of the government; and it was in this compound capacity, under this two-fold monstrous
shape, that they had exercised, over the religion and property of the country, 1385
the most grievous oppressions. What then remained to protect them but their
power?—Right they had none,—and power! it is a mortifying consideration,
but I will ask if Bonaparte, (nor do I mean in the question to imply any thing to ▶
his honour,) had been in the place of Sir Hew Dalrymple, what would he have
thought of their power?—Yet before this shadow the solid substance of *justice* 1390
melted away.

And this leads me from the contemplation of their errors in the estimate and application of means, to the contemplation of their heavier errors and worse blindness in regard to ends. The British Generals acted as if they had no pur- 1395 pose but that the enemy should be removed from the country in which they were, upon *any* terms. Now the evacuation of Portugal was not the prime ob- ject, but the manner in which that event was to be brought about; this ought to have been deemed first both in order and importance;—the French were to be subdued, their ferocious warfare and heinous policy to be confounded; and in this way, and no other, was the deliverance of that country to be accomplished. 1400 It was not for the soil, or for the cities and forts, that Portugal was valued, but for the human feeling which was there; for the rights of human nature which might be there conspicuously asserted; for a triumph over injustice and op- pression there to be atchieved, which could neither be concealed nor disguised, and which should penetrate the darkest corner of the dark Continent of Europe 1405 by its splendour. We combated for victory in the empire of reason, for strong- holds in the imagination. Lisbon and Portugal, as city and soil, were chiefly prized by us as a *language;* but our Generals mistook the counters of the game for the stake played for. The nation required that the French should surrender at discretion;—grant that the victory of Vimiera had excited some unreasona- 1410 ble impatience—we were not so overweening as to demand that the enemy should surrender within a given time, but that they should surrender. Every thing, short of this, was felt to be below the duties of the occasion; not only no service, but a grievous injury. Only as far as there was a prospect of forcing the enemy to an unconditional submission, did the British nation deem that they 1415 had a right to interfere;—if that prospect failed, they expected that their army would know that it became it to retire, and take care of itself. But our Generals have told us, that the Convention would not have been admitted, if they had not judged it right to effect, even upon these terms, the evacuation of Portu- gal—as ministerial to their future services in Spain. If this had been a common 1420 war between two established governments measuring with each other their regular resources, there might have been some appearance of force in this plea. But who does not cry out at once, that the affections and opinions, that is, the souls of the people of Spain and Portugal, must be the inspiration and the power, if this labour is to be brought to a happy end? Therefore it was worse 1425 than folly to think of supporting Spain by physical strength, at the expence of moral. Besides, she was strong in men; she never earnestly solicited troops from us; some of the Provinces had even refused them when offered,—and all

had been lukewarm in the acceptance of them. The Spaniards could not *ulti-*
mately be benefited but by allies acting under the same impulses of honour, 1450
rouzed by a sense of their wrongs, and sharing their loves and hatreds—above ▶
all, their *passion* for justice. They had themselves given an example, at Baylen,
proclaiming to all the world what ought to be aimed at by those who would
uphold their cause, and be associated in arms with them. And was the law of
justice, which Spaniards, Spanish peasantry, I might almost say, would not 1455
relax in favour of Dupont, to be relaxed by a British army in favour of Junot?
Had the French commander at Lisbon, or his army, proved themselves less
perfidious, less cruel, or less rapacious than the other? Nay, did not the pride
and crimes of Junot call for humiliation and punishment far more importu-
nately, inasmuch as his power to do harm, and therefore his will, keeping pace 1460
with it, had been greater? Yet, in the noble letter of the Governor of Cadiz to
Dupont, he expressly tells him, that his conduct, and that of his army, had been
such, that they owed their lives only to that honour which forbad the Spanish
army to become executioners. The Portugueze also, as appears from various
letters produced before the Board of Inquiry, have shewn to our Generals, as 1465
boldly as their respect for the British nation would permit them to do, what
they expected. A Portugueze General, who was also a member of the regency
appointed by the Prince Regent, says, in a protest addressed to Sir Hew Dalrymple, that he had been able to drive the French out of the provinces of Al-
garve and Alentejo; and therefore he could not be convinced, that such a Con- 1470
vention was necessary. What was this but implying that it was dishonourable,
and that it would frustrate the efforts which his country was making, and de- ▶
stroy the hopes which it had built upon its own power? Another letter from a
magistrate inveighs against the Convention, as leaving the crimes of the French
in Portugal unpunished; as giving no indemnification for all the murders, rob- 1475
beries, and atrocities, which had been committed by them. But I feel that I
shall be wanting in respect to my countrymen, if I pursue this argument further.
I blush that it should be necessary to speak upon the subject at all. And these
are men and things, which we have been reproved for condemning, because
evidence was wanting both as to fact and person! If there ever was a case, 1480
which could not, in any rational sense of the word, be prejudged, this is one.
As to the fact—it appears, and sheds from its own body, like the sun in heaven,
the light by which it is seen; as to the person—each has written down with his
own hand, *I am the man.* Condemnation of actions and men like these is not,

in the minds of a people, (thanks to the divine Being and to human nature!) a 1485
matter of choice; it is like a physical necessity, as the hand must be burned
which is thrust into the furnace—the body chilled which stands naked in the
freezing north-wind. I am entitled to make this assertion here, when the *moral* ▶
depravity of the Convention, of which I shall have to speak hereafter, has not
even been touched upon. Nor let it be blamed in any man, though his station 1490
be in private life, that upon this occasion he speaks publickly, and gives a decisive opinion concerning that part of this public event, and those measures,
which are more especially military. All have a right to speak, and to make their
voices heard, as far as they have power. For these are times, in which the conduct of military men concerns us, perhaps, more intimately than that of any 1495
other class; when the business of arms comes unhappily too near to the fire
side; when the character and duties of a soldier ought to be understood by
every one who values his liberty, and bears in mind how soon he may have to
fight for it. Men will and ought to speak upon things in which they are so
deeply interested; how else are right notions to spread, or is error to be de- 1500
stroyed? These are times also in which, if we may judge from the proceedings
and result of the Court of Inquiry, the heads of the army, more than at any
other period, stand in need of being taught wisdom by the voice of the people.
It is their own interest, both as men and as soldiers, that the people should
speak fervently and fearlessly of their actions:—from no other quarter can 1505
they be so powerfully reminded of the duties which they owe to themselves, to
their country, and to human nature. Let any one read the evidence given before
that Court, and he will there see, how much the intellectual and moral constitution of many of our military officers, has suffered by a profession, which, if not
counteracted by admonitions willingly listened to, and by habits of meditation, 1510
does, more than any other, denaturalize—and therefore degrade the human
being;—he will note with sorrow, how faint are their sympathies with the best
feelings, and how dim their apprehension of some of the most awful truths,
relating to the happiness and dignity of man in society. But on this I do not
mean to insist at present; it is too weighty a subject to be treated incidentally: 1515
and my purpose is—not to invalidate the authority of military men, *positively*
considered, upon a military question, but *comparatively;*—to maintain that
there are military transactions upon which the people have a right to be heard,
and upon which their authority is entitled to far more respect than any man or
number of men can lay claim to, who speak merely with the ordinary profes- 1520

sional views of soldiership;—that there are such military transactions;—and that *this* is one of them.

The condemnation, which the people of these islands pronounced upon the Convention of Cintra considered as to its main *military* results, that is, as a treaty by which it was established that the Russian fleet should be surrendered 1525 on the terms specified; and by which, not only the obligation of forcing the French army to an unconditional surrender was abandoned, but its restoration in freedom and triumph to its own country was secured;—the condemnation, pronounced by the people upon a treaty, by virtue of which these things were to be done, I have recorded—accounted for—and thereby justified.—I will 1530 now proceed to another division of the subject, on which I feel a still more earnest wish to speak; because, though in itself of the highest importance, it has been comparatively neglected;—I mean the political injustice and moral depravity which are stamped upon the front of this agreement, and pervade every regulation which it contains. I shall shew that our Generals (and with 1535 them our Ministers, as far as they might have either given directions to this effect, or have countenanced what has been done)—when it was their paramount duty to maintain at all hazards the noblest principles in unsuspected integrity; because, upon the summons of these, and in defence of them, their Allies had risen, and by these alone could stand—not only did not perform this duty, but 1540 descended as far below the level of ordinary principles as they ought to have mounted above it;—imitating not the majesty of the oak with which it lifts its branches towards the heavens, but the vigour with which, in the language of the poet, it strikes its roots downwards towards hell:—

Radice in Tartara tendit.

The Armistice is the basis of the Convention; and in the first article we find it agreed, "That there shall be a suspension of hostilities between the forces of his Britannic Majesty, and those of his Imperial and Royal Majesty, Napoleon I." I will ask if it be the practice of military officers, in instruments of this kind, to acknowledge, in the person of the head of the government with which they 1550 are at war, titles which their own government—for which they are acting—has not acknowledged. If this be the practice, which I will not stop to determine, it is grossly improper; and ought to be abolished. Our Generals, however, had entered Portugal as allies of a Government by which this title had been acknowledged; and they might have pleaded this circumstance in mitigation of 1555 their offence; but surely not in an instrument, where we not only look in vain

for the name of the Portugueze Sovereign, or of the Government which he appointed, or of any heads or representatives of the Portugueze armies or people
as a party in the contract,—but where it is stipulated (in the 4th article) that the
British General shall engage to include the Portugueze armies in this Conven- 1560
tion. What an outrage!—We enter the Portugueze territory as allies; and, without their consent—or even consulting them, we proceed to form the basis of
an agreement, relating—not to the safety or interests of our own army—but to
Portugueze territory, Portugueze persons, liberties, and rights,—and engage,
out of our own will and power, to include the Portugueze army, they or their 1565
Government willing or not, within the obligation of this agreement. I place
these things in contrast, viz. the acknowledgement of Bonaparte as emperor
and king, and the utter neglect of the Portugueze Sovereign and Portugueze
authorities, to shew in what spirit and temper these agreements were entered
upon. I will not here insist upon what was our duty, on this occasion, to the 1570
Portugueze—as dictated by those sublime precepts of justice which it has been
proved that they and the Spaniards had risen to defend,—and without feeling
the force and sanctity of which, they neither could have risen, nor can oppose
to their enemy resistance which has any hope in it; but I will ask, of any man
who is not dead to the common feelings of his social nature—and besotted in 1575
understanding, if this be not a cruel mockery, and which must have been felt,
unless it were repelled with hatred and scorn, as a heart-breaking insult. Moreover, this conduct acknowledges, by implication, that principle which by his
actions the enemy has for a long time covertly maintained, and now openly and
insolently avows in his words—that power is the measure of right;—and it is 1580
in a steady adherence to this abominable doctrine that his strength mainly lies.
I do maintain then that, as far as the conduct of our Generals in framing these
instruments tends to reconcile men to this course of action, and to sanction
this principle, they are virtually his Allies: their weapons may be against him,
but he will laugh at their weapons,—for he knows, though they themselves do 1585
not, that their souls are for him. Look at the preamble to the Armistice! In what
is omitted and what is inserted, the French Ruler could not have fashioned it
more for his own purpose if he had traced it with his own hand. We have then
trampled upon a fundamental principle of justice, and countenanced a prime
maxim of iniquity; thus adding, in an unexampled degree, the foolishness of 1590
impolicy to the heinousness of guilt. A conduct thus grossly unjust and impolitic, without having the hatred which it inspires neutralised by the contempt, is

made contemptible by utterly wanting that colour of right which authority and power, put forth in defence of our Allies—in asserting their just claims and avenging their injuries, might have given. But we, instead of triumphantly dis- 1595 playing our power towards our enemies, have ostentatiously exercised it upon our friends; reversing here, as every where, the practice of sense and reason;—conciliatory even to abject submission where we ought to have been haughty and commanding,—and repulsive and tyrannical where we ought to have been gracious and kind. Even a common law of good breeding would have served 1600 us here, had we known how to apply it. We ought to have endeavoured to raise the Portugueze in their own estimation by concealing our power in comparison with theirs; dealing with them in the spirit of those mild and humane delusions, which spread such a genial grace over the intercourse, and add so much to the influence of love in the concerns of private life. It is a common saying, 1605 presume that a man is dishonest, and that is the readiest way to make him so: in like manner it may be said, presume that a nation is weak, and that is the surest course to bring it to weakness,—if it be not rouzed to prove its strength by applying it to the humiliation of your pride. The Portugueze had been weak; and, in connection with their allies the Spaniards, they were prepared to become 1610 strong. It was, therefore, doubly incumbent upon us to foster and encourage them—to look favourably upon their efforts—generously to give them credit upon their promises—to hope with them and for them; and, thus anticipating and foreseeing, we should, by a natural operation of love, have contributed to create the merits which were anticipated and foreseen. I apply these rules, 1615 taken from the intercourse between individuals, to the conduct of large bodies of men, or of nations towards each other, because these are nothing but aggregates of individuals; and because the maxims of all just law, and the measures of all sane practice, are only an enlarged or modified application of those dispositions of love and those principles of reason, by which the welfare of indi- 1620 viduals, in their connection with each other, is promoted. There was also here a still more urgent call for these courteous and humane principles as guides of conduct; because, in exact proportion to the physical weakness of Governments, and to the distraction and confusion which cannot but prevail, when a people is struggling for independence and liberty, are the well-intentioned and the wise 1625 among them remitted for their support to those benign elementary feelings of society, for the preservation and cherishing of which, among other important objects, government was from the beginning ordained.

Therefore, by the strongest obligations, we were bound to be studious of a delicate and respectful bearing towards those ill-fated nations, our allies: and 1630 consequently, if the government of the Portugueze, though weak in power, possessed their affections, and was strong in right, it was incumbent upon us to turn our first thoughts to that government—to look for it if it were hidden—to call it forth,—and, by our power combined with that of the people, to assert its rights. Or, if the government were dissolved and had no existence, it was our 1635 duty, in such an emergency, to have resorted to the nation, expressing its will through the most respectable and conspicuous authority, through that which seemed to have the best right to stand forth as its representative. In whatever circumstances Portugal had been placed, the paramount right of the Portu- gueze nation, or government, to appear not merely as a party but a principal, 1640 ought to have been established as a primary position, without the admission of which, all proposals to treat would be peremptorily rejected. But the Por- tugueze *had* a government; they had a lawful prince in Brazil; and a regency, appointed by him, at home; and generals, at the head of considerable bodies of troops, appointed also by the regency or the prince. Well then might one of 1645 those generals enter a formal protest against the treaty, on account of its being ▶ "totally void of that deference due to the prince regent, or the government that represents him; as being hostile to the sovereign authority and independence of that government; and as being against the honour, safety, and independence of the nation." I have already reminded the reader, of the benign and happy 1650 influences which might have attended upon a different conduct; how much good we might have added to that already in existence; how far we might have assisted in strengthening, among our allies, those powers, and in developing those virtues, which were producing themselves by a natural process, and to which these breathings of insult must have been a deadly check and interrup- 1655 tion. Nor would the evil be merely negative; for the interference of professed friends, acting in this manner, must have superinduced dispositions and pas- sions, which were alien to the condition of the Portugueze;—scattered weeds which could not have been found upon the soil, if our ignorant hands had not sown them. Of this I will not now speak, for I have already detained the reader 1660 too long at the threshold;—but I have put the master-key into his possession; and every chamber which he opens will be found loathsome as the one which he last quitted. Let us then proceed.

By the first article of the Convention it is covenanted, that all the places

and forts in the kingdom of Portugal, occupied by the French troops, shall be 1665
delivered to the British army. Articles IV. and XII. are to the same effect—de-
termining the surrender of Portugueze fortified places, stores, and ships, to
the English forces; but not a word of their being to be holden in trust for the
prince regent, or his government, to whom they belonged! The same neglect
or contempt of justice and decency is shewn here, as in the preamble to these 1670
instruments. It was further shewn afterwards, by the act of hoisting the British ◀ ▶
flag instead of the Portugueze upon these forts, when they were first taken possession of by the British forces. It is no excuse to say that this was not intended.
Such inattentions are among the most grievous faults which can be committed;
and are *impossible,* when the affections and understandings of men are of that 1675
quality, and in that state, which are required for a service in which there is any
thing noble or virtuous. Again, suppose that it was the purpose of the generals,
who signed and ratified a Convention containing the articles in question, that
the forts and ships, &c. should be delivered immediately to the Portugueze
government,—would the delivering up of them wipe away the affront? Would 1680
it not rather appear, after the omission to recognize the right, that we had ostentatiously taken upon us to bestow—as a boon—that which they felt to be
their own?

Passing by, as already deliberated and decided upon, those conditions, (Articles II. and III.) by which it is stipulated, that the French army shall not be 1685
considered as prisoners of war, shall be conveyed with arms, &c. to some port
between Rochefort and L'Orient, and be at liberty to serve, I come to that
memorable condition, (Article V.) "that the French army shall carry with it all
its equipments, that is to say, its military chests and carriages, attached to the
field commissariat and field hospitals, or shall be allowed to dispose of such 1690
part, as the Commander in Chief may judge it unnecessary to embark. In like
manner all individuals of the army shall be at liberty to dispose of *their private
property* of *every* description, with full security hereafter for the purchasers."
This is expressed still more pointedly in the Armistice,—though the meaning,
implied in the two articles, is precisely the same. For, in the fifth article of the 1695
Armistice, it is agreed provisionally, "that all those, of whom the French army
consists, shall be conveyed to France with arms and baggage, *and* all their
private property of every description, no part of which shall be wrested from
them." In the Convention it is only expressed, that they shall be at liberty to
depart, (Article II.) with arms and baggage, and (Article V.) to dispose of their 1700

private property of every description. But, if they had a right to dispose of it, *this* would include a right to carry it away—which was undoubtedly understood by the French general. And in the Armistice it is expressly said, that their private property of every description shall be conveyed to France along with their persons. What then are we to understand by the words, *their private prop-* 1705
erty of every description? Equipments of the army in general, and baggage of individuals, had been stipulated for before: now we all know that the lawful professional gains and earnings of a soldier must be small; that he is not in the habit of carrying about him, during actual warfare, any accumulation of these or other property; and that the ordinary private property, which he can be sup- 1710
posed to have a *just* title to, is included under the name of his *baggage;*—therefore this was something more; and what it was—is apparent. No part of their property, says the Armistice, shall be *wrested from them.* Who does not see in these words the consciousness of guilt, an indirect self-betraying admission that they had in their hands treasures which might be lawfully taken from 1715
them, and an anxiety to prevent that act of justice by a positive stipulation? Who does not see, on what sort of property the Frenchman had his eye; that it was not property by right, but their *possessions*—their plunder—every thing, by what means soever acquired, that the French army, or any individual in it, was possessed of? But it has been urged, that the monstrousness of such a sup- 1720
position precludes this interpretation, renders it impossible that it could either be intended by the one party, or so understood by the other. What right they who signed, and he who ratified this Convention, have to shelter themselves under this plea—will appear from the 16th and 17th articles. In these it is stipulated, "that all subjects of France, or of Powers in alliance with France, 1725
domiciliated in Portugal, or accidentally in the country, shall have their property of every kind—moveable and immoveable—guaranteed to them, with liberty of retaining or disposing of it, and passing the produce into France:" the same is stipulated, (Article XVII.) for such natives of Portugal as have sided with the French, or occupied situations under *the French Government.* Here 1730
then is a direct avowal, still more monstrous, that every Frenchman, or native of a country in alliance with France, however obnoxious his crimes may have made him, and every traitorous Portugueze, shall have his property guaranteed to him (both previously to and after the reinstatement of the Portugueze government) by the British army! Now let us ask, what sense the word property 1735
must have had fastened to it in *these* cases. Must it not necessarily have in-

cluded all the rewards which the Frenchman had received for his iniquity, and
the traitorous Portugueze for his treason? (for no man would bear a part in
such oppressions, or would be a traitor for nothing; and, moreover, all the rewards, which the French could bestow, must have been taken from the Portu-   1740
gueze, extorted from the honest and loyal, to be given to the wicked and disloyal.) These rewards of iniquity must necessarily have been included; for, on
our side, no attempt is made at a distinction; and, on the side of the French, the
word *immoveable* is manifestly intended to preclude such a distinction, where
alone it could have been effectual. Property, then, here means—possessions   1745
thus infamously acquired; and, in the instance of the Portugueze, the fundamental notion of the word is subverted; for a traitor can have no property, till
the government of his own country has remitted the punishment due to his
crimes. And these wages of guilt, which the master by such exactions was
enabled to pay, and which the servant thus earned, are to be guaranteed to him   1750
by a British *army!* Where does there exist a power on earth that could confer
this right? If the Portugueze government itself had acted in this manner, it
would have been guilty of wilful suicide; and the nation, if it had acted so, of
high treason against itself. Let it not, then, be said, that the monstrousness of
covenanting to convey, along with the persons of the French, their plunder,   1755
secures the article from the interpretation which the people of Great Britain
gave, and which, I have now proved, they were bound to give to it.—But, con-
ceding for a moment, that it was not intended that the words should bear this
sense, and that, neither in a fair grammatical construction, nor as illustrated by
other passages or by the general tenour of the document, they actually did bear   1760
it, had not unquestionable voices proclaimed the cruelty and rapacity—the
acts of sacrilege, assassination, and robbery, by which these treasures had been
amassed? Was not the perfidy of the French army, and its contempt of moral
obligation, both as a body and as to the individuals which composed it, infamous through Europe?—Therefore, the concession would signify nothing: for   1765
our Generals, by allowing an army of this character to depart with its equipments, waggons, military chest, and baggage, had provided abundant means to
enable it to carry off whatsoever it desired, and thus to elude and frustrate any
stipulations which might have been made for compelling it to restore that which
had been so iniquitously seized. And here are we brought back to the fountain-   1770
head of all this baseness; to that apathy and deadness to the principle of justice,
through influence of which, this army, outlawed by its crimes, was suffered to

depart from the land, over which it had so long tyrannized—other than as a band of disarmed prisoners.—I maintain, therefore, that permission to carry off the booty was distinctly expressed; and, if it had not been so, that the prin- **1775** ciple of justice could not here be preserved; as a violation of it must necessarily have followed from other conditions of the treaty. Sir Hew Dalrymple him- ◄► self, before the Court of Inquiry, has told us, in two letters (to Generals Beresford and Friere,) that "such part of the plunder as was in money, it would be difficult, if not impossible, to identify;" and, consequently, the French could **1780** not be prevented from carrying it away with them. From the same letters we learn, that "the French were intending to carry off a considerable part of their plunder, by calling it public money, and saying that it belonged to the military chest; and that their evasions of the article were most shameful, and evinced a want of probity and honour, which was most disgraceful to them." If the French **1785** had given no other proofs of their want of such virtues, than those furnished by this occasion, neither the Portugueze, nor Spanish, nor British nations would condemn them, nor hate them as they now do; nor would this article of the Convention have excited such indignation. For the French, by so acting, could not deem themselves breaking an engagement; no doubt they looked upon **1790** themselves as injured,—that the failure in good faith was on the part of the British; and that it was in the lawlessness of power, and by a mere quibble, that this construction was afterwards put upon the article in question.

Widely different from the conduct of the British was that of the Spaniards in a like case:—with high feeling did they, abating not a jot or a tittle, enforce the **1795** principle of justice. "How," says the governor of Cadiz to General Dupont in ◄► the same noble letter before alluded to, "how," says he, after enumerating the afflictions which his army, and the tyrant who had sent it, had unjustly brought upon the Spanish nation, (for of these, in *their* dealings with the French, they never for a moment lost sight,) "how," asks he, "could you expect, that your **1800** army should carry off from Spain the fruit of its rapacity, cruelty, and impiety? how could you conceive this possible, or that we should be so stupid or senseless?" And this conduct is as wise in reason as it is true to nature. The Spanish people could have had no confidence in their government, if it had not acted thus. These are the sympathies which prove that a government is **1805** paternal,—that it makes one family with the people: besides, it is only by such adherence to justice, that, in times of like commotion, popular excesses can either be mitigated or prevented. If we would be efficient allies of Spain, nay,

if we would not run the risk of doing infinite harm, these sentiments must not
only be ours as a nation, but they must pervade the hearts of our ministers and 1810
our generals—our agents and our ambassadors. If it be not so, they, who are
sent abroad, must either be conscious how unworthy they are, and with what
unworthy commissions they appear, or not: if they do feel this, then they must
hang their heads, and blush for their country and themselves; if they do not,
the Spaniards must blush for them and revolt from them; or, what would be 1815
ten thousand times more deplorable, they must purchase a reconcilement and
a communion by a sacrifice of all that is excellent in themselves. Spain must
either break down her lofty spirit, her animation and fiery courage, to run side
by side in the same trammels with Great Britain; or she must start off from her
intended yoke-fellow with contempt and aversion. This is the alternative, and 1820
there is no avoiding it.

I have yet to speak of the influence of such concessions upon the French
Ruler and his army. With what Satanic pride must he have contemplated the
devotion of his servants and adherents to *their* law, the steadiness and zeal
of their perverse loyalty, and the faithfulness with which they stand by him 1825
and each other! How must his heart have distended with false glory, while he ▶
contrasted these qualities of his subjects with the insensibility and slackness
of his British enemies! This notice has, however, no especial propriety in this
place; for, as far as concerns Bonaparte, his pride and depraved confidence
may be equally fed by almost all the conditions of this instrument. But, as to 1830
his army, it is plain that the permission, (whether it be considered as by an
express article formally granted, or only involved in the general conditions
of the treaty,) to bear away in triumph the harvest of its crimes, must not only
have emboldened and exalted it with arrogance, and whetted its rapacity; but
that hereby every soldier, of which this army was composed, must, upon his 1835
arrival in his own country, have been a seed which would give back plente-
ously in its kind. The French are at present a needy people, without commerce
or manufactures,—unsettled in their minds and debased in their morals by
revolutionary practices and habits of warfare; and the youth of the country are
rendered desperate by oppression, which, leaving no choice in their occupa- 1840
tion, discharges them from all responsibility to their own consciences. How
powerful then must have been the action of such incitements upon a people so
circumstanced! The actual sight, and, far more, the imaginary sight and handling of these treasures, magnified by the romantic tales which must have been

spread about them, would carry into every town and village an antidote for the   1845
terrors of conscription; and would rouze men, like the dreams imported from
the new world when the first discoverers and adventurers returned, with their
ingots and their gold dust—their stories and their promises, to inflame and
madden the avarice of the old. "What an effect," says the Governor of Cadiz, ◀▶
"must it have upon the people," (he means the Spanish people,) "to know that   1850
a single soldier was carrying away 2580 livres tournois!" What an effect, (he
might have said also,) must it have upon the French!—I direct the reader's attention to this, because it seems to have been overlooked; and because some
of the public journals, speaking of the Convention, (and, no doubt, uttering
the sentiments of several of their readers,)—say "that they are disgusted with   1855
the transaction, not because the French have been permitted to carry off a few
diamonds, or some ingots of silver; but because we confessed, by consenting
to the treaty, that an army of 35,000 British troops, aided by the Portugueze nation, was not able to compel 20,000 French to surrender at discretion." This is
indeed the root of the evil, as hath been shewn; and it is the curse of this treaty,   1860
that the several parts of it are of such enormity as singly to occupy the attention
and to destroy comparison and coexistence. But the people of Great Britain
are disgusted both with the one and the other. They bewail the violation of the
principle: if the value of the things carried off had been in itself trifling, their
grief and their indignation would have been scarcely less. But it is manifest,   1865
from what has been said, that it was not trifling; and that therefore, (upon that
account as well as upon others,) this permission was no less impolitic than it
was unjust and dishonourable.

In illustrating these articles of the Armistice and Convention, by which the
French were both expressly permitted and indirectly enabled to carry off their   1870
booty, we have already seen, that a concession was made which is still more
enormous; viz. that all subjects of France, or of powers in alliance with France,
domiciliated in Portugal or resident there, and all natives of Portugal who have
accepted situations under *the French government,* &c., shall have their *property* of every kind guaranteed to them by the British army. By articles 16th and   1875
17th, their *persons* are placed under the like protection. "The French" (Article
XVI.) "shall be at liberty either to accompany the French army, or to remain
in Portugal;" "And the Portugueze" (Article XVII.) "shall not be rendered
accountable for their political conduct during the period of the occupation of
the country by the French army: they all are placed under the protection of the   1880

British commanders, and shall sustain no injury in their property or persons."

I have animadverted, heretofore, upon the unprofessional eagerness of our ◄ ▶ Generals to appear in the character of negotiators when the sword would have done them more service than the pen. But, if they had confined themselves to mere military regulations, they might indeed with justice have been grievously 1885 censured as injudicious commanders, whose notion of the honour of armies was of a low pitch, and who had no conception of the peculiar nature of the service in which they were engaged: but the censure must have stopped here. Whereas, by these provisions, they have shewn that they had never reflected upon the nature of military authority as contradistinguished from civil. French 1890 example had so far dazzled and blinded them, that the French army is suffered to denominate itself *"the French government;"* and, from the whole tenour of these instruments, (from the preamble, and these articles especially,) it should seem that our Generals fancied themselves and their army to be *the British government.* For these regulations, emanating from a mere military author- 1895 ity, are purely civil; but of such a kind, that no power on earth could confer a right to establish them. And this trampling upon the most sacred rights—this sacrifice of the consciousness of a self-preserving principle, without which neither societies nor governments can exist, is not made by our generals in relation to subjects of their own sovereign, but to an independent nation, our 1900 ally, into whose territories we could not have entered but from its confidence in our friendship and good faith. Surely the persons, who (under the counte- ◄ nance of too high authority) have talked so loudly of prejudging this question, entirely overlooked or utterly forgot this part of it. What have these monstrous provisions to do with the relative strength of the two armies, or with any point 1905 admitting a doubt? What need here of a court of judicature to settle who were the persons (their names are subscribed by their own hands), and to determine ◄ the quality of the thing? Actions and agents like these, exhibited in this con- nection with each other, must of necessity be condemned the moment they are known: and to assert the contrary, is to maintain that man is a being without 1910 understanding, and that morality is an empty dream. And, if this condemnation must after this manner follow, to utter it is less a duty than a further inevitable consequence from the constitution of human nature. They, who hold that the formal sanction of a court of judicature is in this case required before a people has a right to pass sentence, know not to what degree they are enemies to that 1915 people and to mankind; to what degree selfishness, whether arising from their

peculiar situation or from other causes, has in them prevailed over those faculties which are our common inheritance, and cut them off from fellowship with
the species. Most deplorable would be the result, if it were possible that the
injunctions of these men could be obeyed, or their remonstrances acknowl- 1920
edged to be just. For, (not to mention that, if it were not for such prompt decisions of the public voice, misdemeanours of men high in office would rarely
be accounted for at all,) we must bear in mind, at this crisis, that the adversary
of all good is hourly and daily extending his ravages; and, according to such
notions of fitness, our indignation, our sorrow, our shame, our sense of right 1925
and wrong, and all those moral affections, and powers of the understanding, by
which alone he can be effectually opposed, are to enter upon a long vacation;
their motion is to be suspended—a thing impossible; if it could, it would be ◀▶
destroyed.

Let us now see what language the Portugueze speak upon that part of the 1930
treaty which has incited me to give vent to these feelings, and to assert these
truths. "I protest," says General Friere, "against Article XVII., one of the two
now under examination, because it attempts to tie down the government of this
kingdom not to bring to justice and condign punishment those persons, who
have been notoriously and scandalously disloyal to their prince and the country 1935
by joining and serving the French party, and, even if the English army should
be allowed to screen them from the punishment they have deserved, still it
should not prevent their expulsion—whereby this country would no longer
have to fear being again betrayed by the same men." Yet, while the partizans
of the French are thus guarded, not a word is said to protect the loyal Portugu- 1940
eze, whose fidelity to their country and their prince must have rendered them
obnoxious to the French army; and who in Lisbon and the environs, were left
at its mercy from the day when the Convention was signed, till the departure
of the French. Couple also with this the first additional article, by which it is
agreed, "that the individuals in the civil employment of the army," (including 1945
all the agitators, spies, informers, all the jackals of the ravenous lion,) "made
prisoners either by the British troops or the Portugueze in any part of Portugal,
will be restored (*as is customary*) without exchange." That is, no stipulations
being made for reciprocal conditions! In fact, through the whole course of this
strange interference of a military power with the administration of civil justice 1950
in the country of an ally, there is only one article (the 15th) which bears the
least shew of attention to Portugueze interests. By this it is stipulated, "That,

from the date of the ratification of the Convention, all arrears of contributions, requisitions, or claims whatever of the French Government against subjects of Portugal, or any other individuals residing in this country, founded on the occu- 1955 pation of Portugal by the French troops in the month of December 1807, which may not have been paid up, are cancelled: and all sequestrations, laid upon their property moveable or immoveable, are removed; and the free disposal of the same is restored to the proper owners." Which amounts to this. The French are called upon formally to relinquish, in favour of the Portugueze, that to 1960 which they never had any right; to abandon false claims, which they either had a power to enforce, or they had not: if they departed immediately and had *not* power, the article was nugatory; if they remained a day longer and *had* power, there was no security that they would abide by it. Accordingly, loud com- plaints were made that, after the date of the Convention, all kinds of ravages 1965 were committed by the French upon Lisbon and its neighbourhood: and what did it matter whether these were upon the plea of old debts and requisitions; or new debts were created more greedily than ever—from the consciousness that the time for collecting them was so short? This article, then, the only one which is even in shew favourable to the Portugueze, is, in substance, nothing: 1970 inasmuch as, in what it is silent upon, (viz. that the People of Lisbon and its neighbourhood shall not be vexed and oppressed by the French, during their stay, with new claims and robberies,) it is grossly cruel or negligent; and, in that for which it actually stipulates, wholly delusive. It is in fact insulting; for the very admission of a formal renunciation of these claims does to a certain 1975 degree acknowledge their justice. The only decent manner of introducing mat- ter to this effect would have been by placing it as a bye clause of a provision that secured the Portugueze from further molestations, and merely alluding to it as a thing understood of course. Yet, from the place which this specious article occupies, (preceding immediately the 16th and 17th which we have 1980 been last considering,) it is clear that it must have been intended by the French General as honey is smeared upon the edge of the cup—to make the poison, contained in those two, more palateable.

Thus much for the Portugueze, and their particular interests. In one instance, a concern of the Spanish Nation comes directly under notice; and that nation 1985 also is treated without delicacy or feeling. For by the 18th article it is agreed, "that the Spaniards, (4000 in number) who had been disarmed, and were con- ◄ ▶ fined on ship-board in the port of Lisbon by the French, should be liberated."

And upon what consideration? Not upon their *right* to be free, as having been treacherously and cruelly dealt with by men who were part of a power that was **1990** labouring to subjugate their country, and in this attempt had committed inhuman crimes against it;—not even exchanged as soldiers against soldiers:—but the condition of their emancipation is, that the British General engages "to obtain of the Spaniards to restore such French subjects, either military or civil, as have been detained in Spain, without having been taken in battle or in con- **1995** sequence of military operations, but on account of the *occurrences* of the 29th ◀▶ of last May and the days immediately following." "*Occurrences!*" I know not what are exactly the features of the face for which this word serves as a veil: I have no register at hand to inform me what these events precisely were: but there can be no doubt that it was a time of triumph for liberty and humanity; **2000** and that the persons, for whom these noble-minded Spaniards were to be exchanged, were no other than a horde from among the most abject of the French Nation; probably those wretches, who, having never faced either the dangers or the fatigues of war, had been most busy in secret preparations or were most conspicuous in open acts of massacre, when the streets of Madrid, a few weeks **2005** before, had been drenched with the blood of two thousand of her bravest citi- ▶ zens. Yet the liberation of these Spaniards, upon these terms, is recorded (in the report of the Court of Enquiry) "as one of the advantages which, in the contemplation of the Generals, would result from the Convention!"

Finally, "If there shall be any doubt (Article XIV.) as to the meaning of **2010** any article, it shall be explained favourably to the French Army; and Hostages (Article XX.) of the rank of Field Officers, on the part of the British Army and Navy, shall be furnished for the guarantee of the present Convention."

I have now gone through the painful task of examining the most material conditions of the CONVENTION OF CINTRA:—the whole number of the articles **2015** is twenty-two, with three additional ones—a long ladder into a deep abyss of infamy!—

Need it be said that neglects—injuries—and insults—like these which we have been contemplating, come from what quarter they may, let them be exhibited towards whom they will, must produce not merely mistrust and jeal- **2020** ousy, but alienation and hatred. The passions and feelings may be quieted or diverted for a short time; but, though out of sight or seemingly asleep, they must exist; and the life which they have received cannot, but by a long course

1997 twenty–two *Errata:* twenty–three 1809.

of justice and kindness, be overcome and destroyed. But why talk of a long
course of justice and kindness, when the immediate result must have been so **2025**
deplorable? Relying upon our humanity, our fellow-feeling, and our justice,
upon these instant and urgent claims, sanctioned by the more mild one of ancient alliance, the Portugueze People by voices from every part of their land
entreated our succour; the arrival of a British Army upon their coasts was
joyfully hailed; and the people of the country zealously assisted in landing the **2030**
troops; without which help, as a British General has informed us, that landing ▶
could not have been effected. And it is in this manner that they are repaid!
Scarcely have we set foot upon their country before we sting them into self-re-
proaches, and act in every thing as if it were our wish to make them ashamed of
their generous confidence as of a foolish simplicity—proclaiming to them that **2035**
they have escaped from one thraldom only to fall into another. If the French
had any traitorous partizans in Portugal, (and we have seen that such there
were; and that nothing was left undone on our part, which could be done, to
keep them there, and to strengthen them) what answer could have been given
to one of these, if (with this treaty in his hand) he had said, "The French have **2040**
dealt hardly with us, I allow; but we have gained nothing: the change is not
for the better, but for the worse: for the appetite of their tyranny was palled;
but this, being new to its food, is keen and vigorous. If you have only a choice
between two masters, (such an advocate might have argued) chuse always the
stronger: for he, after his evil passions have had their first harvest, confident **2045**
in his strength, will not torment you wantonly in order to prove it. Besides,
the property which he has in you he can maintain; and there will be no risk of
your being torn in pieces—the unsettled prey of two rival claimants. You will
thus have the advantage of a fixed and assured object of your hatred: and your
fear, being stripped of doubt, will lose its motion and its edge: both passions **2050**
will relax and grow mild; and, though they may not turn into reconcilement
and love, though you may not be independent nor be free, yet you will at least
exist in tranquillity,—and possess, if not the activity of hope, the security of ¶
despair." No effectual answer, I say, could have been given to a man pleading
thus in such circumstances. So much for the choice of evils. But, for the hope **2055**
of good!—what is to become of the efforts and high resolutions of the Portugueze and Spanish Nations, manifested by their own hand in the manner which
we have seen? They may live indeed and prosper; but not by us, but in despite
of us.

Whatever may be the character of the Portugueze Nation; be it true or not, **2060**
that they had a becoming sense of the injuries which they had received from the
French Invader, and were rouzed to throw off oppression by a universal effort,
and to form a living barrier against it;—certain it is that, betrayed and trampled upon as they had been, they held unprecedented claims upon humanity
to secure them from further outrages.—Moreover, our conduct towards them **2065**
was grossly inconsistent. For we entered their country upon the supposition
that they had such sensibility and virtue; we announced to them publickly and
solemnly our belief in this: and indeed to have landed a force in the peninsula
upon any other inducement would have been the excess of folly and madness.
But the Portugueze *are* a brave people—a people of great courage and worth! **2070**
Conclusions, drawn from intercourse with certain classes of the depraved inhabitants of Lisbon only, and which are true only with respect to them, have
been hastily extended to the whole nation, which has thus unjustly suffered
both in our esteem and in that of all Europe. In common with their neighbours
the Spaniards, they *were* making a universal, zealous, and fearless effort; and, **2075**
whatever may be the final issue, the very act of having risen under the pressure
and in the face of the most tremendous military power which the earth has ever
seen—is itself evidence in their favour, the strongest and most comprehensive
which can be given; a transcendent glory! which, let it be remembered, no subsequent failures in duty on their part can forfeit. This they must have felt—that **2080**
they had furnished an illustrious example; and that nothing can abolish their
claim upon the good wishes and upon the gratitude of mankind, which is—and
will be through all ages their due. At such a time, then, injuries and insults from
any quarter would have been deplorable; but, proceeding from us, the evil must
have been aggravated beyond calculation. For we have, throughout Europe, the **2085**
character of a sage and meditative people. Our history has been read by the degraded Nations of the Continent with admiration, and some portions of it with
awe; with a recognition of superiority and distance, which was honourable to
us—salutary for those to whose hearts, in their depressed state, it could find
entrance—and promising for the future condition of the human race. We have **2090**
been looked up to as a people who have acted nobly; whom their constitution
of government has enabled to speak and write freely, and who therefore have
thought comprehensively; as a people among whom philosophers and poets,
by their surpassing genius—their wisdom—and knowledge of human nature,
have circulated—and made familiar—divinely-tempered sentiments and the **2095**

purest notions concerning the duties and true dignity of individual and social man in all situations and under all trials. By so readily acceding to the prayers with which the Spaniards and Portugueze entreated our assistance, we had proved to them that we were not wanting in fellow-feeling. Therefore might we be admitted to be judges between them and their enemies—unexception- 2100 able judges—more competent even than a dispassionate posterity, which, from the very want comparatively of interest and passion, might be in its examination remiss and negligent, and therefore in its decision erroneous. We, their contemporaries, were drawn towards them as suffering beings; but still their sufferings were not ours, nor could be; and we seemed to stand at that due point 2105 of distance from which right and wrong might be fairly looked at and seen in their just proportions. Every thing conspired to prepossess the Spaniards and Portugueze in our favour, and to give the judgment of the British Nation authority in their eyes. Strange, then, would be their first sensations, when, upon further trial, instead of a growing sympathy, they met with demonstrations of 2110 a state of sentiment and opinion abhorrent from their own. A shock must have followed upon this discovery, a shock to their confidence—not perhaps at first in us, but in themselves: for, like all men under the agitation of extreme passion, no doubt they had before experienced occasional misgivings that they were subject to error and distraction from afflictions pressing too violently 2115 upon them. These flying apprehensions would now take a fixed place; and that moment would be most painful. If they continued to respect our opinion, so far must they have mistrusted themselves: fatal mistrust at such a crisis! Their passion of just vengeance, their indignation, their aspiring hopes, every thing that elevated and cheared, must have departed from them. But this bad 2120 influence, the *excess* of the outrage would mitigate or prevent; and we may be assured that they rather recoiled from allies who had thus by their actions discountenanced and condemned efforts, which the most solemn testimony of conscience had avouched to them were just;—that they recoiled from us with that loathing and contempt which unexpected, determined, and absolute hos- 2125 tility, upon points of dearest interest will for ever create.

Again: independence and liberty were the blessings for which the people of the Peninsula were contending—immediate independence, which was not to be gained but by modes of exertion from which liberty must ensue. Now, liberty—healthy, matured, time-honoured liberty—this is the growth and pe- 2130 culiar boast of Britain; and nature herself, by encircling with the ocean the

country which we inhabit, has proclaimed that this mighty nation is for ever
to be her own ruler, and that the land is set apart for the home of immortal
independence. Judging then from these first fruits of British Friendship, what
bewildering and depressing and hollow thoughts must the Spaniards and Por- 2115
tugueze have entertained concerning the real value of these blessings, if the
people who have possessed them longest, and who ought to understand them
best, could send forth an army capable of enacting the oppression and baseness
of the Convention of Cintra; if the government of that people could sanction
this treaty; and if, lastly, this distinguished and favoured people themselves 2120
could suffer it to be held forth to the eyes of men as expressing the sense of
their hearts—as an image of their understandings.

But it did not speak their sense—it was not endured—it was not submitted
to in their hearts. Bitter was the sorrow of the people of Great Britain when
the tidings first came to their ears, when they first fixed their eyes upon this 2125
covenant—overwhelming was their astonishment, tormenting their shame;
their indignation was tumultuous; and the burthen of the past would have been
insupportable, if it had not involved in its very nature a sustaining hope for
the future. Among many alleviations, there was one, which, (not wisely, but
overcome by circumstances) all were willing to admit;—that the event was 2130
so strange and uncouth, exhibiting such discordant characteristics of innocent
fatuity and enormous guilt, that it could not without violence be thought of
as indicative of a general constitution of things, either in the country or the
government; but that it was a kind of *lusus naturae* in the moral world—a
solitary straggler out of the circumference of nature's law—a monster which 2135
could not propagate, and had no birthright in futurity. Accordingly, the first
expectation was that the government would deem itself under the necessity of
disannulling the Convention; a necessity which, though in itself a great evil,
appeared small in the eyes of judicious men, compared with the consequences
of admitting that such a contract could be binding. For they, who had signed 2140
and ratified it, had not only glaringly exceeded all power which could be supposed to be vested in them as holding a military office; but, in the exercise
of political functions, they had framed ordinances which neither the government, nor the nation, nor any power on earth, could confer upon them a right
to frame: therefore the contract was self-destroyed from the beginning. It is a 2145

2145 self–destroyed *M.Y.* i. 342: self–destroying
    1809.

wretched oversight, or a wilful abuse of terms still more wretched, to speak of the good faith of a nation as being pledged to an act which was not a shattering of the edifice of justice, but a subversion of its foundations. One man cannot sign away the faculty of reason in another; much less can one or two individuals do this for a whole people. Therefore the contract was void, both from its 2150 injustice and its absurdity; and the party, with whom it was made, must have known it to be so. It could not then but be expected by many that the government would reject it. Moreover, extraordinary outrages against reason and virtue demand that extraordinary sacrifices of atonement should be made upon their altars; and some were encouraged to think that a government might upon 2155 this impulse rise above itself, and turn an exceeding disgrace into true glory, by a public profession of shame and repentance for having appointed such unworthy instruments; that, this being acknowledged, it would clear itself from all imputation of having any further connection with what had been done, and would provide that the nation should as speedily as possible, be purified from 2160 all suspicion of looking upon it with other feelings than those of abhorrence. The people knew what had been their own wishes when the army was sent in aid of their allies; and they clung to the faith, that their wishes and the aims of the Government must have been in unison; and that the guilt would soon be judicially fastened upon those who stood forth as principals, and who (it was 2165 hoped) would be found to have fulfilled only their own will and pleasure,—to have had no explicit commission or implied encouragement for what they had done,—no accessaries in their crime. The punishment of these persons was anticipated, not to satisfy any cravings of vindictive justice (for these, if they could have existed in such a case, had been thoroughly appeased already: for 2170 what punishment could be greater than to have brought upon themselves the sentence passed upon them by the voice of their countrymen?); but for this rea- ◄ ►
son—that a judicial condemnation of the men, who were openly the proximate cause, and who were forgetfully considered as the single and sole originating source, would make our detestation of the effect more signally manifest.   2175

These thoughts, if not welcomed without scruple and relied upon without fear, were at least encouraged; till it was recollected that the persons at the head of government had ordered that the event should be communicated to the inhabitants of the metropolis with signs of national rejoicing. No wonder if,

2172 sentence . . . voice 1809 *cancel* N1:   *cancellandum* N1.
      unremoveable contempt and hatred 1809

when these rejoicings were called to mind, it was impossible to entertain the 2180
faith which would have been most consolatory. The evil appeared no longer
as the forlorn monster which I have described. It put on another shape, and
was endued with a more formidable life—with power to generate and transmit
after its kind. A new and alarming import was added to the event by this open
testimony of gladness and approbation; which intimated—which declared— 2185
that the spirit, which swayed the individuals who were the ostensible and immediate authors of the Convention, was not confined to them; but that it was
widely prevalent: else it could not have been found in the very council-seat;
there, where if wisdom and virtue have not some influence, what is to become
of the nation in these times of peril? rather say, into what an abyss is it already 2190
fallen!

His Majesty's ministers, by this mode of communicating the tidings, indis-
creet as it was unfeeling, had committed themselves. Yet still they might have
recovered from the lapse, have awakened after a little time. And accordingly,
notwithstanding an annunciation so ominous, it was matter of surprise and 2195
sorrow to many, that the ministry appeared to deem the Convention binding,
and that its terms were to be fulfilled. There had indeed been only a choice of
evils: but, of the two, the worse—ten thousand times the worse—was fixed
upon. The ministers, having thus officially applauded the treaty,—and, by suffering it to be carried into execution, made themselves a party to the trans- 2200
action,—drew upon themselves those suspicions which will ever pursue the
steps of public men who abandon the direct road which leads to the welfare of
their country. It was suspected that they had taken this part against the dictates
of conscience, and from selfishness and cowardice; that, from the first, they
reasoned thus within themselves:—"If the act be indeed so criminal as there is 2205
cause to believe that the public will pronounce it to be; and if it shall continue
to be regarded as such; great odium must sooner or later fall upon those who
have appointed the agents: And this odium, which will be from the first considerable, in spite of the astonishment and indignation of which the framers
of the Convention may be the immediate object, will, when the astonishment 2210
has relaxed, and the angry passions have died away, settle (for many causes)
more heavily upon those who, by placing such men in the command, are the
original source of the guilt and the dishonour. How then is this most effectually to be prevented? By endeavouring to prevent or to destroy, as far as may
be, the odium attached to the act itself." For which purpose it was suspected 2215

that the rejoicings had been ordered; and that afterwards (when the people had declared themselves so loudly),—partly upon the plea of the good faith of the nation being pledged, and partly from a false estimate of the comparative force of the two obligations,—the Convention, in the same selfish spirit, was carried into effect; and that the ministry took upon itself a final responsibility, **2220** with a vain hope that, by so doing and incorporating its own credit with the transaction, it might bear down the censures of the people, and overrule their judgment to the superinducing of a belief, that the treaty was not so unjust and inexpedient: and thus would be included—in one sweeping exculpation—the misdeeds of the servant and the master.   **2225**

But,—whether these suspicions were reasonable or not, whatever motives produced a determination that the Convention should be acted upon,—there can be no doubt of the manner in which the ministry wished that the people should appreciate it; when the same persons, who had ordered that it should at first be received with rejoicing, availed themselves of his Majesty's high **2230** authority to give a harsh reproof to the City of London for having prayed "that an enquiry might be instituted into this dishonourable and unprecedented transaction." In their petition they styled it also "an afflicting event—humiliating and degrading to the country, and injurious to his Majesty's Allies." And for this, to the astonishment and grief of all sound minds, the petitioners were **2235** severely reprimanded; and told, among other admonitions, "that it was inconsistent with the principles of British jurisprudence to pronounce judgement without previous investigation."

Upon this charge, as re-echoed in its general import by persons who have been over-awed or deceived, and by others who have been wilful deceivers, I **2240** have already incidentally animadverted; and repelled it, I trust, with becoming indignation. I shall now meet the charge for the last time formally and directly; on account of considerations applicable to all times; and because the whole course of domestic proceedings relating to the Convention of Cintra, combined with menaces which have been recently thrown out in the lower House of Par- **2245**

2242 charge ... by 1809: charge in its general import as reechoed by BM.
2239–40 persons ... deceivers, 1809: a part of the Public BM.
2241 incidentally BM, *Errata:* incidently 1809. animadverted; 1809: animadverted with sober reason BM.
2241 it 1809: it also BM.

2242 indignation 1809: indignation at the outrage committed by it against the understanding and moral feelings of mankind BM.
2242 meet ... charge 1809: both for its relation to this particular question, and for the general importance of the subject, meet it BM.
2243–53 on account ... purposes 1809: *om.* BM.

liament, renders it too probable that a league has been framed for the purpose of laying further restraints upon freedom of speech and of the press; and that the reprimand to the City of London was devised by ministers as a preparatory overt act of this scheme; to the great abuse of the Sovereign's Authority, and in contempt of the rights of the nation. In meeting this charge, I shall shew to **2250** what desperate issues men are brought, and in what woeful labyrinths they are entangled, when, under the pretext of defending instituted law, they violate the laws of reason and nature for their own unhallowed purposes.

If the persons, who signed this petition, acted inconsistently with the princi- ◀▶ ples of British jurisprudence; the offence must have been committed by giving **2255** an answer, before adequate and lawful evidence had entitled them so to do, to one or other of these questions:—"What is the act? and who is the agent?"—or to both conjointly. Now the petition gives no opinion upon the agent; it pronounces only upon the act, and that some one must be guilty; but *who*—it does not take upon itself to say. It condemns the act; and calls for punishment upon **2260** the authors, whosoever they may be found to be; and does no more. After the analysis which has been made of the Convention, I may ask if there be any thing in this which deserves reproof; and reproof from an authority which ought to be most enlightened and most dispassionate,—as it is, next to the legislative, the most solemn authority in the land.   **2265**

It is known to every one that the privilege of complaint and petition, in cases where the nation feels itself aggrieved, *itself* being the judge, (and who else ought to be, or can be?)—a privilege, the exercise of which implies condemnation of something complained of, followed by a prayer for its removal or correction—not only is established by the most grave and authentic charters **2270** of Englishmen, who have been taught by their wisest statesmen and legislators to be jealous over its preservation, and to call it into practice upon every

---

2254–57 acted ... questions 1809, BM³: had violated the principles of British jurisprudence by prejudging the case that is deciding upon it without adequate and lawful evidence, it must have been [?] one or other of these [?] BM: had violated ... it must have been by giving an answer before they were entitled so to do by adequate and [lawful evidence] to one or other of these questions BM².

2258–59 pronounces only 1809: only pronounces BM.

2261–63 After ... any thing 1809: Is there any thing BM: After the [? line or ? hint] which we have taken of [? this transaction] is there any thing BM²: After the examination [analysis BM⁴] which we have made of the convention I may ask if there be any thing BM³.

2263 which BM², 1809: that BM. reproof 1809: that reproof BM.

2264 most enlightened and most dispassionate 1809: the most enlightened and [*tear*] most dispassionate BM.

2265 legislative, the most 1809: Legislati[? ve] [?assembly] [*tear*] most BM.

reasonable occasion; but also that this privilege is an indispensable condition of all civil liberty. Nay, of such paramount interest is it to mankind, existing under any frame of Government whatsoever; that, either by law or custom, it 2275 has universally prevailed under all governments—from the Grecian and Swiss Democracies to the Despotisms of Imperial Rome, of Turkey, and of France under her present ruler. It must then be a high principle which could exact obeisance from governments at the two extremes of polity, and from all modes of government inclusively; from the best and from the worst; from magistrates 2280 acting under obedience to the stedfast law which expresses the general will; and from depraved and licentious tyrants, whose habit it is—to express, and to act upon, their own individual will. Tyrants have seemed to feel that, if this principle were acknowledged, the subject ought to be reconciled to any thing; that, by permitting the free exercise of this right alone, an adequate price was 2285 paid down for all abuses; that a standing pardon was included in it for the past, and a daily renewed indulgence for every future enormity. It is then melancholy to think that the time is come when an attempt has been made to tear, out of the venerable crown of the Sovereign of Great Britain, a gem which is in the very front of the turban of the Emperor of Morocco.—(*See Appendix D*.)   2290

To enter upon this argument is indeed both astounding and humiliating: for the adversary in the present case is bound to contend that we cannot pronounce upon evil or good, either in the actions of our own or in past times, unless the decision of a Court of Judicature has empowered us so to do. Why then have historians written? and why do we yield to the impulses of our nature, hat- 2295 ing or loving—approving or condemning according to the appearances which their records present to our eyes? But the doctrine is as nefarious as it is absurd. For those public events in which men are most interested, namely, the crimes of rulers and of persons in high authority, for the most part are such as either have never been brought before tribunals at all, or before unjust ones: 2300 for, though offenders may be in hostility with each other, yet the kingdom of ▶ guilt is not wholly divided against itself; its subjects are united by a general interest to elude or overcome that law which would bring them to condign punishment. Therefore to make a verdict of a Court of Judicature a necessary condition for enabling men to determine the quality of an act, when the "head 2305 and front"—the life and soul of the offence may have been, that it eludes or rises above the reach of all judicature, is a contradiction which would be too gross to merit notice, were it not that men willingly suffer their understandings

to stagnate. And hence this rotten bog, rotten and unstable as the crude con- ◀ ▶
sistence of Milton's Chaos, "smitten" (for I will continue to use the language 2310
of the poet) "by the petrific mace—and bound with Gorgonian rigour by the
look"—of despotism, is transmuted; and becomes a high-way of adamant for
the sorrowful steps of generation after generation.

Again: in cases where judicial inquiries can be and are instituted, and are
equitably conducted, this suspension of judgment, with respect to act or agent, 2315
is only supposed necessarily to exist in the court itself; not in the witnesses, the
plaintiffs or accusers, or in the minds even of the people who may be present.
If the contrary supposition were realized, how could the arraigned person ever
have been brought into court? What would become of the indignation, the hope,
the sorrow, or the sense of justice, by which the prosecutors, or the people of the 2320
country who pursued or apprehended the presumed criminal, or they who appear
in evidence against him, are actuated? If then this suspension of judgment, by a
law of human nature and a requisite of society, is not supposed *necessarily* to exist—except in the minds of the court; if this be undeniable in cases where the eye
and ear-witnesses are few;—how much more so in a case like the present; where 2325
all, that constitutes the essence of the act, is avowed by the agents themselves,
and lies bare to the notice of the whole world?—Now it was in the character of
complainants and denunciators, that the petitioners of the City of London appeared before his Majesty's throne; and they have been reproached by his Majesty's ministers under the cover of a sophism, which, if our anxiety to interpret 2330
favourably words sanctioned by the First Magistrate—makes us unwilling to
think it a deliberate artifice meant for the delusion of the people, must however
(on the most charitable comment) be pronounced an evidence of no little heed-
lessness and self-delusion on the part of those who framed it.

To sum up the matter—the right of petition (which, we have shewn as a 2335
general proposition, supposes a right to condemn, and is in itself an act of
qualified condemnation) may in too many instances take the ground of absolute condemnation, both with respect to the crime and the criminal. It was
confined, in this case, to the crime; but, if the City of London had proceeded
farther, they would have been justifiable; because the delinquents had set their 2340
hands to their own delinquency. The petitioners, then, are not only clear of all
blame; but are entitled to high praise: and we have seen whither the doctrines
lead, upon which they were condemned.—And now, mark the discord which ◀
will ever be found in the actions of men, where there is no inward harmony of

reason or virtue to regulate the outward conduct.   2345

Those ministers, who advised their Sovereign to reprove the City of London for uttering prematurely, upon a measure, an opinion in which they were supported by the unanimous voice of the nation, had themselves before publickly prejudged the question by ordering that the tidings should be communicated with rejoicings. One of their body has since attempted to wipe away this 2350 stigma by representing that these orders were given out of a just tenderness ▶ for the reputation of the generals, who would otherwise have appeared to be condemned without trial. But did these rejoicings leave the matter indifferent? Was not the *positive* fact of thus expressing an opinion (above all in a case like this, in which surely no man could ever dream that there were any features of 2355 splendour) far stronger language of approbation, than the *negative* fact could be of disapprobation? For these same ministers who had called upon the people of Great Britain to rejoice over the Armistice and Convention, and who reproved and discountenanced and suppressed to the utmost of their power every attempt at petitioning for redress of the injury caused by those treaties, 2360 have now made publick a document from which it appears that, "when the ▶ instruments were first laid before his Majesty, the king felt himself compelled *at once"* (i.e. previously to all investigation) "to express his disapprobation of those articles, in which stipulations were made directly affecting the interests or feelings of the Spanish and Portugueze nations."   2365

And was it possible that a Sovereign of a free country could be otherwise affected? It is indeed to be regretted that his Majesty's censure was not, upon this occasion, radical—and pronounced in a sterner tone; that a council was not in existence sufficiently intelligent and virtuous to advise the king to give full expression to the sentiments of his own mind; which, we may reasonably 2370 conclude, were in sympathy with those of a brave and loyal people. Never surely was there a public event more fitted to reduce men, in all ranks of society, under the supremacy of their common nature; to impress upon them one belief; to infuse into them one spirit. For it was not done in a remote corner by persons of obscure rank; but in the eyes of Europe and of all mankind; by the 2375 leading authorities, military and civil, of a mighty empire. It did not relate to a petty immunity, or a local and insulated privilege—but to the highest feelings of honour to which a nation may either be calmly and gradually raised by a long course of independence, liberty, and glory; or to the level of which it may be lifted up at once, from a fallen state, by a sudden and extreme pressure of 2380 violence and tyranny. It not only related to these high feelings of honour; but to the fundamental principles of justice, by which life and property, that is the means of living, are secured.

A people, whose government had been dissolved by foreign tyranny, and which had been left to work out its salvation by its own virtues, prayed for our 2385 help. And whence were we to learn how that help could be most effectually given, how they were even to be preserved from receiving injuries instead of benefits at our hands,—whence were we to learn this but from their language and from our own hearts? They had spoken of unrelenting and inhuman wrongs; of patience wearied out; of the agonizing yoke cast off; of the blessed 2390 service of freedom chosen; of heroic aspirations; of constancy, and fortitude, and perseverance; of resolution even to the death; of gladness in the embrace of death; of weeping over the graves of the slain, by those who had not been so happy as to die; of resignation under the worst final doom; of glory, and triumph, and punishment. This was the language which we heard—this was 2395 the devout hymn that was chaunted; and the responses, with which our country bore a part in the solemn service, were from her soul and from the depths of her soul.

O sorrow! O misery for England, the land of liberty and courage and peace; the land trustworthy and long approved; the home of lofty example and benign 2400 precept; the central orb to which, as to a fountain, the nations of the earth "ought to repair, and in their golden urns draw light;"—O sorrow and shame for our country; for the grass which is upon her fields, and the dust which is in her graves;—for her good men who now look upon the day;—and her long train of deliverers and defenders, her Alfred, her Sidneys, and her Milton; whose 2405 voice yet speaketh for our reproach; and whose actions survive in memory to confound us, or to redeem!

For what hath been done? look at it: we have looked at it: we have handled it: we have pondered it steadily: we have tried it by the principles of absolute and eternal justice; by the sentiments of high-minded honour, both with refer- 2410 ence to their general nature, and to their especial exaltation under present circumstances; by the rules of expedience; by the maxims of prudence, civil and military: we have weighed it in the balance of all these, and found it wanting; in that, which is most excellent, most wanting.

Our country placed herself by the side of Spain, and her fellow nation; she 2415 sent an honourable portion of her sons to aid a suffering people to subjugate or destroy an army—but I degrade the word—a banded multitude of perfidious oppressors, of robbers and assassins, who had outlawed themselves from society in the wantonness of power; who were abominable for their own crimes, and on account of the crimes of him whom they served—to subjugate or de- 2420 stroy these; not exacting that it should be done within a limited time; admitting even that they might effect their purpose or not; she could have borne either issue, she was prepared for either; but she was not prepared for such a deliverance as hath been accomplished; not a deliverance of Portugal from French oppression, but of the oppressor from the anger and power (at least from the 2425 animating efforts) of the Peninsula: she was not prepared to stand between her ◀▶ allies, and their worthiest hopes: that, when chastisement could not be inflicted, honour—as much as bad men could receive—should be conferred: that them, whom her own hands had humbled, the same hands and no other should exalt: that finally the sovereign of this horde of devastators, himself the destroyer of 2430 the hopes of good men, should have to say, through the mouth of his minister, and for the hearing of all Europe, that his army of Portugal had "DICTATED THE ◀▶ TERMS OF ITS GLORIOUS RETREAT."

I have to defend my countrymen: and, if their feelings deserve reverence, if there be any stirrings of wisdom in the motions of their souls, my task is ac- 2435 complished. For here were no factions to blind; no dissolution of established authorities to confound; no ferments to distemper; no narrow selfish interests to delude. The object was at a distance; and it rebounded upon us, as with force collected from a mighty distance; we were calm till the very moment of transition; and all the people were moved—and felt as with one heart, and spake as 2440 with one voice. Every human being in these islands was unsettled; the most slavish broke loose as from fetters; and there was not an individual—it need not be said of heroic virtue, but of ingenuous life and sound discretion—who, if his father, his son, or his brother, or if the flower of his house had been in that army, would not rather that they had perished, and the whole body of their 2445 countrymen, their companions in arms, had perished to a man, than that a treaty should have been submitted to upon such conditions. This was the feeling of the people; an awful feeling: and it is from these oracles that rulers are to learn wisdom.

For, when the people speaks loudly, it is from being strongly possessed ei- 2450 ther by the Godhead or the Demon; and he, who cannot discover the true spirit ◀ from the false, hath no ear for profitable communion. But in all that regarded the destinies of Spain, and her own as connected with them, the voice of Britain had the unquestionable sound of inspiration. If the gentle passions of pity, love, and gratitude, be porches of the temple; if the sentiments of admiration 2455 and rivalry be pillars upon which the structure is sustained; if, lastly, hatred, and anger, and vengeance, be steps which, by a mystery of nature, lead to the House of Sanctity;—then was it manifest to what power the edifice was consecrated; and that the voice within was of Holiness and Truth.

Spain had risen not merely to be delivered and saved;—deliverance and 2460 safety were but intermediate objects;—regeneration and liberty were the end, and the means by which this end was to be attained; had their own high value; were determined and precious; and could no more admit of being departed from, than the end of being forgotten.—She had risen—not merely to be free; but, in the act and process of acquiring that freedom, to recompense herself, 2465 as it were in a moment, for all which she had suffered through ages; to levy, upon the false fame of a cruel Tyrant, large contributions of true glory; to lift herself, by the conflict, as high in honour—as the disgrace was deep to which her own weakness and vices, and the violence and perfidy of her enemies, had subjected her.   2470

Let us suppose that our own land had been so outraged; could we have been content that the enemy should be wafted from our shores as lightly as he came,—much less that he should depart illustrated in his own eyes and glorified, singing songs of savage triumph and wicked gaiety?—No.—Should we not have felt that a high trespass—a grievous offence had been committed; 2475 and that to demand satisfaction was our first and indispensable duty? Would we not have rendered their bodies back upon our guardian ocean which had borne them hither; or have insisted that their haughty weapons should submissively kiss the soil which they had polluted? We should have been resolute in a defence that would strike awe and terror: this for our dignity:—moreover, 2480 if safety and deliverance are to be so fondly prized for their own sakes, what security otherwise could they have? Would it not be certain that the work, which had been so ill done to-day, we should be called upon to execute still more imperfectly and ingloriously to-morrow; that we should be summoned to an attempt that would be vain?   2485

In like manner were the wise and heroic Spaniards moved. If an Angel from heaven had come with power to take the enemy from their grasp (I do not fear to say this, in spite of the dominion which is now re-extended over so large a portion of their land), they would have been sad; they would have looked round them; their souls would have turned inward; and they would have stood 2490 like men defrauded and betrayed.

For not presumptuously had they taken upon themselves the work of chastisement. They did not wander madly about the world—like the Tamerlanes, or the Chengiz Khans, or the present barbarian Ravager of Europe—under a mock title of Delegates of the Almighty, acting upon self-assumed authority. Their 2495 commission had been thrust upon them. They had been trampled upon, tormented, wronged—bitterly, wantonly wronged—if ever a people on the earth was wronged. And this it was which legitimately incorporated their law with the supreme conscience, and gave to them the deep faith which they have expressed—that their power was favoured and assisted by the Almighty.—These 2500 words are not uttered without a due sense of their awful import: but the Spirit of evil is strong: and the subject requires the highest mode of thinking and feeling of which human nature is capable.—Nor in this can they be deceived; for, whatever be the immediate issue for themselves, the final issue for their Country and Mankind must be good;—they are instruments of benefit and 2505 glory for the human race; and the Deity therefore is with them.

From these impulses, then, our brethren of the Peninsula had risen; they could have risen from no other. By these energies, and by such others as (under judicious encouragement) would naturally grow out of and unite with these, the multitudes, who have risen, stand; and, if they desert them, must fall.—Rid- 2510 dance, mere riddance—safety, mere safety—are objects far too defined, too inert and passive in their own nature, to have ability either to rouze or to sustain. They win not the mind by any attraction of grandeur or sublime delight, either in effort or in endurance: for the mind gains consciousness of its strength to ‹ ▶ undergo only by exercise among materials which admit the impression of its 2515 power,—which grow under it, which bend under it,—which resist,—which change under its influence,—which alter either through its might or in its presence, by it or before it. These, during times of tranquillity, are the objects with which, in the studious walks of sequestered life, Genius most loves to hold intercourse; by which it is reared and supported;—these are the qualities in ac- 2520 tion and in object, in image, in thought, and in feeling, from communion with which proceeds originally all that is creative in art and science, and all that is magnanimous in virtue.—Despair thinks of *safety,* and hath no purpose; fear thinks of safety; despondency looks the same way: but these passions are

far too selfish, and therefore too blind, to reach the thing at which they aim; 2525
even when there is in them sufficient dignity to have an aim.—All courage is
a projection from ourselves; however short-lived, it is a motion of hope. But
these thoughts bind too closely to something inward,—to the present and to
the past,—that is, to the self which is or has been. Whereas the vigour of the
human soul is from without and from futurity,—in breaking down limit, and 2530
losing and forgetting herself in the sensation and image of Country and of the
human race; and, when she returns and is most restricted and confined, her dignity consists in the contemplation of a better and more exalted being, which,
though proceeding from herself, she loves and is devoted to as to another.

In following the stream of these thoughts, I have not wandered from my 2535
course: I have drawn out to open day the truth from its recesses in the minds of
my countrymen.—Something more perhaps may have been done: a shape hath
perhaps been given to that which was before a stirring spirit. I have shewn in
what manner it was their wish that the struggle with the adversary of all that
is good should be maintained—by pure passions and high actions. They for- 2540
bid that their noble aim should be frustrated by measuring against each other
things which are incommensurate—mechanic against moral power—body
against soul. They will not suffer, without expressing their sorrow, that purblind calculation should wither the purest hopes in the face of all-seeing justice. These are times of strong appeal—of deep-searching visitation; when the 2545
best abstractions of the prudential understanding give way, and are included
and absorbed in a supreme comprehensiveness of intellect and passion; which
is the perfection and the very being of humanity.

How base! how puny! how inefficient for all good purposes are the tools
and implements of policy, compared with these mighty engines of Nature!— 2550
There is no middle course: two masters cannot be served:—Justice must either
be enthroned above might, and the moral law take place of the edicts of selfish
passion; or the heart of the people, which alone can sustain the efforts of the
people, will languish: their desires will not spread beyond the plough and the
loom, the field and the fireside: the sword will appear to them an emblem of 2555
no promise; an instrument of no hope; an object of indifference, of disgust,
or fear. Was there ever—since the earliest actions of men which have been
transmitted by affectionate tradition or recorded by faithful history, or sung
to the impassioned harp of poetry—was there ever a people who presented
themselves to the reason and the imagination, as under more holy influences 2560

than the dwellers upon the Southern Peninsula; as rouzed more instantaneously from a deadly sleep to a more hopeful wakefulness; as a mass fluctuating with one motion under the breath of a mightier wind; as breaking themselves up, and settling into several bodies, in more harmonious order; as reunited and embattled under a standard which was reared to the sun with more authentic 2565 assurance of final victory?—The superstition (I do not dread the word), which prevailed in these nations, may have checked many of my countrymen who would otherwise have exultingly accompanied me in the challenge which, under the shape of a question, I have been confidently uttering; as I know that this stain (so the same persons termed it) did, from the beginning, discourage 2570 their hopes for the cause. Short-sighted despondency! Whatever mixture of superstition there might be in the religious faith or devotional practices of the Spaniards; this must have necessarily been transmuted by that triumphant power, wherever that power was felt, which grows out of intense moral suffering—from the moment in which it coalesces with fervent hope. The chains 2575 of bigotry, which enthralled the mind, must have been turned into armour to defend and weapons to annoy. Wherever the heaving and effort of freedom was spread, purification must have followed it. And the types and ancient instruments of error, where emancipated men shewed their foreheads to the day, must have become a language and a ceremony of imagination; expressing, 2580 consecrating, and invigorating, the most pure deductions of Reason and the holiest feelings of universal Nature.

When the Boy of Saragossa (as we have been told), too immature in growth and unconfirmed in strength to be admitted by his Fellow-citizens into their ranks, too tender of age for them to bear the sight of him in arms—when this 2585 Boy, forgetful or unmindful of the restrictions which had been put upon him, rushed into the field where his Countrymen were engaged in battle, and, fighting with the sinew and courage of an unripe Hero, won a standard from the enemy, and bore his acquisition to the Church, and laid it with his own hands upon the Altar of the Virgin;—surely there was not less to be hoped for his 2590 Country from this act, than if the banner, taken from his grasp, had, without any such intermediation, been hung up in the place of worship—a direct offering to the incorporeal and supreme Being. Surely there is here an object which the most meditative and most elevated minds may contemplate with absolute delight; a well-adapted outlet for the dearest sentiments; an organ by which 2595 they may act; a function by which they may be sustained.—Who does not recognise in this presentation a visible affinity with deliverance, with patriotism, with hatred of oppression, and with human means put forth to the height for accomplishing, under divine countenance, the worthiest ends?

Such is the burst and growth of power and virtue which may rise out of excessive national afflictions from tyranny and oppression;—such is the hallowing influence, and thus mighty is the sway, of the spirit of moral justice in the heart of the individual and over the wide world of humanity. Even the very faith in present miraculous interposition, which is so dire a weakness and cause of weakness in tranquil times when the listless Being turns to it as a cheap and ready substitute upon every occasion, where the man sleeps, and the Saint, or the image of the Saint, is to perform his work, and to give effect to his wishes;—even this infirm faith, in a state of incitement from extreme passion sanctioned by a paramount sense of moral justice; having for its object a power which is no longer sole nor principal, but secondary and ministerial; a power added to a power; a breeze which springs up unthought-of to assist the strenuous oarsman;—even this faith is subjugated in order to be exalted; and—instead of operating as a temptation to relax or to be remiss, as an encouragement to indolence or cowardice; instead of being a false stay, a necessary and definite dependence which may fail—it passes into a habit of obscure and infinite confidence of the mind in its own energies, in the cause from its own sanctity, and in the ever-present invisible aid or momentary conspicuous approbation of the supreme Disposer of things.

Let the fire, which is never wholly to be extinguished, break out afresh; let but the human creature be rouzed; whether he have lain heedless and torpid in religious or civil slavery—have languished under a thraldom, domestic or foreign, or under both these alternately—or have drifted about a helpless member of a clan of disjointed and feeble barbarians; let him rise and act;—and his domineering imagination, by which from childhood he has been betrayed, and the debasing affections, which it has imposed upon him, will from that moment participate the dignity of the newly ennobled being whom they will now acknowledge for their master; and will further him in his progress, whatever be the object at which he aims. Still more inevitable and momentous are the results, when the individual knows that the fire, which is reanimated in him, is not less lively in the breasts of his associates; and sees the signs and testimonies of his own power, incorporated with those of a growing multitude and not to be distinguished from them, accompany him wherever he moves.—Hence

those marvellous atchievements which were performed by the first enthusiastic
followers of Mohammed; and by other conquerors, who with their armies have
swept large portions of the earth like a transitory wind, or have founded new 2635
religions or empires.—But, if the object contended for be worthy and truly
great (as, in the instance of the Spaniards, we have seen that it is); if cruelties ▶
have been committed upon an ancient and venerable people, which "shake the
human frame with horror;" if not alone the life which is sustained by the bread
of the mouth, but that—without which there is no life—the life in the soul, has 2640
been directly and mortally warred against; if reason has had abominations to
endure in her inmost sanctuary;—then does intense passion, consecrated by
a sudden revelation of justice, give birth to those higher and better wonders
which I have described; and exhibit true miracles to the eyes of men, and the
noblest which can be seen. It may be added that,—as this union brings back to 2645
the right road the faculty of imagination, where it is prone to err, and has gone
farthest astray; as it corrects those qualities which (being in their essence indifferent), and cleanses those affections which (not being inherent in the constitution of man, nor necessarily determined to their object) are more immediately
dependent upon the imagination, and which may have received from it a thor- 2650
ough taint of dishonour;—so the domestic loves and sanctities which are in
their nature less liable to be stained,—so these, wherever they have flowed
with a pure and placid stream, do instantly, under the same influence, put forth
their strength as in a flood; and, without being sullied or polluted, pursue—exultingly and with song—a course which leads the contemplative reason to the 2655
ocean of eternal love.

I feel that I have been speaking in a strain which it is difficult to harmonize
with the petty irritations, the doubts and fears, and the familiar (and therefore
frequently undignified) exterior of present and passing events. But the theme
is justice: and my voice is raised for mankind; for us who are alive, and for 2660
all posterity:—justice and passion; clear-sighted aspiring justice, and passion
sacred as vehement. These, like twin-born Deities delighting in each other's
presence, have wrought marvels in the inward mind through the whole region
of the Pyrenëan Peninsula. I have shewn by what process these united powers
sublimated the objects of outward sense in such rites—practices—and ordi- 2665
nances of Religion—as deviate from simplicity and wholesome piety; how
they converted them to instruments of nobler use; and raised them to a con-
formity with things truly divine. The same reasoning might have been carried

into the customs of civil life and their accompanying imagery, wherever these also were inconsistent with the dignity of man; and like effects of exaltation and purification have been shewn.

But a more urgent service calls me to point to further works of these united powers, more obvious and obtrusive—works and appearances, such as were hailed by the citizen of Seville when returning from Madrid;— "where" (to use the words of his own public declaration) "he had left his countrymen groaning in the chains which perfidy had thrown round them, and doomed at every step to the insult of being eyed with the disdain of the conqueror to the conquered; from Madrid threatened, harassed, and vexed; where mistrust reigned in every heart, and the smallest noise made the citizens tremble in the bosom of their families; where the enemy, from time to time, ran to arms to sustain the impression of terror by which the inhabitants had been stricken through the recent massacre; from Madrid a prison, where the gaolers took pleasure in terrifying the prisoners by alarms to keep them quiet; from Madrid thus tortured and troubled by a relentless Tyrant, to fit it for the slow and interminable evils of Slavery";—when he returned, and was able to compare the oppressed and degraded state of the inhabitants of that metropolis with the noble attitude of defence in which Andalusia stood. "A month ago," says he, "the Spaniards had lost their country;—Seville has restored it to life more glorious than ever; and those fields, which for so many years have seen no steel but that of the plough-share, are going amid the splendour of arms to prove the new cradle of their adored country."—"I could not," he adds, "refrain from tears of joy on viewing the city in which I first drew breath—and to see it in a situation so glorious!"

We might have trusted, but for late disgraces, that there is not a man in these islands whose heart would not, at such a spectacle, have beat in sympathy with that of this fervent Patriot—whose voice would not be in true accord with his in the prayer (which, if he has not already perished for the service of his dear country, he is perhaps uttering at this moment) that Andalusia and the city of Seville may preserve the noble attitude in which they then stood, and are yet standing; or, if they be doomed to fall, that their dying efforts may not be unworthy of their first promises; that the evening—the closing hour of their freedom may display a brightness not less splendid, though more aweful, than the dawn; so that the names of Seville and Andalusia may be consecrated among men, and be words of life to endless generations.

Saragossa!—She also has given bond, by her past actions, that she cannot forget her duty and will not shrink from it.* Valencia is under the seal of the same obligation. The multitudes of men who were arrayed in the fields of Baylen, and upon the mountains of the North; the peasants of Asturias, and the students of Salamanca; and many a solitary and untold-of hand, which, quitting for a moment the plough or the spade, has discharged a more pressing debt 2710 to the country by levelling with the dust at least one insolent and murderous Invader;—these have attested the efficacy of the passions which we have been contemplating—that the will of good men is not a vain impulse, heroic desires a delusive prop;—have proved that the condition of human affairs is not so forlorn and desperate, but that there are golden opportunities when the dictates 2715 of justice may be unrelentingly enforced, and the beauty of the inner mind substantiated in the outward act;—for a visible standard to look back upon; for a point of realized excellence at which to aspire; a monument to record;—for a charter to fasten down; and, as far as it is possible, to preserve.

Yes! there was an annunciation which the good received with gladness; a 2720 bright appearance which emboldened the wise to say—We trust that Regeneration is at hand; these are works of recovered innocence and wisdom:

> Magnus ab integro seclorum nascitur ordo;
> *Jam* redit et Virgo, redeunt Saturnia regna;
> *Jam* nova progenies coelo demittitur alto. 2725

The spirits of the generous, of the brave, of the meditative, of the youthful and undefiled—who, upon the strongest wing of human nature, have accompanied me in this journey into a fair region—must descend: and, sorrowful to think! it is at the name and remembrance of Britain that we are to stoop from the balmy air of this pure element. Our country did not create, but there was 2730 created for her, one of those golden opportunities over which we have been rejoicing: an invitation was offered—a summons sent to her ear, as if from heaven, to go forth also and exhibit on her part, in entire coincidence and perfect harmony, the beneficent action with the benevolent will; to advance in the career of renovation upon which the Spaniards had so gloriously en- 2735 tered; and to solemnize yet another marriage between victory and justice. How she acquitted herself of this duty, we have already seen and lamented: yet on this—and on this duty only—ought the mind of that army and of the govern-

* Written in February.

ment to have been fixed. Every thing was smoothed before their feet;—Provi- 2740
dence, it might almost be said, held forth to the men of authority in this country
a gracious temptation to deceive them into the path of the new virtues which
were stirring;—the enemy was delivered over to them; and they were unable
to close their infantine fingers upon the gift.—The helplessness of infancy was
their's—oh! could I but add, the innocence of infancy!

Reflect upon what was the temper and condition of the Southern Peninsula 2745
of Europe—the noble temper of the people of this mighty island sovereigns
of the all-embracing ocean; think also of the condition of so vast a region in
the Western continent and its islands; and we shall have cause to fear that ages
may pass away before a conjunction of things, so marvellously adapted to ensure prosperity to virtue, shall present itself again. It could scarcely be spoken 2750
of as being to the wishes of men,—it was so far beyond their hopes.—The
government which had been exercised under the name of the old Monarchy of
Spain—this government, imbecile even to dotage, whose very selfishness was
destitute of vigour, had been removed; taken laboriously and foolishly by the
plotting Corsican to his own bosom; in order that the world might see, more 2755
triumphantly set forth than since the beginning of things had ever been seen
before, to what degree a man of bad principles is despicable—though of great
power—working blindly against his own purposes. It was a high satisfaction to
behold demonstrated, in this manner, to what a narrow domain of knowledge
the intellect of a Tyrant must be confined; that if the gate by which wisdom 2760
enters has never been opened, that of policy will surely find moments when it
will shut itself against its pretended master imperiously and obstinately. To the
eyes of the very peasant in the field, this sublime truth was laid open—not only
that a Tyrant's domain of knowledge is narrow, but melancholy as narrow;
inasmuch as—from all that is lovely, dignified, or exhilarating in the prospect 2765
of human nature—he is inexorably cut off; and therefore he is inwardly helpless and forlorn.

Was not their hope in this—twofold hope; from the weakness of him
who had thus counteracted himself; and a hope, still more cheering, from the
strength of those who had been disburthened of a cleaving curse by an ordi- 2770
nance of Providence—employing their most wilful and determined enemy to
perform for them the best service which man could perform? The work of
liberation was virtually accomplished—we might almost say, established. The
interests of the people were taken from a government whose sole aim it had

been to prop up the last remains of its own decrepitude by betraying those **2775**
whom it was its duty to protect;—withdrawn from such hands, to be committed to those of the people; at a time when the double affliction which Spain
had endured, and the return of affliction with which she was threatened, made
it impossible that the emancipated nation could abuse its new-born strength to
any substantial injury of itself.—Infinitely less favourable to all good ends was **2780**
the condition of the French people when, a few years past, a revolution made
them, for a season, their own masters,—rid them from the incumbrance of
superannuated institutions—the galling pressure of so many unjust laws—and
the tyranny of bad customs. The Spaniards became their own masters: and
the blessing lay in this, that they became so at once: there had not been time **2785**
for them to court their power: their fancies had not been fed to wantonness by
ever-changing temptations: obstinacy in them could not have leagued itself
with trivial opinions: petty hatreds had not accumulated to masses of strength
conflicting perniciously with each other: vanity with them had not found leisure to flourish—nor presumption: they did not assume their authority,—it **2790**
was given them,—it was thrust upon them. The perfidy and tyranny of Napo- ▶
leon "*compelled*," says the Junta of Seville in words before quoted, "the whole
Nation to take up arms and *to choose itself a form of government;* and, in the
difficulties and dangers into which the French had plunged it, all—or nearly
all—the provinces, as it were *by the inspiration of Heaven* and *in a manner* **2795**
little short of miraculous, created Supreme Juntas—delivered themselves up
to their guidance—and placed in their hands the rights and the ultimate fate of
Spain."—Governments, thus newly issued from the people, could not but act
from the spirit of the people—be organs of their life. And, though misery (by
which I mean pain of mind not without some consciousness of guilt) naturally **2780**
disorders the understanding and perverts the moral sense,—calamity (that is
suffering, individual or national, when it has been inflicted by one to whom no
injury has been done or provocation given) ever brings wisdom along with it;
and, whatever outward agitation it may cause, does inwardly rectify the will.

But more was required; not merely judicious desires; not alone an eye from 2785
which the scales had dropped off—which could see widely and clearly; but a
mighty hand was wanting. The government had been formed; and it could not
but recollect that the condition of Spain did not exact from her children, as *a*
first requisite, virtues like those due and familiar impulses of spring-time by

which things are revived and carried forward in accustomed health according 2790
to established order—not power so much for a renewal as for a birth—labour
by throes and violence;—a chaos was to be conquered—a work of creation
begun and consummated;—and afterwards the seasons were to advance, and
continue their gracious revolutions. The powers, which were needful for the
people to enter upon and assist in this work, had been given; we have seen that 2795
they had been bountifully conferred. The nation had been thrown into—rather,
lifted up to—that state when conscience, for the body of the people, is not
merely an infallible monitor (which may be heard and disregarded); but, by
combining—with the attributes of insight to perceive, and of inevitable presence to admonish and enjoin—the attribute of passion to enforce, it was truly 2800
an all-powerful deity in the soul.

Oh! let but any man, who has a care for the progressive happiness of the
species, peruse merely that epitome of Spanish wisdom and benevolence and ▶
"amplitude of mind for highest deeds" which, in the former part of this investigation, I have laid before the reader: let him listen to the reports—which they, 2805
who really have had means of knowledge, and who are worthy to speak upon
the subject, will give to him—of the things done or endured in every corner
of Spain; and he will see what emancipation had there been effected in the
mind;—how far the perceptions—the impulses—and the actions also—had
outstripped the habit and the character, and consequently were in a process of 2810
permanently elevating both; and how much farther (alas! by infinite degrees)
the principles and practice of a people, with great objects before them to concentrate their love and their hatred, transcend the principles and practice of
governments; not excepting those which, in their constitution and ordinary
conduct, furnish the least matter for complaint.   2815

Then it was—when the people of Spain were thus rouzed; after this manner
released from the natal burthen of that government which had bowed them to
the ground; in the free use of their understandings, and in the play and "noble
rage" of their passions; while yet the new authorities, which they had generated, were truly living members of their body, and (as I have said) organs of their 2820
life; when that numerous people were in a stage of their journey which could
not be accomplished without the spirit which was then prevalent in them, and
which (as might be feared) would too soon abate of itself;—then it was that
we—not we, but the heads of the British army and nation—when, if they could
not breathe a favouring breath, they ought at least to have stood at an awful 2825

distance—stepped in with their forms, their impediments, their rotten customs and precedents, their narrow desires, their busy and purblind fears; and called ▶ out to these aspiring travellers to halt—"For ye are in a dream;" confounded them (for it was the voice of a seeming friend that spoke); and spell-bound them, as far as was possible, by an instrument framed "in the eclipse" and sealed "with curses dark."—In a word, we had the power to act up to the most sacred letter of justice—and this at a time when the mandates of justice were of an affecting obligation such as had never before been witnessed; and we plunged into the lowest depths of injustice:—We had power to give a brotherly aid to our allies in supporting the mighty world which their shoulders had **2835** undertaken to uphold; and, while they were expecting from us this aid, we undermined—without forewarning them—the ground upon which they stood. The evil is incalculable; and the stain will cleave to the British name as long as the story of this island shall endure.

Did we not (if, from this comprehensive feeling of sorrow, I may for a **2840** moment descend to particulars)—did we not send forth a general, one whom, since his return, Court, and Parliament, and Army, have been at strife with each other which shall most caress and applaud—a general, who, in defending the armistice which he himself had signed, said in open court that he deemed that the French army was *entitled* to such terms. The people of Spain had, through the Supreme Junta of Seville, thus spoken of this same army: "Ye have, among yourselves, the objects of your vengeance;—attack them;—they ▶ are but a handful of miserable panic-struck men, humiliated and conquered already by their perfidy and cruelties;—resist and destroy them: our united efforts will extirpate this perfidious nation." The same Spaniards had said (speak- **2850** ing officially of the state of the whole Peninsula, and no doubt with their eye especially upon this army in Portugal)—"Our enemies have taken up exactly those positions in which they may most easily be destroyed."—Where then did the British General find this right and title of the French army in Portugal? "Because," says he in military language, "it was not broken."—Of the MAN, and of the understanding and heart of the man—of the CITIZEN, who could think and feel after this manner in such circumstances, it is needless to speak; but to the GENERAL I will say, This is most pitiable pedantry. If the instinctive wisdom of your ally could not be understood, you might at least have remembered the resolute policy of your enemy. The French army was not broken? Break it then—wither it—pursue it with unrelenting warfare   hunt it out of its

holds;—if impetuosity be not justifiable, have recourse to patience—to watchfulness—to obstinacy: at all events, never for a moment forget who the foe
is—and that he is in your power. This is the example which the French Ruler
and his Generals have given you at Ulm—at Lubeck—in Switzerland—over 2865
the whole plain of Prussia—every where;—and this for the worst deeds of ▶
darkness; while your's was the noblest service of light.

　This remonstrance has been forced from me by indignation:—let me explain in what sense I propose, with calmer thought, that the example of our
enemy should be imitated.—The laws and customs of war, and the maxims of 2870
policy, have all had their foundation in reason and humanity; and their object
has been the attainment or security of some real or supposed—some positive
or relative—good. They are established among men as ready guides for the
understanding, and authorities to which the passions are taught to pay deference. But the relations of things to each other are perpetually changing; and 2875
in course of time many of these leaders and masters, by losing part of their
power to do service and sometimes the whole, forfeit in proportion their right
to obedience. Accordingly they are disregarded in some instances, and sink
insensibly into neglect with the general improvement of society. But they often
survive when they have become an oppression and a hindrance which can- 2880
not be cast off decisively, but by an impulse—rising either from the absolute
knowledge of good and great men,—or from the partial insight which is given
to superior minds, though of a vitiated moral constitution,—or lastly from that
blind energy and those habits of daring which are often found in men who,
checked by no restraint of morality, suffer their evil passions to gain extraordi- 2885
nary strength in extraordinary circumstances. By any of these forces may the
tyranny be broken through. We have seen, in the conduct of our Countrymen,
to what degree it tempts to weak actions,—and furnishes excuse for them,
admitted by those who sit as judges. I wish then that we could so far imitate
our enemies as, like them, to shake off these bonds; but not, like them, from 2890
the worst—but from the worthiest impulse. If this were done, we should have
learned how much of their practice would harmonize with justice; have learned
to distinguish between those rules which ought to be wholly abandoned, and
those which deserve to be retained; and should have known when, and to what
point, they ought to be trusted.—But how is this to be? Power of mind is want- 2895
ing, where there is power of place. Even we cannot, as a beginning of a new
journey, force or win our way into the current of success, the flattering motion

of which would awaken intellectual courage—the only substitute which is able ▶
to perform any arduous part of the secondary work of "heroic wisdom;"—I
mean, execute happily any of its prudential regulations. In the person of our 2900
enemy and his chieftains we have living example how wicked men of ordinary
talents are emboldened by success. There is a kindliness, as they feel, in the
nature of advancement; and prosperity is their Genius. But let us know and
remember that this prosperity, with all the terrible features which it has gradually assumed, is a child of noble parents—Liberty and Philanthropic Love. 2905
Perverted as the creature is which it has grown up to (rather, into which it has
passed),—from no inferior stock could it have issued. It is the Fallen Spirit,
triumphant in misdeeds, which was formerly a blessed Angel.

If then (to return to ourselves) there be such strong obstacles in the way
of our drawing benefit either from the maxims of policy or the principles of 2910
justice: what hope remains that the British nation should repair, by its future
conduct, the injury which has been done?—We cannot advance a step towards
a rational answer to this question—without previously adverting to the original sources of our miscarriages; which are these:—First; a want, in the minds
of the members of government and public functionaries, of knowledge indis- 2915
pensible for this service; and, secondly, a want of power, in the same persons
acting in their corporate capacities, to give effect to the knowledge which individually they possess.—Of the latter source of weakness,—this inability as
caused by decay in the machine of government, and by illegitimate forces
which are checking and controuling its constitutional motions,—I have not 2920
spoken, nor shall I now speak: for I have judged it best to suspend my task for
a while: and this subject, being in its nature delicate, ought not to be lightly
or transiently touched. Besides, no *immediate* effect can be expected from the
soundest and most unexceptionable doctrines which might be laid down for the
correcting of this evil.—The former source of weakness,—namely, the want of 2925
appropriate and indispensible knowledge,—has, in the past investigation, been
reached, and shall be further laid open; not without a hope of some result of
immediate good by a direct application to the mind; and in full confidence that
the best and surest way to render operative that knowledge which is already
possessed—is to increase the stock of knowledge. 2930

Here let me avow that I undertook this present labour as a serious duty;
rather, that it was forced (and has been unremittingly pressed) upon me by a
perception of justice united with strength of feeling;—in a word, by that power

of conscience, calm or impassioned, to which throughout I have done reverence as the animating spirit of the cause. My work was begun and prosecuted 2935
under this controul:—and with the accompanying satisfaction that no charge
of presumption could, by a thinking mind, be brought against me: though I had
taken upon myself to offer instruction to men who, if they possess not talents
and acquirements, have not title to the high stations which they hold; who also,
by holding those stations, are understood to obtain certain benefit of experi- 2940
ence and of knowledge not otherwise to be gained; and who have a further
claim to deference—founded upon reputation, even when it is spurious (as
much of the reputation of men high in power must necessarily be; their errors
being veiled and palliated by the authority attached to their office; while that
same authority gives more than due weight and effect to their wiser opinions). 2945
Yet, notwithstanding all this, I did not fear the censure of having unbecom-
ingly obtruded counsels or remonstrances. For there can be no presumption,
upon a call so affecting as the present, in an attempt to assert the sanctity and
to display the efficacy of principles and passions which are the natural birthright of man; to some share of which all are born; but an inheritance which 2950
may be alienated or consumed; and by none more readily and assuredly than
by those who are most eager for the praise of policy, of prudence, of sagacity,
and of all those qualities which are the darling virtues of the worldly-wise.
Moreover; the evidence to which I have made appeal, in order to establish
the truth, is not locked up in cabinets; but is accessible to all; as it exists in 2955
the bosoms of men—in the appearances and intercourse of daily life—in the
details of passing events—and in general history. And more especially is its
right import within the reach of Him who—taking no part in public measures,
and having no concern in the changes of things but as they affect what is most
precious in his country and humanity—will doubtless be more alive to those 2960
genuine sensations which are the materials of sound judgment. Nor is it to be
overlooked that such a man may have more leisure (and probably will have a
stronger inclination) to communicate with the records of past ages.

Deeming myself justified then in what has been said,—I will continue to
lay open (and, in some degree, to account for) those privations in the materials 2965
of judgment, and those delusions of opinion, and infirmities of mind, to which
practical Statesmen, and particularly such as are high in office, are more than
other men subject;—as containing an answer to that question, so interesting at
this juncture,—How far is it in our power to make amends for the harm done?

After the view of things which has been taken,—we may confidently af- **2970**
firm that nothing, but a knowledge of human nature directing the operations
of our government, can give it a right to an intimate association with a cause
which is that of human nature. I say, an I intimate association founded on the
right of thorough knowledge;—to contradistinguish this best mode of exertion from another which might found *its* right upon a vast and commanding **2975**
military power put forth with manifestation of sincere intentions to benefit our
allies—from a conviction merely of policy that their liberty, independence,
and honour, are our genuine gain;—to distinguish the pure brotherly connection from this other (in its appearance at least more magisterial) which such a
power, guided by such intention uniformly displayed, might authorize. But of **2980**
the former connection (which supposes the main military effort to be made,
even at present, by the people of the Peninsula on whom the moral interest
more closely presses), and of the knowledge which it demands, I have hitherto
spoken—and have further to speak.

It is plain *à priori* that the minds of Statesmen and Courtiers are unfavour- **2985**
able to the growth of this knowledge. For they are in a situation exclusive and
artificial; which has the further disadvantage, that it does not separate men
from men by collateral partitions which leave, along with difference, a sense
of equality—that they, who are divided, are yet upon the same level; but by
a degree of superiority which can scarcely fail to be accompanied with more **2990**
or less of pride. This situation therefore must be eminently unfavourable for
the reception and establishment of that knowledge which is founded not upon
things but upon sensations;—sensations which are general, and under general
influences (and this it is which makes them what they are, and gives them their
importance);—not upon things which may be *brought;* but upon sensations **2995**
which must be *met.* Passing by the kindred and usually accompanying influence of birth in a certain rank—and, where education has been pre-defined
from childhood for the express purpose of future political power, the tendency ◄ ►
of such education to warp (and therefore weaken) the intellect;—we may join
at once, with the privation which I have been noticing, a delusion equally com- **3000**
mon. It is this: that practical Statesmen assume too much credit to themselves
for their ability to see into the motives and manage the selfish passions of their
immediate agents and dependants; and for the skill with which they baffle or
resist the aims of their opponents. A promptness in looking through the most
superficial part of the characters of those men—who, by the very circumstance **3005**

of their contending ambitiously for the rewards and honours of government, are separated from the mass of the society to which they belong—is mistaken for a knowledge of human kind. Hence, where higher knowledge is a prime requisite, they not only are unfurnished; but, being unconscious that they are so, they look down contemptuously upon those who endeavour to supply (in 3010 some degree) their want.—The instincts of natural and social man; the deeper emotions; the simpler feelings; the spacious range of the disinterested imagination; the pride in country for country's sake, when to serve has not been a formal profession—and the mind is therefore left in a state of dignity only to be surpassed by having served nobly and generously; the instantaneous ac- 3015 complishment in which they start up who, upon a searching call, stir for the land which they love—not from personal motives, but for a reward which is undefined and cannot be missed; the solemn fraternity which a great nation composes—gathered together, in a stormy season, under the shade of ancestral feeling; the delicacy of moral honour which pervades the minds of a people, 3020 when despair has been suddenly thrown off and expectations are lofty; the apprehensiveness to a touch unkindly or irreverent, where sympathy is at once exacted as a tribute and welcomed as a gift; the power of injustice and inordinate calamity to transmute, to invigorate, and to govern—to sweep away the barriers of opinion—to reduce under submission passions purely evil—to 3025 exalt the nature of indifferent qualities, and to render them fit companions for the absolute virtues with which they are summoned to associate—to consecrate passions which, if not bad in themselves, are of such temper that, in the calm of ordinary life, they are rightly deemed so—to correct and embody these passions—and, without weakening them (nay, with tenfold addition to their 3030 strength), to make them worthy of taking their place as the advanced guard of hope, when a sublime movement of deliverance is to be originated;—these arrangements and resources of nature, these ways and means of society, have so little connection with those others upon which a ruling minister of a long-established government is accustomed to depend; these—elements as it were 3035 of a universe, functions of a living body—are so opposite, in their mode of action, to the formal machine which it has been his pride to manage;—that he has but a faint perception of their immediate efficacy; knows not the facility with which they assimilate with other powers; nor the property by which such of them—as, from necessity of nature, must change or pass away—will, under 3040 wise and fearless management, surely generate lawful successors to fill their place when their appropriate work is performed. Nay, of the majority of men, who are usually found in high stations under old governments, it may without injustice be said; that, when they look about them in times (alas! too rare) which present the glorious product of such agency to their eyes, they have not 3045 a right to say—with a dejected man in the midst of the woods, the rivers, the mountains, the sunshine, and shadows of some transcendant landscape— ▶

> "I see, not feel, how beautiful they are:"

These spectators neither see nor feel. And it is from the blindness and insensibility of these, and the train whom they draw along with them, that the throes 3050 of nations have been so ill recompensed by the births which have followed; and that revolutions, after passing from crime to crime and from sorrow to sorrow, have often ended in throwing back such heavy reproaches of delusiveness upon their first promises.

I am satisfied that no enlightened Patriot will impute to me a wish to dis- 3055 parage the characters of men high in authority, or to detract from the estimation which is fairly due to them. My purpose is to guard against unreasonable expectations. That specific knowledge,—the paramount importance of which, in the present condition of Europe, I am insisting upon,—they, who usually fill places of high trust in old governments, neither do—nor, for the most part, 3060 can—possess: nor is it necessary, for the administration of affairs in ordinary circumstances, that they should.—The progress of their own country, and of the other nations of the world, in civilization, in true refinement, in science, in religion, in morals, and in all the real wealth of humanity, might indeed be quicker, and might correspond more happily with the wishes of the benevo- 3065 lent,—if Governors better understood the rudiments of nature as studied in the walks of common life; if they were men who had themselves felt every strong emotion "inspired by nature and by fortune taught;" and could calculate upon the force of the grander passions. Yet, at the same time, there is temptation in this. To know may seduce; and to have been agitated may compel. Arduous 3070 cares are attractive for their own sakes. Great talents are naturally driven towards hazard and difficulty; as it is there that they are most sure to find their exercise, and their evidence, and joy in anticipated triumph—the liveliest of all sensations. Moreover; magnificent desires, when least under the bias of personal feeling, dispose the mind—more than itself is conscious of—to re- 3075 gard commotion with complacency, and to watch the aggravations of distress with welcoming; from an immoderate confidence that, when the appointed day shall come, it will be in the power of intellect to relieve. There is danger in being a zealot in any cause—not excepting that of humanity. Nor is it to be forgotten that the incapacity and ignorance of the regular agents of long-established governments do not prevent some progress in the dearest concerns of men; and 3080 that society may owe to these very deficiencies, and to the tame and unenterprizing course which they necessitate, much security and tranquil enjoyment. ▶

Nor, on the other hand, (for reasons which may be added to those already given) is it so desirable as might at first sight be imagined, much less is it desirable as an absolute good, that men of comprehensive sensibility and tu- 3085 tored genius—either for the interests of mankind or for their own—should, in ordinary times, have vested in them political power. The Empire, which they hold, is more independent: its constituent parts are sustained by a stricter connection: the dominion is purer and of higher origin; as mind is more excellent than body—the search of truth an employment more inherently dignified 3090 than the application of force—the determinations of nature more venerable than the accidents of human institution. Chance and disorder, vexation and disappointment, malignity and perverseness within or without the mind, are a sad exchange for the steady and genial processes of reason. Moreover; worldly distinctions and offices of command do not lie in the path—nor are they 3095 any part of the appropriate retinue—of Philosophy and Virtue. Nothing, but a strong spirit of love, can counteract the consciousness of pre-eminence which ever attends pre-eminent intellectual power with correspondent attainments: and this spirit of love is best encouraged by humility and simplicity in mind, manners, and conduct of life; virtues, to which wisdom leads. But,—though 3100 these be virtues in a Man, a Citizen, or a Sage,—they cannot be recommended to the especial culture of the Political or Military Functionary; and still less of the Civil Magistrate. Him, in the exercise of his functions, it will often become to carry himself highly and with state; in order that evil may be suppressed, and authority respected by those who have not understanding. The power also 3105 of office, whether the duties be discharged well or ill, will ensure a neverfailing supply of flattery and praise: and of these—a man (becoming at once double-dealer and dupe) may, without impeachment of his modesty, receive as much as his weakness inclines him to; under the shew that the homage is not offered up to himself, but to that portion of the public dignity which is lodged 3110 in his person. But, whatever may be the cause, the fact is certain—that there is an unconquerable tendency in all power, save that of knowledge acting by and through knowledge, to injure the mind of him who exercises that power; so much so, that best natures cannot escape the evil of such alliance. Nor is it less certain that things of soundest quality, issuing through a medium to which 3115 they have only an arbitrary relation, are vitiated: and it is inevitable that there should be a reäscent of unkindly influence to the heart of him from whom the gift, thus unfairly dealt with, proceeded.—In illustration of these remarks, as connected with the management of States, we need only refer to the Empire of China—where superior endowments of mind and acquisitions of learning are 3120 the sole acknowledged title to offices of great trust; and yet in no country is the government more bigotted or intolerant, or society less progressive.

To prevent misconception; and to silence (at least to throw discredit upon) the clamours of ignorance;—I have thought proper thus, in some sort, to strike a balance between the claims of men of routine—and men of original and 3125 accomplished minds—to the management of State affairs in ordinary circumstances. But ours is not an age of this character: and,—after having seen such a long series of misconduct, so many unjustifiable attempts made and sometimes carried into effect, good endeavours frustrated, disinterested wishes thwarted, and benevolent hopes disappointed,—it is reasonable that we should endeav- 3130 our to ascertain to what cause these evils are to be ascribed. I have directed the attention of the Reader to one primary cause: and can he doubt of its existence, and of the operation which I have attributed to it?

In the course of the last thirty years we have seen two wars waged against Liberty—the American war, and the war against the French People in the early 3135 stages of their Revolution. In the latter instance the Emigrants and the Continental Powers and the British did, in all their expectations and in every movement of their efforts, manifest a common ignorance—originating in the same source. And, for what more especially belongs to ourselves at this time, we may affirm—that the same presumptuous irreverence of the principles of justice, and 3140 blank insensibility to the affections of human nature, which determined the conduct of our government in those two wars *against* liberty, have continued to accompany its exertions in the present struggle *for* liberty,—and have rendered them fruitless. The British government deems (no doubt), on its own part, that its intentions are good. It must not deceive itself: nor must we deceive ourselves. In- 3145 tentions—thoroughly good—could not mingle with the unblessed actions which we have witnessed. A disinterested and pure intention is a light that guides as well as cheers, and renders desperate lapses impossible.

Our duty is—our aim ought to be—to employ the true means of liberty and virtue for the ends of liberty and virtue. In such policy, thoroughly understood, 3150 there is fitness and concord and rational subordination; it deserves a higher name—organization, health, and grandeur. Contrast, in a single instance, the two processes; and the qualifications which they require. The ministers of that period found it an easy task to hire a band of Hessians, and to send it across the Atlantic, that they might assist *in bringing the Americans* (according to the 3155 phrase then prevalent) *to reason.* The force, with which these troops would attack, was gross—tangible,—and might be calculated; but the spirit of resist-ance, which their presence would create, was subtle—ethereal—mighty—and incalculable. Accordingly, from the moment when these foreigners landed— men who had no interest, no business, in the quarrel, but what the wages of 3160 their master bound him to, and he imposed upon his miserable slaves;—nay, from the first rumour of their destination, the success of the British was (as hath since been affirmed by judicious Americans) impossible.

The British government of the present day have been seduced, as we have seen, by the same common-place facilities on the one side; and have been 3165 equally blind on the other. A physical auxiliar force of thirty-five thousand men is to be added to the army of Spain: but the moral energy, which thereby *might* be taken away from the principal, is overlooked or slighted; the material being too fine for their calculation. What does it avail to graft a bough upon a tree; if this be done so ignorantly and rashly that the trunk, which can alone supply 3170 the sap by which the whole must flourish, receives a deadly wound? Palpable effects of the Convention of Cintra, and self-contradicting consequences even in the matter especially aimed at, may be seen in the necessity which it entailed ¶ of leaving 8,000 British troops to protect Portuguese traitors from punishment ▶ by the laws of their country. A still more serious and fatal contradiction lies 3175 in this—that the English army was made an instrument of injustice, and was ¶ dishonoured, in order that it might be hurried forward to uphold a cause which could have no life but by justice and honour. The nation knows how that army languished in the heart of Spain: that it accomplished nothing except its re-treat, is sure: what great service it might have performed, if it had moved from 3180 a different impulse, we have shewn.

It surely then behoves those who are in authority—to look to the state of their own minds. There is indeed an inherent impossibility that they should be equal to the arduous duties which have devolved upon them: but it is not

unreasonable to hope that something higher might be aimed at; and that the 3185
People might see, upon great occasions,—in the practice of its Rulers—a more
adequate reflection of its own wisdom and virtue. Our Rulers, I repeat, must
begin with their own minds. This is a precept of immediate urgency; and, if attended to, might be productive of immediate good. I will follow it with further
conclusions directly referring to future conduct.   3190

I will not suppose that any ministry of this country can be so abject, so insensible, and unwise, as to abandon the Spaniards and Portuguese while there is a
Patriot in arms; or, if the people should for a time be subjugated, to deny them
assistance the moment they rise to require it again. I cannot think so unfavourably of my country as to suppose this possible. Let men in power, however, 3195
take care (and let the nation be equally careful) not to receive any reports from
our army—of the disposition of the Spanish people—without mistrust. The ▶
British generals, who were in Portugal (the whole body of them,* according to
the statement of Sir Hew Dalrymple), approved of the Convention of Cintra;
and have thereby shewn that *their* communications are not to be relied upon 3200
in this case. And indeed there is not any information, which we can receive
upon this subject, that is so little trust-worthy as that which comes from our
army—or from any part of it. The opportunities of notice, afforded to soldiers
in actual service, must necessarily be very limited; and a thousand things stand
in the way of their power to make a right use of these. But a retreating army, in 3205
the country of an ally;—harassed and dissatisfied; willing to find a reason for
its failures in any thing but itself, and actually not without much solid ground
for complaint; retreating; sometimes, perhaps, fugitive; and, in its disorder,
tempted (and even forced) to commit offences upon the people of the district
through which it passes; while they, in their turn, are filled with fear and in- 3210
considerate anger;—an army, in such a condition, must needs be incapable of
seeing objects as they really are; and, at the same time, all things must change
in its presence, and put on their most unfavourable appearances.

Deeming it then not to be doubted that the British government will continue its endeavours to support its allies; one or other of two maxims of policy 3215
follows obviously from the painful truths which we have been considering:—
Either, first, that we should put forth to the utmost our strength as a military

---

* From this number, however, must be excepted the gallant and patriotic General
Ferguson. For that officer has had the virtue publicly and in the most emphatic
manner, upon two occasions, to reprobate the whole transaction.

power—strain it to the very last point, and prepare (no erect mind will start at the proposition) to pour into the Peninsula a force of two hundred thousand men or more,—and make ourselves for a time, upon Spanish ground, princi- 3220 pals in the contest; or, secondly, that we should direct our attention to giving support rather in *Things* than in Men.

The former plan, though requiring a great effort and many sacrifices, is (I have no doubt) practicable: its difficulties would yield to a bold and ener- getic Ministry, in despite of the present constitution of Parliament. The Mi- 3225 litia, if they had been called upon at the beginning of the rising in the Pe- ninsula, would (I believe)—almost to a man—have offered their services: so would many of the Volunteers in their individual capacity. They would do so still. The advantages of this plan would be—that the power, which ◀ ▶ would attend it, must (if judiciously directed) insure unity of effort; taming 3230 down, by its dignity, the discords which usually prevail among allied ar- mies; and subordinating to itself the affections of the Spanish and Portuguese by the palpable service which it was rendering to their Country. A further en- couragement for adopting this plan he will find, who perceives that the military power of our Enemy is not in substance so formidable, by many—many degrees 3235 of terror, as outwardly it appears to be. The last campaign has not been wholly without advantage; since it has proved that the French troops are indebted, for their victories, to the imbecility of their opponents far more than to their own discipline or courage—or even to the skill and talents of their Generals. There is a superstition hanging over us which the efforts of our Army (not to speak of 3240 the Spaniards) have, I hope, removed.— But their mighty numbers!—In that is a delusion of another kind. In the former instance, year after year we imagined things to be what they were not: and in this, by a more fatal and more common delusion, the thought of what things really are—precludes the thought of what in a moment they may become: the mind, overlaid by the present, cannot lift 3245 itself to attain a glimpse of the future.

All—which is comparatively inherent, or can lay claim to any degree of permanence, in the tyranny which the French Nation maintains over Europe— rests upon two foundations:—First; Upon the despotic rule which has been es- tablished in France over a powerful People who have lately passed from a state 3250 of revolution, in which they supported a struggle begun for domestic liberty, and long continued for liberty and national independence:—and, secondly, upon the personal character of the Man by whom that rule is exercised.

As to the former; every one knows that Despotism, in a general sense, is
but another word for weakness. Let one generation disappear; and a people 3255
over whom such rule has been extended, if it have not virtue to free itself, ▶
is condemned to embarrassment in the operations of its government, and to
perpetual languor; with no better hope than that which may spring from the
diseased activity of some particular Prince on whom the authority may happen
to devolve. This, if it takes a regular hereditary course: but,—if the succession 3260
be interrupted, and the supreme power frequently usurped or given by election,—worse evils follow. Science and Art must dwindle, whether the power
be hereditary or not: and the virtues of a Trajan or an Antonine are a hollow
support for the feeling of contentment and happiness in the hearts of their
subjects: such virtues are even a painful mockery;—something that is, and 3265
may vanish in a moment, and leave the monstrous crimes of a Caracalla or a
Domitian in its place,—men, who are probably leaders of a long procession of
their kind. The feebleness of despotic power we have had before our eyes in
the late condition of Spain and Prussia; and in that of France before the Revolution; and in the present condition of Austria and Russia. But, in a *new-born* 3270
arbitrary and military Government (especially if, like that of France, it have
been immediately preceded by a popular Constitution), not only this weakness
is not found; but it possesses, for the purposes of external annoyance, a preternatural vigour. Many causes contribute to this: we need only mention that,
fitness—real or supposed—being necessarily the chief (and almost sole) rec- 3275
ommendation to offices of trust, it is clear that such offices will in general be
ably filled; and their duties, comparatively, well executed: and that, from the
conjunction of absolute civil and military authority in a single Person, there
naturally follows promptness of decision; concentration of effort; rapidity of
motion; and confidence that the movements made will be regularly supported. 3280
This is all which need now be said upon the subject of this first basis of French
Tyranny.

For the second—namely, the personal character of the Chief; I shall at
present content myself with noting (to prevent misconception) that this basis
is not laid in any superiority of talents in him, but in his utter rejection of the 3285
restraints of morality—in wickedness which acknowledges no limit but the
extent of its own power. Let any one reflect a moment; and he will feel that a
new world of forces is opened to a Being who has made this desperate leap. It
is a tremendous principle to be adopted, and steadily adhered to, by a man in

the station which Buonaparte occupies; and he has taken the full benefit of it. **3290**
What there is in this principle of weak, perilous, and self-destructive— I may
find a grateful employment in endeavouring to shew upon some future occasion. But it is a duty which we owe to the present moment to proclaim—in
vindication of the dignity of human nature, and for an admonition to men of
prostrate spirit—that the dominion, which this Enemy of mankind holds, has **3295**
neither been acquired nor is sustained by endowments of intellect which are
rarely bestowed, or by uncommon accumulations of knowledge; but that it
has risen from circumstances over which he had no influence; circumstances
which, with the power they conferred, have stimulated passions whose natural
food hath been and is ignorance; from the barbarian impotence and insolence **3300**
of a mind—originally of ordinary constitution—lagging, in moral sentiment
and knowledge, three hundred years behind the age in which it acts. In such
manner did the power originate; and, by the forces which I have described, is it
maintained. This should be declared: and it should be added—that the crimes
of Buonaparte are more to be abhorred than those of other denaturalized crea- **3305**
tures whose actions are painted in History; because the Author of those crimes
is guilty with less temptation, and sins in the presence of a clearer light.

No doubt in the command of almost the whole military force of Europe
(the subject which called upon me to make these distinctions) he has, *at this
moment*, a third source of power which may be added to these two. He him- **3310**
self rates this last so high—either is, or affects to be, so persuaded of its pre-
eminence—that he boldly announces to the world that it is madness, and even
impiety, to resist him. And sorry may we be to remember that there are British ◀ ▶
Senators, who (if a judgement may be formed from the language which they
speak) are inclined to accompany him far in this opinion. But the enormity of **3315**
this power has in it nothing *inherent* or *permanent*. Two signal overthrows in
pitched battles would, I believe, go far to destroy it. Germans, Dutch, Italians,
Swiss, Poles, would desert the army of Buonaparte, and flock to the standard of his Adversaries, from the moment they could look towards it with that
confidence which one or two conspicuous victories would inspire. A regiment 3320
of 900 Swiss joined the British army in Portugal; and, if the French had been
compelled to surrender as Prisoners of War, we should have seen that all those
troops, who were not native Frenchmen, would (if encouragement had been
given) have joined the British: and the opportunity that was lost of demonstrating this fact—was not among the least of the mischiefs which attended the ter- **3325**

mination of the campaign.—In a word; the vastness of Buonaparte's military power is formidable— not because it is impossible to break it; but because it has not yet been penetrated. In this respect it may not inaptly be compared to a huge pine-forest (such as are found in the Northern parts of this Island), whose ability to resist the storms is in it's skirts: let but the blast once make an inroad; **3330** and it levels the forest, and sweeps it away at pleasure. A hundred thousand men, such as fought at Vimiera and Corunna, would accomplish three such victories as I have been anticipating. This Nation *might* command a military force which would drive the French out of the Peninsula: I do not say that we could sustain there a military force which would prevent their re-entering; **3335** but that we could transplant thither, by a great effort, one which would expel them:—*This* I maintain: and it is matter of thought in which infirm minds may find both reproach and instruction. The Spaniards could then take possession of their own fortresses; and have leisure to give themselves a blended civil and military organization, complete and animated by liberty; which, if **3340** once accomplished, they would be able to protect themselves. The oppressed Continental Powers also, seeing such unquestionable proof that Great Britain was sincere and earnest, would lift their heads again; and, by so doing, would lighten the burthen of war which might remain for the Spaniards.

In treating of this plan—I have presumed that a General might be placed **3345** at the head of this great military power who would not sign a Treaty like that of the Convention of Cintra, and say (look at the proceedings of the Board of Inquiry) that he was determined to this by "British interests;" or frame *any* Treaty in the country of an Ally (save one purely military for the honourable preservation, if necessary, of his own army or part of it) to which the sole, or **3350** even the main, inducement was—our interests contradistinguished from those of that Ally;—a General and a Ministry whose policy would be comprehensive enough to perceive that the true welfare of Britain is best promoted by the independence, freedom, and honour of other Nations; and that it is only by the diffusion and prevalence of these virtues that French Tyranny can be **3355** ultimately reduced; or the influence of France over the rest of Europe brought within its natural and reasonable limits.

If this attempt be "above the strain and temper" of the country, there remains only a plan laid down upon the other principle; namely, service (as far as is required) in *things* rather than in men; that is, men being secondary **3360**

3359 principle *M.Y.* i. 343: principles 1809.

to things. It is not, I fear, possible that the moral sentiments of the British Army or Government should accord with those of Spain in her present condition. Commanding power indeed (as hath been said), put forth in the repulse of the common enemy, would tend, more effectually than any thing save the prevalence of true wisdom, to prevent disagreement, and to obviate any tem- 3365 porary injury which the moral spirit of the Spaniards might receive from us: at all events—such power, should there ensue any injury, would bring a solid compensation. But from a middle course—an association sufficiently intimate and wide to scatter every where unkindly passions, and yet unable to attain the salutary point of decisive power—no good is to be expected. Great would 3370 be the evil, at this momentous period, if the hatred of the Spaniards should look two ways. Let it be as steadily fixed upon the French, as the Pilot's eye upon his mark. Military stores and arms should be furnished with unfailing liberality: let Troops also be supplied; but let these act separately,—taking strong positions upon the coast, if such can be found, to employ twice their 3375 numbers of the Enemy; and, above all, let there be Floating Armies—keeping the Enemy in constant uncertainty where he is to be attacked. The peninsular frame of Spain and Portugal lays that region open to the full shock of British warfare. Our Fleet and Army should act, wherever it is possible, as parts of one body—a right hand and a left; and the Enemy ought to be made to feel the 3380 force of both.

But—whatever plans be adopted—there can be no success, unless the execution be entrusted to Generals of competent judgement. That the British ▶ Army swarms with those who are incompetent—is too plain from successive ¶ proofs in the transactions at Buenos Ayres, at Cintra, and in the result of the 3385 Board of Inquiry.—Nor must we see a General appointed to command—and required, at the same time, to frame his operations according to the opinion of an inferior Officer: an injunction (for a recommendation, from such a quarter, amounts to an injunction) implying that a man had been appointed to a high station—of which the very persons, who had appointed him, deemed him un- 3390 worthy; else they must have known that he would endeavour to profit by the experience of any of his inferior officers, from the suggestions of his own understanding: at the same time—by denying to the General-in-Chief the free use of his own judgement, and by the act of announcing this presumption of ¶ his incompetence to the man himself—such an indignity is put upon him, that 3395 his passions must of necessity be rouzed; so as to leave it scarcely possible that

he could draw any benefit, which he might otherwise have drawn, from the local knowledge or talents of the individual to whom he was referred: and, lastly,
this injunction virtually involves a subversion of all military subordination. In ▶
the better times of the House of Commons— a minister, who had presumed to   3400
write such a letter as that to which I allude, would have been impeached.

The Debates in Parliament, and measures of Government, every day
furnish new proofs of the truths which I have been attempting to establish—of the utter want of general principles;—new and lamentable proofs!
This moment (while I am drawing towards a conclusion) I learn, from the   3405
newspaper reports, that the House of Commons has refused to declare that ▶
the Convention of Cintra *disappointed the hopes and expectations of the
Nation.*

The motion, according to the letter of it, was ill-framed; for the Convention might have been a very good one, and still have disappointed the hopes and   3410
expectations of the Nation—as those might have been unwise: at all events, the
words ought to have stood—the *just* and *reasonable* hopes of the Nation. But
the hacknied phrase of '*disappointed hopes and expectations*'—should not
have been used at all: it is a centre round which much delusion has gathered.
The Convention not only did not satisfy the Nation's hopes of good; but sunk it   3415
into a pitfall of unimagined and unimaginable evil. The hearts and understandings of the People tell them that the language of a proposed parliamentary
resolution, upon this occasion, ought—not only to have been different in the
letter—but also widely different in the spirit: and the reader of these pages
will have deduced, that no terms of reprobation could in severity exceed the   3420
offences involved in—and connected with—that instrument. But, while the
grand keep of the castle of iniquity was to be stormed, we have seen nothing
but a puny assault upon heaps of the scattered rubbish of the fortress; nay,
for the most part, on some accidental mole-hills at its base. I do not speak
thus in disrespect to the Right Hon. Gentleman who headed this attack. His   3425
mind, left to itself, would (I doubt not) have prompted something worthier
and higher: but he moves in the phalanx of Party;— a spiritual Body; in
which (by strange inconsistency) the hampering, weakening, and destroying, of every individual mind of which it is composed—is the law which
must constitute the strength of the whole. The question was—whether prin-   3430
ciples, affecting the very existence of Society, had not been violated; and an
arm lifted, and let fall, which struck at the root of Honour; with the aggrava-

tion of the crime having been committed at this momentous period. But what relation is there between these principles and actions, and being in Place or out of it? If the People would constitutionally and resolutely assert their rights, 3435 their Representatives would be taught another lesson; and for their own profit. Their understandings would be enriched accordingly: for it is there—there where least suspected—that the want, from which this country suffers, chiefly lies. They err, who suppose that venality and corruption (though now spread- ing more and more) are the master-evils of this day: neither these nor immod- 3440 erate craving for power are so much to be deprecated, as the non-existence of a widely-ranging intellect; of an intellect which, if not efficacious to infuse truth as a vital fluid into the heart, might at least make it a powerful tool in the hand. Outward profession,—which, for practical purposes, is an act of most desirable subservience,—would then wait upon those objects to which inward 3445 reverence, though not felt, was known to be due. Schemes of ample reach and true benefit would also promise best to ensure the rewards coveted by person- al ambition: and men of baser passions, finding it their interest, would natu- rally combine to perform useful service under the direction of strong minds: while men of good intentions would have their own pure satisfaction; and 3450 would exert themselves with more upright—I mean, more hopeful— cheerful- ness, and more successfully. It is not therefore inordinate desire of wealth or power which is so injurious—as the means which are and must be employed, in the present intellectual condition of the Legislature, to sustain and secure that power: these are at once an effect of barrenness, and a cause; acting, and 3455 mutually re-acting, incessantly. An enlightened Friend has, in conversation, ◀ ▶ observed to the Author of these pages—that formerly the principles of men were better than they who held them; but that now (a far worse evil!) men are better than their principles. I believe it:—of the deplorable quality and state of principles, the public proceedings in our Country furnish daily new proof. 3460 It is however some consolation, at this present crisis, to find—that, of the thoughts and feelings uttered during the two debates which led me to these painful declarations, such—as approach towards truth which has any dignity in it—come from the side of his Majesty's Ministers.—But note again those contradictions to which I have so often been obliged to advert. The Ministers 3465 advise his Majesty publicly to express sentiments of disapprobation upon the Convention of Cintra; and, when the question of the merits or demerits of this instrument comes before them in Parliament, the same persons— who, as advisers of the crown, lately condemned the treaty—now, in their character of representatives of the people, by the manner in which they received 3470 this motion, have pronounced an encomium upon it. For, though (as I have said) the motion was inaccurately and inadequately worded, it was not set aside upon this ground. And the Parliament has therefore persisted in with- ◀ ▶ holding, from the insulted and injured People and from their Allies, the only reparation which perhaps it may be in its power to grant; has refused to sig- 3475 nify its repentance and sorrow for what bath been done; without which, as a previous step, there can be no proof—no gratifying intimation even, to this Country or to its Allies, that the future efforts of the British Parliament are in a sincere spirit. The guilt of the transaction therefore being neither repented of, nor atoned for; the course of evil is, by necessity, persevered in.—But let 3480 us turn to a brighter region.

The events of the last year, gloriously destroying many frail fears, have placed—in the rank of serene and immortal truths—a proposition which, as an object of belief, hath in all ages been fondly cherished; namely—That a numerous Nation, determined to be free, may effect its purpose in despite of 3485 the mightiest power which a foreign Invader can bring against it. These events also have pointed out how, in the ways of Nature and under the guidance of Society, this happy end is to be attained: in other words, they have shewn that the cause of the People, in dangers and difficulties issuing from this quarter of oppression, is safe while it remains not only in the bosom but in the hands 3490 of the People; or (what amounts to the same thing) in those of a government which, being truly *from* the People, is faithfully *for* them. While the power remained with the provincial Juntas, that is, with the body natural of the community (for those authorities, newly-generated in such adversity, were truly living members of that body); every thing prospered in Spain. Hopes of the 3495 best kind were opened out and encouraged; liberal opinions countenanced; and wise measures arranged: and last, and (except as proceeding from these) least of all,—victories in the field, in the streets of the city, and upon the walls of the fortress.

I have heretofore styled it a blessing that the Spanish People became their 3500 own masters at once. It *was* a blessing; but not without much alloy: as the same disinterested generous passions, which preserved (and would for a season still have preserved) them from a bad exercise of their power, impelled them to

3477 intimation even, to *M.Y.* i. 343: intimation,
      even to 1809.

part with it too soon; before labours, hitherto neither tried nor thought-of, had created throughout the country the minor excellences indispensible for the 3505 performance of those labours; before powerful minds, not hitherto of general note, had found time to shew themselves; and before men, who were previously known, had undergone the proof of new situations. Much therefore was wanting to direct the general judgement in the choice of persons, when the second delegation took place; which was a removal (the first, we have seen, 3510 had not been so) of the power from the People. But, when a common centre ▶ became absolutely necessary, the power ought to have passed from the provincial Assemblies into the hands of the Cortes; and into none else. A pernicious Oligarchy crept into the place of this comprehensive—this constitutional—this saving and majestic Assembly. Far be it from me to speak of the Supreme Junta 3515 with ill-advised condemnation: every man must feel for the distressful trials to which that Body has been exposed. But eighty men or a hundred, with a king at their head veiled under a cloud of fiction (we might say, with reference to the difficulties of this moment, begotten upon a cloud of fiction), could not be an ¶ image of a Nation like that of Spain, or an adequate instrument of their power 3520 for their ends. The Assembly, from the smallness of its numbers, must have wanted breadth of wing to extend itself and brood over Spain with a quicken- ¶ ing touch of warmth every where. If also, as hath been mentioned, there was a want of experience to determine the judgment in choice of persons; this same smallness of numbers must have unnecessarily increased the evil—by exclud- 3525 ing many men of worth and talents which were so far known and allowed as that they would surely have been deputed to an Assembly upon a larger scale. Gratitude, habit, and numerous other causes must have given an undue preponderance to birth, station, rank, and fortune; and have fixed the election, more than was reasonable, upon those who were most conspicuous for these 3530 distinctions;—men whose very virtue would incline them superstitiously to re- spect established things, and to mistrust the People—towards whom not only a frank confidence but a forward generosity was the first of duties. I speak not of the vices to which such men would be liable, brought up under the discipline of a government administered like the old Monarchy of Spain: the matter is 3535 both ungracious and too obvious.

But I began with hope; and hope has inwardly accompanied me to the end. ¶ The whole course of the campaign, rightly interpreted, has justified my hope. In Madrid, in Ferrol, in Corunna, in every considerable place, and in every part ¶

of the country over which the French have re-extended their dominion,—we 3540
learn, from their own reports, that the body of the People have shewed against
them, to the last, the most determined hostility. Hence it is clear that the lure,
which the invading Usurper found himself constrained lately to hold out to
the inferior orders of society in the shape of various immunities, has totally
failed: and therefore he turns for support to another quarter, and now attempts 3545
to cajole the wealthy and the privileged. But this class has been taught, by late
Decrees, what it has to expect from him; and how far he is to be confided-in
for its especial interests. Many individuals, no doubt, he will seduce; but the
bulk of the class, even if they could be insensible to more liberal feelings, cannot but be his enemies. This change, therefore, is not merely shifting ground; 3550
but retiring to a position which he himself has previously undermined. Here is
confusion; and a power warring against itself.

So will it ever fare with foreign Tyrants when (in spite of domestic abuses)
a People, which has lived long, feels that it has a Country to love; and where
the heart of that People is sound. Between the native inhabitants of France 3555
and Spain there has existed from the earliest period, and still does exist, an
universal and utter dissimilitude in laws, actions, deportment, gait, manners,
customs: join with this the difference in the language, and the barrier of the
Pyrenees; a separation and an opposition in great things, and an antipathy in
small. Ignorant then must he be of history and of the reports of travellers and 3560
residents in the two countries, or strangely inattentive to the constitution of
human nature, who (this being true) can admit the belief that the Spaniards,
numerous and powerful as they are, will live under Frenchmen as their lords
and masters. Let there be added to this inherent mutual repulsiveness—those
recent indignities and horrible outrages; and we need not fear to say that such 3565
reconcilement is impossible; even without that further insuperable obstacle
which we hope will exist, an establishment of a free Constitution in Spain.—
The intoxicated setter-up of Kings may fill his diary with pompous stories of ◀ ▶
the acclamations with which his solemn puppets are received; he may stuff
their mouths with impious asseverations; and hire knees to bend before them, 3570
and lips to answer with honied greetings of gratitude and love: these cannot
remove the old heart, and put a new one into the bosom of the spectators. The
whole is a pageant seen for a day among men in its passage to the "Limbo ◀ ▶
large and broad" whither, as to their proper home, fleet

All the unaccomplish'd works of Nature's hand,   3575

Abortive, monstrous, or unkindly mix'd,
Dissolv'd on earth.

Talk not of the perishable nature of enthusiasm; and rise above a craving
for perpetual manifestations of things. He is to be pitied whose eye can only
be pierced by the light of a meridian sun, whose frame can only be warmed 3580
by the heat of midsummer. Let us hear no more of the little dependence to be
had in war upon voluntary service. The things, with which we are primarily
and mainly concerned, are inward passions; and not outward arrangements.
These latter may be given at any time; when the parts, to be put together, are
in readiness. Hatred and love, and each in its intensity, and pride (passions 3585
which, existing in the heart of a Nation, are inseparable from hope)—these
elements being in constant preparation—enthusiasm will break out from them,
or coalesce with them, upon the summons of a moment. And these passions are
scarcely less than inextinguishable. The truth of this is recorded in the manners and hearts of North and South Britons, of Englishmen and Welshmen, on 3590
either border of the Tweed and of the Esk, on both sides of the Severn and the
Dee; an inscription legible, and in strong characters, which the tread of many
and great blessings, continued through hundreds of years, has been unable to
efface. The Sicilian Vespers are to this day a familiar game among the boys ¶ ▶
of the villages on the sides of Mount Etna, and through every corner of the 3595
Island; and "Exterminate the French!" is the action in their arms, and the word
of triumph upon their tongues. He then is a sorry Statist, who desponds or
despairs (nor is he less so who is too much elevated) from any considerations
connected with the quality of enthusiasm. Nothing is so easy as to sustain it
by partial and gradual changes of its object; and by placing it in the way of 3600
receiving new interpositions according to the need. The difficulty lies—not
in kindling, feeding, or fanning the flame; but in continuing so to regulate the
relations of things—that the fanning breeze and the feeding fuel shall come
from no unworthy quarter, and shall neither of them be wanting in appropriate
consecration. The Spaniards have as great helps towards ensuring this, as ever 3605
were vouchsafed to a People.

What then is to be desired? Nothing but that the Government and the higher orders of society should deal sincerely towards the middle class and the
lower: I mean, that the general temper should be sincere.—It is not required
that every one should be disinterested, or zealous, or of one mind with his 3610
fellows. Selfishness or slackness in individuals, and in certain bodies of men

also (and at times perhaps in all), have their use: else why should they exist? Due circumspection and necessary activity, in those who are sound, could not otherwise maintain themselves. The deficiencies in one quarter are more than made up by consequent overflowings in another. "If my Neighbour fails," says 3615 the true Patriot, "more devolves upon me." Discord and even treason are not, in a country situated as Spain is, the pure evils which, upon superficial view, they appear to be. Never are a people so livelily admonished of the love they bear their country, and of the pride which they have in their common parent, as when they hear of some parricidal attempt of a false brother. For this cause 3620 chiefly, in times of national danger, are their fancies so busy in suspicion; which under such shape, though oftentimes producing dire and pitiable effects, is notwithstanding in its general character no other than that habit which has grown out of the instinct of self-preservation—elevated into wakeful and affectionate apprehension for the whole, and ennobling its private and baser 3625 ways by the generous use to which they are converted. Nor ever has a good and loyal man such a swell of mind, such a clear insight into the constitution of virtue, and such a sublime sense of its power, as at the first tidings of some atrocious act of perfidy; when, having taken the alarm for human nature, a second thought recovers him; and his faith returns—gladsome from what has 3630 been revealed within himself, and awful from participation of the secrets in the profaner grove of humanity which that momentary blast laid open to his view.

Of the ultimate independence of the Spanish Nation there is no reason to doubt: and for the immediate furtherance of the good cause, and a throwing-off 3635 of the yoke upon the first favourable opportunity by the different tracts of the country upon which it has been re-imposed, nothing is wanting but sincerity on the part of the government towards the provinces which are yet free. The first end to be secured by Spain is riddance of the enemy: the second, permanent independence: and the third, a free constitution of government; which will give 3640 their main (though far from sole) value to the other two; and without which little more than a formal independence, and perhaps scarcely that, can be secured. Humanity and honour, and justice, and all the sacred feelings connected with atonement, retribution, and satisfaction; shame that will not sleep, and the sting of unperformed duty; and all the powers of the mind, the memory that broods 3645 over the dead and turns to the living, the understanding, the imagination, and the reason;—demand and enjoin that the wanton oppressor should be driven, with confusion and dismay, from the country which he has so heinously abused.

This cannot be accomplished (scarcely can it be aimed at) without an accompanying and an inseparable resolution, in the souls of the Spaniards, 3650 to be and remain their own masters; that is, to preserve themselves in the rank of Men; and not become as the Brute that is driven to the pasture, and cares not who owns him. It is a common saying among those who profess to be lovers of civil liberty, and give themselves some credit for understanding it,—that, if a Nation be not free, it is mere dust in the balance whether 3655 the slavery be bred at home, or comes from abroad; be of their own suffering, or of a stranger's imposing. They see little of the under-ground part of the tree of liberty, and know less of the nature of man, who can think thus. Where indeed there is an indisputable and immeasurable superiority in one nation over another; to be conquered may, in course of time, be a benefit to 3660 the inferior nation: and, upon this principle, some of the conquests of the Greeks and Romans may be justified. But in what of really useful or honourable are the French superior to their Neighbours? Never far advanced, and, now barbarizing apace, they may carry—amongst the sober and dignified Nations which surround them—much to be avoided, but little to be imitated. 3665

There is yet another case in which a People may be benefited by resignation or forfeiture of their rights as a separate independent State; I mean, where—of two contiguous or neighbouring countries, both included by nature under one conspicuously defined limit—the weaker is united with, or absorbed into, the more powerful; and one and the same Government is extended over both. This, 3670 with due patience and foresight, may (for the most part) be amicably effected, without the intervention of conquest; but—even should a violent course have been resorted to, and have proved successful—the result will be matter of congratulation rather than of regret, if the countries have been incorporated with an equitable participation of natural advantages and civil privileges. Who 3675 does not rejoice that former partitions have disappeared,—and that England, Scotland, and Wales, are under one legislative and executive authority; and that Ireland (would that she had been more justly dealt with!) follows the same destiny? The large and numerous Fiefs, which interfered injuriously with the grand demarcation assigned by nature to France, have long since been united 3680

3671 (for the most part) 1809: always G.
3673 be G[2], 1809: furnish G.
3674–5 if the countries ... privileges G[2], 1809: if arrangements be made for incorporating the

conquered Country according to the principles of justice that is for an equitable participation of natural advantages and civil privileges G.
3680 by nature G[2], 1809: *om.* G.

and consolidated. The several independent Sovereignties of Italy (a country, the boundary of which is still more expressly traced out by nature; and which has no less the further definition and cement of country which Language prepares) have yet this good to aim at: and it will be a happy day for Europe, when the natives of Italy and the natives of Germany (whose duty is, in like **3685** manner, indicated to them) shall each dissolve the pernicious barriers which divide them, and form themselves into a mighty People. But Spain, excepting a free union with Portugal, has no benefit of this kind to look for: she has long since attained it. The Pyrenees on the one side, and the Sea on every other; the vast extent and great resources of the territory; a population numerous enough **3690** to defend itself against the whole world, and capable of great increase; language; and long duration of independence;—point out and command that the two nations of the Peninsula should be united in friendship and strict alliance; and, as soon as it may be effected without injustice, form one independent and indissoluble sovereignty. The Peninsula cannot be protected but by itself: it **3695** is too large a tree to be framed by nature for a station among underwoods; it must have power to toss its branches in the wind, and lift a bold forehead to the sun.

Allowing that the "regni novitas" should either compel or tempt the ◀ ▶ Usurper to do away some ancient abuses, and to accord certain insignificant **3700** privileges to the People upon the purlieus of the forest of Freedom (for assuredly he will never suffer them to enter the body of it); allowing this, and much more; that the mass of the Population would be placed in a condition outwardly more thriving—would be *better off* (as the phrase in conversation is); it is still true that—in the act and consciousness of submission to an im- **3705** posed lord and master, to a will not growing out of themselves, to the edicts of another People their triumphant enemy—there would be the loss of a sensation within for which nothing external, even though it should come close to the garden and the field—to the door and the fire-side, can make amends. The Artisan and the Merchant (men of classes perhaps least attached to their **3710**

3684 happy 1809: glorious G.
3686 the G², 1809: their G. which G², 1809: that G.
3687 mighty G², 1809: free and mighty G.
3688 Portugal G², 1809: Portugal an event most desirable G.
3688–9 she has ... attained it G², 1809: *om.* G.
3691 great 1809: mighty G.

3695 sovereignty. The Peninsula ... sun G², 1809: sovereignty of justice and without a pretext of expediency from unprincipled and sens[e]less ambition G.
3703 more G², 1809: more though most improbable G.
3706 not 1809. not residing in and G.

native soil) would not be insensible to this loss; and the Mariner, in his thoughtful mood, would sadden under it upon the wide ocean. The central or cardi-
nal feeling of these thoughts may, at a future time, furnish fit matter for the
genius of some patriotic Spaniard to express in his own noble language—as ▶
an inscription for the Sword of Francis the First; if that Sword, which was 3715
so ingloriously and perfidiously surrendered, should ever, by the energies of
Liberty, be recovered, and deposited in its ancient habitation in the Escurial.
The Patriot will recollect that,—if the memorial, then given up by the hand of
the Government, had also been abandoned by the heart of the People, and that
indignity patiently subscribed to,—his country would have been lost for ever. 3720

  There are multitudes by whom, I know, these sentiments will not be lan-
guidly received at this day; and sure I am—that, a hundred and fifty years ago,
they would have been ardently welcomed by all. But, in many parts of Europe
(and especially in our own country), men have been pressing forward, for
some time, in a path which has betrayed by its fruitfulness; furnishing them 3725
constant employment for picking up things about their feet, when thoughts
were perishing in their minds. While Mechanic Arts, Manufactures, Agricul- ¶
ture, Commerce, and all those products of knowledge which are confined to
gross—definite—and tangible objects, have, with the aid of Experimental Philosophy, been every day putting on more brilliant colours; the splendour of 3730
the Imagination has been fading: Sensibility, which was formerly a generous

3713 a G[2], 1809: some G.
3714 express 1809: be expressed G.
3716–7 by ... Liberty G[2], 1809: *om.* G.
3718 memorial G[2], 1809: monument G.
3721 There ... not G[3], 1809: These sentiments will
  not I know [hope G[2]] by tens of thousands G.
3726 when 1809: while G.
3727 *After* minds. *the following passage, eventually
  deleted entirely, appears in* G:

  Lord Bacon two hundred years ago
  announced that knowledge was power and
  strenuously recommended the process of
  experiment and induction for attainment of
  knowledge. But the mind of this Philosopher
  was comprehensive and sublime and must
  have had intimate communion of the truth
  of which the experimentalists who deem
  themselves his disciples are for the most part
  ignorant viz. that knowledge of facts conferring
  power over the combinations of things in the

material world has no determinate connection
with power over the faculties of the mind.
Nay so far is such encrease from being a
necessary result that it is scarcely possible
to [? strengthen] and unite the two species
of power in such a manner that the more
noble shall not lag behind in proportion to
the rapid and eager advancement of the less
noble. Let it not be supposed that I am blind
to the power of intellect which has been [?
put forth] in the improvement of experimental
philosophy and the mechanic arts [? or under
subjects] the various and great benefits which
have proceeded from them or may proceed
from these [? inquiries but] in justice [*tear*]
the principles which I have undertaken to
maintain I am [*tear*]mpelled to direct the
Readers attention to these truths, that he may
not overlook the rights and titles of superiority
inherent in things. For the same cause I

nursling of rude Nature, has been chased from its ancient range in the wide domain of patriotism and religion with the weapons of derision by a shadow calling itself Good Sense: calculations of presumptuous Expediency—groping its
way among partial and temporary consequences—have been substituted for **3735**
the dictates of paramount and infallible Conscience, the supreme embracer of
consequences: lifeless and circumspect Decencies have banished the graceful
negligence and unsuspicious dignity of Virtue.

The progress of these arts also, by furnishing such attractive stores of outward accommodation, has misled the higher orders of society in their more **3740**

must add that great and even mighty as is the relative worth of the products of natural science and its industrious associates yet absolute and unconditional worth they have none. They are not even gifted with the power of self-preservation. Innumerable inventions and abilities of this kind and of a very high order perished with the dissolution of morals and consequent wearing-away of intellect, in the declining empire of Rome. Unless as far as these acquisitions are subservient through civil liberty to moral greatness and purity, they are of no more value in the eye of Reason than the shells and pebbles which Caligula gathered up from the shores of Britain and exhibited to his Slaves in the majestic City as a recompense of an expedition and the spoils of a Conquest. ►

Having said this I will not follow it with a charge which I have not, at present, time to substantiate against these pursuits as the cause indirectly of a course of obtuse and mechanical habits of thinking on moral investigations and as a source directly of degrading moral habits, it is enough to suggest to the Reader that while we have been making large encrease of gains on one side these gains have withdrawn our attention from great loss on the other. G.

Lord Bacon two centuries ago announced that knowledge was power and justified by the wrong practice which had till that time generally prevailed and by the wants which were then most pressing he strenuously recommended physical investigation to be carried on by induction and experiment for the attainment of knowledge. But knowledge of facts conferring power over the combinations of things in the material world has no necessary connection with encrease of power in the constitution and faculties of the mind, either in the mind of the individual or in the general mind of the age. Nay so far ... in such manner that ... the less noble. Injustice ... the products of natural science and the mechanic arts its industrious associates ... Innumerable discoveries inventions ... these acquisitions are subservient to moral greatness ... as the cause directly of obtuse feeling towards the nobler moral impressions and of a course of (see the end of last sheet) mechanical thinking on moral investigations and as a source directly of degrading moral habits, thus countenancing and aggravating that evil which [? excess] [of which *del.*] (as I have heretofore proved) [? inseparably] adheres to the minds of ordinary practical statesmen it is enough to suggest that while we have been making large gains on one side ... on the other. G^2.

3727–8 Agriculture, Commerce 1809: agriculture and commerce G.

3730 the splendour ... has 1809: religion and the splendour ... have G.

3732–3 range ... derision 1809: range with the weapons of sneer and derision G.

3734 calculations of G^2, 1809: *om.* G.

3739 also G2, 1809: also (this I venture to assert because no train of reasoning is required to establish the truth) G.

disinterested exertions for the service of the lower. Animal comforts have been rejoiced over, as if they were the end of being. A neater and more fertile garden; a greener field; implements and utensils more apt; a dwelling more commodious and better furnished;—let these be attained, say the actively benevolent, and we are sure not only of being in the right road, but of having successfully **3745** terminated our journey. Now a country may advance, for some time, in this course with apparent profit: these accommodations, by zealous encouragement, may be attained: and still the Peasant or Artisan, their master, be a slave in mind; a slave rendered even more abject by the very tenure under which these possessions are held: and—if they veil from us this fact, or reconcile us **3750** to it—they are worse than worthless. The springs of emotion may be relaxed or destroyed within him; he may have little thought of the past, and less interest in the future.—The great end and difficulty of life for men of all classes, and ¶ ▶ especially difficult for those who live by manual labour, is a union of peace with innocent and laudable animation. Not by bread alone is the life of Man 3755 sustained; not by raiment alone is he warmed;—but by the genial and vernal inmate of the breast, which at once pushes forth and cherishes; by self-support and self-sufficing endeavours; by anticipations, apprehensions, and active remembrances; by elasticity under insult, and firm resistance to injury; by joy, and by love; by pride which his imagination gathers in from afar; by patience, **3760** because life wants not promises; by admiration; by gratitude which—debasing him not when his fellow-being is its object—habitually expands itself, for his elevation, in complacency towards his Creator.

3743 field 1809: Croft G.

3744 benevolent G2, 1809: charitable G.

3746–8 a country ... encouragement 1809: all these G.

3748–50 a slave ... held: 1809: an abject Slave G.

3750–1 or ... it G², 1809: *om*. G.

3753 future. G³, 1809: future. Having no craving he may appear to be contented and deem himself so, but the fullness of his mind is not like the fullness of the pool in the mountains or of the Lake in the [? Vale] ample measure of living and circulating waters, receiving and discharging—its contents are like the basons [basons (*pots of the Lyn*) G²] which the Wanderer by the side of the brooks finds scooped out in the hard rock by the floods which have passed away; such only may be his mind and the stores which it contains—fed by no springs within itself agitated by by [sic] no breezes, exhaled by no sunshine—tranquil, but sullen [joyless G²] in its tranquillity. G.

3753–5 The great ... animation] *In G, written in Wordsworth's hand on the address panel, crossing the address, and with so much alteration as to be almost illegible.*

3757 inmate of 1809: inmate in G.

3758 anticipations] *del. from* G. remembrances; G², 1809: remembrances; by hopes which if not [? manifold] are continuous and which when embodied in action [? fail] not for want of [? alacrity] G.

Now, to the existence of these blessings, national independence is indispensible; and many of them it will itself produce and maintain. For it is **3765** some consolation to those who look back upon the history of the world to know—that, even without civil liberty, society may possess—diffused through its inner recesses in the minds even of its humblest members—something of dignified enjoyment. But, without national independence, this is impossible. ◀ ▶ The difference, between inbred oppression and that which is from without, is **3770** *essential*; inasmuch as the former does not exclude, from the minds of a people, the feeling of being self-governed; does not imply (as the latter does, when patiently submitted to) an abandonment of the first duty imposed by the faculty of reason. In reality: where this feeling has no place, a people are not a society, but a herd; man being indeed distinguished among them from the brute; but **3775** only to his disgrace. I am aware that there are too many who think that, to the bulk of the community, this independence is of no value; that it is a refinement with which they feel they have no concern; inasmuch as, under the best frame of Government, there is an inevitable dependence of the poor upon the rich—of the many upon the few—so unrelenting and imperious as to reduce this other, by **3780** comparison, into a force which has small influence, and is entitled to no regard. Superadd civil liberty to national independence; and this position is overthrown at once: for there is no more certain mark of a sound frame of polity than this; that, in all individual instances (and it is upon these generalized that this position is down), the dependence is in reality far more strict on the side of the wealthy; **3785** and the labouring man leans less upon others than any man in the community.— But the case before us is of a country not internally free, yet supposed capable of repelling an external enemy who attempts its subjugation. If a country have put on chains of its own forging; in the name of virtue, let it be conscious that to itself it is accountable: let it not have cause to look beyond its own limits for **3790** reproof: and,—in the name of humanity,—if it be self-depressed, let it have its pride and some hope within itself. The poorest Peasant, in an unsubdued land, feels this pride. I do not appeal to the example of Britain or of Switzerland, for the one is free, and the other lately was free (and, I trust, will ere long be so again): but talk with the Swede; and you will see the joy he finds in these **3795** sensations. With him animal courage (the substitute for many and the friend of all the manly virtues) has space to move in; and is at once elevated by his im-

3766 those ... look G², 1809: him ... looks G.   3769–76 The difference ... disgrace. 1809: *om.* G.
3767 possess G², 1809: have G.   3778 they feel 1809: *om.* G
3768 even ... members G², 1809: of men G.   3781 has ... and G², 1809: *om.* G.

agination, and softened by his affections: it is invigorated also; for the whole courage of his Country is in his breast.

In fact: the Peasant, and he who lives by the fair reward of his manual **3800** labour, has ordinarily a larger proportion of his gratifications dependent upon these thoughts—than, for the most part, men in other classes have. For he is in his person attached, by stronger roots, to the soil of which he is the growth: ▶ his intellectual notices are generally confined within narrower bounds: in him no partial or antipatriotic interests counteract the force of those nobler sym- 3805 pathies and antipathies which he has in right of his Country; and lastly the belt or girdle of his mind has never been stretched to utter relaxation by false philosophy, under a conceit of making it sit more easily and gracefully. These sensations are a social inheritance to him; more important, as he is precluded from luxurious—and those which are usually called refined—enjoyments.   **3810**

Love and admiration must push themselves out towards some quarter: oth- erwise the moral man is killed. Collaterally they advance with great vigour to a certain extent—and they are checked: in that direction, limits hard to pass are perpetually encountered: but upwards and downwards, to ancestry and to posterity, they meet with gladsome help and no obstacles; the tract is intermi- **3815** nable—Perdition to the Tyrant who would wantonly cut off an independent Nation from its inheritance in past ages; turning the tombs and burial-places of the Forefathers into dreaded objects of sorrow, or of shame and reproach, for the Children! Look upon Scotland and Wales: though, by the union of these with England under the same Government (which was effected without **3820** conquest in one instance), ferocious and desolating wars, and more injurious intrigues, and sapping and disgraceful corruptions, have been prevented; and tranquillity, security, and prosperity, and a thousand interchanges of amity, not otherwise attainable, have followed;—yet the flashing eye, and the agitated voice, and all the tender recollections, with which the names of Prince Llewel- 3825 lin and William Wallace are to this day pronounced by the fire-side and on the public road, attest that these substantial blessings have not been purchased without the relinquishment of something most salutary to the moral nature of Man: else the remembrances would not cleave so faithfully to their abiding- place in the human heart. But, if these affections be of general interest, they **3830** are of especial interest to Spain; whose history, written and traditional, is pre- eminently stored with the sustaining food of such affections: and in no country are they more justly and generally prized, or more feelingly cherished.

In the conduct of this argument I am not speaking *to* the humbler ranks of society: it is unnecessary: *they* trust in nature, and are safe. The People of 3835 Madrid, and Corunna, and Ferrol, resisted to the last; from an impulse which, in their hearts, was its own justification. The failure was with those who stood higher in the scale. In fact; the universal rising of the Peninsula, under the pressure and in the face of the most tremendous military power which ever existed, is evidence which cannot be too much insisted upon; and is decisive 3840 upon this subject, as involving a question of virtue and moral sentiment. All ranks were penetrated with one feeling: instantaneous and universal was the acknowledgement. If there have been since individual fallings-off; those have been caused by that kind of after-thoughts which are the bastard offspring of selfishness. The matter was brought home to Spain; and no Spaniard has of- 3845 fended herein with a still conscience.—It is to the worldlings of our own country, and to those who think without carrying their thoughts far enough, that I address myself. Let them know, there is no true wisdom without imagination; no genuine sense ;—that the man, who in this age feels no regret for the ruined honour of other Nations, must be poor in sympathy for the honour of his own 3850 Country; and that, if he be wanting here towards that which circumscribes the whole, he neither has—nor can have— a social regard for the lesser communities which Country includes. Contract the circle, and bring him to his family; such a man cannot protect *that* with dignified love. Reduce his thoughts to his own person; he may defend himself,—what *he* deems his honour; but it is the 3855 *action* of a brave man from the impulse of the brute, or the motive of a coward.

But it is time to recollect that this vindication of human feeling began from an *hypothesis*,—that the *outward* state of the mass of the Spanish people would be improved by the French usurpation. To this I now give an unqualified de- 3860 nial. Let me also observe to those men, for whose infirmity this hypothesis was tolerated,—that the true point of comparison does not lie between what the Spaniards have been under a government of their own, and what they may become under French domination; but between what the Spaniards may do (and, in all likelihood, will do) for themselves, and what Frenchmen would do for 3865 them. But,—waiving this,—the sweeping away of the most splendid monu- ¶ ments of art, and rifling of the public treasuries in the conquered countries, ▶ are an apt prologue to the tragedy which is to ensue. Strange that there are

3854 love *M.Y.* i. 343: loves 1809.

men who can be so besotted as to see, in the decrees of the Usurper concerning feudal tenures and a worn-out inquisition, any other evidence than that of 3870
insidiousness and of a constrained acknowledgement of the strength which he
felt he had to overcome. What avail the lessons of history, if men can be duped
thus? Boons and promises of this kind rank, in trustworthiness, many degrees
lower than amnesties after expelled kings have recovered their thrones. The
fate of subjugated Spain may be expressed in these words, pillage—depres- 3875
sion—and helotism—for the supposed aggrandizement of the imaginary free-
man its master. There would indeed be attempts at encouragement, that there
might be a supply of something to pillage: studied depression there would
be, that there might arise no power of resistance: and lastly helotism;—but of
what kind? that a vain and impious Nation might have slaves, worthier than 3880
itself, for work which its own hands would reject with scorn.

What good can the present arbitrary power confer upon France itself? Let
that point be first settled by those who are inclined to look farther. The earlier
proceedings of the French Revolution no doubt infused health into the country;
something of which survives to this day: but let not the now-existing Tyranny 3885
have the credit of it. France neither owes, nor can owe, to this any rational
obligation. She has seen decrees without end for the increase of commerce and
manufactures; pompous stories without number of harbours, canals, warehous-
es, and bridges: but there is no worse sign in the management of affairs than
when that, which ought to follow as an effect, goes before under a vain notion 3890
that it will be a cause.—Let us attend to the springs of action, and we shall not
be deceived. The works of peace cannot flourish in a country governed by an
intoxicated Despot; the motions of whose distorted benevolence must be still
more pernicious than those of his cruelty. *"I have bestowed; I have created;
I have regenerated; I have been pleased to organize;"*—this is the language 3895
perpetually upon his lips, when his ill-fated activities turn that way. Now commerce, manufactures, agriculture, and all the peaceful arts, are of the nature of
virtues or intellectual powers: they cannot be given; they cannot be stuck in
here and there; they must spring up; they must grow of themselves: they may
be encouraged; they thrive better with encouragement, and delight in it; but the 3900
obligation must have bounds nicely defined; for they are delicate, proud, and
independent. But a Tyrant has no joy in any thing which is endued with such
excellence: he sickens at the sight of it: he turns away from it, as an insult to
his own attributes. We have seen the present ruler of France publicly addressed

as a Providence upon earth; styled, among innumerable other blasphemies, the   **3905**
supreme Ruler of things; and heard him say, in his answers, that he approved
of the language of those who thus saluted him. (*See Appendix E.*)—Oh folly
to think that plans of reason can prosper under such countenance! If this be
the doom of France, what a monster would be the double-headed tyranny of
Spain!   **3910**

It is immutably ordained that power, taken and exercised in contempt of
right, never can bring forth good. Wicked actions indeed have oftentimes happy issues: the benevolent economy of nature counter-working and diverting
evil; and educing finally benefits from injuries, and turning curses to blessings.
But I am speaking of good in a direct course. All good in this order—all moral   **3915**
good—begins and ends in reverence of right. The whole Spanish People are
to be treated not as a mighty multitude with feeling, will, and judgment; not as
rational creatures;—but as objects without reason; in the language of human
law, insuperably laid down not as Persons but as Things. Can good come from   ¶ ▶
this beginning; which, in matter of civil government, is the fountain-head and   **3920**
the main feeder of all the pure evil upon earth? Look at the past history of our
sister Island for the quality of foreign oppression: turn where you will, it is
miserable at best; but, in the case of Spain!—it might be said, engraven upon
the rocks of her own Pyrenees,

> Per me si va nella città dolente;   **3925**
> Per me si va nell' eterno dolore;   ¶ ▶
> Per me si va tra la perduta gente.

So much I have thought it necessary to speak upon this subject; with a
desire to enlarge the views of the short-sighted, to chear the desponding, and
stimulate the remiss. I have been treating of duties which the People of Spain   **3930**
feel to be solemn and imperious; and have referred to springs of action (in the
sensations of love and hatred, of hope and fear),—for promoting the fulfilment of these duties,—which cannot fail. The People of Spain, thus animated,
will move now; and will be prepared to move, upon a favourable summons,
for ages. And it is consolatory to think that,—even if many of the leading   **3935**
persons of that country, in their resistance to France, should not look beyond
the two first objects (viz. riddance of the enemy, and security of national independence);—it is, I say, consolatory to think that the conduct, which can
alone secure either of these ends, leads directly to a free internal Government.
We have therefore both the passions and the reason of these men on our side   **3940**

in two stages of the common journey: and, when this is the case, surely we are justified in expecting some further companionship and support from their reason—acting independent of their partial interests, or in opposition to them. It is obvious that, to the narrow policy of this class (men loyal to the Nation 3945 and to the King, yet jealous of the People), the most dangerous failures, which have hitherto taken place, are to be attributed: for, though from acts of open treason Spain may suffer and has suffered much, these (as I have proved) can never affect the vitals of the cause. But the march of Liberty has begun; and they, who will not lead, may be borne along.—At all events, the road is plain. 3950 Let members for the Cortes be assembled from those Provinces which are not in the possession of the Invader: or at least (if circumstances render this impossible at present) let it be announced that such is the intention, to be realized the first moment when it shall become possible. In the mean while speak boldly to the People: and let the People write and speak boldly. Let the expectation be 3955 familiar to them of open and manly institutions of law and liberty according to knowledge. Let them be universally trained to military exercises, and accustomed to military discipline: let them be drawn together in civic and religious assemblies; and general communication of those assemblies with each other be established through the country: so that there may be one zeal and one life 3960 in every part of it.

With great profit might the Chiefs of the Spanish Nation look back upon the earlier part of the French Revolution. Much, in the outward manner, might there be found worthy of qualified imitation: and, where there is a difference in the inner spirit (and there is a mighty difference!), the advantage is wholly 3965 on the side of the Spaniards.— Why should the People of Spain be dreaded by their leaders? I do not mean the profligate and flagitious leaders; but those who are well-intentioned, yet timid. That there are numbers of this class who have excellent intentions, and are willing to make large personal sacrifices, is clear; for they have put every thing to risk—all their privileges, their hon- 3970 ours, and possessions—by their resistance to the Invader. Why then should they have fears from a quarter—whence their safety must come, if it come at all?—Spain has nothing to dread from Jacobinism. Manufactures and Commerce have there in far less degree than elsewhere—by unnaturally clustering the people together—enfeebled their bodies, inflamed their passions by 3975 intemperance, vitiated from childhood their moral affections, and destroyed their imaginations. Madrid is no enormous city, like Paris; overgrown, and dis-

proportionate; sickening and bowing down, by its corrupt humours, the frame
of the body politic. Nor has the pestilential philosophism of France made any
progress in Spain. No flight of infidel harpies has alighted upon their ground. A **3980**
Spanish understanding is a hold too strong to give way to the meagre tactics of
the "Système de la Nature;" or to the pellets of logic which Condillac has cast ◁ ▶
in the foundry of national vanity, and tosses about at hap-hazard— self-per-
suaded that he is proceeding according to art. The Spaniards are a people with
imagination: and the paradoxical reveries of Rousseau, and the flippancies of **3985**
Voltaire, are plants which will not naturalise in the country of Calderon and
Cervantes. Though bigotry among the Spaniards leaves much to be lamented;
I have proved that the religious habits of the nation must, in a contest of this
kind, be of inestimable service.

Yet further: contrasting the present condition of Spain with that of France **3990**
at the commencement of her revolution, we must not overlook one characteristic; the Spaniards have no division among themselves by and through themselves; no numerous Priesthood—no Nobility—no large body of powerful
Burghers—from passion, interest, and conscience—opposing the end which is
known and felt to be the duty and only honest and true interest of all. Hostil- **3995**
ity, wherever it is found, must proceed from the seductions of the Invader: and
these depend solely upon his power: let that be shattered; and they vanish.

And this once again leads us directly to that immense military force which
the Spaniards have to combat; and which, many think, more than counterbal-
ances every internal advantage. It is indeed formidable: as revolutionary appe- **4000**
tites and energies must needs be; when, among a people numerous as the people
of France, they have ceased to spend themselves in conflicting factions within
the country for objects perpetually changing shape; and are carried out of it
under the strong controul of an absolute despotism, as opportunity invites, for
a definite object—plunder and conquest. It is, I allow, a frightful spectacle—to **4005**
see the prime of a vast nation propelled out of their territory with the rapid
sweep of a horde of Tartars; moving from the impulse of like savage instincts;
and furnished, at the same time, with those implements of physical destruction
which have been produced by science and civilization. Such are the motions
of the French armies; unchecked by any thought which philosophy and the **4010**
spirit of society, progressively humanizing, have called forth—to determine or
regulate the application of the murderous and desolating apparatus with which
by philosophy and science they have been provided. With a like perversion

of things, and the same mischievous reconcilement of forces in their nature
adverse, these revolutionary impulses and these appetites of barbarous (nay, 4015
what is far worse, of barbarized) men are embodied in a new frame of polity;
which possesses the consistency of an ancient Government, without its embarrassments and weaknesses. And at the head of all is the mind of one man who
acts avowedly upon the principle that every thing, which can be done safely by
the supreme power of a state, may be done (See *Appendix F.*); and who has, at 4020
his command, the greatest part of the continent of Europe—to fulfil what yet
remains unaccomplished of his nefarious purposes.

Now it must be obvious to a reflecting mind that every thing which is desperately immoral, being in its constitution monstrous, is of itself perishable:
decay it cannot escape; and, further, it is liable to sudden dissolution: time 4025
would evince this in the instance before us; though not, perhaps, until infinite
and irreparable harm had been done. But, even at present, each of the sources
of this preternatural strength (as far as it is formidable to Europe) has its corre-
sponding seat of weakness; which, were it fairly touched, would manifest itself
immediately.—The power is indeed a Colossus: but, if the trunk be of molten- 4030
brass, the members are of clay; and would fall to pieces upon a shock which ▶
need not be violent. Great Britain, if her energies were properly called forth
and directed, might (as we have already maintained) give this shock. "Magna
parvis obscurantur" was the appropriate motto (the device a Sun Eclipsed)
when Lord Peterborough, with a handful of men opposed to fortified cities and 4035
large armies, brought a great part of Spain to acknowledge a sovereign of the
House of Austria. We have *now* a vast military force; and,—even without a Peterborough or a Marlborough,—at this precious opportunity (when, as is daily
more probable, a large portion of the French force must march northwards to
combat Austria) we might easily, by expelling the French from the Peninsula, 4040
secure an immediate footing there for liberty; and the Pyrenees would then
be shut against them for ever. The disciplined troops of Great Britain might
overthrow the enemy in the field; while the Patriots of Spain, under wise management, would be able to consume him slowly but surely.

For present annoyance his power is, no doubt, mighty: but lib- 4045
erty—in which it originated, and of which it is a depravation—is far
mightier; and the good in human nature is stronger than the evil. The
events of our age indeed have brought this truth into doubt with some
persons: and scrupulous observers have been astonished and have

repined at the sight of enthusiasm, courage, perseverance, and fidelity, put forth **4050**
seemingly to their height,—and all engaged in the furtherance of wrong. But
the minds of men are not always devoted to this bad service as strenuously as ▶
they appear to be. I have personal knowledge that, when the attack was made
which ended in the subjugation of Switzerland, the injustice of the undertaking
was grievously oppressive to many officers of the French army; and damped **4055**
their exertions. Besides, were it otherwise, there is no just cause for despondency in the perverted alliance of these qualities with oppression. The intrinsic
superiority of virtue and liberty, even for politic ends, is not affected by it. If
the tide of success were, by any effort, fairly turned ;—not only a general de-
sertion, as we have the best reason to believe, would follow among the troops **4060**
of the enslaved nations; but a moral change would also take place in the minds
of the native French soldiery. Occasion would be given for the discontented
to break out; and, above all, for the triumph of human nature, it would *then* be
seen whether men fighting in a bad cause,—men without magnanimity, honour, or justice,—could recover; and stand up against champions who by these **4065**
virtues were carried forward in good fortune, as by these virtues in adversity
they had been sustained. As long as guilty actions thrive, guilt is strong: it has
a giddiness and transport of its own; a hardihood not without superstition, as
if Providence were a party to its success. But there is no independent spring
at the heart of the machine which can be relied upon for a support of these **4070**
motions in a change of circumstances. Disaster opens the eyes of conscience;
and, in the minds of men who have been employed in bad actions, defeat and
a feeling of punishment are inseparable.

On the other hand; the power of an unblemished heart and a brave spirit
is shewn, in the events of war, not only among unpractised citizens and peas- **4075**
ants; but among troops in the most perfect discipline. Large bodies of the British army have been several times broken—that is, technically vanquished—in
Egypt, and elsewhere. Yet they, who were conquered as formal soldiers, stood
their ground and became conquerors as men. This paramount efficacy of moral
causes is not willingly admitted by persons high in the profession of arms; **4080**
because it seems to diminish their value in society—by taking from the importance of their art: but the truth is indisputable: and those Generals are as blind
to their own interests as to the interests of their country, who, by submitting to
inglorious treaties or by other misconduct, hazard the breaking down of those

4103 nature, it *M.Y.* i. 545: nature. It 1809.

personal virtues in the men under their command—to which they themselves, **4085**
as leaders, are mainly indebted for the fame which they acquire.

Combine, with this moral superiority inherent in the cause of Freedom,
the endless resources open to a nation which shews constancy in defensive
war; resources which, after a lapse of time, leave the strongest invading army ▶
comparatively helpless. Before six cities, resisting as Saragossa hath resisted 4090
during her two sieges, the whole of the military power of the adversary would
melt away. Without any advantages of natural situation; without fortifications;
without even a ditch to protect them; with nothing better than a mud wall; with
not more than two hundred regular troops; with a slender stock of arms and
ammunition; with a leader inexperienced in war;—the Citizens of Saragossa 4095
began the contest. Enough of what was needful—was produced and created;
and—by courage, fortitude, and skill, rapidly matured—they baffled for sixty
days, and finally repulsed, a large French army with all its equipments. In
the first siege the natural and moral victory were both on their side; nor less
so virtually (though the termination was different) in the second. For, after **4100**
another resistance of nearly three months, they have given the enemy cause
feelingly to say, with Pyrrhus of old,—"A little more of such conquest, and I
am destroyed."

If evidence were wanting of the efficacy of the principles which throughout this Treatise have been maintained,—it has been furnished in overflowing **4105**
measure. A private individual, I had written; and knew not in what manner tens
of thousands were enacting, day after day, the truths which, in the solitude of a
peaceful vale, I was meditating. Most gloriously have the Citizens of Saragossa proved that the true army of Spain, in a contest of this nature, is the whole
people. The same city has also exemplified a melancholy—yea a dismal truth; **4110**
yet consolatory, and full of joy; that,—when a people are called suddenly to
fight for their liberty, and are sorely pressed upon, —their best field of battle is
the floors upon which their children have played; the chambers where the family of each man has slept (his own or his neighbours'); upon or under the roofs
by which they have been sheltered; in the gardens of their recreation; in the **4115**
street, or in the market-place; before the Altars of their Temples; and among
their congregated dwellings—blazing, or up-rooted.

The Government of Spain must never forget Saragossa for a moment. Nothing is wanting, to produce the same effects every where, but a leading mind
such as that city was blessed with. In the latter contest this has been proved; **4120**

for Saragossa contained, at that time, bodies of men from almost all parts of
Spain. The narrative of those two sieges should be the manual of every Spaniard: he may add to it the ancient stories of Numantia and Saguntum: let him
sleep upon the book as pillow; and, if he be a devout adherent to the religion
of his country, let him wear it in his bosom for his crucifix to rest upon.   4125

Beginning from these invincible feelings, and the principles of justice which
are involved in them; let nothing be neglected, which policy and prudence dictate, for rendering subservient to the same end those qualities in human nature
which are indifferent or even morally bad; and for making the selfish propensi-
ties contribute to the support of wise arrangements, civil and military.—Per- 4130
haps there never appeared in the field more steady soldiers—troops which it
would have been more difficult to conquer with such knowledge of the art of
war as then existed—than those commanded by Fairfax and Cromwell: let us
see from what root these armies grew. "Cromwell," says Sir Philip Warwick,
"made use of the zeal and credulity of these persons" (that is—such of the 4135
people as had, in the author's language, the fanatic humour); "teaching them
(as they too readily taught themselves) that they engaged for God, when he
led them against his vicegerent the King. And, where this opinion met with
a natural courage, it made them bolder—and too often crueller; and, where
natural courage wanted, zeal supplied its place. And at first they chose rather to 4140
die than flee; and custom removed fear of danger: and afterwards—finding the
sweet of good pay, and of opulent plunder, and of preferment suitable to activity and merit—the lucrative part made gain seem to them a natural member
of godliness. And I cannot here omit" (continues the author) "a character of
this army which General Fairfax gave unto myself; when, complimenting him 4145
with the regularity and temperance of his army, he told me, The best common
soldiers he had—came out of our army and from the garrisons he had taken in.
So (says he) I found you had made them good soldiers; and I have made them
good men. But, upon this whole matter, it may appear" (concludes the author)
"that the spirit of discipline of warr may beget that spirit of discipline which 4150
even Solomon describes as the spirit of wisdom and obedience." Apply this
process to the growth and maturity of an armed force in Spain. In making a
comparison of the two cases; to the sense of the insults and injuries which, as
Spaniards and as human Beings, they have received and have to dread,—and
to the sanctity which an honourable resistance has already conferred upon 4155
their misfortunes,—add the devotion of that people to their religion as Catho-

lics;—and it will not be doubted that the superiority of the radical feeling is, on their side, immeasurable. There is (I cannot refrain from observing) in the Catholic religion, and in the character of its Priesthood especially, a source of animation and fortitude in desperate struggles—which may be relied upon as 4160 one of the best hopes of the cause. The narrative of the first siege of Zaragoza, ¶ ▶ lately published in this country, and which I earnestly recommend to the reader's perusal, informs us that,—"In every part of the town where the danger was most imminent, and the French the most numerous,—was Padre St. Iago Sass, curate of a parish in Zaragoza. As General Palafox made his rounds through the 4165 city, he often beheld Sass alternately playing the part of a Priest and a Soldier; sometimes administering the sacrament to the dying; and, at others, fighting in the most determined manner against the enemies of his country.—He was found so serviceable in inspiring the people with religious sentiments, and in leading them on to danger, that the General has placed him in a situation where 4170 both his piety and courage may continue to be as useful as before; and he is now both Captain in the army, and Chaplain to the commander-in-chief."

The reader will have been reminded, by the passage above cited from Sir Philip Warwick's memoirs, of the details given, in the earlier part of this tract, concerning the course which (as it appeared to me) might with advantage be 4175 pursued in Spain: I must request him to combine those details with such others as have since been given: the whole would have been further illustrated, if I could sooner have returned to the subject; but it was first necessary to examine the grounds of hope in the grand and disinterested passions, and in the laws of universal morality. My attention has therefore been chiefly directed to these 4180 laws and passions; in order to elevate, in some degree, the conceptions of my readers; and with a wish to rectify and fix, in this fundamental point, their judgements. The truth of the general reasoning will, I have no doubt, be acknowledged by men of uncorrupted natures and practised understandings; and the conclusion, which I have repeatedly drawn, will be acceded to; namely, 4185 that no resistance can be prosperous which does not look, for its chief support, to these principles and feelings. If, however, there should be men who still fear (as I have been speaking of things under combinations which are transitory) that the action of these powers cannot be sustained; to such I answer that,—if there be a necessity that it should be sustained at the point to which it first 4190 ascended, or should recover that height if there have been a fall,—nature will

4163 where *Errata*: were 1809.

provide for that necessity. The cause is in Tyranny: and that will again call forth
the effect out of its holy retirements. Oppression, its own blind and predestined
enemy, has poured this of blessedness upon Spain,—that the enormity of the
outrages, of which she has been the victim, has created an object of love and   4195
of hatred—of apprehensions and of wishes—adequate (if that be possible) to
the utmost demands of the human spirit. The heart that serves in this cause, if it
languish, must languish from its own constitutional weakness; and not through
want of nourishment from without. But it is a belief propagated in books, and
which passes currently among talking men as part of their familiar wisdom,   4200
that the hearts of the many *are* constitutionally weak; that they *do* languish; and ◀ ▶
are slow to answer to the requisitions of things. I entreat those, who are in this
delusion, to look behind them and about them for the evidence of experience.
Now this, rightly understood, not only gives no support to any such belief; but
proves that the truth is in direct opposition to it. The history of all ages; tumults   4205
after tumults; wars, foreign or civil, with short or with no breathing-spaces,
from generation to generation; wars—why and wherefore? yet with courage,
with perseverance, with self-sacrifice, with enthusiasm—with cruelty driving
forward the cruel man from its own terrible nakedness, and attracting the more
benign by the accompaniment of some shadow which seems to sanctify it; the   4210
senseless weaving and interweaving of factions—vanishing and reviving and
piercing each other like the Northern Lights; public commotions, and those in
the bosom of the individual; the long calenture of fancy to which the Lover is
subject; the blast, like the blast of the desert, which sweeps perennially through
a frightful solitude of its own making in the mind of the Gamester; the slowly   4215
quickening but ever quickening descent of appetite down which the Miser is
propelled; the agony and cleaving oppression of grief; the ghost-like haunt-
ings of shame; the incubus of revenge; the life-distemper of ambition;—these
inward existences, and the visible and familiar occurrences of daily life in
every town and village; the patient curiosity and contagious acclamations of   4220
the multitude in the streets of the city and within the walls of the theatre; a procession, or a rural dance; a hunting, or a horse-race; a flood, or a fire; rejoicing
and ringing of bells for an unexpected gift of good fortune, or the coming of
a foolish heir to his estate;—these demonstrate incontestibly that the passions
of men (I mean, the soul of sensibility in the heart of man)—in all quarrels, in   4225
all contests, in all quests, in all delights, in all employments which are either

4213 of fancy *M.Y.* i. 343: *om.* 1809.

sought by men or thrust upon them—do immeasurably transcend their objects. The true sorrow of humanity consists in this;—not that the mind of man fails; but that the course and demands of action and of life so rarely correspond with the dignity and intensity of human desires: and hence that, which is slow to **4230** languish, is too easily turned aside and abused. But—with the remembrance of what has been done, in the face of the interminable evils which are threat- ened—a Spaniard can never have cause to complain of this, while a follower of the Tyrant remains in arms upon the Peninsula.

Here then they, with whom I *hope*, take their stand. There is a spiritual **4235** community binding together the living and the dead; the good, the brave, and the wise, of all ages. We would not be rejected from this community; and therefore do we hope. We look forward with erect mind, thinking and feeling: it is an obligation of duty: take away the sense of it, and the moral being would die within us.—Among the most illustrious of that fraternity, whose encour- **4240** agement we participate, is an Englishman who sacrificed his life in devotion to a cause bearing a stronger likeness to this than any recorded in history. It is the elder Sidney—a deliverer and defender, whose name I have before uttered with reverence; who, treating of the war in the Netherlands against Philip the Second, thus writes: "If her Majesty," says he, "were the fountain; I wold fear, 4245 considering what I daily find, that we shold wax dry. But she is but a means ▶ whom God useth. And I know not whether I am deceaved; but I am fully per- suaded, that, if she shold withdraw herself, other springs wold rise to help this action. For, methinks, I see the great work indeed in hand against the abusers of the world; wherein it is no greater fault to have confidence in man's power, **4250** than it is too hastily to despair of God's work."

The pen, which I am guiding, has stopped in my hand; and I have scarcely power to proceed.—I will lay down one principle; and then shall contentedly withdraw from the sanctuary.

When wickedness acknowledges no limit but the extent of her power, and 4255 advances with aggravated impatience like a devouring fire; the only worthy or adequate opposition is—that of virtue submitting to no circumscription of her endeavours save that of her rights, and aspiring from the impulse of her own ethereal zeal. The Christian exhortation for the individual is here the precept for nations—"Be ye therefore perfect; even as your Father, which is in Heaven, 4260 is perfect."

4249 abusers *M.Y.* i. 343: abuses 1809.

Upon a future occasion (if what has been now said meets with attention) I
shall point out the steps by which the practice of life may be lifted up towards ▶
these high precepts. I shall have to speak of the child as well as the man; for
with the child, or the youth, may we begin with more hope: but I am not in **4265**
despair even for the man; and chiefly from the inordinate evils of our time.
There are (as I shall attempt to shew) tender and subtile ties by which these
principles, that love to soar in the pure region, are connected with the ground-
nest in which they were fostered and from which they take their flight.

The outermost and all-embracing circle of benevolence has inward con- **4270**
centric circles which, like those of the spider's web, are bound together by
links, and rest upon each other; making one frame, and capable of one tremor;
circles narrower and narrower, closer and closer, as they lie more near to the
centre of self from which they proceeded, and which sustains the whole. The
order of life does not require that the sublime and disinterested feelings should **4275**
have to trust long to their own unassisted power. Nor would the attempt consist
either with their dignity or their humility. They condescend, and they adopt:
they know the time of their repose; and the qualities which are worthy of being admitted into their service—of being their inmates, their companions, or
their substitutes. I shall strive to shew that these principles and movements of **4280**
wisdom—so far from towering above the support of prudence, or rejecting
the rules of experience, for the better conduct of those multifarious actions
which are alike necessary to the attainment of ends good or bad—do instinc-
tively prompt the sole prudence which cannot fail. The higher mode of being
does not exclude, but necessarily includes, the lower; the intellectual does not **4285**
exclude, but necessarily includes, the sentient; the sentient, the animal; and
the animal, the vital—to its lowest degrees. Wisdom is the hidden root which
thrusts forth the stalk of prudence; and these uniting feed and uphold "the
bright consummate flower"—National Happiness—the end, the conspicuous
crown, and ornament of the whole.   **4290**

I have announced the feelings of those who hope: yet one word more to
those who despond. And first; *he* stands upon a hideous precipice (and it will
be the same with all who may succeed to him and his iron sceptre)—he who
has outlawed himself from society by proclaiming, with word and act, that he
acknowledges no mastery but power. This truth must be evident to all who **4295**

4294 word and act *M.Y.* i. 545: act and deed
    1809.

breathe—from the dawn of childhood, till the last gleam of twilight is lost in the darkness of dotage. But take the tyrant as he is, in the plenitude of his supposed strength. The vast country of Germany, in spite of the rusty but too strong fetters of corrupt princedoms and degenerate nobility,— Germany—with its citizens, its peasants, and its philosophers—will not lie quiet under the weight **4300** of injuries which has been heaped upon it. There is a sleep, but no death, among the mountains of Switzerland. Florence, and Venice, and Genoa, and Rome,—have their own poignant recollections, and a majestic train of glory in past ages. The stir of emancipation may again be felt at the mouths as well as at the sources of the Rhine. Poland perhaps will not be insensible; Kosciusko **4305** and his compeers may not have bled in vain. Nor is Hungarian loyalty to be ▶ overlooked. And, for Spain itself, the territory is wide: let it be overrun: the torrent will weaken as the water spreads. And, should all resistance disappear, be not daunted: extremes meet: and how often do hope and despair almost touch each other—though unconscious of their neighbourhood, because their **4310** faces are turned different ways! yet, in a moment, the one shall vanish; and the other begin a career in the fulness of her joy.

But we may turn from these thoughts: for the present juncture is most auspicious. Upon liberty, and upon liberty alone, can there be permanent dependence; but a temporary relief will be given by the share which Austria is about **4315** to take in the war. Now is the time for a great and decisive effort; and, if Britain does not avail herself of it, her disgrace will be indelible, and the loss infinite. If there be ground of hope in the crimes and errors of the enemy, he has furnished enough of both: but imbecility in his opponents (above all, the imbecility of the British) has hitherto preserved him from the natural consequences of his **4320** ignorance, his meanness of mind, his transports of infirm fancy, and his guilt. Let us hasten to redeem ourselves. The field is open for a commanding British military force to clear the Peninsula of the enemy, while the better half of his power is occupied with Austria. For the South of Spain, where the first effort of regeneration was made, is yet free. Saragossa (which, by a truly efficient **4325** British army, might have been relieved) has indeed fallen; but leaves little to regret; for consummate have been her fortitude and valour. The citizens and soldiers of Saragossa are to be envied: for they have completed the circle of their duty; they have done all that could be wished—all that could be prayed for. And, though the cowardly malice of the enemy gives too much reason to **4330** fear that their leader Palafox (with the fate of Toussaint) will soon be among

the dead, it is the high privilege of men who have performed what he has
performed—that they cannot be missed; and, in moments of weakness only,
can they be lamented: their actions represent them every where and for ever.
Palafox has taken his place as parent and ancestor of innumerable heroes.   **4335**

Oh! that the surviving chiefs of the Spanish people may prove worthy of
their situation! With such materials,—their labour would be pleasant, and their
success certain. But—though heads of a nation venerable for antiquity, and
having good cause to preserve with reverence the institutions of their elder
forefathers—they must not be indiscriminately afraid of new things. It is their **4340**
duty to restore the good which has fallen into disuse; and also to create, and to
adopt. Young scions of polity must be engrafted on the time-worn trunk: a new
fortress must be reared upon the ancient and living rock of justice. Then would
it be seen, while the superstructure stands inwardly immoveable, in how short
a space of time the ivy and wild plant would climb up from the base, and clasp **4345**
the naked walls; the storms, which could not shake, would weather-stain; and
the edifice, in the day of its youth, would appear to be one with the rock upon
which it was planted, and to grow out of it.

But let us look to ourselves. Our offences are unexpiated: and, wanting
light, we want strength. With reference to this guilt and to this deficiency, **4350**
and to my own humble efforts towards removing both, I shall conclude with
the words of a man of disciplined spirit, who withdrew from the too busy
world—not out of indifference to its welfare, or to forget its concerns—but
retired for wider compass of eye-sight, that he might comprehend and see in
just proportions and relations; knowing above all that he, who hath not first **4355**
made himself master of the horizon of his own mind, must look beyond it
only to be deceived. It is Petrarch who thus writes: "Hæc dicerem, et quicquid
in rem praesentem et indignatio dolorque dictarent; nisi obtorpuisse animos, ◀ ▶
actumque de rebus nostris, crederem. Nempe, qui aliis iter rectum ostendere
solebamus, nunc (quod exitio proximum est) coeci coecis ducibus per abrupta **4360**
rapimur; alienoque circumvolvimur exemplo; quid velimus, nescii. Nam (ut
coeptum exequar) totum hoc malum, seu nostrum proprium seu potius om-
nium gentium commune, IGNORATIO FINIS facit. Nesciunt inconsulti homines
quid agant: ideo quicquid agunt, mox ut coeperint, vergit in nauseam. Hinc ille
discursus sine termino; hinc, medio calle, discordie; et, ante exitum, DAMNATA **4365**
PRINCIPIA; et expleti nihil."

4366 expleti *M. Y.* i. 343: explete 1809.

As an act of respect to the English reader—I shall add, to the same purpose, the words of our own Milton; who, contemplating our ancestors in his day, thus speaks of them and their errors:— "Valiant, indeed, and prosperous to win a field; but, to know the end and reason of winning, injudicious and unwise. Hence did their victories prove as fruitless, as their losses dangerous; and left them still languishing under the same grievances that men suffer conquered. Which was indeed unlikely to go otherwise; unless men more than vulgar bred up in the knowledge of ancient and illustrious deeds, invincible against many and vain titles, impartial to friendships and relations, had conducted their affairs."

THE END

[Wordsworth's] APPENDICES

A (see text page 124).

WHEN this passage was written, there had appeared only unauthorized ac- ▶
counts of the Board of Inquiry's proceedings. Neither from these however,
nor from the official report of the Board (which has been since published), is
any satisfactory explanation to be gained on this question—or indeed on any 5
other question of importance. All, which is to be collected from them, is this:
the Portuguese General, it appears, offered to unite his whole force with the
British on the single condition that they should be provisioned from the British
stores; and, accordingly, rests his excuse for not co-operating on the refusal
of Sir Arthur Wellesley to comply with this condition. Sir A. W. denies the 10
validity of his excuse; and, more than once, calls it a *pretence*; declaring that,
in his belief, Gen. Freire's real motive for not joining was—a mistrust in the
competence of the British to appear in the field against the French. This however is mere surmise; and therefore cannot have much weight with those who
sincerely sought for satisfaction on this point: moreover, it is a surmise of the 15
individual whose justification rests on making it appear that the difficulty did
not arise with himself; and it is right to add, that the only *fact* produced goes
to discredit this surmise; viz, that Gen. Freire did, without any delay, furnish
the whole number of troops which Sir Arthur engaged to feed. However the
Board exhibited so little anxiety to be satisfied on this point, that no positive 20
information was gained.

A reference being here first made to the official report of the Board of
Inquiry; I shall make use of the opportunity which it offers to lay before the
reader an outline of that Board's proceedings; from which it will appear how
far the opinion—pronounced, by the national voice, upon the transactions in 25
Portugal—ought, in sound logic, to be modified by any part of those proceedings.

We find in the warrant under which the Board of Inquiry was to act, and
which defined its powers, that an inquiry was to be made into the conditions ▶
of the "armistice and convention; and into all the causes and circumstances, 30
whether arising from the operations of the British army, or otherwise, which
led to them."

Whether answers to the charges of the people of England were made possible by the provisions of this warrant—and, secondly, whether even these provisions have been satisfied by the Board of Inquiry—will best appear by 40 involving those charges in four questions, according to the following scale, which supposes a series of concessions impossible to those who think the nation justified in the language held on the transactions in Portugal.

1. Considering the perfidy with which the French army had entered Portugal; the enormities committed by it during its occupation of that country; the 45 vast military power of which that army was a part, and the use made of that power by its master; the then existing spirit of the Spanish, Portuguese, and British nations; in a word, considering the especial nature of the service, and the individual character of this war;—was it lawful for the British army, under any conceivable circumstances, so long as it had the liberty of re-embarking, 50 to make *any conceivable* convention? i.e. Was the negative evil of a total failure in every object for which it had been sent to Portugal of worse tendency than the positive evil of acknowledging in the French army a fair title to the privileges of an honourable enemy by consenting to a mode of treaty which (in its very name, implying a reciprocation of concession and respect) must be 55 under any limitations as much more indulgent than an ordinary capitulation, as that again must (in its severest form) be more indulgent than the only favour which the French marauders could presume upon obtaining—viz. permission to surrender at discretion?

To this question the reader need not be told that these pages give a naked 60 unqualified denial; and that to establish the reasonableness of that denial is one of their main purposes: but, for the benefit of the men accused, let it be supposed granted; and then the second question will be

2. Was it lawful for the English army, in the case of its being reduced to the supposed dilemma of either re-embarking or making *some* convention, to 65 make that *specifical convention* which it did make at Cintra?

This is of necessity and *à fortiori* denied; and it has been proved that neither to this, nor any other army, could it be lawful to make such a convention—not merely under the actual but under any conceivable circumstances; let however this too, on behalf of the parties accused, be granted; and then the third ques- 70 tion will be

3. Was the English Army reduced to that dilemma?

4. Finally, this also being conceded (which not even the Gener-

als have dared to say), it remains to ask by whose and by what misconduct did an army—confessedly the arbiter of its own movements and 75
plans at the opening of the campaign—forfeit that free agency—either to the extent of the extremity supposed, or of any approximation to
that extremity?

Now of these four possible questions in the minds of all those who condemn the convention of Cintra, it is obvious that the King's warrant supposes 80
only the three latter to exist (since, though it allows inquiry to be made into the
individual convention, it no where questions the tolerability of a convention
in genere); and it is no less obvious that the Board, acting under that warrant,
has noticed only the last—i.e. by what series of military movements the army
was brought into a state of difficulty which justified a convention (the Board 85
taking for granted throughout—1st, That such a state could exist; 2ndly, That
it actually did exist; and 3rdly, That—if it existed, and accordingly justified
some imaginable convention—it must therefore of necessity justify *this* convention).

Having thus shewn that it is on the last question only that the nation could, 90
in deference to the Board of Inquiry, surrender or qualify any opinion which
it had previously given—let us ask what answer is gained, from the proceedings of that Board, to the charge involved even in this last question (premising
however—first—that this charge was never explicitly made by the public, or
at least was enunciated only in the form of a conjecture—and 2ndly that the 95
answer to it is collected chiefly from the depositions of the parties accused)?
Now the whole sum of their answer amounts to no more than this—that, in the ▶
opinion of some part of the English staff, an opportunity was lost on the 21st
of exchanging the comparatively slow process of reducing the French army by
siege for the brilliant and summary one of a *coup-de-main*.   100

This opportunity, be it observed, was offered only by Gen. Junot's presumption in quitting his defensive positions, and coming out to meet the English army in the field; so that it was an advantage so much over and above
what might fairly have been calculated upon: at any rate, if *this* might have
been looked for, still the accident of battle, by which a large part of the French 105
army was left in a situation to be cut off, (to the loss of which advantage Sir ▶
A. Wellesley ascribes the necessity of a convention) could surely never have
been anticipated; and therefore the British army was, even after that loss, in as
prosperous a state as it had from the first any right to expect. Hence it is to be

inferred, that Sir A. W. must have entered on this campaign with a predetermi- 110
nation to grant a convention in any case, excepting in one single case which he
knew to be in the gift of only very extraordinary good fortune. With respect to
him, therefore, the charges—pronounced by the national voice—are not only
confirmed, but greatly aggravated. Further, with respect to the General who
superseded him, all those—who think that such an opportunity of terminating 115
the campaign was really offered, and, through his refusal to take advantage of
it, lost—are compelled to suspect in him a want of military skill, or a wilful
sacrifice of his duty to the influence of personal rivalry, accordingly as they
shall interpret his motives.

The whole which we gain therefore from the Board of Inquiry is—that 120
what we barely suspected is ripened into certainty—and that on all, which we
assuredly knew and declared without needing that any tribunal should lend us
its sanction, no effort has been made at denial, or disguise, or palliation.

Thus much for the proceedings of the Board of Inquiry, upon which their
decision was to be grounded. As to the decision itself, it declares that no further 125
military proceedings are necessary; "because" (say the members of the board),
"however some of us may differ in our sentiments respecting the fitness of the ▶
convention in the relative situation of the two armies, it is our unanimous declaration that unquestionable zeal and firmness appear throughout to have been
exhibited by Generals Sir H. Dalrymple, Sir H. Burrard, and Sir A. Wellesley." 130
In consequence of this decision, the Commander-in-Chief addressed a letter to
the Board—reminding them that, though the words of his Majesty's warrant
expressly enjoin that the *conditions* of the Armistice and Convention should
be strictly examined and reported upon, they have altogether neglected to give
any opinion upon those conditions. They were therefore called upon then to 135
declare their opinion, whether an armistice was adviseable; and (if so) whether
the terms of *that* armistice were such as ought to be agreed upon;—and to declare, in like manner, whether a convention was adviseable; and (if so) whether
the terms of *that* convention were such as ought to have been agreed upon.

To two of these questions—viz. those which relate to the particular armi- 140
stice and convention made by the British Generals—the members of the Board
(still persevering in their blindness to the other two which express doubt as to
the lawfulness of *any* armistice or convention) severally return answers which
convey an approbation of the armistice and convention by four members, a
disapprobation of the convention by the remaining three, and further a disap- 145

probation of the armistice by one of those three.

Now it may be observed—first—that, even if the investigation had not been a public one, it might have reasonably been concluded, from the circumstance of the Board having omitted to report any opinion concerning the terms of the armistice and the convention, that those terms had not occupied enough of its 150 attention to justify the Board in giving any opinion upon them—whether of approbation or disapprobation; and, secondly,—this conclusion, which might have been made *à priori*, is confirmed by the actual fact that no examination or inquiry of this kind appears throughout the report of its proceedings: and there-fore any opinion subsequently given, in consequence of the requisition of the 155 Commander-in-Chief, can lay claim to no more authority upon these points—than the opinion of the same men, if they had never sat in a public court upon this question. In this condition are all the members, whether they approve or disapprove of the convention. And with respect to the three who disapprove of the convention,—over and above the general impropriety of having, under 160 these circumstances, pronounced a verdict at all in the character of members of that Board—they are subject to an especial charge of inconsistency in hav-ing given such an opinion, in their second report, as renders nugatory that which they first pronounced. For the reason—assigned, in their first report, for deeming no further military proceedings necessary—is because it appears that 165 unquestionable *zeal and firmness* were exhibited throughout by the several General Officers; and the reason—assigned by those three who condemn the convention—is that the Generals did not insist upon the terms to which they were entitled; that is (in direct opposition to their former opinions), the Gener-als shewed a want of firmness and zeal. If then the Generals were acquitted, in 170 the first case, solely upon the ground of having displayed firmness and zeal; a confessed want of firmness and zeal, in the second case, implies conversely a ground of censure—rendering (in the opinions of these three members) further military proceedings absolutely necessary. They,—who are most aware of the unconstitutional frame of this Court or Board, and of the perplexing situation 175 in which its members must have found themselves placed,—will have the least difficulty in excusing this inconsistency: it is however to be regretted; par-ticularly in the instance of the Earl of Moira;—who, disapproving both of the Convention and Armistice, has assigned for that disapprobation unanswerable reasons drawn—not from hidden sources, unapproachable except by judicial 180 investigation—but from facts known to all the world.—The reader will excuse this long note; to which however I must add one word:—Is it not strange that, in the general decision of the Board, zeal and firmness—nakedly considered, and without question of their union with judgment and such other qualities as can alone give them any value—should be assumed as sufficient grounds 185 on which to rest the acquittal of men lying under a charge of military delinquency?

B (*see text page 128*).

It is not necessary to add, that one of these fears was removed by the actual 190 landing of ten thousand men, under Sir J. Moore, pending the negociation: and ▶ yet no change in the terms took place in consequence. This was an important circumstance; and, of itself, determined two of the members of the Board of Inquiry to disapprove of the convention: such an accession entitling Sir H. Dalrymple (and, of course, making it his duty) to insist on more favourable 195 terms. But the argument is complete without it.

C (*see text page 131*)).

I was unwilling to interrupt the reader upon a slight occasion; but I cannot 200 refrain from adding here a word or two by way of comment.—I have said at page [282], speaking of Junot's army, that the British were to encounter the same men, &c. Sir Arthur Wellesley, before the Board of Inquiry, disallowed this supposition; affirming that Junot's army had not then reached Spain, nor could be there for some time. Grant this: was it not stipulated that a messenger 205 should be sent off, immediately after the conclusion of the treaty, to Buonaparte—apprising him of its terms, and when he might expect his troops; and would not this enable him to hurry forward forces to the Spanish frontiers, and to bring them into action—knowing that these troops of Junot's would be ready to support him? What did it matter whether the British were again 210 to measure swords with these identical men; whether these men were even to appear again upon Spanish ground? It was enough, that, if these did not, others would—who could not have been brought to that service, but that these had been released and were doing elsewhere some other service for their master; enough that every thing was provided by the British to land them as near the 215 Spanish frontier (and as speedily) as they could desire.

D (*see text page 161*).

This attempt, the reader will recollect, is not new to our country;—it was ac- 220
complished, at one æra of our history, in that memorable act of an English ▶
Parliament, which made it unlawful for any man to ask his neighbour to join
him in a petition for redress of grievances; and which thus denied the people
"the benefit of tears and prayers to their own infamous deputies!" For the de- 225
plorable state of England and Scotland at that time—see the annals of Charles
the Second, and his successor.—We must not forget however that to this state
of things, as the cause of those measures which the nation afterwards resorted
to, we are originally indebted for the blessing of the Bill of Rights.

E (*see text page 209*).

I allude here more especially to an address presented to Buonaparte (October 27th,
1808) by the deputies of the new departments of the kingdom of Italy; from which
address, as given in the English journals, the following passages are extracted:—

"In the necessity, in which you are to overthrow—to destroy—to disperse
your enemies as the wind dissipates the dust, you are not an exterminating an- 235
gel; but you are the being that extends his thoughts— that measures the face of
the earth—to re-establish universal happiness upon better and surer bases."

      *   *   *   *   *   *

"We are the interpreters of a million of souls at the extremity of your kingdom of Italy."—"Deign, *Sovereign Master of all Things*, to hear (as we doubt 240
not you will)" &c.

The answer begins thus:—

"I *applaud* the sentiments you express in the name of my people of
Musora, Metauro, and Tronto."

245

F (*see text page 212*).

This principle, involved in so many of his actions, Buonaparte has of late explicitly avowed: the instances are numerous: it will be sufficient, in this place,
to allege one—furnished by his answer to the address cited in the last note:—

"I am particularly attached to your Archbishop of Urbino: that prelate, animated with the true faith, repelled with indignation the advice— and braved

the menaces—of those who wished to confound the affairs of Heaven, which **250**
never change, with the affairs of this world, which are modified according to
circumstances of *force* and policy."

SUSPENSION OF ARMS

Agreed upon between Lieutenant-General SIR ARTHUR WELLESLEY, K.B. *on
the one part, and the General-of-Division* KELLERMANN *on the other part;* **255**
*each having powers from the respective Generals of the French and English
Armies.*

Head-Quarters of the English Army, August 22, 1808.

ARTICLE I. There shall be, from this date, a Suspension of Arms between
the armies of his Britannic Majesty, and his Imperial and Royal Majesty, Na- **260**
poleon I. for the purpose of negociating a Convention for the evacuation of
Portugal by the French army.

ART. II. The Generals-in-Chief of the two armies, and the Commander-
in-Chief of the British fleet at the entrance of the Tagus, will appoint a day to
assemble, on such part of the coast as shall be judged convenient, to negociate **265**
and conclude the said Convention.

ART. III. The river of Sirandre shall form the line of demarkation to be
established between the two armies; Torres Vedras shall not be occupied by
either.

ART. IV. The General-in-Chief of the English army undertakes to include **270**
the Portuguese armies in this suspension of arms; and for them the line of demarkation shall be established from Leyria to Thomar.

ART. V. It is agreed provisionally that the French army shall not, in any
case, be considered as prisoners of war; that all the individuals who compose
it shall be transported to France with their arms and baggage, and the whole of **275**
their private property, from which nothing shall be exempted.

ART. VI. No individual, whether Portuguese, or of a nation allied to France,
or French, shall be called to account for his political conduct; their respective
property shall be protected; and they shall be at liberty to withdraw from Por-

tugal, within a limited time, with their property. 280

ART. VII. The neutrality of the port of Lisbon shall be recognised for the Russian fleet: that is to say, that, when the English army or fleet shall be in possession of the city and port, the said Russian fleet shall not be disturbed during its stay; nor stopped when it wishes to sail; nor pursued, when it shall sail, until after the time fixed by the maritime law. 285

ART. VIII. All the artillery of French calibre, and also the horses of the cavalry, shall be transported to France.

ART. IX. This suspension of arms shall not be broken without forty- eight hours' previous notice.

Done and agreed upon between the above-named Generals, the day and 290 year above-mentioned.

(Signed)   ARTHUR WELLESLEY.
KELLERMANN, General-of-Division.

Additional Article.

The garrisons of the places occupied by the French army shall be included in 295 the present Convention, if they have not capitulated before the 25th instant.

(Signed)   ARTHUR WELLESLEY.
KELLERMANN, General-of-Division.
(A true Copy.)

A. J. DALRYMPLE, Captain, Military Secretary.

300

DEFINITIVE CONVENTION FOR THE EVACUATION OF PORTUGAL BY THE FRENCH ARMY

The Generals commanding in chief the British and French armies in Portugal, having determined to negociate and conclude a treaty for the evacuation of Portugal by the French troops, on the basis of the agreement entered into on 305 the 22d instant for a suspension of hostilities, have appointed the under-mentioned officers to negociate the same in their names; viz.—on the part of the General-in-Chief of the British army, Lieutenant-Colonel MURRAY, Quarter-

Master General; and, on the part of the General-in-Chief of the French army, Monsieur KELLERMANN, General-of-Division; to whom they have given au- 310 thority to negociate and conclude a convention to that effect, subject to their ratification respectively, and to that of the Admiral commanding the British fleet at the entrance of the Tagus.

Those two officers, after exchanging their full powers, have agreed upon the articles which follow: 315

ARTICLE I. All the places and forts in the kingdom of Portugal, occupied by the French troops, shall be delivered up to the British army in the state in which they are at the period of the signature of the present Convention.

ART. II. The French troops shall evacuate Portugal with their arms and baggage; they shall not be considered as prisoners of war; and, on their arrival in 320 France, they shall be at liberty to serve.

ART. III. The English Government shall furnish the means of conveyance for the French army; which shall be disembarked in any of the ports of France between Rochefort and L'Orient, inclusively.

ART. IV. The French army shall carry with it all its artillery, of French 325 calibre, with the horses belonging to it, and the tumbrils supplied with sixty rounds per gun. All other artillery, arms, and ammunition, as also the military and naval arsenals, shall be given up to the British army and navy in the state in which they may be at the period of the ratification of the Convention.

ART. V. The French army shall carry with it all its equipments, and all 330 that is comprehended under the name of property of the army; that is to say, its military chest, and carriages attached to the Field Commissariat and Field Hospitals; or shall be allowed to dispose of such part of the same, on its account, as the Commander-in-Chief may judge it unnecessary to embark. In like manner, all individuals of the army shall be at liberty to dispose of their private 335 property of every description; with full security hereafter for the purchasers.

ART. VI. The cavalry are to embark their horses; as also the Generals and other officers of all ranks. It is, however, fully understood, that the means of conveyance for horses, at the disposal of the British Commanders, are very limited; some additional conveyance may be procured in the port of Lisbon; 340 the number of horses to be embarked by the troops shall not exceed six hundred; and the number embarked by the Staff shall not exceed two hundred. At all events every facility will be given to the French army to dispose of the horses, belonging to it, which cannot be embarked.

ART. VII. In order to facilitate the embarkation, it shall take place in three 345
divisions; the last of which will be principally composed of the garrisons of
the places, of the cavalry, the artillery, the sick, and the equipment of the army.
The first division shall embark within seven days of the date of the ratification;
or sooner, if possible.

ART. VIII. The garrison of Elvas and its forts, and of Peniche and Palmela, 350
will be embarked at Lisbon; that of Almaida at Oporto, or the nearest harbour.
They will be accompanied on their march by British Commissaries, charged
with providing for their subsistence and accommodation.

ART. IX. All the sick and wounded, who cannot be embarked with the
troops, are entrusted to the British army. They are to be taken care of, whilst 355
they remain in this country, at the expence of the British Government; under
the condition of the same being reimbursed by France when the final evacuation is effected. The English government will provide for their return to France;
which shall take place by detachments of about one hundred and fifty (or two
hundred) men at a time. A sufficient number of French medical officers shall 360
be left behind to attend them.

ART. X. As soon as the vessels employed to carry the army to France shall
have disembarked it in the harbours specified, or in any other of the ports of
France to which stress of weather may force them, every facility shall be given
them to return to England without delay; and security against capture until 365
their arrival in a friendly port.

ART. XI. The French army shall be concentrated in Lisbon, and within a
distance of about two leagues from it. The English army will approach within
three leagues of the capital; and will be so placed as to leave about one league
between the two armies. 370

ART. XII. The forts of St. Julien, the Bugio, and Cascais, shall be occupied
by the British troops on the ratification of the Convention. Lisbon and its citadel,
together with the forts and batteries, as far as the Lazaretto or Tarfuria on one side,
and fort St. Joseph on the other, inclusively, shall be given up on the embarkation
of the second division; as shall also the harbour; and all armed vessels in it of every 375
description, with their rigging, sails, stores, and ammunition. The fortresses of Elvas, Almaida, Peniche, and Palmela, shall be given up as soon as the British troops
can arrive to occupy them. In the mean time, the General-in-Chief of the British
army will give notice of the present Convention to the garrisons of those places, as
also to the troops before them, in order to put a stop to all further hostilities. 380

Art. XIII. Commissioners shall be named, on both sides, to regulate and accelerate the execution of the arrangements agreed upon.

Art. XIV. Should there arise doubts as to the meaning of any article, it will be explained favourably to the French army.

Art. XV. From the date of the ratification of the present Convention, all 385 arrears of contributions, requisitions, or claims whatever, of the French Government, against the subjects of Portugal, or any other individuals residing in this country, founded on the occupation of Portugal by the French troops in the month of December 1807, which may not have been paid up, are cancelled; and all sequestrations laid upon their property, moveable or immoveable, are 390 removed; and the free disposal of the same is restored to the proper owners.

Art. XVI. All subjects of France, or of powers in friendship or alliance with France, domiciliated in Portugal, or accidentally in this country, shall be protected: their property of every kind, moveable and immoveable, shall be respected: and they shall be at liberty either to accompany the French 395 army, or to remain in Portugal. In either case their property is guaranteed to them; with the liberty of retaining or of disposing of it, and passing the produce of the sale thereof into France, or any other country where they may fix their residence; the space of one year being allowed them for that purpose.

It is fully understood, that the shipping is excepted from this arrangement; 400 only, however, in so far as regards leaving the port; and that none of the stipulations above-mentioned can be made the pretext of any commercial speculation.

Art. XVII. No native of Portugal shall be rendered accountable for his political conduct during the period of the occupation of this country by the French army; and all those who have continued in the exercise of their em- 405 ployments, or who have accepted situations under the French Government, are placed under the protection of the British Commanders: they shall sustain no injury in their persons or property; it not having been at their option to be obedient, or not, to the French Government: they are also at liberty to avail themselves of the stipulations of the 16th Article. 410

Art. XVIII. The Spanish troops detained on board ship in the Port of Lisbon shall be given up to the Commander-in-Chief of the British army; who engages to obtain of the Spaniards to restore such French subjects, either military or civil, as may have been detained in Spain, without being taken in battle, or in consequence of military operations, but 415 on occasion of the occurrences of the 29th of last May, and the days immediately following.

Art. XIX. There shall be an immediate exchange established for all ranks of prisoners made in Portugal since the commencement of the present hostilities.

Art. XX. Hostages of the rank of field-officers shall be mutually furnished 420 on the part of the British army and navy, and on that of the French army, for the reciprocal guarantee of the present Convention. The officer of the British army shall be restored on the completion of the articles which concern the army; and the officer of the navy on the disembarkation of the French troops in their own country. The like is to take place on the part of the French army.   425

Art. XXI. It shall be allowed to the General-in-Chief of the French army to send an officer to France with intelligence of the present Convention. A vessel will be furnished by the British Admiral to convey him to Bourdeaux or Rochefort.

Art. XXII. The British Admiral will be invited to accommodate His Excel- 430 lency the Commander-in-Chief, and the other principal officers of the French army, on board ships of war.

Done and concluded at Lisbon this 30th day of August, 1808.

(Signed)   George Murray,

                                            Quarter-Master-General.   435

                                   Kellermann,

                                            Le Général de Division.

We, the Duke of Abrantes, General-in-Chief of the French army, have ratified and do ratify the present Definitive Convention in all its articles, to be executed according to its form and tenor.   440

(Signed)   The Duke of Abrantes.

Head-Quarters—Lisbon, 30th August, 1808.

Additional Articles to the Convention of the 30th of August, 1808.

Art. I. The individuals in the civil employment of the army made prisoners, either by the British troops, or by the Portuguese, in any part of Portugal, 445 will be restored, as is customary, without exchange.

Art. II. The French army shall be subsisted from its own magazines up to the day of embarkation; the garrisons up to the day of the evacuation of the fortresses.

The remainder of the magazines shall be delivered over, in the usual form, **450** to the British Government; which charges itself with the subsistence of the men and horses of the army from the above-mentioned periods till they arrive in France; under the condition of their being reimbursed by the French Government for the excess of the expense beyond the estimates, to be made by both parties, of the value of the magazines delivered up to the British army. **455**

The provisions on board the ships of war, in possession of the French army, will be taken in account by the British Government in like manner with the magazines in the fortresses.

ART. III. The General commanding the British troops will take the necessary measures for re-establishing the free circulation of the means of subsist- **460** ence between the country and the capital.

Done and concluded at Lisbon this 30th day of August, 1808.

(Signed)   GEORGE MURRAY,

Quarter-Master-General.

KELLERMANN,   **465**

Le Général de Division.

We, Duke of Abrantes, General-in-Chief of the French army, have ratified and do ratify the additional articles of the Convention, to be executed according to their form and tenor.

The Duke of ABRANTES.

470

(A true Copy.)

A. J. DALRYMPLE, Captain, Military Secretary.

Articles of a Convention entered into between Vice-Admiral SENIAVIN, *Knight of the Order of St. Alexander and other Russian Orders, and Admiral Sir* CHARLES COTTON, *Bart. for the Surrender of the Russian Fleet, now anchored* **475** *in the River Tagus.*

ART. I. The ships of war of the Emperor of Russia, now in the Tagus (as specified in the annexed list), shall be delivered up to Admiral Sir Charles Cotton, immediately, with all their stores as they now are; to be sent to England, and there held as a deposit by His Britannic Majesty, to be restored to His Im- **480** perial Majesty within six months after the conclusion of a peace between His Britannic Majesty and His Imperial Majesty the Emperor of all the Russias.

ART. II. Vice-Admiral Seniavin, with the officers, sailors, and marines, under his command, to return to Russia, without any condition or stipulation respecting their future services; to be conveyed thither in men of war, or proper 485 vessels, at the expence of His Britannic Majesty.

Done and concluded on board the ship Twerday, in the Tagus, and on board His Britannic Majesty's ship Hibernia, off the mouth of that river, the 3d day of September 1808.

(Signed)   DE SENIAVIN.   **490**
(Signed)   CHARLES COTTON.
(Counter-signed) By command of the Admiral,
                       L. SASS, Assesseur de Collège.
(Counter-signed) By command of the Admiral,
                       JAMES KENNEDY, Secretary.

[De Quincey's] POSTSCRIPT

ON SIR JOHN MOORE'S LETTERS.

Whilst the latter sheets of this work were passing through the press, there was laid before Parliament a series of correspondence between the English Government and its servants in Spain; amongst which were the letters of Sir 500 John Moore. That these letters, even with minds the least vigilant to detect contradictions and to make a commentary from the past actions of the Spaniards, should have had power to alienate them from the Spanish cause—could never have been looked for; except indeed by those who saw, in the party spirit on this question, a promise that more than ordinary pains would be taken to 505 misrepresent their contents and to abuse the public judgment. But however it was at any rate to have been expected—both from the place which Sir J. Moore held in the nation's esteem previously to his Spanish campaign, and also especially from that which (by his death in battle) he had so lately taken in its affections—that they would weigh a good deal in depressing the general 510 sympathy with Spain: and therefore the Author of this work was desirous that all which these letters themselves, or other sources of information, furnished to mitigate and contradict Sir J. M.'s opinions   should be laid before the public: but—being himself at a great distance from London, and not having within his reach all the documents necessary for this purpose—he has honoured the 515 friend, who corrects the press errors, by making over that task to him; and the reader is therefore apprised, that the Author is not responsible for any thing which follows.

*   *   *   *   *   *

Those, who have not examined these letters for themselves, will have col- 520 lected enough of their general import, from conversation and the public prints, to know that they pronounce an opinion unfavourable to the Spaniards. They will perhaps have yet to learn that this opinion is not supported by any body of *facts* (for of facts only three are given; and those, as we shall see, misrep- resented); but solely by the weight of Sir John Moore's personal authority. 525 This being the case, it becomes the more important to assign the value of that authority, by making such deductions from the present public estimate of it, as are either fairly to be presumed from his profession and office, or directly inferred from the letters under consideration.

As reasons for questioning *à priori* the impartiality of these letters,—it 530 might be suggested (in reference to what they would be likely *omit*)—first— that they are the letters of a *soldier*; that is, of a man trained (by the prejudices of his profession) to despise, or at least to rate secondary, those resources which for Spain must be looked to as supreme and, secondly, that they are the letters of a *general*; that is, of a soldier removed by his rank from the possibil- 535 ity of any extensive intercourse with the lower classes; concerning whom the question chiefly was. But it is more important to remark (in reference to what they would be likely to *mis-state*)—thirdly—that they are the letters of a *com- mander-in-chief*; standing—from the very day when he took the field—in a dilemma which compelled him to risk the safety of his army by advancing, or 540 its honour by retreating; and having to make out an apology, for either issue, to the very persons who had imposed this dilemma upon him.—The reader is requested to attend to this. Sir John Moore found himself in Leon with a force "which, if united," (to quote his own words) "would not exceed 26,000 men." Such a force, after the defeat of the advanced armies,—he was sure—could 545 effect nothing; the best result he could anticipate was an inglorious retreat. That he should be in this situation at the very opening of the campaign, he

saw, would declare to all Europe that somewhere there must be blame: but
where? with himself he knew that there was none: the English Government
(with whom he must have seen that least a part of the blame lay—for sending 550
him so late, and with a force so lamentably incommensurate to the demands
of the service) it was not for him—holding the situation that he did—openly
to accuse (though, by implication, he often does accuse them); and therefore it
became his business to look to the Spaniards; and, in their conduct, to search
for palliations of that inefficiency on his part—which else the persons, to 555
whom he was writing, would understand as charged upon themselves. Writing
with such a purpose—and under a double fettering of his faculties; first from
anxious forebodings of calamity or dishonour; and secondly from the pain he
must have felt at not being free to censure those with whom he could not but
be aware that the embarrassments of his situation had, at least in part, origi- 560
nated—we might expect that it would not be difficult for him to find, in the
early events of the campaign, all which he sought; and to deceive himself into
a belief, that, in stating these events without any commentary or even hints as
to the relative circumstances under which they took place (which only could
give to the naked facts their value and due meaning), he was making no mis- 565
representations,— and doing the Spaniards no injustice.

These suggestions are made with the greater earnestness, as it is probable
that the honourable death of Sir John Moore will have given so much more
weight to his opinion on any subject—as, if these suggestions be warranted,
it is entitled on this subject to less weight—than the opinion of any other in- 570
dividual equally intelligent, and not liable (from high office and perplexity of
situation) to the same influences of disgust or prejudice.

That these letters *were* written under some such influences, is plain throughout: we find, in them, reports of the four first events in the campaign; and, in
justice to the Spaniards, it must be said that all are virtually mis-statements. 575
Take two instances:

1. The main strength and efforts of the French were, at the opening of the
campaign, directed against the army of Gen. Blake. The issue is thus given by
Sir J. M.:—"Gen. Blake's army in Biscay has been defeated—dispersed; and
its officers and men are flying in every direction." Could it be supposed that 580
the army, whose matchless exertions and endurances are all merged in this
over-charged (and almost insulting) statement of their result, was, 'mere peasantry' (Sir J. M.'s own words) and opposed to greatly superior numbers of

veteran troops? Confront with this account the description given by an eye-
witness (Major-Gen. Leith) of their constancy and the trials of their constancy; **585**
remembering that, for ten successive days, they were engaged (under the pressure of similar hardships, with the addition of one not mentioned here, viz.—a
want of cloathing) in continued actions with the French:—"Here I shall take
occasion to state another instance of the patience (and, I will add, the chearful-
ness) of the Spanish soldiers under the greatest privations—After the action **590**
of Soronosa on the 31st ult., it was deemed expedient by Gen. Blake, for the
purpose of forming a junction with the second division and the army of Asturias, that the army should make long, rapid, and continued marches through a
country at any time incapable of feeding so numerous an army, and at present
almost totally drained of provisions. From the 30th of October to the present **595**
day (Nov. 6), with the exception of a small and partial issue of bread at Bilboa
on the morning of the 1st of November, this army has been totally destitute
of bread, wine, or spirits; and has literally lived on the scanty supply of beef
and sheep which those mountains afford. Yet never was there a symptom of
complaint or murmur; the soldiers' minds appearing to be entirely occupied **600**
with the idea of being led against the enemy at Bilboa."—"It is impossible for
me to do justice to the gallantry and energy of the divisions engaged this day.
The army are loud in expressing their desires to be led against the enemy at
Bilboa; the universal exclamation is—The bayonet! the bayonet! lead us back
to Soronosa." 605

2. On the 10th of November the Estramaduran advanced-guard, of about
12,000 men, was defeated at Burgos by a division of the French army *selected*
for the service—and having a vast superiority in cavalry and artillery. This
event, with the same neglect of circumstances as in the former instance, Sir
J. M. thus reports:—"The French, after beating the army of Estramadura, are **610**
advanced at Burgos." Now surely to any unprejudiced mind the bare fact of
2,000 men (chiefly raw levies) having gone forward to meet and to find out
the main French army—under all the oppression which, to the ignorant of
the upper and lower classes throughout Europe, there is in the name of Bonaparte—must appear, under any issue, a title to the highest admiration, such as **615**
would have made this slight and incidental mention of it impossible.

The two next events—viz. the forcing of the pass at Somosierra by the
Polish horse, and the partial defeat of Castanos—are, as might be shewn even
from the French bulletins, no less misrepresented. With respect to the first,—

Sir J. Moore, overlooking the whole drama of that noble defence, gives only **620** the catastrophe; and his account of the second will appear, from any report, to be an exaggeration.

It may be objected that—since Sir J. M. no where alleges these events as proving any thing against the Spaniards, but simply as accounting for his own plans (in which view, howsoever effected, whether with or without due resist- **625** ance, they were entitled to the same value)—it is unfair to say that, by giving them uncircumstantially, he has misrepresented them. But it must be answered, that, in letters containing elsewhere (though not immediately in connexion with these statements) opinions unfavourable to the Spaniards, to omit any thing making *for* them—*is* to misrepresent in effect. And, further, it shall now **630** be shewn that even those three charges—which Sir J. M. *does* allege in proof of his opinions—are as glaringly misstated. ▶

The first of these charges is the most important: I give it to the reader in the words of Sir John Moore:—"The French cavalry from Burgos, in small detachments, are over-running the province of Leon; raising contributions; to **635** which the inhabitants submit without the least resistance." Now here it cannot be meant that no efforts at resistance were made by individuals or small parties; because this would not only contradict the universal laws of human nature,—but would also be at utter variance with Sir J. M.'s repeated complaints that he could gain no information of what was passing in his neighbourhood. **640** It is meant therefore that there was no regular or organised resistance; no resistance such as might be made the subject of an official report. Now we all know that the Spaniards have every where suffered deplorably from a want of cavalry; and, in the absence of that, hear from a military man (Major-Gen. Brodrick) *why* there was no resistance: "—At that time I was not aware how **645** remarkably the plains of Leon and Castille differ from any other I have seen; nor how strongly the circumstances, which constitute that difference, enforce the opinion I ventured to express." (He means the necessity of cavalry reinforcements from England.) "My road from Astorga lay through a vast open space, extending from 5 to 20 or more miles on every side; without a single **650** accident of ground which could enable a body of infantry to check a pursuing enemy, or to cover its own retreat. In such ground, any corps of infantry might be insulted, to the very gates of the town it occupied, by cavalry far inferior in numbers; *contributions raised under their eyes*, and the whole neighbourhood

exhausted of its resources, *without the possibility of their opposing any resist-* **655**
ance to such incursions."

The second charge is made on the retreat to Corunna: "the Gallicians, ▶
though armed," Sir J. M. says, "made no attempt to stop the passage of the
French through the mountains." That they were armed—is a proof that they
had an *intention* to do so (as one of our journals observed): but what encour- **660**
agement had they in that intention from the sight of a regular force—more than
30,000 strong—abandoning, without a struggle, passes where (as an English
general asserts) "a body of a thousand men might stop an army of twenty times
the number?"

The third charge relates to the same province: it is a complaint that 'the 665
people run away; the villages are deserted;' and again, in his last letter,—"They
abandoned their dwellings at our approach; drove away their carts, oxen, and
every thing which could be of the smallest aid to the army." To this charge, in
so far as it may be thought to criminate the Spaniards, a full answer is furnished
by their accuser himself in the following memorable sentence in another part **670**
of the very same letter:—"I am sorry to say that the army, whose conduct I had
such reason to extol in its march through Portugal and on its arrival in Spain,
has totally changed its character since it began to retreat." What do we collect
from this passage? Assuredly that the army ill-treated the Gallicians; for there
is no other way in which an army, as a body, can offend—excepting by an **675**
indisposition to fight; and that interpretation (besides that we are all sure that
no English army could *so* offend) Sir J. Moore expressly guards against in the
next sentence.

The English army then treated its ally as an enemy: and,—though there are
alleviations of its conduct in its great sufferings,—yet it must be remembered **680**
that these sufferings were due—not to the Gallicians— but to circumstances
over which they had no controul—to the precipitancy of the retreat, the in-
clemency of the weather, and the poverty of the country; and that (knowing
this) they must have had a double sense of injustice in any outrages of an
English army, from contrasting them with the professed objects of that army **685**
in entering Spain—It is to be observed that the answer to the second charge
would singly have been some answer to this; and, reciprocally, that the answer
to this is a full answer to the second.

Having thus shewn that, in Sir J. Moore's very inaccurate statements of
facts, we have some further reasons for a previous distrust of any opinion **690**

which is supported by those statements,—it is now time to make the reader acquainted with the real terms and extent of that opinion. For it is far less to be feared that, from his just respect for him who gave it, he should allow it an undue weight in his judgment—than that, reposing on the faithfulness of the abstracts and reports of these letters, he should really be still ignorant of its 695 exact tenor.

The whole amount then of what Sir John Moore has alleged against the ▶ Spaniards, in any place but one, is comprised in this sentence:—"The enthusiasm, of which we have heard so much, no where appears: whatever good-will there is (and I believe amongst the lower orders there is a great deal) is taken 700 no advantage of." It is true that, in that one place (viz. in his last letter written ▶ at Corunna), he charges the Spaniards with "apathy and indifference:" but, as this cannot be reconciled with his concession of *a great deal of good-will*, we are bound to take that as his real and deliberate opinion which he gave under circumstances that allowed him most coolness and freedom of judg- 705 ment.—The Spaniards then were wanting in enthusiasm. Now what is meant by enthusiasm? Does it mean want of ardour and zeal in battle? This Sir J. Moore no where asserts; and, even without a direct acknowledgement of their good conduct in the field (of which he had indeed no better means of judging than we in England), there is involved in his statement of the relative numbers 710 of the French and Spaniards—combined with our knowledge of the time during which they maintained their struggle—a sufficient testimony to that; even if the events of the first campaign had not made it superfluous. Does it mean then a want of good-will to the cause? So from this, we have seen that Sir J. M. admits that there was, in that class where it was most wanted, 'a great deal' 715 of good-will. And, in the present condition of Spain, let it be recollected what it is that this implies. We see, in the intercepted letter to Marshal Soult (transmitted by Sir J. M.), that the French keep accurate registers of the behaviour of the different towns; and this was, no doubt, well known throughout Spain. Therefore to shew any signs of good-will—much more to give a kind welcome 720 to the English (as had been done at Badajoz and Salamanca)—was, they knew, a pledge of certain punishment on any visit from the French. So that goodwill, manifested in these circumstances, was nothing less than a testimony of devotion to the cause.

Here then, the reader will say, I find granted—in the courage and the good- 725 will of the Spaniards—all the elements of an enthusiastic resistance; and cannot therefore imagine what more could be sought for except the throwing out and making palpable of their enthusiasm to the careless eye in some signal outward manifestations. In this accordingly we learn what interpretation we are to ▶ give to Sir J. M.'s charge:—there were no tumults on his entrance into Spain; 730 no insurrections; they did not, as he says, "rally round" the English army. But, to determine how far this disappointment of his expectations tells against the Spaniards, we must first know how far those expectations were reasonable. Let the reader consider, then,

First; what army was this round which the Spaniards were to rally? 735 If it was known by the victory of Vimiera, it was known also to many by the Convention of Cintra: for, though the government had never ventured to communicate that affair officially to the nation, dark and perplexing whispers were however circulated about it throughout Spain. Moreover, it must surely demand some superstition in behalf of regular troops—to see, in an army of 740 26,000 men, a dignity adequate to the office here claimed for it of awakening a new vigour and enthusiasm in such nation as Spain; not to mention that an English army, however numerous, had no right to consider itself as other than a tributary force—as itself tending to a centre—and attracted rather than attracting. 745

Secondly; it appears that Sir J. M. has overlooked one most important circumstance;—viz. that the harvest, in these provinces, had been already reaped; the English army could be viewed only as gleaners. Thus, as we have already seen, Estramadura had furnished an army which had marched before his arrival; from Salamanca also—the very place in which he makes his complaint—there 750 had gone out a battalion to Biscay which Gen. Blake had held up, for its romantic gallantry, to the admiration of his whole army.

Yet, thirdly, it is not meant by any means to assert that Spain has put forth an energy adequate to the service—or in any tolerable proportion to her own strength. Far from it! But upon whom does the blame rest? Not surely upon 755 the people—who, as long as they continued to have confidence in their rulers, could not be expected (after the early fervours of their revolution had subsided) much to overstep the measure of exertion prescribed to them—but solely upon the government. Up to the time when Sir J. M. died, the Supreme Junta had adopted no one grand and comprehensive measure for calling out 760 the strength of the nation;—scarcely any of such ordinary vigour as, in some countries, would have been adopted to meet local disturbances among the people. From their jealousy of popular feeling,—they had never taken any steps, by books or civic assemblies, to make the general enthusiasm in the cause ▶ available by bringing it within the general consciousness; and thus to create 765 the nation into an organic whole. Sir J. M. was fully aware of this:—"The Spanish Government," he says, "do not seem ever to have contemplated the possibility of a second attack:" and accordingly, whenever he is at leisure to make distinctions, he does the people the justice to say—that the failure was with those who should have "taken advantage" of their good will. With the 770 people therefore will for ever remain the glory of having resisted heroically with means utterly inadequate; and with the government the whole burthen of the disgrace that the means were thus inadequate.

But, further,—even though it should still be thought that, in the three provinces which Sir J. Moore saw, there may have been some failures with the peo- 775 ple,—it is to be remembered that these were the very three which had never been the theatre of French outrages; which therefore had neither such a vivid sense of the evils which they had to fear, nor so strong an animation in the recollection of past triumphs: we might accordingly have predicted that, if any provinces should prove slack in their exertions, it would be these three. So 780 that, after all, (a candid inquirer into this matter will say) admitting Sir J. M.'s description to be faithful with respect to what he saw, I can never allow that the conduct of these three provinces shall be held forth as an exponent of the general temper and condition of Spain. For that therefore I must look to other authorities. 785

Such an inquirer we might then refer to the testimonies of Gen. Leith and of Capt. Pasley for Biscay and Asturias; of Mr. Vaughan (as cited by Lord Cas- ▶ tlereagh) for the whole East and South; of Lord Cochrane (himself a most gallant man, and giving *his* testimony under a trying comparison of the Spaniards with English Sailors) for Catalonia in particular; of Lord W. Bentinck for the 790 central provinces; and, for all Spain, we might appeal even to the Spanish military reports—which, by the discrimination of their praises (sometimes giving severe rebukes to particular regiments, &c.) authenticate themselves.

But, finally, we are entitled—after the *actions* of the Spaniards—to dispense with such appeals. Spain might justly deem it a high injury and affront, 795 to suppose that (after her deeds performed under the condition of her means) she could require any other testimony to justify her before all posterity. What those deeds have been, it cannot surely now be necessary to inform the reader:

and therefore the remainder of this note shall be employed in placing before
him the present posture of Spain—under two aspects which may possibly have 800
escaped his notice.

First, Let him look to that part of Spain which is now in the possession of
the enemy;—let him bear in mind that the present campaign opened at the latter
end of last October; that the French were then masters of the country up to the
Ebro; that the contest has since lain between a veteran army (rated, on the low- 805
est estimate, at 113,000 men—with a prodigious superiority in cavalry, artillery, &c.) opposed (as to all *regular* opposition) by unpractised Spaniards, split
into three distinct armies, having no communication with each other, making
a total of not more than 80,000 men;—and then let him inquire what progress,
in this time and with these advantages, the French have been able to make 810
(comparing it, at the same time, with that heretofore made in Prussia, and elsewhere): the answer shall be given from the *Times* newspaper of April 8th—"It ▶
appears that, at the date of our last accounts from France as well as Spain,
about one half of the Peninsula was still unsubdued by the French arms. The
provinces, which retain their independence, form a sort of irregular or broken 815
crescent; of which one horn consists in parts of Catalonia and Valencia, and the
other horn includes Asturias (perhaps we may soon add Gallicia). The broader
surface contains the four kingdoms of Andalusia (Seville, Grenada, Cordova,
and Murcia), and considerable parts of Estramadura, and La Mancha; besides
Portugal."—The writer might have added that even the provinces, occupied by 820
the French, cannot yet be counted substantially as conquests: since they have
a military representation in the south; large proportions of the defeated armies
having retreated thither.

Secondly, Let him look to that part of Spain which yet remains unsubdued.—It was thought no slight proof of heroism in the people of Madrid, 825
that they prepared for their defence—not as the foremost champions of Spain
(in which character they might have gained an adventitious support from the
splendour of their post; and, at any rate, would have been free from the depression of preceding disasters)—but under a full knowledge of recent and
successive overthrows; their advanced armies had been defeated; and their 830
last stay, at Somosierra, had been driven in upon them. But the Provinces in
the South have many more causes for dejection: they have heard, since these
disasters, that this heroic city of Madrid has fallen; that their forts in Catalonia have been wrested from them; that an English army just moved upon

the horizon of Spain—to draw upon itself the gaze and expectations of the 835
people, and then to vanish like an apparition; and, finally, they have heard of
the desolation of Saragossa. Under all this accumulation of calamity, what has
been their conduct? In Valencia redoubled preparations of defence; in Seville ▶
a decree for such energetic retaliation on the enemy,—as places its authors, in
the event of his success, beyond the hopes of mercy; in Cadiz—on a suspicion 840
that a compromise was concerted with their enemy—tumults and clamours of
the people for instant vengeance; every where, in their uttermost distress, the
same stern and unfaultering attitude of defiance as at the glorious birth of their
resistance.

In this statement, then, of the past efforts of Spain—and of her present 845
preparations for further efforts—will be found a full answer to all the charges
alleged, by Sir John Moore in his letters, against the people of Spain, even if
we did not find sufficient ground for rejecting them in an examination of these
letters themselves.

*   *   *   *   *   *

850

The author of the above note—having, in justice to the Spaniards, spoken
with great plainness and freedom—feels it necessary to add a few words, that
it may not thence be concluded that he is insensible to Sir J. Moore's claims
upon his respect. Perhaps—if Sir J. M. could himself have given us his commentary upon these letters, and have restricted the extension of such passages 855
as (from want of vigilance in making distinctions or laxity of language) are
at variance with concessions made elsewhere—they would have been found
not more to differ from the reports of other intelligent and less prejudiced
observers, than we might have expected from the circumstances under which
they were written. Sir J. M. has himself told us (in a letter published since the 860
above note was written) that he thinks the Spaniards "a fine people;" and that
acknowledgement, from a soldier, cannot be supposed to exclude courage;
nor, from a Briton, some zeal for national independence. We are therefore to
conclude that, when Sir J. M. pronounces opinions on "the Spaniards" not
to be reconciled with this and other passages, he speaks—not of the Spanish 865
people—but of the Spanish government. And, even for what may still remain
charged uncandidly upon the people, the writer does not forget that there are
infinite apologies to be found in Sir J. Moore's situation: the earliest of these
letters were written under great anxiety and disturbance of mind from the anticipation of calamity;—and the latter (which are the most severe) under the 870

actual pressure of calamity; and calamity of that sort which would be the most painful to the feelings of a gallant soldier, and most likely to vitiate his judgment with respect to those who had in part (however innocently) occasioned it. There may be pleaded also for him—that want of leisure which would make it difficult to compare the different accounts he received, and to draw the right 875 inferences from them. But then these apologies for his want of fidelity—are also reasons before-hand for suspecting it: and there are now (May 18th) to be added to these reasons, and their confirmations in the letters themselves, fresh ▶ proofs in the present state of Gallicia, as manifested by the late re-capture ¶¶ of Vigo, and the movements of the Marquis de la Romana; all which, from 880 Sir J. Moore's account of the temper in that province, we might have confidently pronounced impossible. We must therefore remember that what in him were simply mis-statements—are now, when repeated with our better information, calumnies; and calumnies so much the less to be excused in us, as we have already (in our conduct towards Spain) given her other and no light mat- 885 ter of complaint against ourselves.

END OF THE APPENDIX.

EDITORIAL APPENDICES

APPENDIX I

ADDRESS ON THE CONVENTION OF CINTRA

In the Wordsworth Library, Grasmere, is preserved a single manuscript sheet, in the hand of either Mary Wordsworth or Sara Hutchinson, which gives, in a much amended draft, the fragment printed here. It is clear from parallels of wording and substance that the document is connected with *Cintra*: cf. *Cintra*, 1085: 'the transaction, considered as a military transaction', and *Address*, 1: 'To what extent, as a military measure, it may be arraigned …'; *Cintra*, 1098: 'looking at this issue merely as an affair between two armies', and *Address*, 5–6: 'Considered, then, as an affair between two armies'; and especially Wordsworth's claim (*Cintra*, 1488 ff.) that, as a private citizen, he is entitled to speak upon public and military matters, and the similar claim in *Address*, 11–42. Since the last words of the fragment define it as part of an 'address', we conjecture that it is part of a draft of an address which Wordsworth proposed to deliver (either orally or in print: note 'reader', 3) at the public meeting projected by himself and his Lake District friends in protest against the Convention (see *Cintra*, Introd.). We have provided a title accordingly.

The draft, even in the edited form presented here, is in the tortuous manner of *Cintra* itself, and is sometimes, especially in the paragraph 11–28, not absolutely coherent or even grammatical (see 32–3: 'the health … are the condition'). The manuscript is inadequately punctuated, and almost all the commas in our text, and some other pointing, are editorial.

[Address on The Convention of Cintra]

To what extent, as a military measure, it may be arraigned; and under what
conditions this charge of incompetence may be justly preferred against those
who condemn this as a military measure (and the reader will recollect that it is
as such only that I have lately been speaking of it); I will now, in justification
of the sentence which I passed upon it above, proceed to determine.—Con- 5
sidered, then, as an affair between two armies, the measure resolves itself into
three elementary parts—

    1st. Matters which, to be justly appreciated, require professional skill and
a thorough knowledge of all local circumstances and exigences of the time;—
whoever decides upon these matters without such qualifications is obnoxious 10
to the charge: but on these I have given no opinion.

    2^{ndly}. A class of measures, and those general ones, on which certain men
may claim a right to give judgement from the joint consideration, first, that
the facts are of high interest—secondly, that the evidence of the facts is, in
its kind, unquestionable (coming only either from the mouths of the men ar- 15
raigned—or universally acknowledged to be unimpeachable authority)—in its
kind unquestionable, and in its degree complete;—thirdly, that the law, these
conditions being presumed, includes in it's constitution the warrant for its own
application—inasmuch as it is nothing more than an abstract from every parallel case found in history—the [?train] of conduct held in such cases—and 20
[*tear*]ons pronounced by all men who, in recording such [? cases, have] taken
neither the narrow view of a purely military scrutiny, nor the wide and comprehensive one of moral man appealing to elementary and universal principles

MS. *begins*: Arraigning it for the present *del.*
1–3 and under ... measure *ins.*
4 such *del. and restored*; in this light *ins. and del.*
4 have ... of it *subs. for* [1] am now viewing it [2]
    am now looking at it
4–7 I will now ... parts—*subs. for the following,
    which is undeleted except as indicated*: [will
    appear from the *del.*] [my own *del.*] [for the
    subs. for* in] justification of the sentence which

I have passed upon it above I am now called
    upon to [shew *del.*] state: and this I shall do
    by shewing that
6 resolves *subs. for* divides
7 elementary *subs. for* dif[ferent]
9 on these I have not presumed to give an opinion
    del. after time;—
16 or *del. after* authority)
21 all men *subs. for* men

of his nature, but have spoken in the character of politicians and calculators of gross general expediency:—Such character, and the consequent right to pro- 25 nounce sentence upon this second class of measures, I may surely claim, if I have any right to speak to the public at all upon public affairs; and, accordingly, I have spoken without reserve.

3^{rdly}. and lastly: a class of military measures of paramount importance, sinking the rest, in comparison with them, into insignificance— measures which, 30 though formally military, are in their [   ] moral; which cannot be thought of in separation from moral feelings and powers;—where the health of the moral feelings and powers are the condition of the military strength:—These are measures which every man may be entitled to decide upon who has little or no acquaintance with past ages, and only a general knowledge, with a deep 35 feeling of the struggle as a contest of justice with the most atrocious oppression.—On the rights of this class of judges I most earnestly insist; to them I chiefly appeal; theirs is the authority of most weight; by the principles of courage—independence—honor—and dignity inherent in them is the question mainly to be tried; and to encourage these principles, and to sustain them 40 by calling them to their proper exercise—is one of the primary objects of this present address.

27 affairs *subs. for* measures
33 military *subs. for* moral —this is a division of
    the subject *del. after* measures

APPENDIX II

pp. 1–16: a fairly clean version of *Ap. Cintra*, 566–end. This is the longest continuous draft in the MS.; most (but not all) of the emendations are in the direction of
the text of 1809; the order of paragraphs is identical with that of 1809; there is one
large–scale variant at 678–87.

pp. 17–18: a version of 850–end.

p. 19: versions of 672–4, 678–77.

p. 20: details of proof–corrections to the text of 1809, pp. 193–200

pp. 21–4: a version of 519–75.

pp. 25–7: a version of 734–72–840, omitting 745–51.

pp. 28–31: a version of 566–647.

p. 32: summaries of arguments developed elsewhere: on internal inconsistencies
in Moore's letters (cf. 700–04, 853–6); on parts of Spain not under French control
(cf. 773–84); on the guilt of governments; on testimony other than Moore's; on the
'energy and patriotism of Spain' (cf. 823–43).

p. 33: a version of 832–43; and a short passage similar in drift to 801–10.

pp. 34–6: versions of 529–75 and 609–19.

p. 37: extracts from Moore's letters, with dates of letters and of their publication.

p. 38: a discussion of Moore's veracity, hinting at the matter of 529–41; and a draft
combining the matter of 745–51 and 610–5.

pp. 39–40: a version of 793–830. At the top of p. 40, upside-down, a version of
519–20; at the bottom, upside-down, a version of 497–8.

p. 41: two passages which are evidently drafts of De Quincey's note on Saragossa;
see *Cintra*, 2705 ff., and n. The upper third of the page, written upside-down, reads
after emendation as follows:

> & if carefully examined it is not Saragossa—a walled city—that he
> has possessed himself of—but Saragossa a lazarhouse and a tomb!
>
> it is thought necessary therefore to account to the reader for retaining the
> here referred to

the passage relating to that city by stating that the great distance of the author from London made it impossible for his friend (to whom the correcting of the proof–sheets has been entrusted) to wait for the slight alterations occasionally demanded in the allusions to passing occurrences without very long and inconvenient

The lower two–thirds of the page reads after emendation as follows:

for the proof of which assertion the reader who may [?inconsiderately] have adopted any opinion pronounced upon the Army or the Heroic Governor of Saragossa in the calumnious statement of their enemy, is referred with entire confidence to the facts detailed (though no doubt with the greatest possible injustice to the Spaniards) in the same document.

Whilst this sheet was under revisal, the 33rd bulletin of the French Army in Spain was received in London—announcing, in sum, that three divisions of that Army had at length possessed themselves of the ruins of Saragossa.—It is thought proper therefore to inform the reader that, from the author's great distance from London, it was not possible to apply to him for an alteration without considerable inconvenience, and this the reviser deemed the less necessary as being well assured that his friend would make no further alteration than [?] declare, in a more full and solemn tribute of honor to Saragossa, that of all the high anticipations [?] of her she had most faithfully acquitted herself; having then only ceased to be the champion of the Spanish cause when she became its glorious martyr: since even upon the testimony of her [?base] and calumnious enemy

p. 41 verso: In a large hand:

> Convention of Cintra
> all in confusion
> Is this Wordsworths
> hand or my Fathers

p. 42: a version of 572–75; a space for examples; a version of 688–95.

pp. 43–5: a version of 696–800.

p.46: versions of 605–15 and 616–8.

p. 47: a version of 576–84. p. 47 ends: 'For Sir D. Baird, it is still more difficult to find an excuse, who, in'; and p. 46 begins: 'this instance, had—in the letter of Capt. Pasley of the Engineers—a fuller testimony to the merits of this army than was Sir J. M.

'2. The defeat of the Estramaduran advanced–guard' etc.

It is clear that the order of pp. 46 and 47, recto and verso of one sheet, should be reversed.

pp. 48–9: a version of 529–65.

pp. 50–1: a version of 700–51–804, omitting 734–44.

pp. 52–3: a version of 656–97.

p. 54: versions of 685–7, 667–70.

pp. 55^r, 55^v: extracts from *The Courier*, 12 November 1808, for Appendices E and F.

pp. 56–7: *Cintra*, 4288–94, transcribed by De Quincey. See Introd.

p. 58: version of, or notes for, 529–65.

p. 59: versions of, or notes for, 730–2, 745–7, 754–65. Upside-down, near the bottom, a version of 861–4. Last line of page: 'that approach to equality which makes [?superiority pleasant]'.

p. 60: versions of 626–9, 572–5; and this passage, apparently referring to Moore's comments on the defeat of Blake (576 ff.):

> The true reason for all these misrepresentations must be sought in these two circumstances:
>
> 1st that the English army, in it's upper ranks, was in many sympathies and communities of thinking more nearly allied to it's enemy than it's ally: thus we find Sir J. M. more than once quoting with approbation intercepted French letters—2nd—It was a gallant [?army]

p. 61: a version of 872–end.

p. 62: a version of 850–72; at the foot, upside–down, a version of 566–71. The order of pp. 61 and 62, recto and verso of the same sheet, should perhaps be reversed, though the verbal connection is not quite exact.

pp. 63–5: a version of 785–846. p. 63, beginning 'of Gen. Leith and Capt. Pasley', may be intended to follow p. 27, which ends (in its third line) 'refer to the testimonies'. pp. 66^r, 66^v: a version of 529–65. These pages are numbered (by De Quincey) 3 and 4, and seem to be intended to precede the version of 566 ff. beginning on p. 1, the first ten pages of which are numbered 5–14 by De Quincey.

p. 67: versions of 808–10, 823–37.

pp. 68–71: extracts from and summaries of official correspondence on the campaign.

pp. 72–4: versions of 495–517, 525–33, 529–30.

COMMENTARY: *CINTRA*

Title–page. Qui didicit … ducis.] Horace, *Ars Poetica*, 312–15. On the earlier form of the title–page, see Introd.

Motto. See textual n., and cf. *M.Y.* i. 328. The passage is from *An Advertisement touching the Controversies of the Church of England*, in Bacon, *Works* (London, 1740), iv. 460. This edition, 'To which is prefixed, A New Life of the Author, By Mr. Mallet', gives the text as Wordsworth wished it to be printed. From Jordan, pp. 192–5 (31 May 1809), it appears that De Quincey prepared the passage for the press; he explains that 'Mr Wordsworth said that the reason why he did not send me the extract was that he did not exactly know where to look for it.' This letter also indicates Mallet's edition as a source of Wordsworth's version; De Quincey, in a long discussion of the readings 'hate' and 'zeal', is concerned lest Mallet's 'hate' should be less authentic than 'zeal', which he transcribed from other, supposedly more authoritative, texts. Wordsworth was seeking a copy of 'Lord Bacon's Works' in July 1808 (*M.Y.* i. 257).

Advertisement

6–7. two portions … Courier] *Cintra*, 1–187, appeared in *The Courier* for Tuesday, 27 Dec. 1808, p. 2, cols. 2–4, under the heading: 'Concerning the Convention of Cintra, in Reference to the Principles by which the Independence and Freedom of Nations must be Preserved or Recovered.' It was signed 'G.'. *Cintra*, 188–503, appeared in *The Courier* for Friday, 13 Jan. 1809, p. 1, col. 4,–p. 2, col. 4, under the heading, 'Concerning the Convention of Cintra, in Relation to the Principles by which alone the Independence and Freedom of Nations can be Maintained or Recovered. Section II. Continued from Tuesday's Courier, 27th ult.' It is again signed 'G.', and concludes with '(To be continued)'.

9–11. otherwise … work] This seems to refer to the promise at *Cintra*, 228 ff, to cite from Spanish documents, which is repeated at 497–503 and not fulfilled until 504 ff. It is not, however, clear what this has to do with the 'previous publication', except that the reprinting of the Spanish documents would have been an uneconomical way to fill the columns of the newspaper from which Wordsworth had already taken the citations.

13. pressure of public business] Wordsworth probably refers to the examination of Mrs. Clarke before a Committee of the House of Commons. Mary Anne Clarke (1776–1852), *née* Thompson, mistress of Frederick, Duke of York, from about 1803, was under examination from 1 February until 20 March 1809, on the ground that she had received money for using her influence with the Duke in connection with promotions in the Army. The charges were brought before the House by Colonel Gwylym Lloyd Wardle on 27 January; those against the Duke were not proved, but he resigned his appointment as Commander–in–Chief. Reports of the examination occupy most of the space in *The Courier* from 2 February, except on rare occasions such as 22 February, when the debate on the Convention of Cintra is fully reported. On the 'loss of several sheets' (11), see Introd.

23–29. I must ... corrected.] An insertion made on ? 26 March 1809 (*M.Y.* i. 300). Wordsworth's letter reads 'a change' instead of 'changes' (28).

29. On the additions, see Introd.; for examples of corrections see notes on *Cintra*, 2298–9, 3795, 4061, etc.

CONCERNING THE CONVENTION OF CINTRA

67–8. This just and necessary war] Cf. Freeholders, 431, 498–500. A commonplace of the time; see, for instance, the royal 'Proclamation, for General Fast', in *London Gazette*, No. 16214 (31 Dec. 1808—3 Jan. 1809), p. 1: 'We, taking into Our most serious Consideration the just and necessary War in which We are engaged ... do ... hereby command, that a Publick Day of Fasting and Humiliation be observed ... on Wednesday the Eighth Day of February next ensuing.' In the nineties Coleridge had toyed with the phrase in his political writings: see *Collected Works*, i, ed. L. Patton and P. Mann (London and Princeton, 1971), pp. 51, 54, 69, 287.

69–70. before the Treaty ... Switzerland] Between 1798 and 1802.

72 ff. and this justice etc.] Wordsworth draws on his own reactions to the war with France: see *Prel.* X. 228 ff.; and with 'and that enemy ambition' (75–9), cf. *Prel.* X. 792 if. The tone of *Cintra*, in passages such as 'Their conduct was herein consistent [against] the spirit of selfish tyranny and lawless ambition' (84–9), is more confident than that of *Prel.* X. 798–805. See also *L.Y.*, pp. 56–7 (Dec. 1821):

> If I were addressing those who have dealt so liberally with the words Renegado Apostate, etc., I should retort the charge upon them, and say, *you* have been deluded by *Places* and *Persons*, while I have stuck to *Principles*—I abandoned France, and her Rulers, when *they* abandoned the struggle for Liberty, gave themselves up to Tyranny, and endeavoured to enslave the world. I disapproved of the war against France at its commencement ... but after Bonaparte had violated the Independence of Switzerland, my heart turned against him, and

against the Nation that could submit to be the Instrument of such an outrage.

Cf. also the drift of Coleridge's 'France: An Ode'.

95. evil communications] I Cor. 15 : 33: 'Evil communications corrupt good manners.'

127. the moment of the rising] In Madrid, 2 May 1808; subsequently Asturias (24 May) and Galicia (30 May). Asturian envoys were in London seeking British assistance by 7 June.

131. We have inspected, or had reports on, nine copies of 1809 in an effort to establish the correct reading here. In all copies the last letter of the group which we print as 'of a' is printed without a space between it and 'of', and is followed by a space for about three letters. In the copies in the British Museum (Ashley 4628), Yale University Library, and New York Public Library, the letter is certainly 'a'; it is almost certainly 'a' in the copies in the British Museum (C. 114. d. 2), Wordsworth Library (Grasmere), and Turnbull Library (Wellington, New Zealand); in the copies at St. John's College, Cambridge, and Cornell, all that survives is a form like a Greek iota which, from the angle of the spur at the foot, is probably the remains of an 'a'. In the Bodleian copy, Godw. Pamph. 1980 (15), the letter can be read as a 't' at first glance, because of a smear emerging to the right of the minim; but the smear is too low to be the cross of a 't', the spur is that of an 'a' not a 't', and we think that the bow of an 'a' can be seen impressed into the paper but not inked. Wells (pp. 68–9) reports copies reading 'oft' as well as copies reading 'ofa', but his descriptions of those reading 'oft' are so qualified that we suspect that the true reading is 'ofa' in each instance. If a clear case of 'oft' should be found, we should assume an attempt to emend 'of a' (as in *Courier*) to 'of the', which is the reading of most reprints of *Cintra* (Wells, p. 68), though no copy of 1809 known to us or reported by Wells gives authority for this reading. It would indeed be remarkable if such an attempt should be made to emend a text already satisfactory in sense, with a damaged type (Wells, p. 68) replacing another damaged type, and without the necessary 'he'; it seems much more likely that in all copies the uncertain letter is 'a' in various states. Our text accordingly reads 'of a', and our assumption is that 1809 rightly repeats, or attempts to repeat, the reading of *Courier*, the only errors lying in the spacing of the types and in the use of a defective type for 'a'.

132–3. 'this corruptible ... immortality'] 1 Cor. 15: 53.

147–51. Britain and Spain were technically at war in 1808. A peace treaty was signed on 14 January 1809 (*Courier*, 28 Mar. 1809).

159–61. See Introd., sect. I.

174–5. their Sovereign] Charles IV (abdicated 19 March 1808); or more likely his son, Ferdinand VII, who is constantly referred to in Spanish documents of the kind cited below (504 ff.) as the lawful sovereign of Spain.

186. victory of Vimiera] 21 August 1808. Modern authorities give the place-name as 'Vimiero'; we have preserved Wordsworth's spelling throughout.

207–8. opposition ... Marathon] The defence of Thermopylae by the Spartans under Leonidas against the Persians took place in 480 B.C.; see Herodotus, *Hist.* vii. 175–228, especially 210–28. Cf. 429 below. In 490 B.C. the Athenians and Plataeans defeated a Persian reargard near Marathon, and thereby secured the defence of Athens (Herodotus, vi. 102–17).

241. present disaster] At the date of writing, presumably 3 January 1809 (see Introd., sect. II), the most obvious 'disaster' was the ill–fortune of Sir John Moore's army in Spain.

273 ff. paper entitled "PRECAUTIONS**"**] Printed in *Courier*, 4 July 1808, under the heading: 'Precautions which it will be proper to observe throughout the different Provinces of Spain, in the necessity to which they have been driven by the French, of resisting the unjust and violent possession which their Armies are endeavouring to take of the Kingdom'. The original reads 'or even the hope' (279). Clause 2 reads: 'A war of partisans is the system which suits us; the embarrassing and wasting the enemy's armies by want of provisions, destroying bridges, throwing up entrenchments in proper situations, and other similar means. The situation of Spain, its many mountains, and the passes which they present, its rivers and torrents, and even the collocation of its provinces, invite us to carry on this species of warfare successfully.'

334. Thirdly, ... See note to line 356 below

338. battle of Rio Seco] 13–14 July 1808; the French under Bessières defeated the army of Galicia under Blake and Cuesta, mainly because of the latter's incompetence. This battle, which cleared French communications from Bayonne into Spain, was the only notable French success in the early stages of the war.

338–41. returned ... troops.] *Courier*, 9 Aug. 1808, quotes a letter from Blake to Bessières dated 28 July 1808:

> Signior Marshal—I have received your Excellency's letter with due respect, and renew to you my acknowledgments for your having set at liberty the 400 or 500 prisoners taken in the battle of Rio Seco, whom your Excellency calls peasants of Gallicia. They are, however, real soldiers. They are recruits incorporated in the regiments of the line, though they did not wear uniforms. I explain this circumstance, not to exempt myself from acknowledging the generous conduct of your Excellency towards these men, but lest any equivocal idea should, at another time, bring on them a treatment they would not deserve.

340. Blake] Joachim Blake, of Irish descent, general of the Galician forces.

356–478. not merely ... the latter.] Coleridge to Thomas Poole, 3 Feb. 1809 (*C.L.* iii. 174), claims that in the instalments of *Cintra* which appeared in *The Courier* for 13 January 1809, 'The two last Columns of the second, excepting the concluding Paragraph, were written all but a few sentences by me.' The passage concerned is that indicated above. Coleridge summarizes its content in a letter to Stuart of 8–9 January 1809 (*C.L.* iii. 164). [According to *EOT* 3: 98–103 the passage which Coleridge claims to have re-composed from Wordsworth's notes may begin at line 334—RG.]

400. moral qualities ... nature] Cf. *E.E.* II. 55 ff., and n.

404. bodies of the Angels] *Paradise Lost*, VI. 328–3. [c.f. Sonnets to National Independence and Liberty, XXX]

428. ABDIEL] *Paradise Lost*, V. 800 ff.; VI. ill ff.

429. LEONIDAS] Commander of the Spartans against Xerxes at Thermopylae, 480 B.C. (Herodotus, *Hist.* vii. 204). Cf. 231–2 above.

461. late Austrian or Prussian resistance to France] Resistance crushed by Napoleon's campaigns of 1805–6, in his victories at Ulm, Austerlitz, Jena, and Auerstädt.

482–3. all knowledge ... repose] Cf. *Reply to Mathetes,* 427–9.

487 "the sea–mark ... sail"] *Othello*, v. ii. 267.

504. the first to rise] Apart from the riots in Madrid on 2 May 1808; see 127, n.

506–24. "Loyal Asturians ... to arms!"] *The Times*, 29 June 1808, almost verbatim, under heading 'Proclamation of the Council General of the Principality of Asturias'.

524–42. Supreme Junta ... against him."] *Courier*, 8 July 1808, almost verbatim.

544. manifesto of the Court] *Courier*, 11 Aug. 1808: 'Manifesto of the Prince Regent of Portugal against France, Or Justificatory Exposition of the conduct of the Court of Portugal with respect to France, from the commencement of the Revolution to the time of the Invasion of Portugal, and of the motives that compelled it to declare War against the Emperor of the French, in consequence of that Invasion, and the subsequent Declaration of War, made after the Report of the Minister of Foreign Affairs.' The document lists, inter alia, the following French demands: '1st, To shut up the ports of Portugal against England; 2d, to detain all Englishmen who resided in Portugal; and 3d, to confiscate all English property; or, in case of refusal, to expose itself to an immediate war with France and Spain.' It proceeds: 'General JUNOT, without any previous declaration, without the consent of the Prince Regent of Portugal, entered the kingdom with the vanguard of his army, assuring the people in the country that he was marching through it, to succour his Royal Highness against an invasion of the English, and that he entered Portugal as the General of a friendly and allied power.' On the behaviour of the Portuguese court under French pressure, see Introd.

546–77. Address of the Supreme Junta … to action."] *Courier*, 8 July 1808, under heading 'Address to the People of Portugal'. The latter portion of the document is quoted in part below, *Cintra*, 824–35.

579–92. proclamation … shot."] All but the first sentence quoted appears in *Courier*, 15 Aug. 1808, in a fuller version than Wordsworth gives here. *The Times* of the same date supplies the missing sentence as: 'You yourselves have asked him for a king, who, aided by this all–powerful and great Monarch, might be able to recover your unhappy country, and place it in the rank to which it belongs.' Neither journal gives Wordsworth's version exactly.

592–624. bulletins … in chief."] *Courier*, 10 Oct. 1808, under heading: 'The following Bulletins, relative to the commencement of the resistance to the French in Portugal, were since published by the authority of General JUNOT'. 'We entered … burned.' (595–8) is from No. II, dated 2 July 1808; 'The spirit … Portugal.' (598–601) is from No. III, dated 7 July 1808; the remaining passages, quoted with omissions and adaptations, are from No. IV, dated 18 July 1808. Beia was sacked by Maransin on 26 June, Guerda (Guarda) and Alpedrinha by Loison in early July. These events took place as outlying French detachments fought their way back Lisbon for concentration there when Junot found himself isolated Portugal by the Spanish revolt.

609. 13000 dead] So *Courier*, 10 Oct. 1808; *The Times* of same date reads '3000 dead'.

625–31. Address … course."] *Courier*, 1 Oct. 1808, reporting 'a general and extraordinary Junta of the Province of Biscay [at Bilbao] and under the Presidency … of his Excellency Don JOSEPH DOMINGO DE MASSAREDO, Captain–General of the Navy, Minister for Maritime Affairs, &c,':

> Biscayans! his Majesty has ordered me to assemble you, 1st, To know from yourselves what share you have had in the insurrection excited in the city of Bilboa; whether you approved of, or abhorred it.—2d. To assure you in case you disapprove of it, that his Majesty has consigned to oblivion, the mistakes and errors of the insurgents, and that he will punish only the heads and beginners of the insurrection, with regard to whom the law must take its course, for the purpose of preventing them in future from disturbing your repose and prosperity.

644–66. address … enemies, &c."] *The Times*, 28 June 1808, in different translation. 'Resolved to get together something like a representative body which might vote away the liberty of Spain, Napoleon nominated, in the Madrid Gazette of May 24,

150 persons who were to go to Bayonne and there ask him to grant them a king ... no less than ninety–one of the nominees were base enough to obey the orders given them, to go to Bayonne and there crave as a boon that the weak and incompetent Joseph Bonaparte might be set to govern their unhappy country' (Oman, i. 63–4).

668–77. address ... exist?"] *The Times*, 30 June 1808, in this translation, with minor variants. This passage is the basis of the opening lines of *Nat. Ind. and Lib.* II. xxvii (*P.W.* iii. 137).

719–22. Council ... correction."] *The Times*, 30 Aug. 1808, under heading: 'Proclamation of the Council of Castile, to the People of Madrid, on the Departure of the French', dated 5 August 1808: 'Let us, therefore [i.e. because of Spanish victories outside Madrid], cast off our lethargy, and purify our manners, which were arrived almost at the pitch of complete corruption. Let us acknowledge the calamities which the kingdom and this great capital have endured, as a punishment necessary for our correction.'

722–9. General Morla ... loaded."] Morla was in command in Cadiz in 1808, and, according to Napier (i. 172–3), who accuses him of double dealing, declined British assistance there. The passage is quoted from an address dated 15 June 1808, in *Courier*, 16 July 1808.

731–41. "The defence ... formed them."] *Courier*, 15 Sept. 1808, almost verbatim.

745–54. The names ... progenitors."] *Courier*, 1 July 1808, under heading: 'Address from the Council of Leon to the Spanish nation.'

761–71. "Life or Death ... enjoy."] We have not found the source of this quotation.

774–82. The next ... disgrace."] From Clause 9 of *Precautions*, verbatim from *Courier*, 4 July 1808; see n. on 273 ff.

789–99. "All Europe ... preserved."] *Courier*, 12 July 1808, with minor variants.

803–24. Address ... just cause."] *The Times*, 30 June 1808, in this translation.

824–35. address ... like men."] *Courier*, 8 July 1808, continuing almost immediately after the passage quoted in 546–7. With omissions and slight adaptation. Cf. 2846–50.

836–47. "Precautions ... laws, &c. &c."] From Clause 11 of the document; *Courier*, 4 July 1808, almost verbatim. The italics are Wordsworth's.

848–57. proclamation ... herself."] *The Times*, 4 Aug. 1808, almost verbatim.

864–5. the voice ... God] Cf. *E.S.* 855—62: 'The voice that issues from this Spirit is that Vox Populi which the Deity inspires', whereas there is nothing infallible in 'the clamour of that small though loud portion of the community … which, under the name of the Public, passes itself, upon the unthinking, as the People.'.

882–3. the knowledge … forefathers] Similarly, *Prel.* (1850), VI. 448–50: 'Past and future [are] the wings / On whose support harmoniously conjoined / Moves the great spirit of human knowledge'. Cited in *E.S.* 851–3.

886–9. The stream … strengthen it] Cf. *Llandaff*, 273–5.

897. those heights of magnanimity] Cf. 75 ff.

924–33. dispatches … cannon, &c. &c."] Reprinted from the *Gazette* of 2 September in *Courier*, 3 Sept. 1808. The 'second letter' is dated 'Vimiera, Aug. 21, 1808'. Wordsworth quotes verbatim. The first letter (17 Aug. 1808) describes the action against Laborde at Roliça. The 'official communication' (933) does not seem to be reprinted; but cf. Courier, 5 Sept. 1808: 'After this action [Vimiera], on the next day, Gen. KELLERMAN arrived at Sir ARTHUR WELLESLEY's headquarters, to treat for terms of submission.'

925–6. two several engagements] Roliça and Vimiera (17 and 21 Aug. 1808).

943. losses … sustained in Spain] Primarily in the defeat of Dupont at Baylen in mid–July; see n. on 1452.

950. Maida] Some 210 miles south of Naples; scene of an engagement between British and French troops on 4 July 1806, in which the British force under General Sir John Stuart was successful.

957–63. proclamation … England."] *The Times*, 3 Sept. 1808:

His Britannic Majesty our most gracious King and Master has, in compliance with the wishes and ardent supplication for succour from all parts of Portugal, sent to your aid a British army directed to co-operate with his fleet already on your coast. The English soldiers who land upon your shore do so with equal sentiments of friendship, faith, and honour. The glorious struggle in which you are engaged is for all that is dear to man; the protection of your wives and children; the restoration of your lawful Princes; the independence, nay, the very existence of your kingdom; and the preservation of your holy religion. Objects like these can only be attained by distinguished examples of fortitude and constancy. The noble struggle against the tyranny and usurpation of France will be jointly maintained by Portugal, Spain, and England; and, in contributing to the success of a cause so just and glorious, the views of his Britannic Majesty are the same as those by which you are yourselves animated.

985–90. Sir Arthur … disappointed.] *Courier*, 18 Nov. 1808, citing a dispatch of Wellesley dated 16 Aug. 1808, read before the Board of Inquiry:

It had been the wish of [the Portuguese] Government that the British stores should be employed for the maintenance of the Portuguese troops; and the dispatch stated the refusal of compliance on the part of Sir Arthur Wellesley, who intimated to the Portuguese General that the British forces would not be under

> the necessity of obtaining bread from them, but would require that nation to supply the British with beef, wine, and forage. It also contained an account of … some extraordinary messages sent respecting the supplies, in which General Friere expressed his anxiety on that subject. Sir Arthur Wellesley received a proposition from General Friere, respecting a new plan of operations, which went to separate the Portuguese from the British troops; and the pretext for this proceeding was the probable want of supplies, notwithstanding Sir Arthur Wellesley had expressly stated to him the contrary. Sir Arthur Wellesley attributed this wish of General Friere to his apprehension that the British were not sufficiently strong for the enemy. … If Sir Arthur had been furnished with the supplies, he would have acceded to the request, but he found that the British Commissariat had not sufficient stores to enable him to do so. Besides, he did not believe that the motives stated by General Friere were what led to his determination.

Wellesley's and Freire's motives are analysed by Napier, i. 197–8. Oman calls Freire 'a pretentious and incapable person . . . a self-willed and shifty man' (i. 212, 233). He was murdered by his own troops at Braga in March 1809, during the second French invasion of Portugal (Oman, ii. 233).

997–1044. Now there is … event.] Cf. editorial comment in *Courier*, 22 Sept. 1808:

> There is [in the Convention] a studied abstinence from any thing that can in the least degree wound even the *feelings* of the enemy, as if we were *fearful* he would not accept the conditions. … Could we imagine the French General to have sat down for the purpose of inventing terms of an agreement which should not only wipe off every stain which his character had sustained from a previous defeat, but which would transfer that stain from his own to his adversary's character, he could not have done it more effectively than by the present convention. Nothing that can gratify the pride and vanity of Junot and his Master is omitted.—The former is the *Duke of Abrantes*, and the latter *is his Imperial and Royal Majesty Napoleon the First!!*—Oh! this hateful Convention.

Again, *Courier*, 27 Sept. 1808, editorial comment:

> In the very outset of the negociation we acknowledge Junot as Duke of Abrantes—This was a most singular imprudence. … At the very time we were reconquering the Country for its legitimate Sovereign, from the Usurper of his authority, we recognise as legal an act of that Usurper against the legitimate Sovereign—we recognise Junot as the rightful possessor of a Portuguese title and territory, bestowed upon him, not by the Prince Regent of Portugal, from whom alone such a gift could have justly proceeded, but from Bonaparte, who had no right to grant it.

Cf. also Southey to Humphrey Senhouse, 15 Oct. 1808 (*Life and Correspondence*, iii. 175): 'the high treason against all moral feeling, in recognising Junot by his usurped title'.

1048–50. The night before … news.] *Courier*, 16 Sept. 1808: 'The Park and Tower Guns were fired between eight and nine o'clock.—Undoubtedly it is a matter of great and deep rejoicing, that the main object of the expedition has been accomplished. …

But here joy and congratulation cease; for it must be confessed that the terms were not such as the public had expected.'

1052. such a burst … indignation] Meetings of public bodies demanding inquiry into the Convention are reported in *The Times*, 13 Oct. 1808 (City of London); 20 Oct. (Reading, Winchester); 21 Oct. (City of Westminster); 29 Oct. (Essex); 4 Nov. (Hampshire); 12 Nov. (Middlesex); 17 Nov. (Rochester); and others. It was from Lord Lonsdale's pressure against such a meeting in Westmorland that *Cintra* arose; see Introd.

1085–6. the Russian fleet] See the Convention between Seniavin and Cotton, Appendix, 472–94.

1085–90. the Russian fleet … Sweden] Cf. *Courier*, 16 Sept. 1808: 'As to the Russian Fleet, nine sail of the line, and of the Russian line, more or less, are of little importance to such a Navy as ours.—But holding in deposit is not a term to be found in our Naval Dictionary. … And the Seamen! they are to be sent back to Russia without conditions; of course they may serve immediately against us and our Allies, as the French may'; *The Times*, 16 Sept. 1808: 'Are then the Russian Officers and seamen to be indeed sent home by us—or, in other words, to be conveyed to attack the King of SWEDEN, our most faithful Ally?' Oman (i. 224) calls 'our most faithful Ally' 'the hairbrained King of Sweden'. Cf. *Nat. Ind. and Lib.* I. vii, and Wordsworth's and de Selincourt's notes (*P.W.* iii. 112, 453–4); II. xx and xxi (*P.W.* iii. 133–4).

1090. a French army] See Convention, arts. II–X, pages 387–8, above.

1090–3. a French army … it] Cf. *Courier*, 16 Sept. 1808: 'But still, whatever inconveniences we might have been subject to [after Vimiera], the enemy were subject to the same, if not to greater, and their force was inferior:—the country all round them was hostile.' Junot's communications had been cut by the Spanish uprising in general and by the defeat of Dupont at Baylen in particular.

1094–6. to be transported … immediately!] Cf. *Courier*, 16 Sept. 1808: 'But here we find the French obtaining the favourable terms of being allowed to evacuate Portugal, retaining their baggage, that is, their plunder … the moment they reach France they may set out upon their march to resume hostilities against this very Portugal which they have but just evacuated'; *The Times*, 20 Oct. 1808: 'For see, now, the result of the memorable Armistice and Convention of Cintra: the first body of the French troops were embarked on board the British transports about the 8th of last month, six weeks ago. These men, therefore, may be in Spain; and notwithstanding the arts which have been used to conceal the terms of the Portuguese Convention, the Spaniards may have already learned them from the bayonets of those troops which we have sent to aid in their destruction.'

1098. as an affair between two armies] Cf. *Address*, 6 (p. 405, above).

1118–20. The motive ... famine] *Courier*, 17 Sept. 1808, quoting a letter from Dalrymple to Castlereagh of 3 September 1808:

> my own opinion in favour of the expediency of expelling the French army from Portugal by means of the Convention ... was principally founded on the great importance of time, which the season of the year rendered peculiarly valuable.... When the suspension of arms was agreed upon, the army under the command of Sir John Moore had not arrived, and doubts were even entertained whether so large a body of men could be landed on an open and dangerous beach; and that being effected, whether the supply of so large an army with provisions from the ships could be provided for, under all the disadvantages to which the shipping were exposed.

Cf. *Courier*, 16 Sept. 1808: 'A respectable Morning Paper hints, that a fleet of transports off the coast of Portugal was in a dangerous state; that the difficulty of landing provisions from the victuallers was very great, and highly precarious, from the state of the surf; besides which considerable dread was entertained in respect of the approaching equinox.'

1122. The nation ... discretion] Cf. *Courier*, 16 Sept. 1808: the British public 'expected from the decisive victory of the 21st, gained by a British force which had afterwards been strengthened by 15,000 men, that JUNOT would have been compelled to an unconditional surrender'.

1124–9. It has ... termination.] *Courier*, 15 Dec. 1808, reporting Colonel Torrens under examination by Sir Arthur Wellesley:

> Immediately after we had defeated the right column of the French army, which had made its attack on our left, Sir Arthur Wellesley rode to Sir Harry Burrard, and said, "Sir Harry, now is your time to advance, the enemy are completely beaten, and we shall be in Lisbon in three days. We have a large body of troops which have not been in action: let us move them from the right on the road to Torres Verdas [*sic*], and I'll follow the enemy with the left." Sir H. Burrard replied that he thought a great deal had been done, very much to the credit of the troops; but that he did not think it advisable to move off the ground in pursuit of the enemy. [Ibid., reporting Wellesley:] On the 21st the enemy being completely defeated at all points, he had repeatedly proposed to Sir H. Burrard to advance in pursuance of his original plan of operations. His reasons for thinking that to advance would be beneficial, were before the Court ... [but this opportunity having been lost on 21 August, he did not consider the Convention an unreasonable solution, since the French had recovered by 22 August].

1125–9. Sir Arthur ... termination] *Courier*, 22 Nov. 1808: 'Q[uestion]. Did you consider the army under your command adequate to the dispersion of Junot's force, when you advised Sir Harry Burrard to march to cut off the enemy's retreat?—

A[nswer, by Wellesley]. I did consider the force which marched under my command to be sufficient to drive the French from Lisbon, and from the forts upon the Tagus.'

1136. his letter] Presumably that of 3 September 1808, cited in n. on 1118–20.

1136. A want of cavalry] *Courier*, 13 Dec. 1808, reporting Burrard: 'The want of cavalry, and the insufficiency of the artillery horses to drag the artillery, appeared to him to be insuperable objections to advancing. ... The difficulties which arose from the want of cavalry were rendered evident by that action [Vimiera] ...'; *Courier*, 22 Nov. 1808, reporting Dalrymple: 'the great loss which we sustained in our very small body of cavalry'; *Courier*, 3 Jan. 1809 (report of Board of Inquiry): 'a superior cavalry retarding our advance ... the want of a sufficient body of cavalry was the cause of [the enemy's] suffering but little loss in the plain. ... He succeeded in effecting his retreat in good order, owing principally to [Wellesley's] want of cavalry.'

1138–9. certain failures ... horses] *Courier*, 22 Nov. 1808, reporting Dalrymple's narrative to the Board of Inquiry: 'It was ... hard to move with rapidity when, as it was stated by Sir A. Wellesley, the artillery horses were by no means in proper condition—when a great proportion of them were horses furnished by the Irish Commissariat from the cast horses of the cavalry, many of them blind and lame.'

1142. difficulties] *Courier*, 18 Nov. 1808, reporting Wellesley's dispatch to Castlereagh of 1 August 1808: 'he had commenced his disembarkation in that river on the day of writing that letter, but ... the landing was attended with some difficulty, and it would have been quite impossible, had it not been for the zeal of the people of the country, and the activity of the Officers of the navy and army'; *Courier*, 21 Nov. 1808, reporting Wellesley's narrative to the Board of Inquiry: 'The landing [at Mondego Bay] was ... attended with considerable difficulties, on account of the surf.' Naval witnesses were called by the Board to testify to the difficulties (*Courier*, 22 and 23 Nov. 1808).

1146–7. heavy ordnance ... needed.] *Courier*, 26 Nov. 1808: 'Major General SPENCER answered [to Wellesley], that the *Alfred* was ordered for the express purpose of supplying whatever heavy ordnance the Commander in Chief might require'; *Courier*, 15 Dec. 1808: 'how did you propose to get heavy cannon?—[Wellesley.] From the ships. It had been so settled before I left England, and a store-ship lay off for that purpose.'

1158. the proclamation] See 957–63, and n.

1176–8. in Sir Hew ... enemies] Wordsworth thought that this passage might be libellous (*M.Y.* i. 341).

1185. talents, genius] See *E.S.* 1, textual n., and n. In 1812, H.C.R notes, W 'observed of himself that he has comparatively but little talent [compared with Coleridge]; genius is his characteristic quality'. H.C.R. corroborates and expands on this judgement.

1195. "bold, bad men"] Spenser, *Faerie Queene*, i. i. 37, and Shakespeare, *Henry VIII*, II. ii. 44. Cf. *Prel.* VII. 322, where the quotation is directly from Spenser; but the reference to Wolsey in Shakespeare is nearer Wordsworth's meaning in the present passage.

1218–9. Phocion, Epaminondas, and Philopœmen] All subjects of Lives by Plutarch (Epaminondas in *Pelopidas*). There do not seem to be any obvious verbal borrowings from Plutarch. Phocion is said to have refused a present of 100 talents from Alexander and bribes from Harpalus (*Phocion*, XVIII, XXI). Note also *Pelopidas*, IV. 3: 'And the true reason for the superiority of the Thebans was their virtue, which led them not to aim in their actions at glory or wealth, which are naturally attended by bitter envying and strife; on the contrary, they were both filled from the beginning with a divine desire to see their country become most powerful and glorious in their day and by their efforts, and to this end they treated one another's successes as their own' (trans. Perrin, in Loeb edn., London, 1917, v. 349). On Philopœmen see the Life, III: 'it was the energy, sagacity, and indifference to money in Epaminondas which he strenuously imitated' (ed. cit., x. 261); and Life, IV, on his intense interest in military matters. 'Wordsworth was seeking a translation of Plutarch's *Lives* in July 1808 (*M.Y.* i. 257).

1219–20. Sidney ... *dealing*] Fulke Greville, *The Life of the Renowned Sr. Philip Sidney* (London, 1652), in *Works*, ed. Grosart (privately printed, 1870), iv. 38: 'Besides which honour of unequal nature and education, his very waies in the world, did generally adde reputation to his prince and Country, by restoring amongst us the ancient majestie of noble and true dealing.' Wordsworth was seeking Greville's *Life* in February 1809 (*M.Y.* i. 289), though he had quoted from it in 1806 (*P.W.* iii. 122, 456–7).

1223. Lord Peterborough] Charles Mordaunt, third Earl of Peterborough (1658–1735), commanded British forces in Spain in 1705–6, with notable incompetence, according to modern authorities. Wordsworth's favourable opinion probably derives from the *Memoirs of an English Officer ... By Capt. George Carleton* (London, 1727), edited by Walter Scott in 1809, and read by Wordsworth early in that year (*M.Y.* i. 303). An edition of 1743 is recorded in Rydal Mount Catalogue, lot 96. Coleridge refers to the book favourably in 1809 (*C.L.* iii. 200, cf. iii. 241). See n. on 4582–5.

1252, fn. Cf. *M.Y.* i. 289 (Feb. 1809): 'Buonaparte may rather be said *to inflict upon* than *to propose* terms to his adversaries.'

1257. it has been urged] Perhaps from *Courier*, 25 Nov. 1808 (examination of General Ferguson):

> He was then asked—Suppose the Armistice had been rejected upon the 22d, and the French attacked in their positions, whether it was not his opinion, that from the known character of the French General, and the mode in which French armies were accustomed to conduct themselves, the city of Lisbon would not have been in great danger of destruction?—General Ferguson replied, that he had no reason to suppose that a French army and a French commander would have acted at all differently from what any other army or any other Commander would have done in similar circumstances.

1267. further effusion of human blood] *Courier*, 15 Dec. 1808, reporting Dalrymple's answer to questions on Junot's motives for accepting the Convention: Junot 'doubtless thought he saw some advantages in it to the French interest which I could not discern, exclusively of the great motive that must influence upon all such occasions—to spare the useless effusion of blood'.

1286–7. ignoble ease and darling sloth] *Paradise Lost*, II. 227: 'Counsel'd ignoble ease, and peaceful sloath'.

1308. submit or yield] *Paradise Lost*, I. 108: 'And courage never to submit or yield'.

1321–2. purified and exalted] Cf. *P.L.B.* 130–1, and [115]: 'affections strengthened and purified'; 'taste exalted' (by the perception of general truth in poetry). So *E.S.* 715–16.

1353–62. manifesto … contributions] See n. on 544. *Courier*, 11 Aug. 1808:

> General JUNOT, without any previous declaration, without the consent of the Prince Regent of Portugal, entered the kingdom with the vanguard of his army, assuring the people of the country that he was marching through it, to succour his Royal Highness against an invasion of the English, and that he entered Portugal as the General of a friendly and allied power. [Whereupon the Prince Regent, though he could have resisted, removed to Brazil, so that his resistance should not be made an excuse for reprisals on his people. Since then he has heard of] pillage and plunder practised in [Portugal] … the raising of an exorbitant contribution demanded from a country which opposed no kind of resistance to the entry of the French troops.

1388–90. but I will … power?] Cf. the drift of the passage from *Courier*, 4 Jan. 1809, cited in n. on 2860–7.

1409–15. The nation … submission] Cf. *Courier*, 16 Sept. 1808, cited in n. on 1122.

1417–20. our Generals … Spain] *Courier*, 22 Nov. 1808, reporting Dalrymple:

> If, however, he had understood that the objects of the expedition were merely limited to Portugal, and that there was no other motive for it, except the reduction of that particular force which occupied that country; he would allow, in such

> a case, that the Convention would be improper, for if the British army had no
> ulterior object, or nothing else to do, there could be no question but that by the
> delay of many months, they would be able completely to reduce the French force
> under Junot; but he always conceived that a co-operation with the Spanish army
> was not only the ultimate, but by many degrees the principal object for which
> the expedition was originally intended; and as to the expulsion of the French
> from Portugal, he only considered that as a preliminary step to a co-operation
> of the British army in the defence of Spain.

Courier, 23 Nov. 1808, reporting Wellesley: 'The object of the British Government
… had been to lose as little time as possible in Portugal, and to proceed to co–operate
with the Spanish armies. By this Convention, there were liberated for the same purpose
4000 Spaniards, who were on board of the Russian fleet.'

1452. Baylen] On 13 July 1808, and following days, the Spaniards under Castanos
defeated the French under Dupont at Baylen, and a convention was agreed by 22 July.
Wordsworth's observation on 'justice' refers to the fact that Dupont's force became
prisoners of war, whereas Junot's did not. According to Napier, i. 125, 'The French
troops, instead of being sent to France [according to the terms of the Convention],
were maltreated, and numbers of them murdered in cold blood … all who survived
the march to Cadiz … were cast into some hulks, where the greatest number perished
in lingering torments: a few hundreds … contrived to escape.' Cf. Oman, i. 200ff.

1454–6. And was … Junot?] Cf. *Courier*, 17 Sept. 1808: 'in reading the first of
these Articles [of the Convention], our readers we fear will be immediately disposed
to compare it with the very different result of the operations of the Spanish army
against DUPONT—DUPONT'S was a larger army than JUNOT'S, and the army of CASTANOS
was an army composed almost of raw levies; yet these levies forced DUPONT to an
unconditional surrender, and to disgorge all the plunder they had acquired.'

1461–4. noble letter … executioners] Two letters, dated Cadiz, 10 and 14 August
1808, are printed in *Courier*, 12 Sept. 1808. The drift of the first is that transport out of
Spain, required by the terms of Dupont's surrender to Castanos, cannot be provided;
that Castanos had no means of guaranteeing to Dupont safe passage through the
British blockade, that Castanos must have known this, and that Dupont must have
known it also. The substance of Wordsworth's summary is in this letter, but he draws
verbally on Morla's recapitulation in the second: 'Your Excellency will lay aside such
false expectations and congratulate yourself that the Spanish people, as I have already
said, have so noble a character, that they will abstain from exercising the vile office
of executioners.' A glance at the complete text in the sources quoted, or in Oman, i.
624–5, will show that Oman's characterization of the letter as 'most shameless and
cynical' is more apt than Wordsworth's 'noble'. Morla was subsequently concerned

in the surrender of Madrid to Napoleon in early December.

1467–71. A Portugueze … necessary.] *Courier*, 21 Nov. 1808, reporting documents read to the Board of Inquiry:

> a letter from a Portuguese General, whose name we could not collect, who was also a Member of the Regency appointed by the PRINCE REGENT. He protested against the Armistice, and said, that from the 19th of June, when he had taken the command in the Algarves, he had been able to drive the French completely out in that province, to free the province of Alentejo, and to establish his head-quarters on the South of the Tagus. He therefore could not be convinced that such an Armistice was absolutely necessary.

1473–6. Another letter … by them.] Courier, 21 Nov. 1808:

> The next letter that was read was a sort of protest against the Convention, addressed by a Judge of a district in Portugal (the name of which we did not hear) to Sir Hew Dalrymple. This letter, although coming from an individual, was allowed to be his act as a Magistrate speaking the sentiments of the people of his district. It inveighed against the Convention, as leaving the crimes of the French in Portugal unpunished; as giving no indemnification for all the murders, robberies, and atrocities which had been committed by them.

Wordsworth, not unnaturally, omits the passage immediately following in The *Courier*: 'Next followed a letter from the same Judge to Sir Hew Dalrymple, dated only ten days after. In this second letter, the Judge expressed his satisfaction and unqualified admiration of the British, and made an invocation to the genius of Pope and Milton.'

1478–80. Wordsworth hints at the King's rebuff to the City of London; see n. on 2231–8.

1483–4. each has written … man.] Cf. *The Times*, 21 Sept. 1808: 'We do not say that the proofs of [Wellesley's] guilt are conclusive; but they are such, that the grand inquest of his country has found "a true bill against him." His own hand-writing stares him in the face.'

1488–1522. I am entitled … one of them.] Cf. *Address*, 12 ff.

1545. Radice … tendit] Vergil, *Georgics*, ii. 292. Lines 126–33 of this poem are cited in *M. Y.* i. 302 (? 26 Mar. 1809), as part of the draft of a note which Wordsworth eventually cancelled.

1549–53. I will … abolished.] Cf. the passage from *Courier*, 22 Sept. 1808, cited in n. on 997–1044.

> Junot found a salve for his injured pride by remembering that he had slipped a mention of Napoleon as 'Emperor of the French,' into the text of the suspension of hostilities: in this he thought that he had won a great success, for the British Government had hitherto refused to recognize any such title, and had constantly irritated its adversaries by alluding to the master of the Continent as 'General Bonaparte,' or the 'actual head of the French executive' [Oman, i. 272, where it

is pointed out that the objectionable phrase did not recur in the Convention].

1561–6. We enter ... agreement.] Cf. *Courier*, 24 Sept. 1808: 'Why were not the Portuguese our Allies consulted? It is true that the battle of Vimiera was gained by British valour: but surely it would have been but delicate and proper to have made the Portuguese a party to the Negociations'; Southey to Humphrey Senhouse, 15 Oct. 1808 (*Life and Correspondence*, iii. 175): '[Dalrymple] presuming to grant stipulations for the Portuguese which no government ever pretended to have power to make for an independent ally ...'.

1580. power is the measure of right] Cf. 4019–21, and Appendix F; *M.Y.* i. 299–300 (26 Mar. 1809): 'the blasphemous address to Buonaparte made by some Italian deputies ... and his answer [containing] the avowal which he has so repeatedly made to the Spaniards, that power is, in his estimation, the measure of right'.

1645–50. one of those ... nation."] *Courier*, 26 Sept. 1808, under heading: 'Protest Made by Bernardin Freire de Andrade, General of the Portuguese Troops.' Wordsworth quotes with minor omissions and adaptations.

1671–3. It was ... intended.] *Courier*, 22 Nov. 1808: 'As to the hoisting of the English colours, instead of the Portuguese, on the entrance of the British into Lisbon, [Dalrymple] declared it was entirely without his knowledge; and when he heard of it, he ordered the Portuguese to be hoisted.'

1777–85. Sir Hew ... to them."] *Courier*, 21 Nov. 1808:

> Sir Hew Dalrymple, in his answer to General Beresford, declared that he was determined that no Article of the Convention should be violated by the French; that their conduct on this occasion had been most shameful, and had evinced a want of probity and honour which was most disgraceful to them. It seemed to be their intention to go away, leaving all their debts unpaid, and carrying off a considerable part of their plunder, by calling it public money, and saying it belonged to their military chest. As to any plunder that could be identified, it must be restored. He regretted, however, much, that part of their plunder, which was in money, it would be difficult, if not impossible, to identify.

1796–1803. "How ... senseless?"] See n. on 1461–4. This passage is adapted from Morla's letter of 14 August 1808:

> It is with extreme surprise that I received your Excellency's letter of yesterday, in which you make a demand of the equipages, money, horses and various commodities belonging to you and the General who accompanied you, which the populace of Santa Maria plundered and destroyed ... [He regrets the action of the mob, indeed he had made suggestions previously for the safety of Dupont and his baggage.] But it never was my intention, still less of the Supreme Junta, that your Excellency and your army should carry out of Spain the fruit of your rapacity, cruelty, and impiety. How could your Excellency conceive this possible? How could you imagine us to be so stupid and senseless? Can a capitulation, which speaks only of your equipage, give you a property in the treasures which your

army has accumulated by means of assassinations, cruelty, and sacrilege of the most horrid kind, at Cordova, and other cities? [etc., etc.]

The Times, 12 Sept. 1808, reprints a dispatch from Madrid dated 23 August 1808:

> On the 14th inst. General Dupont arrived with the Staff of his army at the port of Santa Maria, in order to embark in the armed vessels, in which they were to remain till means could be found to transport them to France. The people beheld with indignation the robbers of their riches, the sacrilegious plunderers of the temples, and the profaners of every law, human and divine; but they repressed their just indignation through respect for the Government. But while the baggage was actually embarking, it happened that there fell out of a bag a chalice and a paten; the sight of these sacred utensils about to be thus sacrilegiously transported, roused their sentiments of zeal for our holy religion, the instantaneous effects of which it was impossible to repress. [The French were attacked and the loot recovered.] Nevertheless, the insolent Dupont had the audacity to make a formal demand of his Excellency the Governor of Cadiz, that he and his army should be indemnified for the loss they had sustained. This occasioned the letter of General Morla.

1826. How must ... glory] *Paradise Lost*, I. 571–3: 'And now his heart / Distends with pride, and hardning in his strength / Glories.'

1830–49. But, as to ... the old.] Cf. Coleridge to T. G. Street, 7 Dec. 1808 (*C.L.* iii. 137): 'Buonaparte were a fool, if he sent Junot's army immediately into Spain—they are doing him more service in France, where every Soldier with his Plunder is acting the part of a Recruiting Serjeant.'

1849–51. "What an effect ... tournois!"] See n. on 1461–4. Wordsworth quotes Morla's letter of 10 August 1808 verbatim.

1882. I have animadverted] See 1325 ff. Cf. *The Times*, 18 Oct. 1808, commenting on a proclamation to the inhabitants of Lisbon signed by Lieutenant–General John Hope: 'Our Commanders have, in fact, assumed the civil government of Lisbon.... We believe, that most of the people of England thought, that the duty of the British army in Portugal was to beat and drive away the French ... instead of which, having liberated JUNOT'S army at Lisbon, we have, it appears, most kindly condescended to take their places.'

1902–4. See n. on 2231–8.

1907. the persons] Cf. 1482–4, 2226 ff.

1928. their motion ... suspended] For the phrasing cf. 'Tintern Abbey', 44–5 (*P. W.* ii. 260).

1932–9. "I protest ... men."] *Courier*, 26 Sept. 1808, with minor variants.

1987. the Spaniards] Spanish troops under General Caraffa, who had entered Portugal as part of Junot's invading force, stationed at Lisbon and discreetly disarmed by Junot on 9 June 1808, after the first Portuguese rising in Oporto, which had been viewed favourably by Spain. Wordsworth conveniently ignores the reason for the presence of these troops in Lisbon.

1996. occurrences of the 29th of last May] Like Wordsworth, we are unable to identify these events. Oman, i. 627, says that 'the persons intended were primarily General Quesnel, his staff, and escort, who had been seized in Portugal and then taken into Spain. The clause also covered some French officers and commissaries who had been seized at Badajoz and elsewhere while making their way to Lisbon, at the moment when the insurrection broke out.' But Oman, i. 208, appears to indicate that the capture of Quesnel took place on 6 June; unless, therefore, the capture of the 'officers and commissaries' took place on 29 May, the clause remains dark.

2005. a few weeks before] During the first rising in Madrid, 2 May 1808. With Wordsworth's comment (2003–7), cf. *The Times*, 27 Sept. 1808: 'We may ... easily judge what kind of wretches these are whose liberation JUNOT has thus bargained for, by the surrender of honourable Spanish troops. They are spies, assassins, and corrupters, employed by BUONAPARTE, and seized to answer for their crimes.'

2030–2. and the people ... effected.] *Courier*, 18 Nov. 1808; cited above, n. on 1142.

2053. if not ... despair."] Probably suggested by *Paradise Lost*, I. 187–91: 'Consult ... / What reinforcement we may gain from Hope, / If not what resolution from despare.'

2067. we announced] In the proclamation of Cotton and Wellesley; see 957–63, n.

2172. sentence ... countrymen] See textual n. The alteration, which resulted in the cancel N1, was made because Wordsworth feared that the uncancelled text was libellous; see *M. Y.* i. 327–34, 336–7. 'The change, sent by M Wordsworth [*M. Y.* i. 329], was adopted—only leaving out the word already which, M St[uart] observed, had occurred just before' (Jordan, p. 153; 9 May 1809).

2231–8. City of London ... investigation."] On Tuesday, 4 October 1808, at Guildhall, Mr. Waithman moved:

> That an Humble and Dutiful Address and Petition be presented to his Majesty, expressing our grief and astonishment at the extraordinary and disgraceful Convention lately entered into by the Commanders of his Majesty's Forces in Portugal and the Commander of the French Army in Lisbon, praying his Majesty to institute such an Enquiry into this dishonourable and unprecedented transaction, as will lead to the discovery and punishment of those by whose misconduct and incapacity the Cause of the Country and its Allies have been so shamefully sacrificed. ... The question was ... put and carried unanimously, not a single hand having been held up against it [*Courier*, 5 Oct. 1808].

The Address and Petition were presented to the King on 12 October (*Courier*, 13 Oct.

1808); the operative paragraph reads:

> We therefore humbly pray your Majesty, in justice to the outraged feelings of a brave, injured, and indignant people, whose blood and treasure have been thus expended, as well as to retrieve the wounded honour of the country, and to remove from its character so foul a stain in the eyes of Europe, that your Majesty will be graciously pleased immediately to institute such an inquiry into this dishonourable and unprecedented transaction, as will lead to the discovery and punishment of those by whose misconduct and incapacity the cause of the Country and its Allies have been so shamefully sacrificed. [The King's reply reads:] I am fully sensible of your loyalty and attachment to my Person and Government. I give credit to the motives which have dictated your Petition and Address, but I must remind you that it is inconsistent with the principles of British Justice to pronounce judgment without previous investigation. I should have hoped that recent occurrences would have convinced you, that I am at all times ready to institute inquiries on occasions in which the character of the Country, or the honour of my Arms is concerned, and that the interposition of the City of London could not be necessary for inducing me to direct due inquiry to be made into a transaction, which has disappointed the hopes and expectations of the Nation [*Courier*, 13 Oct. 1808].

2239–65. Upon ... land.] A deleted draft of this passage (see Introd. and textual notes) appears in Wordsworth's hand at the head of his letter to Daniel Stuart of 'Sunday Evening' (5 Feb. 1809; p.m. 9 Feb. 1809; *M.Y.* i. 288; B.M. Add. MS. 34046, fol. 207). In the letter Wordsworth says that he has had to 'recompose' the passage, presumably to include the reference to 'menaces ... recently thrown out in the lower House of Parliament' concerning the freedom of the press (2245–7). The 'menaces' arose from the initial debate (27 Jan. 1809) on the case of the Duke of York and Mrs. Clarke, when Mr. Secretary Canning, speaking in favour of an Inquiry by a Committee of the House, rather than a private one, attacked the national press for its 'calumnies ... against his Royal Highness'; they were

> only a part of a system of abuse, which for foulness and aspersion had never before disgraced the press of this country, so that it might create a doubt amongst those who love the freedom of the press, whether liberty was not on such terms too dearly purchased. But, by the proceedings of that day, the doubt would be renewed [? removed], as it would appear that the evil was only transient, whilst the good was permanent. Every man must be sensible of the cowardliness, the baseness, and the wretchedness of the calumnies which had been vented in the publications of the day during the last six months against the Duke of York ... those in the highest station ... should not be attacked with such slanderous malevolence [*Courier*, 28 Jan. 1809].

The Courier of the same date comments in its editorial:

> But we warn the public to prepare for some measures, which seem to be desired if not in contemplation, to fetter the Press of this Country, *the only free Press in the World*—Our warning is founded upon some expressions that fell in the course of last night's debate—It is supposed that the free discussion of the

> Cintra Convention has given mortal offence—The Press will be fettered, upon the old pretence of its being licentious—but let the public recollect, that there are laws in existence sufficiently powerful to punish any offence of which the Press may be guilty.

The Times, 30 Jan. 1809, carries similar editorial comment.

2241. I have … animadverted] See 1902 ff.

2254 ff. If the persons, etc.] Cf. *The Times*, 20 Oct. 1808:

> But, we are subverting the maxims of the English law: we "are condemning unheard." Strange assertion! Have we the power to condemn? And is there no difference between condemnation and accusation? We condemn no one, but we accuse all, connected in any way either with the Armistice … or the Convention. It belongs, therefore, to persons accused, against whom there is presumptive evidence of guilt, such as the signature of their names [cf. *Cintra*, 1483–4, 1907] or the sanction of their approbation, to prove their innocence.

2300. unjust [tribunals]] Cf. *Prel.* X. 378; *Samson Agonistes*, 695.

2305. "head and front"] *Othello*, I. iii. 80: 'The very head and front of my offending'. Cf. *Subl. and Beaut.* 159.

2309. crude consistence] *Paradise Lost*, II. 941; the quotation following is from *Paradise Lost*, X. 293 ff.:

> The aggregated Soyle
> Death with his Mace petrific, cold and dry,
> As with a Trident smote, and fix't as firm
> As *Delos* floating once; the rest his look
> Bound with *Gorgonian* rigor not to move.

2330–5. under the cover … framed it.] A passage rewritten by De Quincey because Wordsworth thought it possibly libellous: 'speaking of the King's reproof to the City of London, I said they had been condemned under a sophism insidiously or ignorantly applied. Pray was that altered? If not surely it ought to be—some way in this manner, "as might be said if the words were not entitled to deference by having been put into his Majesty's mouth insidiously or ignorantly, etc."' (*M.Y.* i. 340–1). De Quincey writes on 13 May 1809 (Jordan, p. 163): 'The "insidiously or ignorantly employed" &c. passage—I had altered myself according to Mr. Wordsworth's direction; clumsily enough, I fear; but not so as by any torture, I think, to be racked into a libel.'

2343–5. And now … conduct.] Cf. *E.E.* III. 11–24.

2350. One of their body] The incident is referred to in Castlereagh's speech of 19 January 1809 in the House of Commons (*Courier*, 21 Jan. 1809):

> But the Hon. Gentleman thought an extreme contrast existed between the disapprobation expressed by his Majesty in his Speech of some parts of the Convention of Cintra, and the part which Government took in ushering in to the Public, by the usual mark of approbation and joy (the firing of guns) the intelligence which they had received of the evacuation of Portugal by the French. Was it

unnatural that Government, feeling that the great object of the expedition had
been thus attained, should afford to the Public their testimony that such a great
good had been accomplished?

2354–7. Was not the *positive* **... disapprobation?**] *The Times*, 14 Oct. 1808, makes
a similar point by juxtaposing the clause from the King's reply to the City ('I must
remind you that it is inconsistent with the principles of British justice, to pronounce
judgment without previous investigation') with the presentation of Wellesley to the
King on his return from Portugal: 'is "a gracious reception at Court" ... no prejudication
of a man against whom there are apparent, we do not mean to say conclusive, proofs
of guilt?'

2361–5. a document ... nations."] Printed in *Courier*, 21 Jan. 1809, under
head–note: 'The following are the terms in which his MAJESTY has expressed his
disapprobation to Sir H. DALRYMPLE, of certain parts of the Convention of Cintra':

> The King has taken into his consideration the Report of the Board of Inquiry,
> together with the documents and opinions thereunto annexed. While his Majesty
> adopts the unanimous opinion of the Board, that no farther Military proceeding
> is necessary to be had upon the transactions referred to in their investigation,
> his Majesty does not intend thereby to convey an expression of his Majesty's
> satisfaction at the Terms and Conditions of the Armistice and Convention. When
> those instruments were first laid before his Majesty, the King, reserving for in-
> vestigation those parts of the Definitive Convention in which his Majesty's imme-
> diate interests were concerned, caused it to be signified to Sir Hew Dalrymple,
> by his Majesty's Secretary of State, that his Majesty, nevertheless, felt himself
> compelled at once to express his disapprobation of those articles, in which stipu-
> lations were made, directly affecting the interests and feelings of the Spanish
> and Portuguese nations. At the close of the Enquiry, the King, abstaining from
> any observations upon other parts of the Convention, repeats his disapprobation
> of those articles; his Majesty deeming it necessary that his sentiments should
> be clearly understood, as to the impropriety and danger of the unauthorised ad-
> mission, into Military Conventions, of articles of such a description, which, espe-
> cially when incautiously framed, may lead to the most injurious consequences.
> His Majesty cannot forbear further to observe, that Lieutenant–General Sir Hew
> Dalrymple's delaying to transmit for his information the Armistice concluded on
> 22d Aug. until the 4th September, when he, at the same time, transmitted the
> ratified Convention, was calculated to produce great public inconvenience, and
> that such inconvenience did in fact result therefrom.

The King's disapproval was similarly referred to in the Speech from the Throne
opening the Parliamentary session (*Courier*, 19 Jan. 1809).

2401–2. to which ... light;") Cf. *Prel.* XI. 383–5: 'All these were spectacles and
sounds to which / I often would repair and thence would drink, / As at a fountain.'
The quotation is from *Paradise Lost*, VII. 364–5: 'Hither as to thir Fountain other
Starrs / Repairing, in thir gold'n Urns draw Light.'

2405. Sidneys] Philip (1554–86) and Algernon (1622–82).

2413. weighed ... wanting] Dan. 5:27: 'Thou art weighed in the balances, and art found wanting.' Cf. *Prel.* III. 65–6.

2426. animating] De Quincey on 1 April 1809 (Jordan, p. 136) suggested that this should be 'animated'. Wordsworth means that the 'efforts of the Peninsula' animated Englishmen: cf. 124–6: 'we were instantaneously animated' by 'the rising of the people of the Pyrenean peninsula'.

2432–3. "DICTATED ... RETREAT."] *Courier*, 15 Nov. 1808, reporting an 'Exposition of the Situation of the French Empire', delivered by M. Crelet, Minister of the Interior, on 3 November 1808: 'What presage does the heroic army of Portugal afford, which, contending against double its numbers, was able to erect trophies of victory upon the very ground where it fought with so much disadvantage, and to dictate the conditions of a glorious retreat.' *The Times*, 16 Nov. 1808, comments that this passage 'contains a melancholy truth'.

2450–1. For, when ... Demon] Cf. *The Friend*, No. 7 (28 Sept. 1809), p. 111: 'Sir Philip Sidney ... was so deeply convinced that the Principles diffused through the majority of a Nation are the true Oracles from which Statesmen are to learn wisdom, and that "when the People speak loudly it is from their being strongly possessed either by the Godhead or the Dæmon," that in the Revolution of the Netherlands he considered the universal adoption of one set of Principles, as a proof of the divine Presence.' Coleridge goes on to cite the passage from Sidney's letter to Walsingham used by Wordsworth in 4245–51 below, and to recommend *Cintra* to his readers. The passage cited above reappears in essentials in *On the Constitution of Church and State* (3rd edn., London, 1839), pp. 43–4. It is not quite clear whether Coleridge is adapting *Cintra*, or Wordsworth adapting Coleridge, or whether both have a common source in Sidney, which we have not found.

2451. discover] Wells (p. 75) reports that in a copy owned by him and corrected in De Quincey's hand, this word has been altered to 'distinguish'. As we have found no Wordsworthian authority for this emendation, and as the text is intelligible, we have preferred to let the reading of 1809 stand.

2473. illustrated] 'illuminated, made famous'. Cf. *Reply to Mathetes,* 45.

2514–8. for the mind ... before it] Cf. *Prel.* VIII. 756: 'all objects, being / Themselves capacious, also found in me / Capaciousness and amplitude of mind; / Such is the strength and glory of our Youth'; *Prel.* p. 576: 'He feels that, be his mind however great / In aspiration, the universe in which / He lives is equal to his mind, that each / Is worthy of the other'; *P. 1815,* 352—7; Owen, *Wordsworth as Critic,* ch. VIII.

2551. two masters ... served] Matt. 6:24: 'No man can serve two masters.' Cf. *E.S.* 90–1.

2552. take place of] 'take precedence of' (*O.E.D.*, s.v. *place*, sb., sense 27 c); so *R.M.* 444–5; *Subl. and Beaut.* 163. Knight (*Prose Works*, i. 209), evidently not understanding the idiom, prints 'take the place of'.

2583–90. Boy of Saragossa ... Virgin] Cf. *Courier*, 7 Jan. 1809:

> Letters from Valencia state the following trait of the most heroic valour, on the part of a boy, fourteen years of age, which deserves to be recorded in the military annals of his country:—
> During the last inlistment in Saragossa, the said boy was rejected as unfit for service, but animated by the most fervent patriotism, and anxious to share in the glory of the gallant defenders of their country, he continued to mix with the troops who attacked the French, and behaved with so much intrepidity and valour, that he took a stand of colours, which, in the sight of the army, he carried to the church of Pilar, placed them on the high altar, and rejoined the troops, who were still closely engaged with the enemy.—*Corunna Diary, December 30.*

2638–9. "shake ... horror"] From the Address of the Junta of Seville to the people of Madrid, 809 above.

2639. Cf. Matt. 4:4: 'Man shall not live by bread alone, but by every word that proceedeth out of the mouth of God'; Deut. 8:3; 3755 below.

2641. abominations .... sanctuary] Ezek. 5:11: 'thou hast defiled my sanctuary ... with all thine abominations.'

2652–6. wherever ... love.] For the image cf. *E.E.* I. 67–77.

2664. I have shewn] See 2566–618.

2674–93. citizen of Seville ... glorious!"] We have not found the source of this passage.

2705 ff. This passage, as the footnote to 2706 states, was written in February 1809, before the fall of Saragossa (20 Feb.) was reported in Britain. On 10 March De Quincey first read reports of the fall, which he received at first with incredulity, but which were soon confirmed (Jordan, pp. 112, 117; 14 and 21 Mar. 1809). He consequently thought it incumbent upon him to alter or annotate this passage:

> On the passage relating to Saragossa I have, in consequence [*here a lacuna of about nine lines*] I thought of substituting—Saragossa!—She also, the wasted and twice [   ] city, has borne witness—in her glorious martyrdom—to the efficacy of these passions. [   ] had pledged herself to the same self-devotion. The Multitudes of men, who were [   ]ed in the fields of Baylen—!—or something to that purpose. But this, on consideration, seemed improper on 2 accounts; 1st. that it was to do a grievous injustice to Saragossa; and 2ndly. that, as [the] pamphlet could not be supposed to have been written since that news was received, it looked too much like an artifice to make [   ] thing. Therefore, on the whole, I have thought it right to do as follows:—[   ] footnote, as from

a friend of the author's employed to correct the press errors [that, whilst that sheet was passing through the press, the 33ᵈ bulletin had been received—containing an account of the enemy's having possessed himself of the ruins of Saragossa;—that, in a pamphlet adverting perpetually to passing occurrences, it seemed necessary to notice this,—that it's date might be [   ];—but that, from the distance of the author it was impossible to [   ] [wi]thout occasioning a very serious delay:—that, finally, this was the less necessary as the friend of the author was well assured that he would wish to make no other change than to declare, in a more full and solemn tribute to Saragossa, that all which had been prophesied of her she had faithfully ratified: and that, for the truth of this assertion, the reader—if unwarily he had adopted the *conclusions* of the French,—was referred with the greatest confidence the statements made even by that base enemy upon which those conclusions professed to be grounded [*here another lacuna of about nine lines*] [Jordan, p. 117; Mar. 1809].

On 25 March (Jordan, p. 119), De Quincey says that, as he has received no instruction on the subject, he proposes to print the note; but on ?26 March (*M.Y.* i. 298), Wordsworth brushes aside De Quincey's efforts in this matter, and orders him 'to *cancel* the page with the footnote'. This instruction, and Wordsworth's seeming misunderstanding of the drift of the note, brought De Quincey to the verge of a quarrel with him, and on 1 April (Jordan, p. 132) he complains 'of the very great injustice which [Wordsworth] had done me in what relates to Saragossa'. The rupture was healed in subsequent correspondence. Fragmentary drafts of De Quincey's proposed note are preserved in the Cornell MS. of De Quincey's Postscript on Moore's letters; see our Appendix II.

2706, fn. This replaces De Quincey's suggested footnote; see previous note and *M.Y.* i. 309.

2723–5. Magnus ... alto.] Vergil, *Ecl.* iv. 5–7: [in T F Royd's Everyman's library translation: 'A mighty roll of generations new / Is now arising. Justice now returns / And Saturn's realm, and from high heaven descends / A worthier race of men'].

2792–8. "compelled ... Spain."] Cf. 731–41, and n.

2785. eye ... off] Acts 9:18: 'there fell from his eyes as it had been scales.'.

2802–3. progressive ... species] Cf. Prospectus to *The Recluse* (*P. Exc.* 122–3): 'the progressive powers ... / Of the whole species'.

2804. "amplitude ... deeds"] *Paradise Regained*, II. 139: 'And amplitude of mind to greatest Deeds'.

2818. "noble rage"] Gray, *Elegy Written in a Country Church-Yard*, 51.

2828. "For ye are in a dream;"] We have not found the source of this quotation.

2830–1. "in the eclipse ... dark."] *Lycidas*, 101: 'Built in th'eclipse, and rigg'd with curses dark.'

2841–5. a general ... terms] The general was Wellesley; see *M.Y.* 289 (? 5 Feb.

1809), referring to an article in *The Courier*: 'What you say upon Wellesley, as to the french being *entitled* to such terms …'. Wellesley was received at Court on his return from the Peninsula, and received votes of thanks in the Lords (23 Jan. 1809; Earl of Liverpool's motion) and Commons (25 Jan. 1809; Castlereagh's motion). Attempts to have Burrard's name included in these votes (motions of Lord Moira and Mr. Whitbread) were discussed and eventually withdrawn.

2845, 2855. the French army … terms … "Because … broken."] *Courier*, 21 Nov. 1808: Wellesley agreed with Dalrymple 'in the propriety of signing a Convention for the evacuation of Portugal, because … by the customs of war, the French army, being then unbroken, had a fair claim to treat for the evacuation of Portugal'. See also n. on 3348.

2846–50. "Ye have … nation."] From the Address of the Junta of Seville the Portuguese of 30 May 1808; see 546–77, 824–35. More or less verbatim from *Courier*, 8 July 1808.

2852–3. "Our enemies … destroyed."] *Courier*, 12 July 1808, under heading 'Proclamation of the Supreme Junta of Seville': 'The positions they [the French] have taken are exactly those in which they can be conquered and defeated in the easiest manner.' The passage quoted above, 789–99, follows almost immediately.

2860–7. The French army … light] The Board of Inquiry pointed out that the generals had cited the example of procedure in Egypt in 1801, when a similar convention was granted to the French. On this parallel *Courier*, 4 Jan. 1809 (see n. on 3173–5), comments:

> we wish they had rather referred to the practise of Bonaparte, who as the most successful Captain of the times, is consequently the highest authority. Has it been policy to send back to their country with their arms, equipments, and even plunder, the armies whom he has "signally defeated." Has not on the contrary, the signal defeat of an army and its annihilation been with him one and the same thing, except when on some occasions he has gained greater advantages by a Treaty, such as at Marengo, thereby extirpating the army wholly. After he had signally defeated the Prussians at Jena, he would make no convention to spare any of them.—The Prussian General Blucher, with his brave army, was pursued even to annihilation. At Ulm, the Austrians had one of their finest armies, nearly equal in numbers to the French, strongly posted in chosen situations, commanded by chosen Generals, equipped in the best manner. This army had not been signally defeated; it was unbroken. And yet Bonaparte would not send it back by Convention into Austria with arms, ammunition, and baggage, as an unbroken and even a triumphant army. No, he insisted on making the whole prisoners of war, and he wholly annihilated the army. … What a pity our Generals could not feel the wisdom of pursuing the same policy at Cintra, having so rare and glorious an opportunity before them! Had Bonaparte been in their situation, he would have talked as much as they about his love of tranquillity and sparing of the effusion of

innocent blood; but he would have fought his enemies day and night, hotly and vigorously attacking them until they were all either slain or surrendered prisoners at discretion. Had our own Commanders acted in this way, we should not now have had to contemplate Junot's army at Vittoria, preparing under very different circumstances to revenge upon the British their disgrace at Vimiera.

2865–6. at Ulm ... Prussia] The fortress of Ulm under Mack von Leiberich surrendered to Napoleon in October 1805. Napoleon's Prussian campaign took place in October 1806. Lübeck was the scene of Blucher's surrender, 7 November 1806. Switzerland was occupied in 1798. Cf. *Nat. Ind. and Lib.* I. xxvii (*P.W.* iii. 122).

2899. "heroic wisdom;"] Milton, Digression to *History of Britain*, in *Works*, x (New York, 1932), 324, and xviii (New York, 1938), 254: 'But to do this and to know these exquisit proportions, the heroic wisdom which is requir'd surmounted far the principles of narrow politicians.' Cf. nn. on 3358, 4369–76. Wordsworth was seeking Milton's Prose Works in July 1808 (*M.Y.* i. 257).

2930. is to increase] Altered by De Quincey from 'or to increase'; see Jordan, pp. 97, 137.

2998–9. the tendency ... intellect] Some alteration, 'omitting what is said about "shutting out from common sympathies and genuine knowledge"', was made by Wordsworth on ? 26 March 1809 (*M.Y.* i. 300).

3048. "I see ... they are:"] Coleridge, 'Dejection: An Ode', 38.

3068. "inspired by nature and by fortune taught;"] Adapted or misquoted from Dryden, *Absolom and Achitophel*, 883: 'Endew'd by nature and by learning taught'. The following passage, 3071–73, may have been suggested by Dryden's description of Achitophel, *Abs. Ach.* 153–63, 198–9, though there are no obvious verbal parallels except Wordsworth's 'Great talents' and Dryden's 'Great Wits' (*Abs. Ach.* 163). Cf. also the character of Oswald as presented in *The Borderers*; note especially *P. Bord.*: 'to such a mind those enterprizes which are the most extraordinary will in time appear the most inviting ... he frequently breaks out into what has the appearance of greatness.'

3083. those already] Altered by De Quincey from 'those which I have already' (Jordan, p. 97; 5 Mar. 1809).

3087–100. The Empire ... leads.] Cf. *R.M.* 249–54, 429–46.

3173–5. the necessity ... country.] *Courier*, 4 Jan. 1809, reprints extracts from the Report of the Board of Inquiry with interspersed comments. Among these is the following:

[Report:] It appears, that pains were taken to misrepresent and raise a clamour in Portugal against this Convention; but when it was generally known, and its effects felt, the people of Lisbon, and of the country, seem to have expressed their gratitude and thanks for the benefits attending it. [Comment:] Gratitude and thanks, by being so discontented as to render it necessary that we should leave 10,000 men in Portugal to keep them quiet!

3176. the English army] Altered by De Quincey from 'this army', 'for the sake of euphony; but, on reading the whole paragraph over, it seems to me to improve the emphasis of the passage, from a feeling of the opposition between what is *English*— and *dishonor*' (Jordan, p. 110; 14 Mar. 1809).

3198, fn. See *M.Y.* i. 300–1 (26 Mar. 1809): 'I have done injustice to Gen. Ferguson, by not mentioning in the body of the work his marked disapprobation of the Convention of Cintra.' Wordsworth proposed to mention Ferguson in a projected note on 'the French Bulletin on Saragossa' (*M.Y.* i. 301–2), but later abandoned the note (*M.Y.* i. 305); whereupon De Quincey took the opportunity of introducing this note into the body of the work rather than into the Appendix (Jordan, p. 158; 5 Apr. 1809), adapting Wordsworth's suggested phrasing (*M.Y.* i. 302). In the debate on the Convention in the Commons, Ferguson 'was aware that many General Officers of great eminence had approved of this Convention. He was not of rank to be consulted upon it; but if he had been so consulted, he had no hesitation in saying, that it should have met his decided negative' (*Courier*, 22 Feb. 1809).

3199. Sir Hew Dalrymple … Cintra] Wellesley stated to Castlereagh that he was in disagreement on details, but approved the general plan for a French evacuation of Portugal. Dalrymple repeated before the Board that the negotiations had begun two hours before his arrival (*Courier*, 21 Nov. 1808, and elsewhere). Again (*Courier*, 23 Nov. 1808), Wellesley stated: 'That the Negociation should not originally extend beyond the suspension of hostilities. … That instead of private property, the words arms and baggage should be substituted. … That nothing should be introduced about the Russian Fleet.—On the two first of these the Commander differed from him.' Castlereagh, in the debate on the Convention, asserted that 'it was rather presumptuous to oppose the opinion of the whole Staff in Portugal with respect to the propriety of granting to the French the liberty of retiring from that country' (*Courier*, 22 Feb. 1809).

3214 ff. Wordsworth's 'two maxims of policy' were mentioned as 'two extreme opinions' by Castlereagh in the debate on the campaign in Spain in the Commons on 24 February 1809: one was that Spain 'was sufficiently powerful as to men; and that our co–operation need go no further than supplies of arms, money, clothing, ammunition, and whatever other necessaries might be wanting'; the other, 'that there was no medium between a great effort, and the whole effort, and … that not a soldier should be kept at home … [this] would be in itself impracticable' (cf. *Cintra*, 3223–

4). The Government rejected both these policies. In the same debate Mr. Windham recommended a force of 100,000 men (cf. *Cintra*, 3331), based on Gibraltar; such a force (though he 'disliked the practice') could be recruited 'from the militia' (cf. *Cintra*, 3225–6). 'The effect of such an army, ably conducted [cf. *Cintra*, 3345 ff.], was not to be spoken lightly of … when we talked of Buonaparte's numbers, we must recollect where these numbers were to act [cf. *Cintra*, 3241]. A force raised to the greatest possible amount to which the mind and means of the country,—then elevated above itself and exalted to something of a preternatural greatness … could have carried it, should have been placed in Spain' (cf. *Cintra*, 3271–20). Since no single newspaper report we have seen gives all the above details, we cite the report in Cobbett's *Parliamentary Debates*, xii (1809), cols. 1078–9, 1111–12. That Wordsworth studied this debate as well as that of 21 February on the Convention (see n. on 3405–8) is clear from his reference to 'the two debates' (3462).

3229. power, which] Altered by De Quincey from 'power, that' (Jordan, p. 110; 14 Mar. 1809).

3254. every one … weakness] Cf. *Prel.* X. 160–8: 'the commonplaces of the Schools, / A theme for boys … that tyrannic Power is weak'.

3263–7. Trajan … Antonine … Caracalla … Domitian] Emperors of Rome in A.D. 98–117, 138–61, 211–17, and 81–96 respectively.

3285–6. his utter rejection … morality] Cf. 1823–8; Coleridge to Sir George Beaumont, 14 Dec. 1808 (*C.L.* iii. 147): 'reflect only on the enormous power, which for a small time a mere Individual can acquire by the total emancipation of the will from all the Laws of general Morality. What then must be the power, when one pre–eminently wicked Man wields the whole strength and cunning of a wicked Nation?'; *C.N.B.* ii. 3230 (1807–10): 'What then is the secret of the French Power? of the vicious French? Consistency, unanimity in vice & energy'; passage from *The Friend*, No. 6 (21 Sept. 1809), 84–5, cited in n. to *E.E.* III. 14–15. The association of Napoleon with the Miltonic Satan is common in Coleridge's writings of this and later dates.

3313–5. And sorry … opinion] Cf. *Freeholders*, 482–5: 'the Opposition were taking counsel from their fears, and recommending despair they continued to magnify without scruple the strength of the Enemy, and to expose, misrepresent, and therefore increase the weaknesses of their country.'

3320–1. A regiment of 900 Swiss] Oman, i. 238, reports that members of the 4th Swiss battalion in Junot's force deserted to the British before and during the battle of Roliça (17 Aug. 1808), and after the Convention of Cintra. They numbered 985, according to a French return of 15 July (Oman, i. 235, 243). We have not found

Wordsworth's source for this information.

3348. "British interests;"] *Courier*, 15 Dec. 1808, reporting Wellesley under interrogation by Lord Moira, who hinted that Junot would not have signed the Convention had he not considered this a better course than continuing to fight, which (as the British generals admitted under examination) he could have done after 22 August 1808:

> When I considered the expediency of allowing the French to evacuate Portugal by sea, I took into my contemplation British interests and British objects only, with the objects of our allies as connected with those of Great Britain. I considered that the French army, from the relative situation of the two armies in Portugal, and from its having the military possession of the country, had a fair military right to withdraw by sea with their arms and baggage; and I do not think it necessary for me to account for the motives which induced General Junot to prefer the evacuation by sea to another line of operations.

3358. "above the strain and temper"] Milton, Digression to *History of Britain*, in *Works*, x (New York, 1932), 324: 'what wonder then if they sunke as those unfortunate Britans before them, entangl'd and oppress'd with things too hard and generous above thir straine and temper.' Cf. 2899, and n.

3384. those who are incompetent] Cf. the comments on the Army in *M.Y.* i. 296 (?26 Mar. 1809). Daniel Stuart, seeking possible libels in *Cintra*, thought this passage libellous, but deferred to the judgement of De Quincey and of Baldwin, the printer of the pamphlet. For details, see Jordan, pp. 164–6 (16 May 1809). Wordsworth was displeased by De Quincey's opposition to Stuart in this matter (*M.Y.* i. 342–4); De Quincey defended himself at length in late May (Jordan, pp. 196–8).

3385. transactions at Buenos Ayres] An expedition sent against Buenos Ayres under General Beresford in 1806 had surrendered to the local inhabitants. A second force under Lt.–Gen. John Whitelocke attacked Buenos Ayres in June–July 1807, but withdrew, by agreement with the Spanish commander, after sustaining considerable losses in prisoners. Whitelocke was court–martialled (Jan.–Mar. 1808) and cashiered.

3394–5. announcing … himself] Altered by De Quincey from 'making this avowal of incompetence … himself', 'since, as it stood, the *incompetence* seemed to be the minister's—not Sir H[ew] D[alrymple]'s incompetence', and for other reasons (Jordan, pp. 110–11; 14 Mar. 1809).

3400. such a letter] Sir Hew Dalrymple reported to the Board of Inquiry that

> He afterwards, upon the 2d of August, received another dispatch from Lord Castlereagh … pointing out to him the general outlines of the measures to be pursued, after the French force should have been subdued or expelled from Portugal. … He saw no reason for assuming the responsibility of measures which ap-

peared to have been confided peculiarly to Sir Arthur Wellesley. Sir A. had been recommended by Lord Castlereagh to his most particular confidence; and great confidence was expressed in the dispatch to have been given by Government to his well–known talents, and a sort of wish that every attention which the rules of the service would allow should be paid to his advice and opinion. He, for his part, felt perfectly disposed to pay every attention to the opinion of a man of Sir Arthur Wellesley's talents, who had also distinguished himself by an important victory [*Courier*, 22 Nov. 1808].

This matter raised adverse comment in the debate on the Convention in the Commons: from Lord Henry Petty, moving the motion referred to below (3405–8), from General Tarleton, and from Wellesley himself, who said that he 'should have felt uncomfortable' had he been aware of such instructions from Castlereagh (*The Times*, 22 Feb. 1809).

3405–8. This moment ... Nation.] The motion was moved in the House of Commons on 21 February 1809 by Lord Henry Petty: 'That the Convention of Cintra, and also that entered into by Adm. Cotton, had disappointed the hopes and expectations of the country—and this resolution the Noble Lord announced his intention to follow up with another, "that these events were to be attributed to the misconduct of his Majesty's Ministers."' It was lost, after debate, by 203 votes to 153 (*Courier*, 22 Feb. 1809).

3456. An enlightened Friend] Presumably Coleridge, who makes this observation in his *Lay Sermon* of 1817 (2nd edn., London, 1839, p. 310): 'A long and attentive observation had convinced me that formerly men were worse than their principles, but that at present the principles are worse than the men.' The germ of this appears to be in *C.N.B.* ii. 2627: 'Pasley remarked last night (2nd Aug. 1805) ... that *men* themselves in the present Age were not so much degraded, as their *sentiments* ... almost all men nowadays act and feel more nobly than they think.'

3473–4. in withholding] Altered by De Quincey from 'to withhold', the altered version 'seeming to me the English idiom' (Jordan, p. 110; 14 Mar. 1809).

3510. the second delegation] The transfer of power from local Juntas to the Supreme Junta at Aranjuez in the summer of 1808; see Oman, i. 342–66.

3519. begotten ... fiction] Cf. *E.S.* 552–4 [WW's joke about Ossian as a 'Phantom begotten by the snug embrace of an impudent Highlander upon a cloud of tradition'].

3522–3. breadth of wing ... every where.] Perhaps suggested by *Paradise Lost*, 1. 19–22: 'Thou ... with mighty wings outspread / Dove–like satst brooding on the vast Abyss / And mad'st it pregnant.'

3537 ff. But I began, etc.] See Introd.

3539. In Madrid ... Corunna] Madrid was reoccupied by the French under

Napoleon in early December 1808. Corunna surrendered to Soult on 19 January 1809, after the embarkation of Sir John Moore's army, and Ferrol on 26 January. As Soult marched south in February into Portugal, Galicia rose in revolt, at the instance of local ecclesiastics and of the Marquis de la Romana, who was gradually assembling a force about Monterey at this time.

3568. The intoxicated setter–up of Kings] Cf. 'an intoxicated Despot', 3893 below, and *Burns*, 478–9 ['the downfall of an intoxicated despot'].

3573–7. "Limbo … earth.] *Paradise Lost*, III. 495, 455–7. Cf. *Burns*, 457–8.

3594. Sicilian Vespers] On 31 March 1282 the people of Palermo rose against their French rulers (under Charles I of Anjou), and a general revolt spread through Sicily, with considerable slaughter of the French population. We have not found the source of Wordsworth's information; but it may well have been Coleridge, whose obscure entry in *C.N.B.* ii. 2675, as illuminated by Miss Coburn's note, indicates that he knew details of the event.

3699. "regni novitas"] *Aeneid*, i. 563–4: 'Res dura et regni novitas me talia cogunt / Moliri, et late fines custode tueri' [where Dido is using the 'newness of the kingdom' to excuse the reception experienced by the Trojans].

3715. Sword of Francis the First] *Courier*, 12 May 1808, from the Madrid Gazette of 5 April:

> His Imperial Highness, the Grand Duke of Berg, having intimated to his Excellency Don Pedro Cevallos, First Secretary of State, that his Imperial Majesty the Emperor of the French and King of Italy, would be pleased in the possession of the Sword that Francis I. King of France, surrendered in the famous battle of Pavia, in the reign of the Emperor Charles V. in Spain, which was kept in due estimation in the Royal Armory, since the year 1525, desiring that it might thus be represented to our Lord the King. His Majesty being informed of this, and desirous of availing himself of every opportunity to testify to his intimate Ally the Emperor of the French, his high regard for his august person, and the admiration his unheard of deeds inspire him with, immediately ordered the aforementioned sword to be remitted to his Imperial and Royal Majesty.

'Perfidious' (cf. 3717) occurs twice in a Spanish document on this subject printed in *The Times*, 10 Sept. 1808. Wordsworth queries 'deposited Escurial' (3718) in *M.Y.* i. 300 (? 26 Mar. 1809).

3727, textual n. Lord Bacon … power] From *Meditationes Sacrae: De Haeresibus*, in *Works* (London, 1740; see n. on *Cintra*, motto), ii. 402: certain heretics 'statuunt … latiores terminos scientiae Dei quam potestatis, vel potius ejus partis potestatis Dei (nam & ipsa scientia potestas est) qua scit, quam ejus qua movet & agit, ut praesciat quaedam otiose, quae non praedestinet & praeordinet'. The rest of the general Baconian doctrine in Wordsworth's sentence does not appear in the *De Haeresibus*.

3727 (on 2nd page of textual note), shells and pebbles ... a Conquest] The episode occurred in A.D. 40 during Caligula's visit to Gaul. See Suetonius, *Caligula*, XLVI; Dio Cassius, *Roman History*, LIX, which mentions, as Suetonius does not, that Caligula behaved 'as if he were going to conduct a campaign in Britain', and that the shells were taken to Rome 'for the purpose of exhibiting the booty to the people there as well' (trans. Cary, Loeb edn., London, 1924, vii. 339). Wordsworth's version seems to derive from inaccurate recollection, or reporting, of this account; no authority known to us places the episode in Britain. He refers to it in a letter of 1791 (*E.Y.* p. 56).

3753, textual n. pots of the Lyn] *pots* = 'the deep circular holes which the action of a river forms amongst the rocks of the Duddon', cited as Lakeland usage in *E.D.D.*, s.v. *pot*, sb.² Wordsworth could have observed the Devon river Lyn during his walk with Cottle and Coleridge in May 1798 (Moorman, i. 373).

3755. Not by bread ... sustained] Matt. 4:4; cf. 2639 above.

3769–76. The difference ... disgrace] Added on 28 March 1809 (*M.Y.* i. 304, reading 'mind' for 'minds').

3795. Swede] 'or Norwegian', following, was deleted, according to *M.Y.* i. 300.

3804. his intellectual ... bounds] Cf. *P.L.B.* 80: 'the sameness and narrow circle of their intercourse'.

3805–6. of those nobler ... Country] Supplied by De Quincey to cover an omission in the manuscript, in which the sentence ended with 'force' (Jordan, p. 135; 1 Apr. 1809; cf. *M.Y.* i. 315).

3811–2. Love ... killed] Cf. *Exc.* IV. 763: 'We live by Admiration, Hope, and Love'; and *Prel.* p. 571, lines 3–5.

3825–60. Prince Llewellin, *ob.* 1240, Prince of North Wales, active against English pressure on North Wales under King John, 1211–15, and subsequently in Wales generally, until the last years of his life, 1237–40. William Wallace (?1272–1305) engaged in similar operations on behalf of Scotland against Edward I, from 1297 until his capture and execution in 1305. Cf. *Prel.* I. 213–19.

3866. the sweeping away] Napoleon 'extorted from [Joseph Bonaparte] fifty of the choicest pictures of the royal gallery at Madrid; but in compensation Joseph was invited to annex all that he might choose from the private collections of the exiled Spanish nobility and the monasteries of the capital' (Oman, ii. 16). We have not found Wordsworth's source. *Courier*, 30 Aug. 1808, prints a dispatch from Madrid, dated 3 August, on the departure of the French: Joseph 'goes laden with the rich booty of the Royal Palaces, the cash of the Treasury, and Chest of Consolidation'.

3869. feudal tenures ... inquisition] *Courier*, 7 Jan. 1809, reports a decree of

Napoleon dated Madrid, 4 December 1808, abolishing 'the feudal rights ... in Spain' and 'All personal dues, all exclusive rights of fishery, or other rights of the same nature, on the coasts, rivers, and banks of rivers, all bannalities of mills'. Another decree of the same date abolishes 'The Tribunal of the Inquisition ... as contrary to the Civil Sovereignty and Authority'. Cf. Oman, i. 475–6. In March 1809 Wordsworth's landlord, Mr. Crump, praised such activities of Napoleon (*M.Y.* i. 306).

3893–4. an intoxicated Despot] Cf. 3568 and n.

3919. not as Persons but as Things] A distinction common in Coleridge's political writings; see John Colmer, *Coleridge: Critic of Society* (Oxford, 1969), pp. 100, 141.

3926. Per me ... gente.] Dante, *Inferno*, III. 1–3 [In H. F. Cary's translation: 'Through me you pass into the city of woe: / Through me you pass into eternal pain: / Through me among the people lost for aye.' RG].

3982. Système ... Condillac] Paul Heinrich Dietrich, Baron D'Holbach (1723–89), contributor to the *Encyclopédie*, published *Le Système de la Nature*, an attack on Christianity, and religion in general, in 1770. The item 'Systime [*sic*] de la Nature' appears as item 126 in manuscript 'Inventory of Books, Prints, and Pictures, of the late Wᵐ Wordsworth, Esq. of Rydal Mount taken by me [John Hudson], this 7th day of May 1850', preserved in the Wordsworth Library, Grasmere. Étienne Bonnot de Condillac (1715–80), follower of Locke and friend of Rousseau; Wordsworth perhaps refers especially to his *Logique* (1780).

4030. The power ... clay] Dan. 2:32–3: 'The image's ... belly and his thighs of brass, ... his feet part of iron and part of clay.'

4033. "Magna ... Austria.] See n. on 1223. The Carleton *Memoirs*, pp. 160–1, read: 'Accordingly, next Morning, the first of May, 1706, while the Sun was under a total Eclypse, in a suitable Hurry and Confusion, they [King Philip's forces] broke up ... [In commemoration of the subsequent relief of Barcelona,] The next Orders were for recasting all the damag'd brass Cannon which the Enemy had left; upon every one of which was, by order, a Sun eclyps'd, with this Motto under it: *Magna parvis obscurantur*.'

4053. I have personal knowledge] How and when Wordsworth acquired such knowledge we have not discovered.

4061 ff. a moral change ... This paramount efficacy ... who, by submitting] Altered on 28 March 1809 (*M.Y.* i. 304).

4076–7. Large bodies ... elsewhere.] See Jordan, pp. 134–6 (1 Apr. 1809): 'It is said, in speaking of the English Troops, that they were *broken* at *Corunna*—in

Egypt—and *elsewhere.*' De Quincey challenges the statement with respect to Corunna, and remarks that 'many [will read the pamphlet] who were present in that battle and who therefore, if it be a misstatement, will instantly detect it.' On the affair in Egypt, his recollection is that 'the Scotch Regiment—which was penetrated by the French Cavalry—was scarcely broken; and if it was—and that should be thought equivalent to being *vanquished*, still it restored itself as *technically* as it was defeated—viz. by *rallying* into groupes—and taking advantage of the French who found themselves unable to act from the *ruins* among which the Scotch Reg. had been posted.' He thinks that the reference to Corunna at least ought to be deleted. Wordsworth agrees, after argument (*M.Y.* i. 319, 320).

4090. Saragossa] The first siege of Saragossa, by Lefebvre–Desnouettes and Verdier, lasted from June to August 1808; it ended with the withdrawal of the French. The second siege began on 20 December 1808 under Moncey and Mortier; it continued under Mortier, Junot, and eventually Lannes, until the fall of the city on 20 February 1809.

4092 ff. The details mentioned here may have been gathered from R. Vaughan's *Narrative of the Siege of Zaragoza* (see 4161 and n.):

> [p. 2:] The walls of Zaragoza appear to have been constructed merely to facilitate the means of levying taxes upon every article brought into the town for sale; the gates … are of the most simple construction, and the *alignment* between them, is in some places preserved by the mud–wall of a garden, in others by … the remains of an old Moorish wall, which has a slight parapet, but without any platform even for musquetry. … [p. 4:] At the time when Don J. Palafox assumed the command in Aragon, he had very little acquaintance with military affairs; for though he had been in the Spanish guards all his life, he had never seen actual service. … [p. 5:] Palafox mustered the regular troops quartered at Zaragoza, and found that they amounted to two hundred and twenty men. … [p. 9:] Zaragoza['s] fortifications consisted merely of mud–walls; it was destitute of heavy artillery, and without troops that could undertake sorties against the enemy's works. … [p. 19:] [Palafox] caused corn–mills worked by horses, to be established in various parts of the city, and ordered the monks to be employed under skilful directors in manufacturing gunpowder. All the sulphur which the place afforded was put into immediate requisition, the earth of the streets was carefully washed in order to furnish saltpetre; and charcoal was made of the stalks of hemp [cf. *Cintra*, 4097] … [pp. 26–7:] For eleven successive days the most sanguinary conflict was continued from street, to street, from house, to house, and from room to room, (the enraged populace always gaining by degrees upon the disciplined troops of the French,) until the space occupied by the enemy was gradually reduced to about one-eighth part of the city [cf. *Cintra*, 4113–8].

4095. a leader inexperienced in war] Joseph Palafox is criticized by Oman for his 'refusal to make sorties on a large scale during the first half of the [second] siege, while he was still in possession of great masses of superfluous fighting–men …if [he] had saved up all the volunteers whom he lost by tens and twenties in small and fruitless attacks on the trenches, he could have built up with them a column–head that would have pierced through the French line at any point that he chose' (Oman, ii. 141).

4102. Pyrrhus ... destroyed."] After the battle of Asculum, 279 B.C.; Plutarch, *Pyrrhus*, XXI.

4112–5. their best field ... up–rooted.] In the first siege the Spaniards had successfully exploited a technique of house–to–house fighting; in the second, they continued these tactics, but they were successfully, though laboriously, countered by the French, who advanced by mining buildings, occupying them when the mines had cleared them, and using them as bases for further mining. See Oman, ii. 123 ff.

4121–2. bodies ... Spain.] This is confirmed by the analysis in Oman, ii. 622–4; but we have not found the source of Wordsworth's information. Vaughan's *Narrative* (1st edn., p. 13; see n. on 4726) says of the first siege that 'In the last few days of the month of June, four hundred soldiers of the regiment of Estramadura, small parties from other corps, and a few artillerymen, contrived to reinforce Zaragoza. To the artillerymen were added, two hundred of the militia of Logrono. ...'

4123. Numantia and Saguntum] Numantia, near Soria in Old Castile, was much besieged by the Romans in the wars of 154–133 B.C., until reduced by famine in the siege under Scipio Aemilianus, 134–133 B.C. (Appian, *Iber.* 84–98). Saguntum, mod. Sagunto, near Valencia, in alliance with Rome just before the second Punic War, was attacked and taken by Hannibal in 219 B.C. after a siege of eight months (Livy, XXI. vi–xv). Cf. Southey to Grosvenor C. Bedford, 9 Nov. 1808 (*Life and Correspondence*, iii. 182): 'there will be many and dreadful defeats of the patriots [in Spain], and such scenes as have never been witnessed in Europe since the destruction of Saguntum and Numantia may perhaps be renewed there.'

4134–51. "Cromwell ... obedience."] *Memoires of the Reigne of King Charles I* (London, 1701), pp. 252—3: 'Now from [Cromwell's] personall temper wee will reflect on the temper of his whole army; for they had all either naturally the phanatick humour, or soon imbibed it ... he himselfe ... made use of the zeal and credulity of those persons', etc., with omissions and minor variants.

4161. The narrative] Charles Richard Vaughan, *Narrative of the Siege of Zaragoza* (three editions, all dated London, 1809). Vaughan's Preface is dated 25 January 1809. The passage cited is on pp.27–8 of the second and third editions; it does not appear in the first. After 'of his country.—' (4168), Wordsworth omits: 'from his energy of character and uncommon bravery, the commander in chief reposed the utmost confidence in him during the siege: wherever any thing difficult or hazardous was to be done, Sass was selected for its execution; and the introduction of a supply of powder, so essentially necessary to the defence of the town, was effected in the most complete manner, by this clergyman, at the head of forty of the bravest men in Zaragoza.'

4201–6. the hearts ... civil] Emended on ? 6 March 1809, not exactly as printed here (*M.Y.* i. 294—5).

4224–30. the passions ... human desires] Cf. *Exc.* IV. 136–9: ''tis a thing impossible to frame / Conceptions equal to the soul's desires; / And the most difficult of tasks to keep / Heights which the soul is competent to gain.'

4245–51. "If ... work."] Sidney to Sir Francis Walsingham, 24 Mar. 1586, in *Works*, ed. Feuillerat, iii (Cambridge, 1923), 166; verbally as Wordsworth gives it, except 'faithfully' for Wordsworth's 'fully'.

4255–9. When wickedness ... zeal] Cf. *Exc.* IV. 307–19, especially 313–16: 'Virtue / Will, to her efforts, tolerate no bounds / That are not lofty as her rights; aspiring / By impulse of her own ethereal zeal.'

4260–1 Be ye . . . perfect] Matt. 5:48.

4263. I shall point out] This obscure promise is perhaps most easily explained as reflecting a projected continuation of *Cintra*; see Introd. De Quincey on 5 April 1809 (Jordan, p. 139) questions it, and observes that 'no direction is given [by Wordsworth] for erasing it.' Wordsworth may have retained it through oversight, or because he thought the promise would be honoured in *The Prelude*, or in *The Recluse* generally, or because he was already meditating matter which shortly appeared in *R.M.*, where he deals with childhood, with his rejection of 'despair even for the man' (or at least the young man), and with 'the inordinate evils of our time'.

4268–70. Cf. the imagery of 'To a Skylark' (*P.W.* ii. 266).

4272–4. circles ... self] Emended on ? 6 March 1809 (*M.Y.* i. 295).

4288–9. "the bright consummate flower"] *Paradise Lost*, V. 479–82: 'So from the root / Springs lighter the green stalk, from thence the leaves / More aerie, last the bright consummate floure / Spirits odorous breathes.'

4306. Kosciusko] Tadeusz Andrzej Bonawentura Kosciusko (1746–1817), Polish soldier and statesman, fought for the Americans in the War of Independence, and commanded Polish forces against Russia and Prussia in 1794, until his defeat at Maciejowice, 10 October 1794. After his release from Russia in 1796 he continued to work in the political field for the independence of Poland. [For his disillusionment with Napoleon's predatory instincts as regards Poland, see Helen Maria Williams in *A Narrative of the Events which have taken place in France; with an account of the* *present state of society and public opinion* (2nd ed. London: John Murray, 1816), 149–52.]

4316. Austria] See *M.Y.* i. 302 for a potential alteration. Austrian troops advanced against the French on 9 April 1809.

4332. Palafox] Jose de Palafox y Melzi (1780–1847), Captain General of Aragon and commander of Saragossa during its two sieges. He was captured at the end of the second, and imprisoned at Vincennes until December 1813. Cf. *Nat. Ind. and Lib.* II. xiii, xvi, xxii, xxiii (*P.W.* iii. 131 ff.).

4332. Toussaint] Pierre-Dominique Toussaint L'Ouverture, a leader against local French authority in Haiti in 1791; governor and commander-in-chief under French authority against Spanish and British intervention in the mid-nineties; self-appointed governor-general in 1801; captured in April 1802 by Napoleon's forces, and died in prison in the Château de Joux, 7 April 1803. Cf. *Nat. Ind. and Lib.* I. viii (*P.W.* iii. 112).

4358–67. "Hæc ... nihil."] Petrarch, *De Vita Solitaria*, I, in *Prose*, ed. G. Martellotti *et al.* (Milan and Naples, 1955), p. 394, with an omission after 'nauseam' (4958). Coleridge's *Prospectus to The Friend*, dated 2 February 1809, concludes with a quotation from this work, ed. cit., p. 328. [Petrarch's quotation communicates the utmost political despair. Translated by Ted Kenney (formerly Kennedy Professor of Latin in the University of Cambridge) the passage runs:

> This is what I should be saying, with whatever else grief and indignation at the present state of affairs might dictate, were it not that I believe that our minds have become numbed and that it is all up with us. I mean that we who once used to show others the right way, now (and this is close on utter ruin) are being blindly carried away headlong by blind leaders and are enmeshed by foreign example, not knowing what we want. For, to finish what I have begun, this evil, whether it is peculiar to us or common to all nations, is wholly caused by ignorance of our goal. When ill-advised, men do not know what to do, so that whatever they do, as soon as it is begun, turns to disgust. Hence comes that running this way and that; hence, in mid-way, dissension; and before any result is reached, principles have gone to the devil and nothing has been fully achieved.]

4370–77. "Valiant ... affairs."] Milton, Digression to *History of Britain*, in Works, x (New York, 1932), 325. Cf. n. on 2899.

COMMENTARY: APPENDIX

4. report of the Board] On 21 March 1809 (Jordan, p. 116), De Quincey says that 'the *Appendix* A which I got about that time [14 March] from the [*tear*] it was quite necessary shou[ld be] remodeled since the appearance of an official Report of the Board of Inquiry's proceedings.' The Board's summary of the evidence it had heard, and its conclusions, had been published in *Courier*, 3 Jan. 1809; but De Quincey is here referring to a *Copy of the Proceedings upon the Inquiry relative to the Armistice and Convention, &c. made and concluded in Portugal, in August 1808, between the Commanders of the British and French Armies;—held at the Royal Hospital at Chelsea, on Monday the 14th of November; and continued by Adjournments until the 27th of December 1808. Ordered by the House of Commons, to be printed, 81st January 1809.* This publication contains a full verbatim report of the Inquiry, and full texts of relevant documents; the 'Report' itself, i.e. the matter printed in newspapers of 3 January, begins on p. 111. How far De Quincey's remodelling proceeded cannot now be determined; it may have been confined to 'verify[ing] some quotations' and the like (Jordan, p. 116), though Wordsworth's 'thanks for ... trouble about the note on the Board of Inquiry' and 'The note on the Board of Inquiry is a clencher for that business' (*M.Y.* i. 300, 348) might suggest more thorough recasting. In the absence of firm evidence, we have assumed that De Quincey's revisions were minimal, and in the following notes we have quoted newspaper reports as Wordsworth's probable source; but we have added references to the *Copy*, and occasionally drawn on its texts of written documents.

7–19. the Portuguese General ... feed] This matter is summarized by the Board: 'It appears, that hitherto the Portuguese had moved on [Wellesley's] left, extending towards the Tagus, but they now [16 August 1808] raised such difficulties about subsistence and proceeding on the manner Sir A. Wellesley thought most advisable, that he dispensed with their co–operation, on condition they would send him 1600 men, to be at his disposal, and to whom he was to furnish bread' (*Courier*, 3 Jan. 1809; *Copy*, pp. 113–14). Wellesley's narrative to the Board (*Copy*, p. 27) states:

> Colonel Trant ... informed me of the General's [Freire's] intention to halt at Leyria, unless I should consent to supply the Portuguese troops with provisions from the British commissariat on the march to Lisbon ... I pointed out the impossibility of my complying with the demand for provisions ... I then proposed to him,

> that ... he should send to join me 1,000 regular infantry, all his light troops and his cavalry, which troops I engaged to feed [cf. *Ap. Cintra*, 20] as the utmost I could undertake to perform in that way. These troops, in numbers 1,000 regular infantry, 400 light troops, and 250 cavalry, joined me at Alcobaça.

Wellesley to Castlereagh, 16 Aug. 1808 (*Copy*, p. 155) gives the above information, and proceeds: 'General Freire has been apprized of this state of the resources; and yet he perseveres in his plan; and I acknowledge that I can attribute it only to his apprehensions, which, however, he has never hinted to me, that we are not sufficiently strong for the enemy. I don't believe the motive stated [by Freire] is that which has caused the determination to which I have adverted.'

28–32. the warrant ... to them."] *Courier*, 15 Nov. 1808; *Copy*, p. 10. The operative part reads:

> We think it necessary that an enquiry should be made . . . into the conditions of the said Armistice and Convention, and into all the causes and circumstances (whether arising from the previous operations of the British army or otherwise), which led to them, and into the conduct, behaviour, and proceedings of the said Lieutenant–General Sir HEW DALRYMPLE, and of any other officer or officers who may have held the command of our troops in Portugal; and of any other person or persons, as far as the same were connected with the said Armistice and Convention, in order that the said General Officers [of the Board] may report to Us, touching the matters aforesaid for our better information.

97–100. Now the whole ... coup–de–main.] This matter is summarized by the Board (*Courier*, 8 Jan. 1809; *Copy*, pp. 119—20):

> It is further urged by the Generals, as much more than probable, that if the enemy had been required to lay down their arms, and surrender prisoners of war, they would not have complied; but if driven to extremity, that they would have retired upon Lisbon, reinforced by six thousand Russians, who must have been thus compelled to share their fate; and in the temporary attack of this city, much calamity and destruction must have ensued.
>
>   Also, that masters of the Russian fleet, and of the boats and shipping in the Tagus, the passage of the river was ensured to them: that they could have defended, for a considerable time its East Bank, and prevented the occupation of the Tagus by our fleet: that with the strong fortresses of Alentejo in their possession, they could have protracted a destructive war, to the great detriment of Portugal and the Spanish cause, by finding employment for the greater part of the British Army, for the remainder of the year, and whose difficulties and losses in such operation [*sic*] must have been very considerable.

106–7. Sir A. Wellesley ascribes] See n. on *Cintra*, 1268–73.

126.–30. "because ... Wellesley."] *Courier*, 3 Jan. 1809; *Copy*, p. 121; reading 'howsoever' and spelling Christian names in full.

131. the Commander–in–Chief] Frederick, Duke of York. The letter reads in part (*Courier*, 3 Jan. 1809; *Copy*, pp. 121–2):

upon a due consideration of the whole matter, it certainly appears that your opinion upon the conditions of the Armistice and Convention, which the words of his Majesty's warrant expressly enjoin should be strictly examined, enquired into, and reported upon, has been altogether omitted. [The Board is asked] to subjoin to the opinion ... already given ... whether, under all the circumstances which appear in evidence before you, on the relative situation of the two armies, on the 22d of August, 1808, it is your opinion that an Armistice was advisable, and if so, whether the terms of that Armistice were such as ought to have been agreed upon [; and similarly with regard to the Convention].

The Armistice was then approved by all members of the Board except the Earl of Moira; the Convention was approved by Nugent, Heathfield, Craig, and Dundas, disapproved by Nicholls, Pembroke, and Moira. Those who disapproved gave reasons, Nicholls and Pembroke briefly, Moira at length. The burden of their disapproval is that the British case was greatly strengthened by the arrival of reinforcements, so that harder terms might well have been extracted from the French. See 193–6.

190–31. the actual landing] *Courier*, 3 Jan. 1809; *Copy*, p. 116: 'It appears that Sir J. Moore did arrive at Mondego on the 20th [August]—that he began to disembark—that on the 22d he received an order from Sir H. Burrard, to re-embark such as he had landed, and proceed to Maciera—that he arrived on the 24th at Maciera Bay, and that he disembarked his corps on the days from the 25th to the 29th.'

193. two of the members] In fact all three who disapproved (Nicholls, Pembroke, Moira) mentioned the reinforcement by Moore's corps (*Courier*, Jan. 1809; *Copy*, pp. 122–8).

194–6. such ... terms.] 'I think, considering the great increase of our force from the first suspension of hostility to the definitive signing of the Convention, added to the defeat the enemy had suffered, Sir HEW DALRYMPLE was fully entitled to have insisted upon more favourable terms' (Nicholls disapproving of the Convention; see previous n.).

203–5. Sir Arthur Wellesley ... time] *Courier*, 23 Nov. 1808, reporting Wellesley's comments on Dalrymple's narrative:

The object of the British Government ... he conceived, had been to lose as little time as possible in Portugal, and to proceed to co–operate with the Spanish armies. By this Convention, there were liberated for the same purpose 4000 Spaniards, who were on board of the Russian fleet. Besides these, 16,000 British troops had been rendered disposable for the same purpose; and, of the French liberated, who, it was alledged, would so speedily find their way into Spain, not a single man had arrived there, or could expect to be brought to the frontiers of Spain for some time to come.

In the debate in the Commons on the Convention Lord Henry Petty alleged that 'the only French Officer who had been taken at the battle of Corunna was found, to the grief, shame, and disgust of our brave army, to be one who was also taken prisoner at the battle of Vimiera' (*The Times*, 22 Feb. 1809).

221. that memorable act] Wordsworth evidently refers to 'An Act against Tumults and Disorders, upon Pretence of preparing or presenting public Petitions, or other Addresses, to his Majesty or the Parliament' (1661; 13 Charles II, st. 1, c. 5):

> ... no Person or Persons whatsoever shall, from and after the First of *August*, one thousand six hundred sixty and one, solicite, labour, or procure the getting of Hands, or other Consent, of any Persons above the Number of Twenty or more, to any Petition, Complaint, Remonstrance, Declaration, or other Addresses to the King, or both or either Houses of Parliament, for Alteration of Matters established by Law in Church or State, unless the Matter thereof have been first consented unto and ordered by Three or more Justices of that County, or by the major Part of the Grand Jury of the County, etc. [*Statutes at Large*, London, 1786, iii. 189].

For the Bill of Rights (1689), which lays it down that 'it is the Right of the Subjects to petition the King', see *Statutes at Large*, iii. 416–19. Cf. *M.Y.* i. 299. We have not traced the quotation '"the benefit ... deputies!"' 'On 6 April De Quincey reported (Jordan, p. 138): 'The note upon Charles II$^{nd's}$ parliaments, I have not placed at the foot of the page, but in the Appendix:—it seemed to me quite *digressional* enough to warrant (or even require) this.'

230–51. an address ... policy] Verbatim from *Courier*, 12 Nov. 1808, under heading: 'Paris, Oct. 29. The Deputies of the new Departments of the Kingdom of Italy, the Musora, the Tronto and the Metauro, presented the day before yesterday to the Emperor and King, pronounced the following Speech.' The note, or at least the quotation, is evidently due to De Quincey, who was asked to supply the quotation by Wordsworth (*M.Y.* i. 299–300). De Quincey's transcript of the quotation is in the Cornell MS. (see n. on 495 ff., below), p. 55. The passage quoted in Appendix F (249–51) is also from *Courier*, 12 Nov. 1808, almost verbatim.

252–494. The text of these documents was taken from official prints (perhaps the *Copy of the Proceedings* mentioned above, n. to 4) supplied to the printer by De Quincey (Jordan, p. 157; 10 May 1809); though on 28 March (Jordan, p. 121) he mentioned transcribing 'the Armistice & Convention from authorised copies'. The version given here differs slightly from that printed in *Courier*, 17 Dec. 1808.

495 ff. The Postscript on Moore's letters, as the text makes clear (550–7), is the work of De Quincey. In the Cornell Wordsworth Collection is preserved a manuscript of De Quincey (item 2804 in the Catalogue of G. H. Healey) which shows various parts of the work in various stages of development and which contains other matter connected with its compilation. To attempt a complete critical apparatus would, we are convinced, be pointless in an edition of Wordsworth's prose; we have therefore confined ourselves to the summary of the contents of the manuscript which is given in our Appendix II.

499. the letters of Sir John Moore] Moore's letters to Castlereagh, and other relevant documents, were laid on the table of the House of Commons in late March 1809. *The Courier* began to print them on 24 March, and Wordsworth saw them there (*M.Y.* i. 307). Since, however, De Quincey refers to *The Times* (*Ap. Cintra*, 868), since *The Times* gives a fuller presentation of the letters than *The Courier*, and since De Quincey on 12 May 1809 praises *The Times* at the expense of *The Courier* (Jordan, p. 160), we have usually preferred to give references to *The Times* as De Quincey's probable source. Most of the documents are conveniently collected in Cobbett's *Parliamentary Debates*, xiii (1809), ccxc ff. De Quincey's criticisms in this Postscript are often based on the views of Wordsworth expressed in his letter of 29 March 1809 (*M.Y.* i. 307 if.); parallels are noted below. De Quincey admits that he wrote 'making a point to prepare the course of what I was saying to receive nearly all of Mr. Wordsworth's thoughts … and sometimes his words' (Jordan, p. 167).

537–41. the letters … upon him] Cf. *M.Y.* i. 307: 'First to remind the reader of the situation in which Sir J. Moore stood, and of the purpose for which these Letters were written—namely, under a conviction that his army could accomplish nothing; and to save himself and it from reproach in that quarter by which he had been sent—the Ministry.'

543. "which … 26,000 men"] Moore's letter of 5 December 1808 (*The Times*, 25 Mar. 1809): 'which when united does not exceed 26,000 men'. Transcribed by De Quincey in Cornell MS., p.37. Moore means the junction of his own force with Sir David Baird's corps, which had landed at Corunna on 13 October 1808 but which did not join Moore until 20 December.

548–53. the English Government … Spaniards] Cf. *M.Y.* i. 307: 'Now it was clear that the best way to succeed in this, was not to charge those who had sent him with blame, but to fling the whole upon the Spaniards.'

578–9. "Gen. Blake's … direction."] Moore's letter of 24 November 1808; *The Times*, 25 Mar. 1809; transcribed in Cornell MS., p.37; criticized by Wordsworth, *M.Y.* i. 307. Blake was defeated by Lefebvre at Zornosa on 31 October 1808, and by Victor at Espinosa on 11 November, after some Spanish success on 10 November. There followed a disastrous retreat through the mountains until the remnant of Blake's army reached Leon, where he gave up his command to La Romana.

581. 'mere peasantry'] Moore's letter of 24 November 1808; *The Times*, 25 Mar.

1809; Cornell MS., p. 37.

584. Major-Gen. Leith] 'Military Agent … in the Asturias' (*The Times*, 25 Mar. 1809, whence the following extract, 587–604, is taken); Cornell MS., p. 71. This was among the third body of papers laid on the table of the House of Commons; *The Times* prints only an extract (of which De Quincey gives most), 'as it gives an interesting account of the sufferings of General BLAKE and his army, and the resolution with which they were sustained'.

605–7. The Estramaduran force, under the Conde de Belvedere, numbered just under 11,000, according to Oman, i. 421. They were opposed by Soult with some 22,000 men, including 4,500 cavalry; the total French force available in the advance on Burgos was nearly 70,000. De Quincey's information is from Lord William Bentinck to Castlereagh, 14 Nov. 1808 (*The Times*, 24 Mar. 1808; Cornell MS., p. 68).

609–10. "The French … at Burgos."] Moore's letter of 24 November 1808; *The Times*, 25 Mar. 1809; Cornell MS., p. 37. Criticized by Wordsworth, *M.Y.* i. 307. With what follows (610–15), cf. *M.Y.* i. 307: Moore 'seems to be surprized that these raw levies could not stand their ground, upon all occasions, against the practised troops of Buonaparte'.

616–21. The two next … exaggeration] Moore's letters of 29 November and 5 December 1808 (*The Times*, 25 Mar. 1809; Cornell MS., p. 37): 'I received yesterday evening a letter … announcing the total defeat of the army of Castanos and Palafox … I had the honour to address your Lordship on the 29th November, and to inform you with the determination I had come to in consequence of the defeat of the army of General Castanos. … The French attacked and carried the pass of Soma Sierra on the 29th.' Cf. *M.Y.* i. 307: 'the fate [fact MS.] of Castanos is totally misrepresented— inasmuch as his centre only was defeated, his two wings being untouched.' On the Polish cavalry at Somosierra, where a squadron was wiped out by Spanish artillery, in one of Napoleon's more theatrical military gestures, and where French infantry carried the day, see Oman, i. 456 ff. Castanos was defeated by Lannes at Tudela on 23 November 1808. According to Oman, 1. 443, and Napier, i. 403, the Spanish right wing was defeated, and the left wing appears to have been 'untouched' mainly because it failed to fight. Oman, i. 442, says that 'Palafox was not on the field'; Napier, i. 403, that he fled to Saragossa 'with the right wing and the centre'.

633–5. "The French cavalry … resistance."] Moore's letter of 24 November 1808; *The Times*, 25 Mar. 1809. With De Quincey's comment, cf. *M.Y.* i. 308: 'This fact I cannot believe upon the evidence of any General,—because my knowledge of human nature teaches me beforehand that it is impossible. That the resistance might fall far below what a superficial thinker would expect I can easily believe—things of this sort, where regular arrangements have not been made to preclude such inactivity … depend upon accident.'

644–55. "—At that time … *incursions*."] Broderick's letter to Castlereagh dated Reynosa, 10 September 1808 (*The Times*, 25 Mar. 1809), almost verbatim.

656–8. "the Gallicians … mountains."] Moore's letter of 13 January 1809 (*The Times*, 10 Apr. 1809): 'The people of the Galicias, though armed', etc.

662–3. "a body … number?"] *The Times*, 23 Mar. 1809; printed as a translation of 'part of the following enclosure, &c. which we know not how has found its way into these Documents'. After the translation, *The Times* inserts the following comment: 'We cannot help again expressing our surprize at the introduction of such a document as this in an official correspondence. If it is meant to attack General MOORE, why not do it openly? if not, to what purpose is it to tell Lord WILLIAM BENTINCK, in French, that a small force can defend Gallicia against a large one?' The original is an enclosure in Castlereagh to Lord William Bentinck, 30 Sept. 1808 (also printed in *The Times*, 23 Mar. 1809); it is a memorandum, in French, from the Marquis de la Romana (see 879 below, and n.), designed for the general assistance of British forces in Spain. The French text (Cobbett, *Parliamentary Debates*, xiii, ccciv) reads: '… la grande route qui mène de Castille en Galice, et qui est tellement rétrécie par les montagnes de droite et de gauche qu'un Corps de mille hommes pourrait arrêter une armée de vingt mille.' Why De Quincey attributes this to 'an English general', and why, in his transcript from *The Times's* translation (Cornell MS., p. 68), he marks off the phrase 'an army of twenty times the number' as a quotation, we have not discovered.

665. 'the people … deserted;'] Moore's letter of 31 December 1808; *The Times*, 25 Mar. 1809; Cornell MS., p. 71.

665–7. "They abandoned … army."] Moore's letter of 13 January 1809; *The Times*, 10 Apr. 1809; and so "I am sorry … retreat" (670–72).

697–700. "The enthusiasm … advantage of."] Moore's letter of 24 November 1808; *The Times*, 25 Mar. 1809; Cornell MS., p. 37.

701. "apathy and indifference:"] Moore's letter of 13 January 1809 (*The Times*, 10 Apr. 1809): 'I was sensible … that the apathy and indifference of the Spaniards would never have been believed.'

716. letter to Marshal Soult] A letter from Berthier to Soult, dated Chamartin, 10 December 1808, sent with Moore to Castlereagh, 16 Dec. 1808; *The Times*, 25 Mar. 1809. The passage referred to seems to be: 'Valladolid is a fine city, and has conducted itself well', which is hardly an 'accurate register of the behaviour of the different towns'.

720. Badajoz and Salamanca] Moore concentrated his own forces at Salamanca in November–December 1808; Badajoz was the base of Hope's corps. In Moore to Castlereagh, 8 Dec. 1808 (*Courier*, 24 Mar. 1809; not in *The Times*), Moore says that in Salamanca 'no one stirs, and yet they are well inclined.' We have not found any source for a similar view of Badajoz, nor anything to contradict it.

730. "rally round"] Probably from Moore's letter of 5 December 1808 (*The Times*, 25 Mar. 1809): 'it was my intention … to march upon Madrid, from whence, getting behind the Tagus, we should have given the Spaniards an opportunity of rallying round us, and have shared their fortunes'; cf. also his letter of 24 November 1808 (ibid.): 'if the Spaniards, roused by their misfortunes, assemble round us, and become once more enthusiastic and determined, there may still be hopes of expelling the French.' Neither passage is transcribed in the Cornell MS.

765–7. "The Spanish Government … attack:"] Moore's letter of 24 November 1808; *The Times*, 25 Mar. 1809; Cornell MS., p. 37.

785. Leith] See n. on 584 above.

786. Pasley] De Quincey extracted the 'testimony' from Broderick to Castlereagh, 22 Nov. 1808 (*The Times*, 25 Mar. 1809); his note (Cornell MS., p. 69) says that the letter 'states the substance of Captn. Pasley's of the Royal Engineers detail of Blake's actions in Biscay'. Broderick gives 'details [of actions in Biscay] contained in a letter I received yesterday from Capt. Pasley of the Royal Engineers. [There follows a factual report of the battle of 31 October 1808 between Blake and Lefebvre.] The Asturians, who principally composed the beaten wing, being raw troops, and one of their Generals killed, and the other wounded, and several of their officers having gone off, Captain Pasley remarks, that their conduct on that day ought not to excite surprize. They had fought very well on the former days.' For Pasley see *M.Y.* i. 370, n. 2.

786. Mr. Vaughan] Castlereagh to Moore, 16 Dec. 1808 (*The Times*, 23 Mar. 1809): 'Mr. Vaughan, who has travelled over the greater part of Spain, describes the southern and eastern provinces as full of ardour and enthusiasm.' Cornell MS., p. 68. Charles Vaughan, author of the *Narrative of the Siege of Zaragoza* (see n. on *Cintra*, 4161); for a brief account of his exploits in Spain see Oman, i. iv—vi.

787. Cochrane] In the frigates *Impérieuse* and *Cambrian* he bombarded Duhesme's force aimed at Barcelona in July and August 1808. In early November a French force under St. Cyr marched to relieve Duhesme, and on 7 November besieged Rosas, which held out until 5 December. The Spanish garrison was materially assisted by the guns of Cochrane's ships and by British sailors and marines therefrom. Cochrane's observations can be found in his dispatch to Collingwood, 5 Dec. 1808, printed in the

London Gazette, No. 16235 (7–11 Mar. 1809), p. 307:

> The Garrison [of Rosas, on 23 November 1808,] consisted of about Eighty Span-
> iards, and were on the Point of surrendering; accordingly I threw myself into it,
> with Fifty Seamen and Thirty Marines of the Imperieuse ... The Spanish Garrison
> being changed, gave good Assistance; and Lieutenant Bourman, of the Regi-
> ment of Ultonia, who succeeded to the Command of the Spanish Soldiers in the
> Castle on Captain Fitzgerald's being wounded in the Hand, deserves every Thing
> his Country can do for an active and gallant Officer. Innocenti Maranger, Cadet of
> the same Regiment, particularly distinguished himself by his Zeal and Vigilance.
> As to the Officers, Seamen, and Marines of this Ship, the Fatigues they under-
> went, and the gallant Manner in which they behaved, deserve every Praise.

We have not found this dispatch reprinted in the newspapers that we have consulted; at the relevant date they are still almost wholly occupied with the affairs of the Duke of York. From Jordan, p. 177, it appears that De Quincey sometimes read the *Gazette* itself.

789. Bentinck] Letter to Castlereagh, 14 Nov. 1808 (*The Times*, 24 Mar. 1809; Cornell MS., p. 68): 'This army [of Castanos and Palafox] is also in want of clothing, of money, and of provisions. Its spirit, however, is represented to be excellent; and Colonel Graham, in whose opinion I have great reliance, speaks very confidently of the event of a battle ... Notwithstanding I think ill of the present moment, and that the Spaniards have not the means at present to repel the danger that threatens, still I have confidence in the unconquerable spirit of the nation.' Earlier, Bentinck says: 'I must not disguise from your Lordship that I think very unfavourably of the affairs of Spain.' Bentinck was the British military representative in Madrid in late 1808.

811–19. "It appears ... Portugal."] Almost verbatim from *The Times*, 8 Apr. 1809.

824–30. Madrid was attacked by Napoleon on 2 December 1808, and capitulated on 4 December. The authorities appear to have envisaged a house-to-house defence as in Saragossa, but the city was unsuited to such tactics.

832–3. forts in Catalonia] Rosas fell on 5 December 1808 (see above, n. on 787). St. Cyr moved about the Barcelona district until March 1809, but we have not discovered what other 'forts' he took.

837–43. Preparations for the defence of Valencia as of 9 December 1808 are reported in *The Times*, 11 Jan. 1809, but De Quincey seems to refer to a later report which we have not discovered. He writes on 1 April 1809 (Jordan, pp. 136–7): 'Last night I read, with great pleasure, the Decree for giving no quarter to the French Troops (under particular limitations)'; *Courier*, 31 Mar. 1809, reports this decree of 7 February 1809 under the heading: 'Decree of the Supreme Junta against the French'; after listing various atrocities, it decrees: 'That no quarter shall be given to any French soldier, Officer, or General, who may be made prisoner in any town or district, in which acts contrary to the laws of war have been committed by the enemy, but that such persons shall be immediately put to the sword, as an example to their companions, and a satisfaction to outraged humanity.' *The Times*, 23 Mar. 1809, reports 'serious tumults' in Cadiz,

> from a suspicion on the part of the people, too well justified by fatal experience in other quarters, that their magistrates were unfaithful to the cause of their country. The immediate occasion is understood to be the following:—Some of the French prisoners, who, under that description, had been so long confined at Cadiz, made the suspicious offer of their services to garrison the town, and to make this proposal palatable, declared themselves to be Poles, and not French-men. The Marquis de Vıʟʟᴇʟ, Governour of the place, was disposed to accept of this offer, against which the inhabitants mutinied.

A longer report in *Courier*, 25 Mar. 1809, citing a dispatch from Cadiz of 22 February.

860. **"a fine people:"**] Moore's letter of 28 November to J. H. Frere; *The Times*, 15 Apr. 1809.

879. **Vigo**] Its capture in early February 1809 is reported in a French bulletin of 17 February (*The Times*, 6 Mar. 1809). The recapture, on 27 March, by local forces with the assistance of the British navy, is reported in *The Times*, 14 Apr. 1809. A dispatch from Captain George M'Kinley ends: 'It also becomes most gratifying that I am enabled to inform you of the spirit and determination of the Spaniards to expel from their country the invaders of all that is dear to a brave and loyal people ... The ardour of the peasantry is beyond all description.'

879. **Marquis de la Romana**] Pedro Caro y Sureda, commanded Spanish troops in French service in Denmark, rescued thence with his troops by the British navy in August 1808. He returned to Spain and took over Blake's command in November 1808, after Blake's failures at Zornosa and Espinosa. Sir John Moore made more or less abortive attempts to co-operate with him during his Spanish campaign. He had been building up forces about Monterey since January 1809; at the time of which De Quincey is writing, he was pursuing Fabian tactics further east, and captured Villa–franca from a small French garrison on 17 March.

Also from Humanities-Ebooks

John Beer, *Coleridge the Visionary*

John Beer, *Blake's Humanism*

Jared Curtis, ed. *The Fenwick Notes of William Wordsworth* *

Richard Gravil, ed., *Master Narratives: Tellers and Telling in the English Novel*

Richard Gravil and Molly Lefebure, eds, *The Coleridge Connection: Essays for Thomas McFarland*

John K. Hale, *Milton as Multilingual*

Simon Hull, ed., *The British Periodical Text, 1796–1832*

W. J. B. Owen, *Understanding The Prelude*

W. J. B. Owen and J. W. Smyser, eds, *Wordsworth's Political Writings* *

W. J. B. Owen and J. W. Smyser, eds, *The Prose Works of William Wordsworth, Volume 1* *

Wordsworth's Political Writings, Keith Sagar, *D. H. Lawrence: Poet* *

In Preparation

Pamela Perkins, ed. *Francis Jeffrey: Unpublished Tours*

*ALSO AVAILABLE IN PRINT

http://www.humanities-ebooks.co.uk